NOT ALL WHO ARE LOST
WANT TO BE FOUND . . .

"Solid gold suspense!"
—#1 *New York Times* Bestselling Author
LEE CHILD on *Live to Tell*

"Classic Staub, at the top of her game."
—**GREG HERREN,**
author of *Garden District Gothic*

THE GOOD SISTER

LITTLE GIRL LOST

By Wendy Corsi Staub

Mundy's Landing Series
BONE WHITE
BLUE MOON
BLOOD RED

And
LITTLE GIRL LOST
THE BLACK WIDOW
THE PERFECT STRANGER
THE GOOD SISTER
SHADOWKILLER
SLEEPWALKER
NIGHTWATCHER
HELL TO PAY
SCARED TO DEATH
LIVE TO TELL

WENDY CORSI STAUB

LITTLE GIRL LOST

wm

WILLIAM MORROW
An Imprint of HarperCollinsPublishers

Excerpt from *Little Boy Blue* copyright © 2019 by Wendy Corsi Staub.

LITTLE GIRL LOST. Copyright © 2018 by Wendy Corsi Staub. All rights reserved. Printed in the United States of America. No part of this book may be used or reproduced in any manner whatsoever without written permission except in the case of brief quotations embodied in critical articles and reviews. For information, address HarperCollins Publishers, 195 Broadway, New York, NY 10007.

First William Morrow mass market printing: August 2018

Print Edition ISBN: 978-0-06-274205-6
Digital Edition ISBN: 978-0-06-274202-5

Cover design by Amy Halperin
Cover photograph © Tara Moore / Getty Images (woman's silhouette);
© Ivelina Petkova / EyeEm / Getty Images (background)

William Morrow and HarperCollins are registered trademarks of Harper-Collins Publishers in the United States of America and other countries.

FIRST EDITION

18 19 20 21 22   QGM   10 9 8 7 6 5 4 3 2 1

For my graduating godchildren,
Hannah Rae Koellner, SUNY Fredonia, Class of 2018
Rick Peyton Corsi, Dunkirk High School, Class of 2018
For my husband, Mark, on his milestone birthday,
And for my boys, Brody and Morgan, with love.

Acknowledgments

With gratitude to my editor, Lucia Macro, for going above and beyond with this one,

To her assistant, Carolyn Coons, and to all the crew at William Morrow;

To my agent, Laura Blake Peterson—so ready to take that lunch raincheck now,

To my film agent, Holly Frederick and the gang at Curtis Brown;

To Cissy, Degan, Susan, and Celeste at Writerspace;

To Carol Fitzgerald and the gang at Bookreporter;

To Noah Leiboff for the website work;

To Morgan Staub for the research and notes;

To Chris Spain for dropping his life to bail me out when I'd written myself into a corner;

And to the enchanting Seretha Tuttle for the guided tour of St. Helena Island. I will be back!

LITTLE
GIRL
LOST

Chapter One

May 12, 1968
New York City

Footsteps approach the bed.

She cowers under the covers, clutching the doll she got from her Sunday school teacher back in December, along with some candy canes and homemade doll clothes and a little plastic ornament of the baby Jesus. She tried to hand that back.

"We don't have a Christmas tree. Mommy hates Christmas."

"Keep it, sugar. Remember, He is always with you."

Plastic baby Jesus is tucked under her pillow, sleeping so peacefully.

Please keep me safe, she tells him, clutching the doll, who's wearing a pretty blue dress with ruffles tonight. Her name used to be Chatty Cathy. The girl renamed her Georgy Girl, after Daddy and that song Mommy liked to hear on the radio before she started turning sad and scary.

If you pull a ring on Georgy Girl's back, she says things like, "*Tell me a story*" and "*Let's play house.*" The girl never tires of pulling the cord. It's extended in her hand right now, frozen in place as the footsteps stop by the bed.

Georgy Girl is silent. Mommy is muttering.

The little girl keeps her eyes squeezed shut, thinking of Jesus—plastic Jesus, real Jesus.

Please don't let her hurt me this time.

"Don't you just lie around here! Come on!"

Mommy yanks off the covers, wrenches the doll from her hands, and hurtles it across the room. The cord winds down. "*I love y—*"

The doll hits the wall and drops to the floor, shattering the sweet, familiar phrase.

"No! Georgy Girl!"

"Shut up!" Something glows in the darkness—the tip of a cigarette? It bobs around as Mommy waves her hand, shouting. "It's laundry day! Get up and help me! Do you hear me?"

Hot tears spill over. "It isn't day, Mommy. It's nighttime! Please—"

"Don't you sass, young lady!"

"I'm sorry! Please—"

Her mother pulls her up by her hair.

The little girl's tears sizzle and her right cheek explodes in searing pain, burned by the thing in her mother's hand—not the tip of a cigarette, but the red indicator light of an electric iron.

ACCORDING TO ITS cornerstone, freed slaves built the Park Baptist Church of Harlem precisely one hundred years ago.

According to Marceline LeBlanc, the Gullah Geechee priestess who recently moved into an apartment two blocks up and around the corner on 129th Street, the church is haunted as a low-country graveyard at midnight.

"It's built on a burial ground," she told Calvin Crenshaw in her Creole patois the first time they met, deep crow's-feet crinkling her narrowed black eyes. "*Ooooold* bones there."

"How do you know that?"

"I know. I *feeeeel* it. Here." Her bony fingertip staccatoed her temple between a swath of purple turban and wide earrings that jangled like wind chimes. "Spirits are vengeful."

Ms. LeBlanc, Calvin decided, was full of bull. Maybe full of the devil, too. Yet she's oddly unavoidable, even in a city populated by millions.

Like an alley cat he once made the mistake of feeding, she seems to be everywhere he goes, lurking, prowling, staring. Yesterday morning at this hour, she sprang from murky shadows and scared the bejesus out of him. He was climbing the wide stone steps into the church; she was coming from God-knows-where. Not the butcher shop at 5 a.m., though she carried a small brown paper parcel oozing what appeared to be . . .

Blood?

He might have been wrong, but it sure did look like blood.

She stood on a patch of sidewalk just beyond the streetlight's yellow glow, barefoot on cracked concrete littered with beer bottle caps, saliva-scummed cigarette butts, ant-infested food wrappers, and worse.

"Moon is full," she said, pointing toward it, high above the church spire. "Dangerous to go in alone."

"It's my job to clean the place."

"Some stains, you cannot scrub away."

He shrugged off the cryptic remark and left her there, unlocking the door with his janitor's key ring and then locking it again behind him, just in case . . .

In case Marceline isn't merely a harmless addition to the neighborhood—colorful and slightly off, like the lone cobalt panel in the muted blue stained-glass mosaic window behind the altar.

Calvin himself had replaced that broken piece a few

summers ago, after sweeping away blue shards dotted with metallic pellets. Mischievous neighborhood kids, probably. Fooling around with a BB gun on a fire escape, aiming for a rat or pigeon. No one, not even an outsider, would deliberately deface a century-old sacred landmark.

That's what he thought then; what he'd like to think now. But things are changing out there, where the night air is often thick with sirens, shouts, shrieks, and a haze of marijuana smoke; where morning-after gutters are awash in a hideous flotsam—syringes, used condoms, human waste.

Calvin snaps on thick yellow rubber gloves and rolls his creaky bucket of sudsy water toward the altar.

Yesterday, his gloves were white cotton, and he pushed the pine casket with five fellow pallbearers. They halted right here at the front pew. On the left, his friend Ernie Fields's black-veiled widow, Shirley, sat sobbing with their four anguished teenaged daughters. On the right, the Harlem political powerhouse Gang of Four—Basil Paterson, Charles Rangel, David Dinkins, and Manhattan Borough president Percy Sutton—wiped their eyes with crisp white handkerchiefs. The famous writer James Baldwin, a neighborhood fixture and close childhood friend of Calvin's late daddy, gave a soul-stirring eulogy that began with the same words that have been running through Calvin's mind ever since he heard about Ernie's murder.

"There but for the grace of God . . ."

Calvin held his own emotions in check until the choir sang "Swing Low, Sweet Chariot." Even now, tears sting his eyes as he swishes his mop in the bucket, blurring the tall stained-glass windows where lightning flares as if God Himself is enraged.

The *New York Times* hadn't bothered to cover the story about a humble negro bellhop killed in a hot rod hit and run, and the NYPD sure as heck isn't conducting a citywide manhunt for the killers, white punks cruising for trouble.

This weekend, the esteemed paper and local police are more concerned with escalating race riots, Vietnam protestors, a Brooklyn arson fire that had killed a young firefighter and left another with life-threatening burns, and a string of unsolved murders. The latest victims, a couple, their twelve-year-old son, and the wife's elderly mother, had been stabbed in their beds Friday night. A teenaged daughter, brutally raped, lies in Coney Island Hospital. No known enemies or motives, no witnesses. The culprit, now known in the press as the Brooklyn Butcher, is thought to be responsible for two similar cases this year.

When well-off white people die, headlines scream and detectives mobilize, establishing a tip hotline with talk of a task force, even the FBI. But Ernie's death was just one more violent crime in these dangerous times. No one beyond the neighborhood seems to even—

An unearthly wail stops Calvin cold, reverberating through the cavernous nave.

Marceline and her mambo mumbo-jumbo seep in as it fades.

Wide-eyed, clutching his mop handle like a weapon, he gazes over the century-old carved wooden pews, the shadowy pulpit, and the locked vestibule.

Maybe it was that damned alley cat. Probably snuck in to get out of the storm.

Except, it sounded human.

Maybe a hobo—hungry, harmless . . .

Crying?

All right, then who—*what*—is it? A ghost?

No such thing as ghosts.

He's alone, as always, within the arched plaster walls. The sound must have come from outside.

Unlike the dead, the city doesn't sleep. Cars splash along Lenox Avenue. Pedestrians, shrouded in rain bonnets or holding umbrellas, sidestep streaming channels in galoshes. Some are calling it a night, others working the graveyard shift or beginning a new day. Even in this weather, desperate souls prowl in search of a fix, a good time, easy cash. Eventually, the junkies, streetwalkers, and hoodlums will pass out in grimy doorways until the harsh glare of morning or a beat cop's flashlight bring a rude awakening.

Calvin dips the mop into the water. The scent of Pine-Sol mingles with vintage wood, musty hymnals, and the cloying perfume of funeral lilies.

Lightning flashes again. He listens for another phantom cry in its wake; hears only a resounding crackle of thunder.

Jaw clenched, Calvin mops his way along the altar, shoulders burning as though he's nearing the end of his shift, instead of just beginning it. He hasn't slept much the last few nights. Since April, really, when the Reverend King was gunned down in Memphis. He admired the civil rights leader, but didn't know him personally. Not like Ernie.

Last night, Calvin had lain awake past midnight, thinking about the funeral, the murder. When at last he slept, he drifted into a nightmare. He was Ernie—running, running, running through dark streets, screaming for help, chased by a racing engine and taunting shouts.

At four, the alarm jarred him back to reality. He splashed cold water on his face, pulled on his tattered overalls, and left Bettina sleeping soundly and his good black suit waiting on a hanger.

He'll return for both, and an umbrella, before the nine o'clock service begins. By then, he'll have polished the woodwork and erased smudges and yesterday's muddy footprints. If only he could scrub away the horror and grief, as well.

Some stains, you cannot scrub away.

He shoves his wheeled bucket over to the corner beside the choir stall. He doesn't want to think any more about his dead friend, or the teetering world, or—least of all—about Marceline and her vengeful spirits. For him, as for many, the church is sacred ground; a haven amid the tempest of hatred raging beyond its limestone walls; a place to pray and count your blessings.

Calvin has many, though fatherhood isn't among them, despite years of beseeching the good Lord to bestow a child. But he and Bettina have each other, their health, a roof over their heads, food on the table, and their work—five jobs between them.

Weekdays, Calvin drives a bus and Bettina is a housekeeper. Weeknights, he buses tables at Sylvia's while she works the token booth at the 116th Street subway station.

Weekend wee hours, he's the custodian here at Park Baptist.

The meager pay has grown the nest egg they started when they married a decade ago. Back then, they were saving for the larger place they'd need when children came along. Now, they're just saving for a rainy day.

Today is one of them. Sunday, a day of rest. Mother's Day.

Calvin swings the mop from the bucket. It hits the floor with a wet *slap*.

On its heels, another wail pierces the air, so close this time that he whirls around, expecting to see someone in the choir stall.

The rows of wooden seats beyond the carved rail are vacant.

He thinks of the violence swirling out there in the darkness; rage that has yet to cross the sanctity of this place. Thinks of shattered blue glass and BB pellets scattered like confetti.

Of his dead friend Ernie.

"Anybody here?"

He hears only his own uneasy breathing and the hard rain pattering high above the rib-vaulted ceiling.

Fool. You're imagining things. You need a nice long nap today, and maybe to get these ears of yours checked out by a doctor, and that is that.

He shoves the mop along, creating a gleaming swath on the scarred hardwood. He thinks about working hard, and growing older. If you live a long life and are blessed with loved ones, loss is inevitable. People die before their time, some more violently than others. Let yourself dwell in that dark reality, and you'll never move on.

He thinks about Ernie, about Mama three years in her grave, about Bettina's stillborn son ten years ago. About this being Mother's Day, and all these years trying, trying, trying for another pregnancy . . .

You try, and you hope, and you hold tight to what you have. Even if it's nothing more than faith and hope, life itself, and love.

Calvin is no teeny-bop Beatles fan, but they sure got it right last year when they sang "All You Need Is—"

He whirls around, startled by a choking little gasp.

It came from down near the floor toward the back of the choir stall.

Resisting the instinct to flee, he closes his eyes, asking the Lord for guidance.

Someone may be lying in wait there. Someone with

hatred in his cold heart for men like Calvin, Ernie, the Reverend King . . .

Or someone might need help.

Calvin opens his eyes and relinquishes his mop handle, letting it fall against the rail.

"Hey," he calls, into the shadows. "Are you all right?"

The question is met with a whimper.

He moves closer and leans in to look, expecting to find a woman crouched on the floor.

Instead, he sees a small bundle. At a glance, it appears to be someone's coat or wrap left behind on the seat. Then it makes another wailing sound, and Calvin knows, before he reaches into the folds of fabric, exactly what it is.

A baby.

Chapter Two

The D train was standing room only when Oran boarded in the Bronx just past four o'clock on this stormy Sunday morning. He dozes as it winds into Manhattan and back out again into the wilds of Brooklyn, dispersing the raucous after-hours bar crowd and world-weary shift workers along the way. When the conductor announces the end of the line, Oran wakes to find himself sharing the car with a lone woman.

Elderly, dressed all in black, holding an open Bible, she meets his gaze as the train slows. When the doors open, she escapes on thick-soled old lady shoes.

"Don't worry!" he calls, ambling along behind, galoshes squeaking on the tile floor. "I'm harmless!"

To you, anyway. You're way too far past your prime.

The Stillwell Avenue station has been spared the wrecking ball that shattered neighboring landmarks. When Oran was a boy, it was a grand place. Now it's bathed in urine-colored light that seeps over scarred floors and peeling paint, falling short of dingy corners. He passes a vagrant sleeping on the shoe shine stand near the shuttered Philips Candy Shop, where he'd beg his mother, Pamela, to stop for saltwater taffy. Once, while he waited for her to come out of the restroom, a man who'd overheard his fruitless pleas bought him some. Oran accepted, being the kind of kid who took candy from a stranger and lacked the manners to say thank you. Pamela was just a kid herself; too young and frivolous to keep him close by her side in public places, or give much thought to social etiquette, rules, and warnings . . . laws.

He will never allow his own daughter to wander the way he used to. Terrible things can happen to a child. Terrible.

He remembers trailing behind his mother as they walked out toward the boardwalk, cramming his mouth full of taffy, wincing as the sticky sugar zapped his cavities. When he tried to swallow the sodden mass, it lodged in his windpipe. He clawed frantically at his throat, searching for Pamela's high blond ponytail, red lipstick, bobby sox, and saddle shoes. He spotted her up ahead in the throng surrounding Nathan's Famous hot dog stand on the corner of Stillwell and Surf Avenue. She was laughing with a handsome man whose blond crew cut tufted high above his tanned, handsome face.

He turned out to be Eddie. Later—weeks, months later—Oran realized he was the reason they'd come to Coney Island on that summer Saturday. It was Eddie who noticed Oran turning blue just before he lost consciousness, suffocated by the forbidden treat. Eddie who saved his life.

Eddie who destroyed his mother's.

Oran thinks of his former stepfather now as he snaps open an umbrella and exits the station into the pouring rain, heading south to cross Surf Avenue. Is he still alive in prison?

What about his mother? She's likely dead by now, although you never know.

The sky is still dark above the patchwork of dripping billboards that proclaim the iconic hot dog stand as The Only Original Nathan's and urge pedestrians to Follow the Crowd.

No crowd today, here or on the puddle-pooled board-walk beyond. Near the spot where Steeplechase Park once stood, a flag whips in the wet sea wind, hooks clanging a desolate rhythm against the metal pole. Oran closes his eyes. He hears the triple carousel's calliope, and penny arcade buzzers and bells. He smells sausage, cotton candy, roasted peanuts, fried dough, fried oysters, fried everything, all mingling with hot tar and damp marine air.

His soul tickles with the same butterflies that would flutter whenever he glimpsed the Pavilion of Fun. In his mind's eye, the legendary Steeplechase Funny Face glimmers high in the glass façade, its broad, painted grin beaming the promise of a glorious day. His heart gallops in rhythm with the carved mechanical horses that once circled the amusement park's vast circumference— magical creatures that could whisk him away to a better place, if only for the eponymous ride's duration.

He thought about those horses and the smiley face long after Pamela and Eddie had wrenched him out of Brooklyn.

Two years ago, Fred Trump, a scandal-ridden real estate developer, threw a party—a party!—to celebrate the park's bulldozing. Sulking after the city had denied zoning permits to build fancy occanfront apartment towers at the site, surrounded by bikini-clad models and reporters, the millionaire handed out champagne along with bricks for gleeful onlookers to hurtle through the Pavilion of Fun's stained-glass façade. Oran was there that day, on the boardwalk. He watched the joyful smile crack and shatter, raining razor shards onto hallowed ground, and his soul.

He walks on past the Parachute Jump ride, a relic left to weather the salt air, rising like a tombstone above twisted scrap metal. It's all that remains of the glorious park. The promised towers have yet to materialize.

He hums "The First Cut Is the Deepest," his favorite song from the latest Cat Stevens album. Most fitting, these days.

He passes the pier, Astroland, the Wonder Wheel and the Cyclone, the New York Aquarium. Turning north along Ocean Parkway, he spots Coney Island Hospital three blocks up and quickens his pace, thinking of Margaret Costello.

He managed to stay away all day yesterday, smothering his urges in salacious press coverage of Friday night's triple homicide in Bensonhurst. This time, the "Brooklyn Butcher" had slain four family members in their beds: Joe and Rose Costello, their twelve-year-old son, Danny, and Rose's mother, Margarita, who lived with them. Seventeen-year-old Margaret had been raped.

The case echoes similar crimes committed over the past several months: the Myers family of Sheepshead Bay and the Sheeran family of Bay Ridge. In both of those cases, a teenaged daughter was the lone survivor. Christina Myers and Tara Sheeran were released from the hospital within days of their families' murders, and Margaret will be out soon, as well. Her wounds aren't life threatening, just cuts and bruises received in the struggle with her rapist.

At the main entrance, Oran lowers the umbrella, removes his hat and trench coat, and strides inside. A middle-aged woman sits behind the desk. He was hoping to find someone younger, inexperienced. Visiting hours don't start for another hour, but he's not just any visitor, as long as she buys his story.

She looks up from her magazine. He greets her with brisk efficiency, and explains why he's here. She directs him to the hospital's Burn Unit on the third floor, saying, "I read about that in the newspaper yesterday. That poor young firefighter's family will be glad to see you."

He thanks her and heads for the elevator. Inside, he presses the button for the third floor, and then the second, his real destination. Just before the doors close, a young nurse in a white uniform slips in, presses the button for seven, and flashes him a smile.

"Still raining out there?" She gestures at his umbrella, its gleaming metal prong speared in a puddle that trickles like blood across the tile floor.

"Like cats and dogs."

She sighs. "I hope it lets up by the time I finish my shift."

"When is that?"

"Noon. My husband is taking me out to brunch for Mother's Day. It's my first one."

"Congratulations. Boy or girl?"

"Girl. She's the sweetest, most precious little thing in the whole world."

"I'll bet. I have a—" he starts to say, then catches himself, as the doors slide open at the second floor. He steps out, changing it to, "You have a happy Mother's Day."

"I will, thanks."

In the deserted corridor, he can hear a transistor radio playing somewhere, quiet conversation from the nurses' station. They smile as he passes.

He returns the smile and walks briskly, noting the exits along the way. He scans the patient names taped to the doors until he reaches hers.

Margaret Costello

He's expecting a police guard posted outside the room, as he'd found when he'd attempted to visit Tara. That day, he gave the officer a polite nod and kept right on walking, rounding the corner at the end of the hall. There, he pushed through the stairwell doors and tore down onto the street, propelled by an irrational burst of panic.

The guard couldn't have recognized him. There had been no witnesses at the Sheeran house that night, just as there had been none at the Myerses' the month before. No one had glimpsed the masked intruder who crept into sleeping households to slaughter all but the precious, precious daughters.

Oran finds a chair positioned in the hall outside Margaret's room, but the guard must have stepped away. No sign of him down the hall, nor in the dim room, but, ah . . . there she is, sound asleep. Her arms, bared in a hospital gown, are bruised and scratched. One is bent, hand fisted beneath her chin. The other stretches along her side, an IV needle protruding from a vein.

Oran hurries over to her. Her face is scraped and there's a bandage on her temple, yet she appears serene. Are her dreams pleasant? She must be sedated. How else would someone sleep so soundly after what she's endured?

Soon the medication will wear off, and she'll wake to the nightmare again. Poor sweet baby.

A thin clump of long dark hair straggles across her mouth. His fingers itch to brush it away, but he doesn't dare touch her.

He reaches into his pocket, pulls out the packet, and tucks it under her pillow. The movement is painstaking, so as not to disturb her, but something is already under there.

It drops out onto the floor as he pulls his hand away. It's a small cross, looped and woven from yellowed palm fronds.

A memory flashes: an usher handing him a pair of long green strips as he walked into church with his grandparents on Palm Sunday. In the pew, his grandfather folded and turned them in his hands and his grandmother didn't scold him for fidgeting. Oran noticed many other parishioners doing the same thing with their fronds, fashioning them into cross shapes. Grandfather handed his to Oran with a smile and a nod. Back home after mass, his grandmother told him to tuck it under his pillow.

"Why?"

"It's what we do. It will keep you safe."

But it was no more a magic talisman than the rosary beads his grandmother slipped into his bag when his mother moved him out of their house one volatile night. Having taken off a few days earlier with Eddie, she came back to collect her things and—almost an afterthought—her child.

"If you leave this house to go live with that scoundrel," his grandfather screamed, "don't ever come back!"

"Don't worry! We won't!"

A few years later, Oran ran away and returned to his grandparents' house. Surely they wouldn't hold him responsible for his mother's sins. Surely they'd provide a safe haven, if only until he could heal his wounds—not just the lacerations that covered his frail body.

A sob of relief clogged his throat when he rounded the corner and spotted the familiar clapboard row house. But as he drew closer, he saw children playing on the front walk, and a strange man sitting on the stoop watching them. The door opened, and an unfamiliar apron-clad redhead poked her head out to call them all inside to dinner.

Oran never did find out what had become of his grandparents. They no longer mattered. The new family that had moved into their home would live—albeit not for very long—to regret it.

Seething at the memory, he reaches to snatch up the

palm cross lying on the floor beside Margaret's bed. His arm bumps the tray alongside the bed. The rattle is deafening. Her eyes pop open, and she looks at him. He braces himself for the scream, accusation, shout for help.

Her eyes drift closed again.

Bolting from the room, Oran finds the stairwell exit blocked by an orderly clattering along with a cart, and is forced to stroll in the opposite direction, past the nurses' station. Still engrossed in their conversation, they don't seem to notice him.

He presses the down button on the elevator and waits, pulse throbbing, hand clenched around the wooden umbrella handle. When the doors slide open, there are no other passengers. He rides back down to the first floor, head bowed, inhaling through his nose, holding the breath, and exhaling through his mouth.

Calm down. Calm down!

Margaret had looked at him, but had she *seen* him? Later, when—*if*—she remembers what happened, she might think she'd been hallucinating from the drugs piped into her arm. Even lucid, she might not connect him to what happened Friday night. Maybe she's blocked that out anyway. Trauma can trigger protective amnesia.

He has to escape without calling attention to himself. And he has to stay away from here, from her, until the time comes. A lot can happen between now and next winter, but if all goes as planned . . .

The doors open, and he forces himself to walk, not run, back to the entrance. The woman at the desk has finished her magazine and set it aside. Now he can see that it's this week's copy of *Life*, with the Columbia riots and Paul Newman on the cover. He played Cool Hand Luke.

The magazine is a sign. They're everywhere, if you know how to recognize them. Oran had seen the film at least five, ten times back in November, mesmerized and inspired by the charismatic character who triumphed over what some might interpret as a metaphorical crucifixion to become a savior. If Luke, faced with a harsh prison sentence, could persevere to lead the downtrodden on the path to glorification, Oran can do the same.

Beyond the plate glass, the rain is still pouring down. He pauses to put on his hat and raincoat before heading for the doors, umbrella at the ready.

"Have a pleasant Sunday," he tells the woman at the desk.

She looks up with a smile.

"Thank you, Father. You, too."

Chapter Three

Saturday, March 7, 1987
New York City

Stepping off the elevator shortly before midnight, Amelia Crenshaw spots her father. Calvin is straddling the threshold—one foot in her mother's room and the other in the hall.

"Sorry I'm late getting back," she calls, hurrying past the nurses' station and a small solarium where the sun never shines. If she looks in, she'll see a somber family, or maybe a gaunt, hairless patient, fixated on the television or window, swaddled in too many layers for this overheated place.

She doesn't look. You learn not to. Amelia's first bleak February journey down this hallway at Morningside Memorial Hospital had exposed a priest bestowing last rites, an old man's withered backside bared between gaping gown flaps, orderlies joking around as if the sheet-covered corpse on a gurney between them were a checkerboard. Now she sees only what's right in front of her—if that.

The room feels emptier, as if someone has departed in her absence. But both patients—her mother and the stranger who lies on the other side of the curtain—are still here, still alive. Barely.

She sets her heavy backpack in the space vacated by

Calvin's duffel bag. It holds the bus driver's uniform he'd been wearing when he arrived six hours ago. Now he's in janitor's coveralls, pulling on his jacket. Amelia hangs her own over the back of the visitor's chair and sinks onto the warm vinyl cushion.

"You're not going home to sleep for a bit, Daddy?" she asks as he leans over the bed and presses a tender kiss to Bettina's forehead.

"No. Just going to get my work done and get right back here as soon as I can," he says—to them both, though Amelia is certain her mother could no longer hear.

Calvin gives his wife a long last look, then leaves for his custodial job at Park Baptist, giving Amelia's shoulder a pat on his way to the door.

Tag—you're it.

She settles in with her philosophy text so that her brain, in contemplating her mother's impending death, can also attempt to absorb applied normative ethics and Dewey's theory of valuation. She earned a 4.0 in her first semester at Hunter College. Her second was scarcely underway when her mother was diagnosed. So much for As. She could have passed English Comp, History of Jazz, and Intro to Acting without opening a book, but she's struggling with philosophy, and midterms loom.

She reads a page, and then reads it again, toying with her necklace. It's the finest thing she owns. The tiny fourteen-carat gold signet ring, anyway—not the cheap chain from which it dangles. At least this one doesn't turn her neck green like the first, bought from a sidewalk vendor who claimed it was gold and sold it for a dollar.

Amelia had been hoping for a blue linde star sapphire ring as a high school graduation gift. Instead, her parents presented her with the ring. It does have two sapphires, but they're so small you can barely see them, on either side of an engraved, blue enamel-filled *C* for Crenshaw.

"It was yours," Bettina told her, "when you were just a tiny little baby."

Her flash of disappointment had given way to sweet sentimentality, and appreciation that despite all the hard times, they'd never resorted to selling it.

She turns the page of her text, realizes she still hasn't absorbed what she read, goes back for a third pass, and gives up. Snapping the book closed, she slumps back in the chair, half expecting her mother to say, "Sit up straight, child."

Bettina is always nitpicking. Posture is a big concern. "Be proud of your height. When I was your age, I'd have given anything to be tall."

Just under six feet in her bare feet even before she started high school, Amelia would have given anything not to tower over both her parents, all the girls, and plenty of the guys. Her mother's comments never helped. "Go on, try some of this honey fried chicken," or, "Tall girls can afford to eat pecan pie. Y'all carry a few extra pounds like it's nothing at all."

Like her culinary skills, Bettina's accent is drenched in rich Southern sugar.

"Mama, you know I don't like sweets."

"It's chicken."

"It's sweet chicken. I'm not hungry, and I don't need any extra pounds."

"Neither do I, child. Neither do I."

Never a thin woman, Bettina hasn't been sick long enough to waste away. Even now, her figure beneath the beige blanket appears to be its usual ample self. Her face, always chubby, is still swollen from a new drug that should have given her a good shot at survival. The doctor was optimistic back in January, and sent Bettina home before that first treatment with stacks of information about scientific studies and clinical trials.

She didn't give them a second glance, but Amelia pored over them.

"See that? I'll be cured in no time. The doctor said so."

"Really? He said you'd be cured?"

"Sure he did. I haven't even been sick for more than a week."

"But the statistics say that the odds aren't—"

"Don't you worry about statistics, child. The doctor said I'm younger and healthier than all those people who didn't beat it. I'll take some medicine, and I'll get better."

The treatments failed to halt the malignant march. By mid-February, the doctor called them off.

"Keep fighting, baby," Amelia overheard a devastated Calvin urging her as they wept together behind their closed bedroom door. "You know we believe in miracles."

Bettina's response was cryptic. "We got ours twenty years ago. We need to talk about—"

"All we need to talk about is getting you better. Don't you waste an ounce of energy on anything else."

"But—"

"None of it matters right now. You have to beat this. You *have to*! Amelia and I will do whatever it takes to—"

"You have three jobs. She has college. You can't—"

"We can. We will. Whatever it takes!"

Bettina fell silent. Was that the moment she decided to expedite her own death sentence?

One of the regular nurses bustles in to check her vital signs and administer morphine. She's in her thirties, maybe early forties, with a Caribbean accent, complicated braids, and an unusual name Amelia keeps forgetting.

Catching sight of Amelia, she gives a nod. "You're back. Did you get some sleep?"

"Yes," she lies. "Any change since I left?"

"No."

"Are you sure? Because something seems . . . different."

The nurse shrugs, busy writing something in her folder.

She closes it, and Amelia clears her throat. "Um, how long do you think . . ."

"Could be anytime. Tonight, tomorrow . . ."

"*Tomorrow*?" White-hot accusation flares. "Yesterday you said that it would be yesterday, and this morning you said—"

"I said it could be anytime now. That's all I can tell you. It's all I know. It's all anyone knows. Your mama's just hangin' on. Sometimes they do that." She looks at Amelia like she wants to say something more, then shakes her head, saying only, "I'm sorry."

She moves past the dividing curtain to check Bettina's comatose roommate, who never has any visitors. That first day, just over a week ago, Amelia assumed that she must not have any family.

Now she isn't so sure. What if the woman's loved ones just can't take it anymore? What if they can't endure another day or hour or minute of sitting and watching and waiting? What if they can't stand to see a once robust woman lying motionless and pale as the pillow, hearing her lungs gasp for every tortured breath? Trying to think of meaningful things to say, wondering if she'll hear, wondering whether she's in pain, wondering what life will be like afterward. Terrified of being here when she passes; terrified of not being here. Either way, the patient will never know. Maybe they've decided to remember her as she'd once been and simply walked away, back to the world.

For Amelia, there's no escaping the terrible vigil. Calvin expects her to stay with Bettina whenever he's working. He works a lot.

"What about school?" she'd asked in the beginning.

"Bring your books to the hospital and study. If your teacher needs a note, I can—"

"It's college, Daddy! It's not like that!"

He wouldn't know. He'd never made it past high school, and her mother hadn't even gotten that far. Amelia had heard stories—schoolgirl Bettina, skipping barefoot on dusty antebellum lanes, until her family needed her to drop out and go to work.

Both her parents have told her how fortunate she is to have CUNY, with free tuition for impoverished students like her. But you don't get to stay if you don't do well. When this is over, she can turn things around, especially if it happens before midterms.

The nurse steps back around the curtain, flashes a rare smile at Amelia to make up for her earlier terse attitude, and pauses to tuck in the blanket at the foot of Bettina's bed. As if the patient had kicked it askew in her absence. As if the patient might be capable of something more than struggling for breath or contorting her facial muscles in the slightest indication of pain. As if her daughter isn't sitting here wishing she'd hurry up and die already.

"You okay?" she asks Amelia. "You want some water?"

"No, thanks."

"I'll get you water. You need to hydrate." She sets down her paperwork and disappears into the hall with a brown plastic pitcher no one has bothered—needed—to fill for days.

Amelia looks at her mother, ashamed, swallows hard, and whispers, "I love you."

She isn't a terrible person. She's a good person.

She *was*, anyway. Before her mother got sick.

Really? Before the blindside diagnosis, she was her sweet, humble self?

No, she's been grappling for a while now with this deep-seated yearning, not even sure what it is that she wants. It isn't just about material possessions, but about comfort, peace of mind, leisure, stability, freedom, opportunity . . .

She wants a different kind of life, one built around those elusive facets so many people lack in her world, and take for granted beyond it. Things her parents can't, or won't, provide.

The nurse returns with the pitcher, pours some water, and hands her the paper cup. "Drink. We don't want you to get dehydrated."

We, as in the nurse and . . . who? Her mother? The hospital staff?

The implication of broad concern irritates Amelia, as if meant to reassure her that her own physical well-being is relevant at a time like this, in a room like this. As if she will ever matter again, to anyone, now that the person who's always taken care of her is . . .

Gone.

Bettina has already departed, her body vacated like a house whose residents stole away in the night. The figure in the bed is a hollow shell. It's all over but the dying.

Amelia watches the nurse leave the room, wishing she could stop her and confide that she doesn't want to lose her mother today, tomorrow, ever. But it's going to happen. Bettina's soul can't live on in this disease-infested body. No further medical intervention or prayer will alter the fact that her organs are shutting down and the next labored breath might be her last.

"Every moment we have her is a gift," Calvin said earlier, before she left him sitting in this awful chair, clasping one of his wife's hands in both his own. Amelia didn't dare dispute it. She just bowed her head and asked God for a merciful end to the suffering.

Mouth dry, she sips from a waxy cup already gone soggy. The water is tepid, with an institutional silkiness.

Bring on the dehydration.

She looks around for a place to set the cup and sees the patient folders, forgotten on the bedside table. Bettina's file is right on top. She reaches for it without hesitation, opens it, and scans the staff's scribbled notes.

No clue to her mother's condition; no preordained timeline for her demise.

She turns the pages. Bettina's medical history is meticulously outlined on forms detailing not just her diagnosis and illness, but other information, as well. Basic questions like height, weight, date of birth, plus—

Wait a minute.

Total number of pregnancies carried to term . . .

One?

Amelia's first thought is that someone—her mother? The hospital?—forgot to count her unnamed brother who'd only lived for a few hours.

But the date in the file, 1957, coincides with his birth, and death.

Something is missing.

Amelia is missing.

"*LIFE COMES DOWN to a series of choices*," the wisest man Stockton Barnes has ever known once told him. "*Make the wrong one at any given moment, and you find yourself at a dead-end. If you're lucky, someone will come along and pull you back onto the right track.*"

He was lucky.

Smoking a cigarette, striding through the rain toward Morningside Memorial, he spots a kid shuffling toward him, hands in his pockets, hood up, head down. When he gets closer, he glances up through narrowed eyes, looking for trouble.

Ah, yes. Barnes himself at fifteen.

He meets the kid's gaze, sending a silent message. *Don't mess with me.*

They move on past each other. Barnes tosses his soggy Marlboro into a puddle and enters the hospital. It's across town from the East Harlem one where his father had died fifteen years ago, and that had happened at high noon, not midnight. Barnes thinks of him nonetheless, remembering their last moments together at the kitchen table, wishing they'd been more remarkable. Wishing they'd been having a meaningful conversation instead of gobbling toaster waffles drenched in butter and syrup, Stockton thinking about basketball and his father unaware that his heart was about to give out. It happened so fast—one moment he was sitting there, the next, he was on the floor, fork still in hand, and Mom was shrieking.

Barnes pushes the memory from his mind as he approaches the reception desk, manned by an elderly black man with a bushy white mustache. Seeing the NYPD uniform, he straightens in his chair. "Hi, Officer. If you're here about the gang shooting, they're all in—"

"Just visiting a friend. He was admitted a few hours ago. George Washington."

"George . . ."

"Washington. Right."

"Hell of a name to live up to."

"He does." Barnes flashes a brief smile.

"Room 707. Lucky sevens—that's a good sign."

"Let's hope so."

He walks toward the elevator, inhaling the stuffy, antiseptic air. Wash must hate it. He's the kind of guy who likes the windows wide open, regardless of escalating crime rates.

A little over a decade ago, Barnes had been part of the problem. They called him Gloss, back then. Slick. Smooth. Nothing ever seemed to stick. He got away with shoplifting and worse—escapades he now recognizes as criminal mischief. He blamed grief over his father, poverty, being surrounded by bad influences . . . everything but his own lousy choices.

Rounding a corner, he passes an orderly rolling a new mother toward the exit in a wheelchair. Plump and disheveled, she's gazing down at a blue bundle in her arms. A man trails, his face almost obscured by several bags, a couple of blue-tinted carnation arrangements, and a blue ribbon bobbing with a Mylar helium balloon proclaiming, It's a Boy! Yeah, no kidding. Feeling for the brother, Barnes meets his gaze, but he grins back, giddy as his wife.

To each his own. At the elevator bank, Barnes pushes the up button and rocks back and forth on his heels, wondering what's going on with Wash. Yesterday, his friend left a message at the precinct saying not to come over when he got off duty, as was Barnes's Friday night habit.

Wash left another message today. Not at the precinct, but on Barnes's home answering machine.

"Stockton, I'm at Morningside Memorial. I came in for some tests, and they admitted me. The guy in the other bed got the damned window. Other than that, I'm fine."

He didn't sound fine. His breathing was labored, words strangled as if he was trying not to cough. He ended the call telling Barnes not to worry, and not to come. Of course, Barnes hurried right over.

The elevator dings, doors glide open, and a young woman barrels right into him.

"Sorry!" they say in unison.

Always one to appreciate a beautiful woman, he smiles at this one, tall and lithe, wearing baggy jeans and a bright pink blouse with lengths of gold chain dangling beneath either side of the collar as if someone yanked it in two. She doesn't smile back. Her eyes are anguished, face ravaged with grief, or terror, or fury—difficult to discern in passing, but none of those emotions would be unusual in a place like this, at an hour like this. Terrible tales are unfolding all over the hospital.

Barnes spends his workdays seeing strangers through

their darkest hours. Tonight, he has to help Wash. He allows the girl to disappear, running from her tragedy as he steps into the elevator to face his.

It might just be bronchitis, but lately he's had a feeling . . .

Wash hasn't been well in a while. He's been coughing and wheezing since Christmas. Longer. Too long for bronchitis.

Barnes presses the button for lucky seven. The doors close and he looks at the paneled ceiling, asking anyone who might be listening up there to let Wash be okay. His grandmother? His father? Almighty God Himself?

You guys never listen, though.

He sighs and stares at his shoes, in need of a shine at the end of a slushy March day on the streets. Something glints on the muddy tile alongside them. He reaches down and picks up a miniature gold signet ring. It's engraved with a *C*, the letter filled in with a gleaming, bright blue enamel, and there are tiny blue stones on either side of it.

It's far too small to fit on an adult's hand, or even a child's. It must be meant for a baby. He thinks of the couple with the newborn son. Or maybe it had fallen from the girl's broken chain. At the rate this elevator is going, they'll all be long gone by the time he can get back down to the lobby.

C . . .

His father's name was Charles. Can it be a sign?

The hospital will have a lost and found. Barnes will turn in the ring downstairs, after he sees Wash. For now, he clasps it in his pocket and looks heavenward again.

"Hey, Dad. If you're up there and you can hear me . . . you know what to do."

RAIN-SOAKED, SHIVERING, BREATHLESS, Amelia bursts into Park Baptist Church.

Calvin is there alone, mopping the aisle. He sees her rushing toward him and drops to his knees. "She's gone?"

Amelia's question is simultaneous. "Was I adopted?"

"Is your mother gone?" he asks as if he hadn't heard, gaping up at her, tears streaming down his cheeks.

"She isn't my mother! She lied to me. You both did. I—"

"Tell me if she's gone, girl! Tell me right now!"

"No, she didn't—she's . . . alive."

He exhales and buries his face in his hands, murmuring a prayer. She watches as if from a great distance as he pulls himself to his feet, his work-roughened hand quaking on the mop handle like it's a crutch.

"I told you not to leave your mother alone, Amelia."

She turns away from the glint of accusation, muttering, "She isn't my mother."

"What did you say?"

"I *said*—" She whirls back. "I saw her file at the hospital."

"What are you talking about? What file?"

"She's not my mother. And you're not my—"

"No! That isn't true!"

She exhales in relief. She should have known there was some mistake. It must have been someone else's file, although . . .

Her brother's birthdate was there. All right, then she must have misinterpreted the information. Lord knows she couldn't even read a textbook page tonight.

"I am your father, and your mother is your mother, Amelia. We raised you. That's all that matters. We love you. It doesn't matter how you came to us."

"What?"

No mistake, then.

Total number of pregnancies carried to term: one.

"How . . ." The rest snags on a monstrous ache in her throat.

How did I come to you?

No wonder she doesn't look like them. No wonder they rarely talk about the past. No wonder she's always felt unsettled, though she's never known any other home but theirs.

"It doesn't matter how," he says.

"It does to me. If I was adopted, I deserve to know more about—"

"Now is not the time for that. Go back to her."

"But I—"

"I said, *go.* I'll be there as soon as I'm finished here."

She shakes her head, standing her ground. "I need to know."

"You need to be with her. She can't die alone!"

"*You* go. She's your wife."

"I have a job to do."

"Does it matter more than she does?"

"*Nothing* matters more than she does."

"I know!" She's sobbing now. "I don't want to watch her die, either, okay? Just go!"

He bows his head, looking for a long time at his worn shoes, at the clean patch of wet floor, and the waiting, dusty patch of dry.

Then he hurtles the mop toward the altar with a strangled cry. It clatters to the floor, spattering dirty water.

He grabs her arm and pulls her down the aisle, out the door.

"I'm going home," Amelia cries on the church steps, struggling in his grip.

"You're coming with me and apologizing to your mother for leaving her."

"She can't even hear me! She can't see me, she can't talk to me, she can't—" She breaks off, turning away.

She can't apologize to me for lying.

Her gaze falls on someone standing on the street, just

beyond the lamppost light. Marceline LeBlanc gazes up at them through the curtain of freezing rain.

Calvin sees her, too, and mutters, "Let's go."

"Everything okay over there?" Marceline calls in her island dialect.

No, everything is not okay over here, Amelia wants to scream. *Everything will never be okay again!*

Calvin ignores the question. He leads her down the steps and past Marceline, who meets Amelia's sorrowful gaze and asks where they're going.

"To the hospital. My—"

"Hush!" Calvin squeezes her arm. "It's nobody's business."

They splash on past in solemn silence.

When they reach Morningside Memorial, the rain has become snow, and the cornrowed Caribbean nurse is waiting.

They're too late.

LUCKY SEVEN MY ass, Barnes thinks, peeking into Wash's room.

The curtain is drawn between the beds, obscuring the guy with the window view. Wash is asleep, mouth open, wheeze-snoring loudly. That doesn't sound good. Worse than the bronchitis he's been battling. Pneumonia? Worse than pneumonia?

Shaken, he settles into the guest chair. Wash didn't look this frail last week. Has he deteriorated so quickly? Or is it because he was awake, full of spit and vinegar as always? A man, asleep, allows a glimpse of vulnerability. Mortality.

Barnes has only seen Wash as a stalwart conqueror. A lesser man couldn't have saved a kid like him.

Barnes had been about to swing a lead pipe through the window of a parked car when Wash burst from the shadows and collared him. Certain he was going to call the cops, Barnes later discovered that he *was* a cop. Though six inches shorter than a lanky teenaged Barnes, he had a steely grip and delivered one hell of a dressing-down.

"And I don't ever want to see you out on the street again unless you're going to school! Got it?"

No meek terror for that kid. Only belligerence, delivered with a glare. "I don't go to school. I dropped out."

"Who throws away an opportunity to get an education? What's wrong with you, son?"

"Ain't nothin' wrong with me. What's wrong with y—"

"Listen to me. I don't want to see you again out here unless you're picking up litter with the Boy Scouts. You got it?" He was shouting again. "Got it? Can you hear me, son?"

"Yeah, I hear you!" He wasn't a Boy Scout, either, but the belligerence was dribbling away.

"Okay, then. Good."

And then he did the thing that Barnes would never forget. If the course of his life changed in a moment, in a gesture, that was it.

Wash released him and extended a hand.

YEARS AGO, HIS father had taught him to stand tall, look people in the eye, and give a solid handshake. "It's how you show you're a man," he said, and then scoffed at Barnes's first few efforts. "Ain't nobody wants to grab on to a wussy wet noodle like that, boy."

It had been years since anyone had wanted to shake his hand.

The man's grasp was firm and warm. He introduced himself.

"*Wash?* What kind of fool name is that?"

"Wash is a hell of a lot better than George Washington.

I think we agree *he* was nobody's fool. That's my real name, by the way."

"George Washington?"

"Yeah. My ancestors were slaves on his plantation down in Virginia a million years ago, so they took his name. That's how things worked back then."

"A million years ago?"

"Something like that. Still trying to figure out whether my parents had a mean streak or a sense of humor. What do you think?"

Barnes shifted his weight, prepared to bolt.

But then Wash said, "Your name's Stockton, right?"

"How'd you know that?"

"Met your dad a time or two. I'm sorry for your loss."

The unexpected condolences were the first pull on Barnes's adolescent heartstrings in ages. Yet mere words couldn't release his tangled emotions like a slipknot tug. That complicated snarl of grief and fury would take time and persistence to unravel.

Wash was a patient man. Thanks to him, Barnes has grown into one. Without his mentor, he would never have chosen a career in law enforcement. Without Wash . . .

He can't imagine life without Wash. He has to be okay.

Eyes swimming, he reaches for the tissue box on the bedside table. Wash stirs and looks at him. A familiar gap-toothed grin spreads beneath the oxygen tubes poking from his nostrils.

"What are you doing here?"

He shoves the tear-dampened tissue into his pocket. "That's my question for you."

"They're crazy." Wash waves a gnarled hand at the door. "Should'a just ignored them and gone home. I can't sleep in this place."

"You were doing a decent job of it. What did the doctor—"

"Is it snowing out there yet?"

"Just raining. What did—"

"Supposed to snow, though, right?"

"I don't know. What—"

"You know what's funny?"

"How you keep interrupting me?"

"Snow. See, if this was the other end of the year, we'd be all excited about it. Nothing like that first snowfall. Scrubs away the grime, makes everything fresh and pretty. But in March it's a different story. In March, that snow buries every hint of springtime. It's all about the timing, Stockton, you see? Same snow, but whether we welcome it depends on when it shows up."

"Wash. What did the doctor say?"

A pause. "I'll be all right."

Is that the answer to Barnes's question? Or is it unrelated commentary; merely what Wash wants to believe—or wants Barnes to believe?

"Is it the bronchitis?"

"No."

"What, then? Did it turn into pneumonia?"

"Aren't you supposed to be at Hogan's Pub for a retirement party?" No one can change a subject like Wash.

"What? No."

"Sure you are. You said something about it the other day. Bub Carson's retiring, right? Moving to Arizona?"

"Guess we can rule out Alzheimer's. How about pneumonia?"

Wash shakes his head, covering a cough that turns into a full-blown spell.

Barnes pours a cup of water from the brown plastic pitcher and holds it out to him.

"I can't drink that lying flat on my back. Can't have a conversation this way, either." He presses a button, and the top half of the bed sinks, tilting him backward. He curses and fiddles with the control. It rises, nearly folding him in half. He lowers it to a more comfortable position, grumbling, "Damned thing goes up when I want to go down, and down when I want to go up."

"You'll get the hang of it."

"I don't want to. I want to go home."

"Yeah. You said." He hands Wash the water. "What's going on, exactly?"

"I don't want to talk about it, Stockton. You learn anything interesting at school today?"

On Saturdays, Barnes takes a Race and Gender class at John Jay College of Criminal Justice. It was Wash's idea. He's already earned his associate degree, but the NYPD likes to see initiative, and Barnes is gunning for a promotion.

"I learned a lot. I'm starting to think there's only one thing in this world more challenging than being a black man."

"Being a black woman?"

"Ah, you took the same course?"

"Oldest story there is." Wash shakes his head. "Back when I was coming up, we didn't take classes like you do now."

"Guess it was a lot easier back then to make detective."

"You just work hard on the job and keep up with your course work, Stockton. You'll get that gold shield one of these days."

"More like one of these years. This millennium would be good."

"Be patient. I guarantee it'll happen. There's no finer man in the NYPD."

They talk awhile longer, about everything but Wash's diagnosis, though the conversation is stalled by several coughing fits. Every time Barnes brings up his health, Wash changes the subject. Finally, he says, "Get out of here now. You still have time to go to that party."

Barnes looks at his watch. "Do you know what time it is?"

"They'll be there till dawn."

He's right, but Barnes isn't in the mood for socializing. "I'd rather stay—"

"Yeah, well, you can't. I need my . . ." Wash huffs, catches his breath ". . . beauty sleep. But thanks for coming to see me."

"You're welcome. And thank you."

"For what?"

"For thinking I'm going to make detective. For being the only person who ever believed in me."

"Your mother does."

"Not like you. There's nothing in it for you."

His mother is hoping he might eventually earn enough to bail her out of her ongoing financial crisis. But Wash? He simply loves Barnes and wants the best for him.

He rides the elevator back downstairs, exits the hospital, and lights a cigarette.

The rain has turned to snow—fat, feathery flakes, coming down hard. March snow.

He still doesn't feel like socializing, but he's not ready to go home. He doesn't want to be alone tonight.

Instead of walking toward East Harlem, he makes his way on slick sidewalks to the subway. The platform is crowded. At this time of night, trains are few and far between. Approaching the turnstile, he feels around in his pocket for a token, and his fingers encounter the little gold ring.

Damn. He forgot to turn it in at the hospital's lost and found. He starts back toward the shadowy stairway, then hears the rumble of an approaching downtown train. If he doesn't get on this one, there's no telling how long he'll have to wait for the next.

He'll have to keep the ring until tomorrow. He slides it onto his key ring for safekeeping.

ORAN ROLLS OVER on his creaky cot, over again, and then back. Sleep is evasive, not just because of the lumpy mattress and blanket too flimsy for the clammy draft. He can't stop thinking about what lies ahead. Soon, like Cool Hand Luke, he'll be called upon to lead his followers to salvation. Unlike his long-ago movie hero, Oran will survive in the end.

He always looks forward to chapel on Sundays, but he doesn't typically get to anticipate visitors. Tomorrow, he will. Make that today, if midnight has already come and gone. He's pretty sure it has.

Alone in the dark cell, a man has no way of knowing the hour, but after nearly two decades, you develop a sense for telling time without a clock or watch. You learn the rhythm of this overcrowded hellhole—guards' footsteps, inmates' audible bodily functions, cooking smells, the rumble of distant traffic and train whistles out in the night. Every day, every night, the same events unfold in the same damned order.

A few years ago, there was a blip. Protesting the atrocious conditions, rioting inmates took seventeen guards hostage on a Saturday evening. It happened during recreational hour for maximum security prisoners, as Oran was delivering a sermon to a basketball-dribbling inmate. He couldn't tell whether the fellow was paying attention, but he always liked to think he was getting through to someone. From there, he couldn't see the chaos unfolding over on B Block, where they keep the newcomers. But he could feel it even before it reverberated through the facility.

The ensuing standoff disrupted the routine that evening, and the next day. It was resolved without violence during the wee hours Monday morning, but even in the aftermath, the air was charged with a different kind of energy.

Eventually, life—as in a life sentence, six consecutive for Oran—settled back to regimented normalcy. But as a result of the siege, Governor Cuomo and the state corrections officials stepped up prison renovation and reform. That means Oran has access to the outside world—not via a Cool Hand Luke–style escape, but through formerly forbidden print media.

He still reads his Bible daily. But now he can also peruse publications that used to be censored by the warden and clergy. Now he knows what's going on out there beyond the concrete and razor wire.

Now it isn't just the Bible warning him that Judgment Day is coming—it's the newspapers. They're filled with evidence that his days here are numbered. He hasn't mentioned his findings to anyone, not even the chaplain or fellow members of his Christian study group. He doesn't trust them.

He doesn't trust anyone, other than his own flesh and blood. That's why he's summoned his firstborn child here tomorrow. It's time to resume the mission that began in 1968, when he crept into a slumbering Brooklyn household and slaughtered the first of four families.

Chapter Four

Bettina's body has already been moved from the shared room to a smaller one at the end of the hall. "To give you privacy," the Caribbean nurse tells Amelia and Calvin, pressing neatly folded tissues into their hands, "so you can say your goodbyes."

As they walk past her old room, Amelia glimpses a young woman methodically stripping the sheets from Bettina's bed. She looks like a bored housewife preparing the guest room for in-laws who are on their way, regardless of whether anyone wants them.

To the staff, death is all in a day's work. They moved Bettina because they needed her bed.

Amelia expects to find that a sense of peace has settled over her mother's face now that her suffering has ended and she's gone home to be with Jesus, as Calvin put it after they got the news.

Indeed, the tubes and wires are gone, as is the perpetual gasp for breath. Yet she looks no different—clasped hands clenched on top of the white sheet, mouth set as if in resignation, brow furrowed.

Calvin lets out a wail and goes to her.

Amelia shudders. The window is open, a wet, cold wind blowing in like death itself. She moves to close it, but the nurse stops her.

"We do that when someone passes," she says quietly, "to let the spirit escape."

Amelia, too, longs to escape. But she dutifully sits in one of the two wooden chairs beside the bed as Calvin sobs into his dead wife's shoulder. She reaches to toy with her necklace.

It isn't there.

It's as if Bettina, leaving this world, had snatched that tiny gold ring from her along with everything she'd ever believed about who she is.

Numb with exhaustion and shock, grief and anger, she clasps her hands on her lap and stares dry-eyed out at the storm that swirls with the dead woman's spirit and the words *Some Kind of Wonderful.*

That's the name of the movie lit up on the marquee at the theater across the street. Amelia saw it with a guy from her psych class. Not here. He'd taken her to the Beekman on the Upper East Side, where the seats are cushy and the curtains open like in a fancy theater. It was a rare real date, with a nice guy who wanted to see her again. She'd have liked that, except . . .

This happened. He's moved on, and she doesn't blame him. Who wants to wait around for a girl on deathwatch? *Some Kind of Wonderful . . .*

Oh, the irony on this terrible night when her life has transformed into some kind of nightmare.

She hates herself for hating Bettina when she should be mourning her, with sorrow untainted by wrath. And Calvin—she hates him, too. She turns away from the window to see him sit back at last, spent, rubbing his miserable eyes and blowing his nose into his handkerchief.

"You have to tell me."

He gapes at her.

"About my adoption. I have to know—"

She turns toward a soft knock on the open door. The nurse is back, accompanied by an orderly and a long trolley of some sort. On it, a pile of linens.

"We're going to get her ready to go downstairs now."

Calvin redirects his bewilderment to her. "Downstairs?"

"To the mortuary. You can wait right out here in the hall and come along with her."

As if they're tagging along to a party.

Amelia follows Calvin from the cold, wet room and settles beside him on a bench. The nurse closes the door, and she and the orderly go about their gruesome work.

Her father is sobbing again.

Amelia leans back against the tile wall, staring at the ceiling.

At last, his tears subside. He takes a deep breath and she feels him looking at her, but keeps her eyes trained on the cold fluorescent light overhead.

"First, you weren't adopted."

She pounces. "Don't lie! Please, Daddy . . ." Her voice breaks. "I saw the file. It said she only had one baby, and it wasn't me!"

"That's true."

"Then how—"

"We found you. That's how. *I* found you."

"What?"

"I was working in the church one Saturday night— Sunday morning," he amends. "Mother's Day. I heard a sound, and there you were. Just an itty-bitty baby, lying there like Moses in a basket."

She gasps. He found her. He found her. Like some . . .

Like something someone lost, or threw away.

"I knew I had to get you out of there, get you someplace safe. But, *lawd*, it was raining like the dickens. So I got a bunch of rags to cover you and keep you dry."

"Rags?"

"Clean ones. I carried you out of that church and straight home, and never told a soul where you'd come from. You should have seen Bettina's face. Oh, Bettina." The name is hoarse, as if he'd momentarily forgotten she was gone. He lowers his head again and wipes his eyes.

Amelia can only focus on the lies he'd told. Lies *they'd* told. It had been bad enough to assume she'd been adopted, but this?

She'd found a dollar on the street once, a few years ago, as they were crossing the street for Sunday services. It was Christmastime, and she'd been saving pennies in a jar hidden under the couch, hoping to have enough to buy her parents each a Woolworths plastic candy cane filled with M&M's.

She started to put the dollar into her pocket, but Bettina stopped her. "What are you doing? And right in front of Jesus's house?"

"Jesus wanted me to have it!"

"You don't keep what isn't yours," she said firmly. "That would be stealing, and stealing is a sin."

Apparently, that applies only to cold, hard cash. Her mother made her put the dollar into the collection plate.

"So you found me, and you didn't even bother to take me to a hospital?" she asks Calvin when he looks up at last.

"You were healthy."

"Why wouldn't you have a doctor check me out and make sure?"

"They would have asked where you came from. The police would have taken you away, tried to find the person who left you there."

"Exactly!"

If they hadn't acted so selfishly, she might have found her way back to her real parents. She's a human being, not some forgotten treasure chest they'd stumbled across and greedily decided to keep for themselves.

"Don't you see, Amelia? Whoever did that didn't deserve you! But your mother and I . . ." He pauses again, collects his emotions. "You were the answer to our prayers. We knew Jesus had sent you into our arms. You were wearing your ring, and it was etched with a *C* . . ."

Her ring. Gone.

"*C*, for Crenshaw. You were meant to be ours. Who were we to question His gift?"

"Didn't anyone else ask where I'd come from?"

"They didn't even know you were there at first. Summer of '68—we had the war, assassinations, protests, riots . . . the whole city was on edge. The whole world. But especially in this neighborhood. We didn't go out for a long, long time, except to work."

"Because you were hiding me."

"A lot of folks stayed locked away inside that summer, out of trouble—or what the cops might decide was trouble." He shakes his head. "Terrible times for the black man back then."

"Yeah, times are just super for the black man now."

"We have come a long, long way, Amelia. You don't know—"

"I know that we have a long, long way to go," she said, thinking of what happened in Howard Beach in December. "So you kept me locked away in the apartment . . . for how long?"

"I don't know. It was probably sometime that fall when we took you to church the first time. I went down to Woolworths in midtown and got you a little pink jumpsuit to wear, and your mama dressed you up and showed you off."

"And no one said, 'Hey, why didn't you tell us you were pregnant?'"

"Back then, folks didn't ask nosy personal questions like they do now. Pregnancy and childbirth were nobody's business but the parents'."

"So that's why it was okay to lie."

"No lies. Everyone figured Bettina must have had a baby, so . . ."

"So you let them."

At his shrug, a thousand accusations spring to Amelia's lips.

But the door opens, and the sheet-covered trolley rolls out, and it's time to resume the business of Bettina Crenshaw's death.

As WASH HAD predicted, the retirement party is still going strong when Barnes makes it to Hogan's in midtown. Most everyone in his own circle has already left, either stuck with the overnight shift, or headed home to counties north and west of the city—far more affordable, and far snowier.

His friend Marsha remains. She lives on the Upper East Side with a doctor roommate—not bad for a girl who, like Barnes, grew up in the East Harlem projects. Plus-sized and attractive, with a headful of cornrows and a quick smile, she's a few years older than Barnes. She's one of the few women at work—or anywhere, really—who doesn't flirt with him. Maybe because she's not interested in the opposite sex, though that assumption makes him seem ridiculously full of himself . . . even to himself.

But women are drawn to him, and Barnes has always found female company to be one of life's greatest pleasures. It's the only one that's come without a struggle, though the problem isn't the coming. It's the going.

He's never met a woman who doesn't eventually want a long-term commitment—nor a woman he couldn't let go, faced with an ultimatum. He's just not cut out to be a husband, a father, a family man. He wouldn't be good at it, and if you can't excel at something, you should have the wisdom to walk away.

"Walk away? How is that wise?" asked the most recent woman with whom he shared that theory. "Practice makes perfect. If at first you don't succeed . . ."

"Maybe that's true if you're working on a jump shot. But not in relationships, where other people can get hurt."

The words were suitably noble. Sometimes, his intentions are not.

If he ever meets a woman he can't let go . . . well, maybe he'd attempt monogamy. But the rest? No way. No wedding rings. No kids.

He congratulates Bub Carson, who ropes him into doing a couple of shots—not that he protests. Haunted by concern for Wash, he doesn't want to think about what might be ailing his friend if it isn't pneumonia. After the shots, Bub's longtime partner on the Missing Persons Squad, Frank DeStefano, buys a round of drinks. Barnes requests his usual, Jack Daniel's on the rocks.

"Get the good stuff, kid," Stef says.

"That is good stuff."

"There's better stuff, and it's on me."

A minute later, Barnes finds himself sipping Wild Turkey as Stef shares a couple of anecdotes, including a dirty joke about Bub and a case involving a missing stripper.

It results in more squirms than laughter, and Barnes raises a brow at Marsha.

She rolls her eyes and heads over to the bar, settling on an empty stool.

Barnes joins her. "Not a great joke for him to tell in mixed company, huh?"

"Or, you know . . . *ever*." She shakes her head. "Stef's not known for his tact. I feel sorry for Jason."

"Who?"

"His new partner. Jason Sturgis. Didn't you hear? He just got his shield."

Stone sober, Barnes probably would have been happy for the kid. Or at least, pretended to be. He has nothing against Sturgis, a young, earnest sort, and it's always nice to see a fellow officer succeed. Still . . .

"I should've gotten that. I've been here a few years longer. And I'm definitely a few years older."

"But you"—Marsha points a finger at him—"are the wrong color for Stef."

"What? You mean . . ."

"I mean you're not white."

"So?"

"So he lives out in Howard Beach."

The Queens neighborhood has become synonymous with racial tension. Just before Christmas, a gang of white high school kids attacked a trio of stranded black motorists. One victim fled in terror onto the Belt Parkway and was killed in traffic. The resulting marches and protests, uncooperative witnesses, and unfolding murder trial are national news and tabloid fodder, featuring the outspoken Mayor Koch perpetually at odds with the equally outspoken Reverend Al Sharpton.

"Come on, Marsha. Living in Howard Beach doesn't make someone a racist. If you think that, then you're just as guilty as—"

"Look, Stef goes way back with the families of a couple of the kids who were arrested for murder, okay? He's been saying the whole story hasn't come out, that it was self-defense—"

"He said that to you?"

"He never says anything directly to me. *Us*. Just about us."

Barnes looks over at Stef. Then he takes a long sip of his bourbon. Smooth.

"I don't know . . . I think he's just old-school. You know . . . conservative."

"You say conservative, I say misogynistic racist." Marsha plunks her beer bottle onto the bar. Bud Light. For as long as Barnes has known her, she's been trying to shed the excess pounds fleshing out her waistline, hips, and pretty face.

"I'll buy you another," he offers.

"Can't. I gotta get home and walk Krypto."

"What about your roommate?"

"She's working the late shift."

"Come on, stick around for one more. I just got here. The night is young."

"So is my Great Dane. And you don't want to know what he'll do if I leave him alone for much longer."

"What about me?"

"Are you going to barf the sock I've been missing onto the rug? Eat a shoe? Poop on my bed?"

Barnes laughs and shakes his head.

"Then you, my friend, will be just fine on your own. See ya, Barnes."

He lifts his glass in a silent farewell, in no hurry to follow Marsha out into the swirling snow beyond the plate glass window. Should he order another drink? He's off tomorrow. But he needs to see Wash again first thing, try to find out what—

"Excuse me?"

He turns to see a fine-looking woman with a halo of honey-dyed Jheri curl, short skirt, long legs, bountiful cleavage.

"Someone sittin' here?"

"All yours."

She looks at the bar stool, and then at him. "The seat?"

His grin is slow and easy as a bourbon buzz. "That, too."

AFTER THEIR SLEEPLESS night, Calvin goes to church on Sunday morning. He expects Amelia to join him, but she refuses, and for once, he doesn't force her to obey him. Home alone, she lets the bitter tears fall, grieving not just because Bettina died, but because she'd lied.

Huddled on the couch in pajama pants and a moth-bitten olive green sweater, hair still matted from the rain and snow, Amelia is startled by a knock on the door. Too soon for Calvin to be back. Maybe one of the neighbors has already heard about Bettina. Bad news always travels fast around here. She ignores the knocking until a familiar female voice calls her name.

Startled, she hastily dries her eyes on her sleeve and opens the door to Marceline LeBlanc, wearing a bright cobalt turban and dangling earrings big as dinner plates. She holds a big cardboard carton and a bouquet of blue and white wildflowers that look like they've just been picked in a meadow.

"Come to pay respects," she tells Amelia with a nod.

"Who told you?"

"No one."

"Then how did you know?"

"I just do."

Her accent is far thicker than Bettina's ever was, laced with a dialect born in some foreign tongue.

"My father isn't home right now, Miss LeBlanc, so if you come back—"

Marceline has already crossed the threshold into the untidy apartment as though she's been here a thousand times before. Amelia follows her to the kitchen, where she sets the cardboard box on the cluttered countertop.

The sink is full of dirty dishes, and the trash can is full of garbage that's spilled onto the floor around it. Bettina would be furious, having company see the place in such disarray.

No, that's not why she'd be furious.

How could you let that voodoo crackpot into my house? Bettina demands in Amelia's head.

I didn't, Mama. I opened the door, and somehow she was just . . . in. And even though you never gave Marceline the time of day, she's paying her respects. Because that's what people do—people who do the right thing. You didn't care much about that, though, did you, Mama. About doing the right thing?

Marceline picks up a pickle jar lying on the floor near the garbage can, filled with green liquid. She rinses it, fills it with fresh water, and sets the wildflowers in it. Then she reaches into the sink and grabs a cleaver Calvin had used to hack the last salty bits of flesh from a ham bone.

In that moment, Amelia wishes she hadn't opened the door; wishes she'd heeded Bettina's long-ago warnings about evil and voodoo. Trembling, she takes a step backward, and then another, wondering if she can reach the door before Marceline—

But the old woman has turned her attention to the box on the counter. Dark smudges ooze along the sides. She uses the blade to slice neatly across the masking tape sealing the box, then tosses the cleaver back into the sink. She sets a pair of roaster pans on the table, peels back the foil, and beckons Amelia.

"What . . . what is it?"

"*Supshun.*"

"What?"

"*Supshun . . .*" She flashes a rare smile and rubs her belly. "It means good for you. Not like that *buckrahbittle.*"

"What?" Amelia asks yet again.

"*Buckrahbittle*." Marceline points at a cereal box on the counter. "White man's food, we say where I come from."

"Where do you come from?"

"Down south, like your mama. This is Frogmore," she goes on, pointing to one pan, "and that's Hoppin' John."

The words mean nothing to Amelia, but the food smells delicious. She takes a few cautious steps forward and leans in to see shrimp, sausage, rice, corn . . .

So the stain on the box was grease, and not . . .

Whatever grisly item her imagination had conjured, thanks to Bettina's dire warnings over the years.

The gesture is so ordinary—a meal, a condolence call, flowers, a meal.

"Eat, child."

Child.

Bettina always called her that, too.

Amelia is struck by a sudden and profound longing for the woman who had raised her, despite the lies, despite . . .

Dammit. The tears are back.

Marceline makes no move to console her, not even when she wipes her streaming nose on her sweater's frayed cuff. She just stands watching her.

Oddly, Amelia finds the lack of sentiment more comforting than if Marceline were to hug her and tell her how sorry she is about her mother. Is she keeping a respectful distance, or simply unsympathetic? Maybe a little of both, along with a keen awareness that Amelia doesn't want to be touched or comforted in this moment.

"She wasn't my real mother, you know," she blurts, and Marceline nods, as if she's not surprised to hear it, or maybe . . .

"Did you know that?"

Another nod.

Stunned, Amelia asks, "Who told you?"

"No one told me." She heads for the door. "I just know."

"Wait! Miss LeBlanc! How—"

"Not the time for questions," she says firmly, opening the door. "Time to mourn the dead."

With that, she's gone, leaving Amelia to mourn the dead and wonder if she's just uncovered the real reason Bettina warned Amelia away from Marceline all these years.

SHE WAITS WITH the other inmates' family members in a drab room where nothing wonderful has ever happened. No, she can't know that for certain, but the pall hangs thicker than the fog she left behind in northern Maine. No one is talking, not even the people who came together. They mill around or sit on hard benches avoiding eye contact. Most wear shabby clothing. Her own distressed denim and scuffed combat boots are a fashion statement, while the others are merely poor, and some of them smell. The whole place reeks of noxious cleaning chemicals that can't mask body odor or unsavory food or dank filth.

When she got his letter requesting this meeting, she was tempted to ignore it. Hadn't she just been here three months ago, on Christmas? Won't she be back in another three months, on Father's Day? Doesn't he know how long and difficult a road lies between the prison and her cabin in northern Maine? Hasn't she dutifully visited him twice a year, every year, since she was fifteen years old?

Back then, she didn't have far to go—half an hour by bus across the Tappan Zee Bridge from Rockland County. The trip became more complicated when she went to college in New England, but she managed then, and in all the years since, even though she lives seven hundred miles away now—treacherous ones, especially at this time of year.

At thirty-three, she's spent more than half her Christmases in this place, along with countless June Sundays when other families were picnicking in the sunshine. Here she's sat, across from a grizzled man in an orange jumpsuit and shackles who bears no resemblance to the handsome hero who was once her whole world. After his arrest, the system took over: foster care for her, corrections for him. Same difference, she thought then. But now that she has her freedom, and he has no hope of getting his . . .

Not really the same. Her own grim days are a distant memory. His march to infinity. That's why, when he summoned her, she made the trip. She set out yesterday morning, not sure what to expect of the drive that took at least twelve hours in June and often twice as many in December. Some mountain roads were closed due to snow, and it was ice by the time she reached Boston.

The room stirs with expectation. Guards are congregating. Doors buzz, clank, and open. The inmates have arrived.

For every six months she sees her father, he ages at least a couple of years. His hair and razor stubble are always grayer; his ashen skin more creviced; posture increasingly hunched.

Today, however, it's the opposite. He seems taller, younger, almost cheerful. So he didn't summon her here to share bad news, as she'd speculated?

Now that she thinks of it, what would constitute bad news when he's serving six consecutive life sentences without parole? Even a terminal illness would be a reprieve. He told her that once, when she was young enough to go home and cry for him. She hasn't done that in years—cried for him, or for anyone else, including herself.

They follow the rules, as always—a brief embrace before they sit across from each other, hands resting on the table in full view.

"I'm glad you came."

"Of course I came. You asked me to." As if she hadn't hesitated.

He studies her, and she shifts her gaze away from his. No one else in this world is capable of making her uneasy. But her father cultivated omniscience long before they parted ways, and she sometimes believes he can read her mind.

Now that the other families have settled in with their incarcerated loved ones, they're sneaking curious glances in this direction. Oran Matthews is arguably the facility's most notorious current inmate, if not of all time.

He, however, is focused only on his daughter. "You read my letter?"

"Of course I read it!"

"And . . . ?"

"And you asked me to come, so I came."

"What about the rest?"

She frowns, thinking of his note scrawled in longhand on loose leaf paper. Had she missed something?

"The Bible passages!"

Ah, yes. As always, he'd closed with several verses. She'd merely skimmed them, knowing them by heart, of course.

He glances around and lowers his voice. "The prophecy has come to pass. War, drought, famine, epidemic, natural disasters . . . you know what it means."

"Yes." All her life, he's been preparing her for the end of their time here on earth, and eternal salvation—not for all, but for the chosen few. Oran, and his offspring.

"Are the resources in place?"

Resources—money, and manpower. She nods. She knows where to find both; has been laying the groundwork for years, though she wasn't entirely convinced that her father's prophecies, or even the Bible's, would come to pass in her lifetime.

He gives an approving nod. "All right, then. Go forth now and find your sisters and brothers. Assemble them and wait."

She and Oran may have studied the same Bible, but her interpretation differs from his.

She'll find them, all right.

Find them, and destroy them.

Chapter Five

The diner, on Tenth Avenue in Hell's Kitchen, is no frills, with a stool-lined counter, Formica-and-vinyl booths, and a glass case filled with rotating triangles of pie. Seven mornings a week, Red orders a slice of apple and a cup of coffee for breakfast. On six of them, Barb, the tired-eyed waitress, offers Red the same greeting. "What's new, pussycat?"

Tuesdays through Fridays, when Red leaves, she says without fail, "Have a great day at work."

Saturdays and Sundays, she says, "Enjoy the rest of your weekend."

Mondays, she's off, volunteering at a local animal shelter.

Right on schedule, Barb bustles over to the booth to clear the empty plate and cup and asks how breakfast was.

"Great," Red says, same as always.

"Great." She smiles and drops the check.

No need to look at it. Four dollars and fifteen cents, totaled alongside a smiley face and "thanks!"

Red usually leaves a five on the table.

Today . . .

What the hell? It's not my money, and this might be the last day.

Red drops a ten-dollar bill and heads outside to take the subway to the East Village.

Steam rises from a manhole as if the gates of hell yawn beneath. An emaciated woman weeps on the dirty sidewalk beside a hand-lettered cardboard banner that reads *AIDS, PLEASE HELP.* Overhead, a hedonistic porn marquee advertises Wet Tramps. Steeped in ignorance, pedestrians hurry blindly past prostitutes, thieves, and beggars.

Stocks Plunge 508 Points, the *New York Times* had screamed on Tuesday, and the city—the whole world—was stunned. Not Red, thanks to White.

It was just as foretold in Revelations: *Woe! Woe to you, great city, where all who had ships on the sea became rich through her wealth! In one hour she has been brought to ruin!*

The media is calling it Black Monday. The irony is not lost on Red.

Beyond the Bowery, Alphabet City lies steeped in lethargy and stink, like a vagrant sleeping off last night's binge. Many are doing just that on rubble-and-syringe-strewn streets, as the neighborhood's dwindling population of respectable residents—students, immigrants, old-timers—go about their business.

Red settles into a handbill-papered alley to watch the tenement across East Sixth Street, having learned the hard way not to venture inside. You don't wander up and down the corridors of a building like this without being propositioned and threatened, roughed up, and robbed.

After a long time, hours, Margaret appears. She's wearing a man's suit coat that on anyone else might be the height of current fashion, plucked from one of the vintage clothing boutiques that dot the Village. Hanging on her emaciated frame, it's just shabby.

She'd once been a pretty girl, with enormous dark eyes

and deep dimples, smiling from her senior class portrait printed in a 1968 newspaper article about the murders. Her long hair had been teased high above a prominent widow's peak, the ends flipped above slender shoulders bared between a classy black drape and pearls.

Later photos, snapped by the press at the trial, depict a haunted young woman visibly pregnant beneath a bulky winter coat. The one printed in the *Daily News* on January 7, 1969, showed her leaving the hospital with a newborn baby. The picture is black-and-white, but the caption mentions a pink blanket, indicating the child was a girl. That was the last public sighting, as portrayed in the media.

She'd been harder to track down than the others, her identity uncertain even when Red had finally found her here. Her beauty, dimples and all, has sunk into that haggard face like diamonds in quicksand. She'd have been completely unrecognizable if not for the distinct widow's peak atop a mass of stringy dark hair.

Red slips from the shadows, knife in hand as she scuttles out onto the street and around the corner onto Avenue D. She's desperate for her fix, same as every other day. But today will be her last.

Red trails her into the lawless epicenter of East Village blight. Tompkins Square Park had been swampland before its nineteenth century transformation into a grassy, gaslit oasis in this overcrowded immigrant neighborhood. It's seen its share of controversy in Red's lifetime—wartime neglect, racially charged turf wars, counterculture protests. Street gangs and hippies have been eclipsed by drug dealers, junkies, prostitutes, and a vast homeless population encamped on graffiti-covered benches.

Mayor Koch, the Parks Department, and the NYPD are threatening to turn things around in this socioeconomic wasteland, but it's hardly a priority. No one will bat an eye later when another dead addict is found near the decaying fountain littered with drug paraphernalia and human waste.

But Red spots a couple of police sedans on the outskirts of the park, and uniformed officers on foot patrol. The woman sees them, too, and slows her pace, seeming to weigh her options before joining a group of regulars on a bench. She's either going to wait out the authorities or furtively do what she has to do and hope she doesn't get busted.

Red can't risk being seen. Can't wait around, either. The day holds a far more important task, one that must be performed according to schedule.

Nothing to do but leave Margaret Costello there in the park, unaware that her life has just been spared. For now.

"LOOKING FORWARD TO some excitement tonight?" the deli guy asks, wrapping a meatball sub in a layer of foil.

Barnes nods, though he's experienced more than his share of excitement lately, thanks to a wrong move that coulda-shoulda-woulda ended his detective career—and his life—in a Hell's Kitchen alleyway three weeks ago.

On October 4, at precisely 4:36 a.m., Barnes foolishly lifted his head, the perp fired, and Detective Frank DeStefano dove on top of him.

Maybe not in that order.

Whenever Barnes looks back on it, he's nearly certain that Stef instinctively pushed him down a split second before the gun went off. But his partner wasn't interested in analyzing whether the life-saving move was simultaneous or even preemptive; a lucky coincidence, as opposed to reaction to an action. All in a day's work, as far as he was concerned.

The perp is now in jail and this newbie detective's knuckleheaded head is intact.

"Kid got off without a scratch," Stef bragged to everyone at the precinct, seizing the opportunity to bare the angry red welt on his abdomen where he'd been knifed as a rookie because *his* older, wiser partner hadn't intervened.

The deli counter guy isn't referring to Missing Persons Squad excitement, though. He's talking about tonight's World Series Game Five between the Minnesota Twins and the Saint Louis Cardinals. "Game Six on Saturday no matter who wins," he tells Barnes as he tucks the sub into a paper bag with some napkins. "That's my day off. How about you?"

"I'll probably be working."

An hour ago, he and Stef returned a disgruntled teen runaway to her mother's custody. Another case will come along any minute now. This time, maybe a disoriented senior citizen who can't find her way home from her weekly mahjong game. Or a child who took hide-and-seek a little too far, or a college kid sleeping off a weekend binge in someone else's bed . . .

Those are the cases you want. The ones that end with no one getting hurt.

He pays for his sandwich and heads out into the dusk, trudging several steep uphill blocks toward home. They call this neighborhood Washington Heights for a reason. Perched at the top of Manhattan, it's home to the island's highest natural elevation. A little over two hundred years ago, General George Washington was headquartered here. Now it's an ethnic melting pot, with lower rents attracting newcomers like Barnes, who might have been the only black man in his building a decade or two ago.

The broad, tree-lined blocks and prewar elevator buildings fall away. Now he's in his territory, a more rundown—yet up-and-coming, if you believe the Realtors—

part of the Heights. He hasn't been mugged in the three months since he moved in, but it's probably only a matter of time. Still, it's safer here than East Harlem. More space, too, in his new place, on the top floor of a yellow brick walk-up.

He moved up here in July. The weather was beautiful, Wash was still feeling pretty good, and Barnes had been promoted at last.

"Guess he's not a racist, after all," he told Marsha when he learned he'd be partnered with Stef.

"Don't be so sure about that."

According to her, Barnes's short-lived predecessor, the young, white, earnest Jason Sturgis, had considered filing a complaint about Stef's bigotry.

"But he didn't."

"Not because it wasn't valid. Word got around, and someone obviously convinced him the code of silence is more important."

Barnes isn't surprised. It's one thing to report a fellow officer for a major infraction. But for anything less, you look the other way.

"Anyway, I heard the same someone—or *someones*—convinced Sturgis that law enforcement wasn't for him. Next thing you know, he's out."

"And I'm in. So you're saying I'm supposed to teach Stef a lesson in tolerance?"

"Maybe. Or maybe, if he tolerates you, you'll come in handy if a complaint ever does pop up. Look, I don't want to put a damper on your promotion. I'm happy for you. Just watch your back."

He has, but Stef has his back.

He proved it when he saved my life.

Barnes lets himself into the building and climbs the stairs, keys in hand. Every time he looks at them, he sees the little gold baby ring he found at the hospital back in March. He'd forgotten to turn it in to lost and found the next day.

Or had he? Maybe he selfishly wanted to keep it, because the *C* reminded him of his father. Maybe it was his father's way of letting him know he's still around. That everything is going to be okay with Wash.

Even though it isn't.

As Barnes reaches his door, the one across the hall opens and a neighbor sticks her curly gray head out.

"I've been waiting for you, Stockton."

"I can see that, Mrs. Klein. Do you need help moving something?" Yesterday, he'd wrestled a marble coffee table from one end of her living room to the other. Not a great distance, but she decided she wanted it back in the original position . . . and then, predictably, returned to the new location.

"I just wanted to give you this. I signed for it this morning. It's from a lawyer's office. Do you know what it is?"

"No, but thank you."

"You're welcome. I hope it's nothing too serious."

She's fishing for more information, but Barnes isn't about to speculate. He takes the envelope, thanks her again, and closes the door. It has to be about his mother's tangled finances. At least this time, it's not from the IRS.

Flicking on the kitchen light, he sees Connie scurrying for cover. That's his pet name for the fat cockroach that's been keeping him company the last couple of days. Maybe it's not always Connie, but he'd prefer to think there's just one.

"Yeah, I wish I could hide, too." He tosses the sandwich on the counter with his keys and the letter. "Lawyers never send good news, do they, Connie?"

He opens a cupboard to find the bottle of Jack Daniel's he bought Monday, and it takes him a moment to remember why it's nearly empty. Tuesday, he'd invited a woman back here for a nightcap. He drank Jack, and she had a couple of the wine coolers he keeps stashed in the fridge for female guests. She was a fair-skinned, quick-witted redhead. He's always had a weakness for women like her. They shared a few drinks, laughs, and hours in his bed before she left at sunrise. Though he dutifully exchanged numbers, he hasn't heard from her since, and he doesn't plan to call. It was an unremarkable encounter he finds appealing for its lack of consequence, aside from having depleted this week's whiskey supply.

He takes a swig from the bottle before tearing open the envelope. Whatever it is . . .

This too shall pass, he hears Wash saying, as he so often does.

He's never heard of the firm engraved at the top of the letterhead, or the name scrawled with swagger at the bottom. He scans the dense paragraphs. The attorney is contacting him on behalf of . . .

Who? Who the heck is . . .

Oh. Right. Barnes remembers *her.* Tall and attractive, with big hair and big . . .

Yeah. Just his type.

And now, according to her lawyer, she's pregnant with his child.

SPRUNG FROM THE low-budget self-service West Side parking garage where it's been stashed the last few hours, the Mercedes zips along in the northbound lanes of the Henry Hudson Parkway. Rush hour is long over. Up ahead, the George Washington Bridge glitters like an emerald crown at the top of Manhattan, its swooping suspension cables lit in green tonight.

Even from here, it's easy to see that taillights on the upper span are moving toward New Jersey more quickly than those on the lower. Good, because the upper span has the walkways, and is of course preferable for suicide.

Not many people who watch *M*A*S*H* on television know the dark lyrics to the instrumental theme song. Those who do shouldn't believe them. Suicide is not painless, unless you do it right.

Take slitting your wrists. Mother had bled out on the kitchen floor—excruciating and messy. There are better, more efficient ways to go.

Not hanging. Unless you tie the knot just right to snap your neck, you'd slowly strangle. Not overdose, either, because you might vomit the lethal dosage before it takes hold. Plus, there's lag time, after you swallow the pills, during which you might think second thoughts.

Gunshot? No. You can fire a bullet into your mouth, but it's not easy to take steady aim in that position. What if your hand slips at the last moment and you miss the spot that would kill you? You might live on indefinitely, maimed, physically paralyzed, unable to see, hear, speak. Trapped, no way out.

Jumping is the ideal method. You're pretty much guaranteed to die instantly if you hurtle yourself from a sufficiently high spot. Like the upper span of the George Washington Bridge. They might not find your body in the Hudson River for days. If ever.

Yeah, jumping is perfect.

So is this plan, though not foolproof.

The Mercedes hugs the on-ramp curves like a dream, speeding across the first half of the span before slowing.

To the south, beyond the concrete divider, eastbound headlights, and pedestrian walkway, Manhattan's skyline dazzles. To the north, past another walkway bordered by low railings, the Hudson Highlands hug the river on both sides.

When you're three quarters of the way across, park

the car, leave the keys, wait till the coast is clear and get out.

But how clear can it be in the middle of a busy bridge?

A lull, then. When there's a lull, you make your move.

But—

Don't worry. Even if a few people spot you, they're zipping past. They won't think anything of it, and you'll be out of there in no time.

Sure. Easy for someone to say when they're not stuck taking this monumental risk.

Park.

Done.

Leave the keys in the ignition.

Done.

Wait, with one gloved hand on the door handle, eyes on the rearview mirror . . .

Wait . . .

Wait . . .

At last, there's a break in the rushing headlights. The perfect moment to open the door and climb out, if not entirely without notice, then at least without getting mowed down by passing traffic.

A fierce gust grabs the car door, making it difficult to push closed. Forget jumping—on a stormy night, a careless person might very well blow off the bridge.

Hurry, hurry.

One sneaker over the railing, the other foot, and hit the eight-foot-wide pathway running, back toward Manhattan. Anyone who now notices the abandoned Mercedes might assume that if the Jersey-bound driver had car trouble, he would just walk the remaining distance, a quarter mile at most, to find help at the Fort Lee Bridge Plaza. Later, when he doesn't turn out to have done that, they'll assume that he'd jumped.

One thing is fairly certain: no one who comes along

now is going to connect the absent Mercedes driver with a jogger running back toward Manhattan, dressed in a bright purple sweat suit, hood up against the chill.

The sprint along the span is exhilarating. So much to think about, so many things to look forward to, and zero complications.

On this brisk October night, as expected, the northern walkway is otherwise deserted. The Port Authority opened it to cyclists last May, in an effort to separate speeding bikes from ambling walkers who use the other side. But who wants to lug a bike up and down the steep stairways on either end? Most bikers have ignored the new regulation and stuck with the other side, where there are just ramps.

Just before the end of the bridge, a roadside assistance truck passes, flashing yellow lights. It's undoubtedly en route to assist the stranded Mercedes.

And so it begins.

But the risky part ends with the descent from view, along the steep, unlit stairwell leading back to 177th Street.

Almost to safety.

Halfway down, a figure pounces from the shadows, brandishing a switchblade, demanding money.

"Just don't hurt me, okay?" The fright-laced plea isn't entirely contrived. In all the imagined scenarios, a garden-variety thief never disrupted the sprint to freedom. Cops were the main threat. Good Samaritans, sure. Fellow pedestrians, nosy motorists . . .

But an armed mugger?

"Shut up and give me your wallet."

"Please, I don't have . . ."

"Then give me whatever you've got."

"Some cash. That's all. It's in my pocket."

Slowly, slowly, reach in, and then—

A single shot. The mugger collapses.

The pistol goes back into the jacket pocket and then, on second thought, over the railing.

It lands far below and the splash, like the shot, is lost in the rush of traffic above.

WRAPPED IN A sweater and clutching a blue Milk of Magnesia bottle she'd rescued from the trash, Amelia walks Lexington Avenue, looking for Marceline LeBlanc.

Sometimes, she's out here, sometimes not. She isn't the sort of person who keeps a schedule.

Familiar neighborhood faces, innocuous by day, are baleful in the wee hours of a Harlem morning. An acquaintance of Calvin's greets her with a lewd proposition. Her father would be furious if he knew Amelia is even out here at this hour, but he's at work. He's always at work, and Amelia is always alone. Most of the time she prefers it that way. Not that she has much choice.

She drifted from her old neighborhood pals after she went to college and they did not. She's not on campus much this semester, and she has yet to cross paths with the friends she'd made last year. She doesn't feel like seeking them out, or meeting new people, or dating, though a few guys have seemed interested.

When you get to know someone, you have to talk about your past—who you are, where you come from. It's easier to keep to herself, isolated by her secret.

She continues on toward Park Baptist, drawn to the church ever since Calvin had told her that it was where he'd found her. And it's where Amelia often finds Marceline. Tonight, the old woman is there, sitting on the steps, feeding an alley cat from a paper cup of raw chicken innards.

"Past your bedtime, child," Marceline greets her.

"I don't have a bedtime anymore. I brought you a present." She holds out the bottle, scrubbed clean.

Marceline stares at it, turning it over in her hands.

"It's for your bottle tree," Amelia explains, and the woman looks up sharply.

"You seen my bottle tree?"

"No. You told me about it, remember?"

Marceline often speaks of the Gullah Geechee community she left behind on some coastal island down south, where everyone seems to believe in hexes and spells, potions and herbs, omens and spirits and mojo. Amelia was fascinated by the Gullah tradition of placing empty blue bottles upside down over crepe myrtle branches, preferably just outside the front door, also painted blue. The color is believed to ward off evil spirits and bad luck.

There's no crepe myrtle here in New York, but Marceline said there's an oak growing beyond her fire escape, and she stuck blue bottles over the branches she can reach. Amelia has kept an eye out for the tree in her travels, wondering where Marceline lives. She won't say. She doesn't like to answer questions. She prefers to share stories about magic, and the past—not necessarily her own, and certainly not Amelia's.

Looking pleased with her gift, Marceline tucks the bottle into the pocket of her dress. "T'engky."

It means "thank you." When Amelia first got to know her, she couldn't comprehend the strange Gullah dialect even if it is plain old English. The more she hears it, the easier it is to understand, though there are some foreign phrases—like *supshun*, and *buckrahbittle*—that she'd never be able to translate. Her favorite is *day-clean*. Marceline told her it means "early morning, after dawn breaks"—a fresh start, with yesterday's troubles scrubbed away.

"Miss LeBlanc, when I found the bottle, it got me thinking about my baby ring. It was gold, with blue stones, and the letter *C* etched in blue. Maybe it was supposed to keep the evil away, but . . ." She shrugs.

No response. Marceline just sits there, allowing the cat to slurp innards from her hand.

She isn't the type to pepper a conversation with questions, prompts, or even acknowledgment. Amelia used to wonder if she was even listening. Now she knows the woman doesn't miss a thing.

"I lost it the night my mother died," Amelia goes on, watching her closely. "A few days later, I even went back to the hospital to see if anyone had turned it in, but it wasn't there. My only clue, and it's gone forever, and now I keep thinking about the letter *C*. Maybe it wasn't some grand plan God had, like they said—that someone named Calvin Crenshaw was supposed to find me. Maybe it was my real name."

A subtle shift. Marceline is still sitting there, her hand outstretched for the cat, but the animal stops slurping, poised ears twitching like antennae.

"Every time I bring up the past, you change the subject. But you were around here back then, in '68. You already told me you knew Bettina wasn't my real mother, but you never told me who told you?"

"Sometimes we don't know what we know because someone tells us, or because we *know*. You see?"

Amelia doesn't see at all. Marceline often speaks in this mystical way. Tonight, she doesn't have the patience.

"How can someone know something that she really can't know? That doesn't make sense."

"It do to me."

"Well, it don't to me. Doesn't." *College girl.*

Yes, she's smart. Too smart not to ask questions of the one person who might be willing to answer them.

"Tell me what you know about how I was found."

"Ask your daddy. He was there."

"I think you were there, too. And he won't talk about it, and Bettina is dead, so who else am I going to ask?" She refuses to let emotion break her voice, aware that tears wouldn't budge Marceline, but repel her. She's a tough old woman, and Amelia has earned her friendship and respect by being a tough young one.

Marceline is silent, weighing something as Amelia and the cat watch her. At last, she gives a little nod. "It's like he said. He found you in the church that night. I saw him go in alone. I saw him carry you out."

Amelia presses a fist to her mouth. "You saw me?"

"I saw a big ol' bundle of rags. But I heard a baby."

Rags. Calvin had told the truth.

"Did you ask him why he suddenly had a baby in his arms?"

"No. He didn't see me there." She gestures at the side of the church steps.

"Is that where you were? Hiding?"

"No hiding!" she says, indignant. "Just there."

"And then what happened?"

"He went home. I went home. That's it."

"You didn't say anything to him? Or tell anyone?"

Marceline shakes her head and gets to her feet. The cat slips off into the shadows beneath the steps.

"Wait, where are you going?"

"Time for me to go. I got things to do before dayclean."

Marceline descends the steps without looking back.

Amelia knows better than to follow.

She's certain the woman knows more than she's telling.

But now that she's broken down the wall, it's only a matter of time before she learns more.

She walks slowly home, seeing the first hint of light in the eastern sky.

Dayclean.

Chapter Six

Friday, October 23, 1987

Another day, another missing person. This time, it's not a teenaged runaway or a confused mahjong lady, but a Park Avenue millionaire named Perry Archibald Wayland III.

Sitting in the passenger's seat as Stef inches the dark sedan along East Seventy-Third Street, Barnes is reasonably certain Wayland didn't jump off the George Washington Bridge, though his Mercedes had been abandoned on the upper span overnight. He wouldn't be leaning toward foul play, either, if there hadn't been a homicide in the area around the same time Wayland's car was found.

A junkie known on the streets as Popper was gunned down in a crime-plagued stairwell leading from the bridge walkway on the Manhattan side. Society is better off, and Popper might be as well, having led a miserable existence in and out of juvie and jail. His murder was likely a drug deal gone bad, gang violence, or maybe even a victim turned vigilante like Bernie Goetz, the New Yorker who'd shot four muggers on the downtown 2 train a few years ago.

Still, the timing and location are close enough to the Wayland disappearance that a connection, while maybe not likely, is possible.

Behind them, squealing brakes pierce the street noise, followed by a loud, sustained car honk and a resounding crash. Stef curses into the rearview mirror and Barnes glances to see a commotion back on Lex.

"Cab rear-ended a Civic," Stef tells him.

"I'll call it in." Barnes reaches for the radio amid shouting and angry beeps from blocked traffic surrounding the accident.

"Nah. Not our problem, kid. I didn't even see it happen, did you?"

"I—"

"You didn't. We've got bigger fish to fry right now. Big fat rich fish who live in the sky above Park Avenue."

Unlike Barnes's Washington Heights neighborhood, this one has a number of private homes, framed by gleaming blue sky and arguably far more autumn foliage than you find elsewhere in Manhattan, save the parks. Most are narrow, four-story structures of brick or limestone. Some have subterranean patios beyond wrought iron gates; others, shallow balconies a level or two above the sidewalk. No one ever seems to use the outdoor space.

The leafy block is thick with town cars transporting residents and visitors; delivery trucks bearing meals, flowers, and gifts. Doormen are stationed beneath tony green awnings that jut toward the curb wherever condo buildings break the row of brownstones. Boys in miniature blazers and shiny leather wing tips spill onto the sidewalk in front of the Buckley School. They're met by women who appear not to have eaten in weeks, or nannies pushing strollers that probably cost more than a cop makes in a month.

There are no fathers.

"Did you ever pick up your kids from school?" he asks Stef, who has three sons, and stayed married for their sake until the youngest joined the marines a couple of years ago.

"What, are you kidding me? I used to stay late at work so I wouldn't have to go to all those damned Little League games and parents' nights. 'Don't you want to meet the teacher?' Judy would ask me, and I'd want to say, 'Depends on what she looks like.'"

He laughs as if Bill Cosby had just delivered a hilarious one-liner, then resumes his recap of last night's Cardinals-Twins showdown. Barnes lights a Marlboro and resumes wondering how the one thing he's always tried so hard to prevent could have happened.

Because you didn't try hard enough, fool.

Abstinence is the only surefire way not to get someone pregnant.

According to Delia Montague's lawyer, she's been trying to track him down for months. Thinking back, Barnes remembers that maybe she *had* tried to get in touch.

"You're never home," her recorded voice accused.

Yes, he was. He was right there by the answering machine, listening to her ramble on about how important it was that he return the call.

Calls. There had been quite a few messages from her.

"Where are you? Away for the holiday? Call me when you get back!"

The last time he heard from her was back around the Fourth of July—or was it Memorial Day?

Must have been, because he'd moved into his new apartment on July first, and she didn't have that number. He'd regretted giving her the old one, never expecting her to use it, just as he never planned to dial hers, jotted on the lengthy bar receipt from their first date.

By all definitions, it was a one-night stand. Barnes assumed she was as comfortable with that as he was, especially since he didn't hear from her following that night in . . .

Barnes could have sworn it was April, maybe May. It had to be warm outside, right? She was wearing a low-cut, sleeveless top and a short skirt that rode up her bare legs.

The baby is due around Thanksgiving. Her attorney claimed they'd met in March.

Barnes supposes that might be possible. Women like Delia don't wear thick down parkas and mukluks, even in the dead of winter.

Okay, so March—that's one month—then April, May, June . . .

Yeah. It could be his.

Her lawyer claims she's lost her cocktail waitress job and her apartment since becoming pregnant. That means a child is about to be born into this harsh world with an unemployed, homeless mother, and no father . . .

Except the likes of me?

Poor kid. You don't stand a chance.

ON FRIDAY AFTERNOONS, Amelia gets out of class at three, walks to the Sixty-Eighth Street subway, takes a fifteen-minute subway ride to Harlem, and is home in time to catch the end of *General Hospital*.

Today, she descends from the street to find a logjam inching toward the turnstiles. The platform is packed beyond, and the loudspeaker blares with gibberish.

"What are they saying?" she asks a man wearing blue scrubs, probably coming from a shift at Weill Cornell Hospital four blocks east. He sticks a cigarette in his mouth, standing so close she can smell stale coffee on his breath. He lights up and treats her to a lungful of secondhand smoke before saying, "Sick passenger."

Bettina, who worked for the MTA, had told her that "sick passenger" is often code for suicide.

"Why don't they just tell the truth, Mama?"

"Because people might get ideas about doing the same thing," she said darkly. "The truth can be dangerous."

Back then, Amelia couldn't believe Bettina would condone a lie any more than she could imagine someone jumping in front of a subway train just because someone else had.

Yeah, well . . . live and learn.

Amelia shoulders her way back through the crowd, up the stairs to the street. This won't be the first time she's walked the fifty-odd blocks home up Lexington Avenue.

She scans pedestrians' features, searching every black face for some resemblance to her own—ideally, someone who shares her own unusual light green eye color.

That tall woman, the one with the high cheekbones . . . ?

Or her companion, a few inches shorter but lighter skinned, like Amelia . . . ?

Maybe the guitar-carrying hippie with a hint of gray in her dreadlocks . . . ?

Are you my mother?

No, no, and no. They all walk on past Amelia without a glimmer of interest. Her mother would be scrutinizing every young black woman on the street, because that's what you do when something is missing. You can't shake the nagging feeling that something is off, and you keep an eye out for the thing you've lost. You don't just keep plowing ahead as though your world is intact. You don't just forget your child. Not if you're a normal, decent human being, and her mother has to be, because—

Squealing brakes, a blast of car horn, a dull metallic crunch.

She turns to see the front fender of a yellow cab crumpled

against a Honda Civic's hatchback. Just one more daily drama that will play out in an overpopulated city, crazily tilted with seven million lives teetering on the edge.

Amelia walks on, preoccupied with her own.

Are You My Mother?

That was the title of her favorite childhood book, and she knew it by heart. Maybe some part of her soul identified with the lost baby bird searching for its missing mama. That story had a simple, happy ending. So will hers.

As she waits to cross onto the final block of Lexington Avenue, she spots a familiar figure on the bus stop bench across the intersection. Even from a distance, on a Harlem thoroughfare crowded with traffic and pedestrians, Marceline LeBlanc's watermelon-colored head wrap sets her apart.

What is she doing out at this hour? Heading downtown, apparently, but why? Mundane pursuits—shopping, visiting a friend—aren't likely for an exotic creature like her. Not in broad daylight, anyway.

She turns abruptly and stares directly at Amelia, as though she's been expecting her to show up in exactly this spot at exactly this moment.

She couldn't have, because Amelia is at least half an hour past her usual arrival time on the block. Anyway, Miss LeBlanc wouldn't know her afternoon habits. Early mornings, late evenings . . . those are the hours when she's out and about, doing whatever it is that a high priestess does.

Maybe she has a doctor's appointment. She always seems perfectly healthy, but she's getting up there in years. She must be in her seventies, at least.

Spotting a handled basket over Marceline's arm and a large red leather satchel at her feet, Amelia feels her apprehension give way to panic.

She isn't going downtown. She's going away. Now, when they have so much to discuss.

"Miss LeBlanc!"

The shout is lost in traffic noise and a blast of music from the opposite corner.

The Carter brothers, ten and twelve, have set a boom box on top of a piece of cardboard by the bus stop, preparing to break dance. The older one holds a tip jar containing a dollar bill. The younger is a dead ringer for Michael Jackson, with silky ringlets and doe eyes, wearing a white suit and fedora.

The Don't Walk light is still on. Farther up the avenue, the bus is approaching. It might reach the stop before Amelia does.

She eyes the cars crawling across the intersection, then steps off the curb to begin weaving her way around fenders. Horns honk as she darts to the opposite sidewalk, and a driver rolls down the window to give her the finger and shout a racial slur.

Ignoring it, she scurries toward Marceline. The bus has stopped a little farther up the avenue to pick up passengers.

"Miss LeBlanc!"

She must be able to hear Amelia now, yet she doesn't respond.

She saw me coming. She knows I'm here. Why would she ignore me? Why would she leave without saying goodbye?

The bus is moving again, edging closer. Marceline picks up her satchel and stands to face it, waiting with her back turned to Amelia.

"Miss LeBlanc!" She rushes along the crowded sidewalk, weaving among pedestrians. "Wait! Miss—"

"What the hell!" A young man turns with a menacing glare as she shoulders into his brick wall of an arm. She apologizes and pushes past him, only to slam an elderly man shuffling along with a Key Food grocery bag. It slips from his grasp, skittering Campbell's soup cans and oranges across the sidewalk.

"Sorry!" Amelia stoops to gather his groceries.

"Slow down, girl," he scolds as she fumbles the bag, trying to open it wide enough for a dented box of Shredded Wheat. "You kids are in such a hurry all the time."

She thrusts the shopping bag at him and rushes away, reaching Marceline just as the bus pulls up.

"Miss LeBlanc!" Amelia touches her shoulder. "Please! Where are you going?"

She turns with resignation as the doors hiss open.

"Home."

"But home is that way!" Amelia gestures uptown.

The woman shakes her head and silently points in the opposite direction.

"You're going down south?"

"Mmm-hmm."

"Why?"

"It time."

"Time for what?"

"Time for me to go."

Passengers are still disembarking. She strains to hold her satchel in one gnarled hand and the basket in the other, a colorful cloth draped over the top. Both appear to be filled with bricks. Or all her worldly possessions.

"Are you coming back?"

No reply.

"But what about me? You were going to tell me!"

The woman glances at the Park Baptist Church across the street. "Tell you what?"

"What you know about . . . me." Amelia swallows an aching lump.

"What I know about you is that you have your daddy, your schooling, your whole life to live."

"Hey, lady, you coming?" the bus driver calls, and Marceline turns away.

"Comin'!" She sets down the basket.

"Let me help you." Amelia reaches toward it, but Marceline grabs it after hefting the satchel onto the bottom step, followed by one foot and then the other, clad in lace-up booties made of supple red leather that almost matches her bag.

"I don't need help."

I do. I need you.

For a wild moment, she imagines hurtling herself onto the bus along with the basket. But then she catches Marceline's eye, and what she sees there stops her, hand poised near the handle. Her gaze isn't cold, exactly. Just detached. As if she's already said her goodbyes and moved on.

Slowly, she takes a step back and watches the old woman climb the steps. The doors close after her, and she's gone.

Gone forever, Amelia knows as she watches the taillights touch and glow, touch and glow down the avenue.

TRAFFIC ON THIS northbound stretch of Interstate 95 has been bumper-to-bumper since Manhattan, with none of the expected trickling off in the Connecticut suburbs. Maybe the city is evacuating to New England and Canada to escape Black Monday's fallout. It's going to take hours just to reach the ferry. But it will be worth it. White is waiting.

Growing up across the river in Rockland County, Red had dreamed of life in Manhattan—a high-powered job, rich, famous friends, a sprawling skyscraper condo . . .

Until White came back, the reality was unemployment,

loneliness, and a dreary, barely affordable Hell's Kitchen walk-up. The place came furnished, though it's strictly utilitarian. Couch, chairs, tables, lamps, a bed. The living room and bedroom are boxes; the windowless kitchen little more than an alleyway between them. The bathroom is closet-sized; there are no closets. That's okay. When you spend the first part of your life in a trailer and the next moving from one group home to another, you don't accumulate possessions.

The landlord, a wiry little man with a cartoon-villain hook nose, had advertised this place as having "river views."

"From where?" Red asked that first day, standing on tiptoes to peer out the two small windows high on the wall above the couch. Nothing to see but other buildings and between them, a fleck of sky—gray that day. Always gray. Here, and back in Rockland, everywhere in between.

"The roof. You can see the river from up there."

"Do the other tenants use it?"

"No, so if you're looking to make friends—"

"I'm not."

Red's a loner, not always by choice. People don't notice that, though, in New York City. Not like back home. Here, you can go days without small talk, or even eye contact. That's a good thing, on good days. On bad days, memories barge in.

One bad day after moving into this place, Red searched for the roof access and found the door locked, marked with a bold RESTRICTED sign.

Trapped. In this building, in this dark world, in this skin . . .

After that, Red explored other options and discovered anyone could take the elevator all the way up to the 107th floor of the World Trade Center's South Tower.

From there, escalators climbed even higher, to a 110th floor outdoor deck called Top of the World. Ironic, to a person who was feeling anything but. Essentially a series of catwalks, the viewing area had blue floors that matched the sky and surprisingly flimsy white railings that were only waist-high. Beyond lay a tranquil sea of skyscrapers, even the Empire State Building far below, and helicopters and birds and wisps of cloud.

On bad days, as the wind whipped and tourists chattered and snapped photos, Red stood gripping the rail with both hands, trying to work up the nerve. Always thinking this would be the time; always leaving a coward, doomed to struggle through another day, until the one when a voice jarred from the past.

This time, it came not from inside Red's head, but there. In real life. *Real.*

"Won't work."

Stunned, Red turned to see familiar translucent violet eyes—backlit, as if the sun were setting behind them and not on New Jersey across the river.

"What . . . what are you doing here?"

"Looking for you."

"But how . . . Did you follow me?"

"I've been following you for a while now."

"Why?"

White shrugged. "Someone has to keep an eye on you. Just like the old days. By the way, unless you can fly, there's only one way down from here. It's suicide-proof. See?"

Below, the tower's flat roof extended well beyond the platform on all sides. If you jumped, you might break a bone, but you'd find yourself sprawled on a broad stretch of roof. It, too, was surrounded by a white railing, well within the footprint. Beyond, yet another railing lay before the edge, where a tall, slanted barrier tilted out into the sky.

Maybe Red always knew it wasn't possible to free-fall over that railing. Does it matter? Not anymore.

"So, can you?" White had asked.

"Can I what?"

"Fly?"

"Look, I don't know why you're—I mean, I didn't say anything about jumping."

"You've had some rough times in your life."

White knows that, better than anyone.

"And you know I'm a really good listener."

Yes. In Red's darkest days, White was there.

"Come on. I'll buy you a drink."

"I don't drink anymore." Turns out alcohol, like drugs, can tear down walls, allowing memories to slip in.

"Coffee, then. Let's go." White reached out a gentle hand.

Red took it, just like the first time.

"You didn't really want to die," White said later.

"Do you think I'm a coward? You're wrong! I *did* want to die. That's why I started going to the tops of tall buildings every day. I was planning to jump."

"But you didn't do it. Not because you're a coward. Because you're brave, and strong, and you were meant to live. You knew deep down that I would come for you."

Red hadn't known. Seeing White again that first day had been a shock.

"But how did you find me?"

"You can find anyone if you have the patience, and the time, and the money. That's what I need from you."

"I don't have any money." Red had inherited some, after Mother died. But it was running out, and time to find a job.

White offered one, handing over an envelope filled with cash, and a list with four names on it.

Margaret Costello
Tara Sheeran
Christina Myers
Bernadette DiMeo

"Hey, aren't they—"

"Yes." White smiled. "Good memory. I need you to find them, and their children."

"For what?"

"Just find them. Watch them. The Bible tells us that false prophets will arise in end times. When the time comes, they'll need to be eliminated. Do you understand?"

"I think so. But I don't think I can—"

"You can. You *have*." White is the only person in the world who knows Red's darkest secret. "Whose salvation is more important? Theirs, or yours? It's that simple. They haven't been chosen. You have."

"All right. I'll do this for you."

"No, it's for us. The four of us. The chosen ones."

The search began with a mountain of old press clippings, records, notes, and true crime books about the Brooklyn Butcher, New York's most notorious serial killer.

Nearly twenty years ago, he'd methodically slaughtered four families as they slept. In every home, a teenaged daughter was the sole survivor. Overburdened in that violent, uneasy summer of 1968, the NYPD assigned every available detective to the case. On the heels of the fourth incident, they'd solved it.

Windows throughout Dyker Heights had been open on the steamy June night when the DiMeo family was murdered. People were up late, too hot to sleep in the heat, or unsettled by Bobby Kennedy's assassination the day before. Several neighbors heard screams and called the police. They arrived too late to save anyone but Bernadette, the teenaged daughter.

But this time, there had been an eyewitness—a milkman who glimpsed a masked figure running from the building and disappearing into the subway as sirens closed in. And this time, the police found several clues at the scene. Most important, Bernadette had recognized and was able to identify her rapist. The fingerprints matched up. An arrest swiftly followed. The suspect was tried, convicted, and sentenced to several consecutive terms of life imprisonment, Governor Rockefeller having abolished the death penalty a few years earlier.

The young women faded into obscurity, though the brutal crime spree hadn't just robbed them of their families and their innocence.

All had been raped. All were pregnant.

Red has located the four, along with two of their offspring. Tara is in Boston with her daughter, Emily. Christina remains in Sheepshead Bay, Brooklyn; her son, adopted in 1969 as a newborn, lives in suburban Westchester County. Both Bernadette and Margaret are in Manhattan. Bernadette had reportedly lost her baby early in the second trimester.

Margaret's is missing.

She'd refused to answer reporters' questions about her obvious pregnancy back in the winter of '68, but court transcripts revealed that she'd admitted it on the stand. She'd eventually carried the pregnancy to term, delivering a daughter that January, unnamed on the birth certificate.

There are no records of her anywhere, not even adoption. Yes, those would be sealed. But like White said, when money is no object, a person can find just about anything. Red failed to find a trace of Margaret's daughter in New York or the tristate area, and Margaret hadn't raised her.

So what did you do with her . . . or to her?

That's the question Red had planned to ask Margaret yesterday in the park, if it hadn't been crawling with police. She was supposed to be the first to die.

"It's okay," White said last night, on the phone, unaware that Margaret's daughter is still missing. "Do the Sheerans first, tomorrow night. Come here, first, on the way to Boston, so that I can see you. I miss you."

"I miss you, too. I wish—"

"I know you do, but soon we'll be together forever."

Off the exit, Red jiggles an anxious right leg, resisting the urge to stop for a bushel of apples at a farm stand heaped with orchard fruit. The rural road winds on toward the coast, past weathered homes bordered by vibrant foliage and remnants of ancient fieldstone walls. It looks like the scenic November photo from a wall calendar that had hung in the trailer, always open to the same page from an earlier, happier year, further in the past than Red's memory can stretch.

A few fast-food chains and service stations cluster near the Post Road intersection, where the remaining stream of traffic turns toward the quaint tourist towns to the north. Red goes right, following *ferry* signs past bait and tackle shops and a clam shack with missing letters on the sign.

The working-class bayside neighborhood is no picturesque calendar scene. Familiar elements from Red's childhood dot the landscape. Clotheslines and rusty pickup trucks; battered-looking indoor furniture on outdoor porches; vinyl siding and windows stapled with plastic sheeting to insulate against the bay wind.

Red remembers drafty Decembers backlit by other people's flashing twinkle lights, with a blaring singsong soundtrack of television commercials advertising toys Santa would never bring.

Once, when Mother wasn't home, Red took the calendar off the wall and flipped through the previous pages. Earlier in the year, there were handwritten appointments with a Dr. Schultz—once, twice, occasionally three times a week. After that November, nothing. Life had stopped moving forward long before it ended for Mother, lying in a pool of blood, her throat slit ear to ear.

Her blubbery flesh bulged beneath the tracksuit she'd lived in for weeks. Her tangled hair was matted with grease and blood. Her left hand clutched her bloody throat, her right, a knife. The same blade had been used to slice Red's after school apple into wedges. Before calling the police, Red ate them, standing over her, then washed the plate, dried it, and put it back into the cabinet.

"How come?" White asked, when Red first shared the story, years ago.

"I was hungry. And it wasn't like she needed an ambulance. She was dead, you know? Her eyes were wide open, just staring."

"If you think your story's bad . . ."

"You don't?"

"I do. It's nasty. But I can top your dead mother," White said, like a poker shark upping the ante.

"I doubt it."

"Oh, yeah? Ever hear of the Brooklyn Butcher?"

Chapter Seven

The towering redbrick apartment building has a Park Avenue address and takes up the entire block. After speaking to the doorman and building manager, neither of whom can shed any light on Perry Wayland's disappearance, Barnes and Stef ride the elevator to the top floor.

Place like this, you expect to be greeted by the help, but the woman who answers the door is no housekeeper.

"Kirstin Wayland?" Stef asks, as they show their badges, and she nods, inviting them in.

Bathed in golden sunshine falling through the skylight, she's attractive, Barnes supposes, if you like your women Aryan and angular. Everything about her is pale—complexion, long hair held back in a narrow velvet band, sweater and pants, even the polish on her toenails. Her left hand is weighted by a hunk of a diamond set in a platinum band.

Barnes is surprised to note that she's barefoot, until she asks them to take off their shoes. He looks down at his polished black oxfords, then at Stef, who speaks for both of them.

"Sorry, can't do that on the job."

She arches a blond brow. "It's just that Wellesley just started crawling, and I worry about germs . . ."

"Wellesley?"

"My youngest," she says, as if he should have known. "It's cold and flu season."

"Ma'am, I'm sorry, but our shoes stay on."

Seeing the flash of indignation in her chalky blue eyes, Barnes speaks up. "If you want, we can talk out in the hallway, or somewhere else."

"I can't leave the apartment, in case Perry calls, or . . . someone asking for ransom. Just wipe your feet really well. But if Wellesley gets sick . . ."

Scraping his soles against the doormat, Barnes dismisses the likelihood of either of those things. Not that he's an expert on crawling babies. Or ever intends to be. But statistically speaking, a ransom demand is unlikely.

He takes in the surroundings as he and Stef follow Kirstin Wayland across presumably sterilized white marble floors. Beyond an archway, the living room is an untouched coloring book—walls, carpet, draperies, furniture, artwork. Even the sky has been stripped of its glorious blue up here, monochromatic beyond three walls of floor-to-ceiling windows and French doors that have surely never been opened. Most people's homes have a distinct smell, and Barnes always makes note of it when he enters. Here, there's not a whiff of food, fragrance, or even furniture polish.

Kirstin invites them to sit in a pair of silvery club chairs facing the matching sofa. She's one of those people, Barnes notes, who keeps an eye on her own image reflected in various surfaces around the room. Some are furtive about it, but Kirstin Wayland might as well be addressing herself, gazing into strategically placed mirrors and spotless windows around the room.

A magazine fan arcs across the glass coffee table, possibly more for show than for reading. The top issue of *Vogue*, featuring Cindy Crawford sporting towering teased hair, features headlines in a foreign language— Dutch? German?

"Can I get you some water? I'd offer you coffee, but my housekeeper is busy keeping the twins out of the way right now. They just got home from school and I don't want them asking any questions just yet."

"So they don't know your husband is—"

"No, they don't. They'll just worry. They're at that fragile age."

Which age, Barnes wants to ask, is the fragile one? Ten? Twelve? Thirteen?

Five, he discovers when he asks instead for the children's names and ages. The twins, Eaton and Gardner, will be six next month. Their baby sister, born on Valentine's Day, is napping in the nursery down the hall. The nanny is there, too, presumably watching her sleep.

Barnes gets the staff's names. "Maria Ruiz and Millie Ruiz—they're related?"

"I think they're cousins. Maybe sisters. Something like that."

"Where do they live?"

"Somewhere up in Harlem. Or the Bronx, maybe?" she asks, as if he might know.

"They live together?"

"I have no idea." Seeing his expression, she adds, "I mean, it's not like I visit them."

"You have addresses and phone numbers for them, though, right?" Stef asks. "Unless you're paying them under the table. That would be illegal, and I know you wouldn't—"

"We wouldn't," she says hastily. "I have it somewhere around here."

"Good, because we'll need to interview them. They know your husband is missing, right?"

"I mentioned that he didn't come home last night, but it would be a waste of time for you to discuss this with them."

"How so?"

"For one thing, they barely speak English."

"Well, Barnes here is bilingual, so don't worry. They'll understand each other perfectly."

Kirstin goes to the kitchen for the water and Barnes looks over the notes he just scribbled in the notebook balanced on his knee. Eaton, Gardner, and Wellesley . . . the Wayland daughters might as well be a law firm.

"Hey, Barnes, you ever hear that phrase 'picture perfect'? 'Cause there it is." Stef gestures at a framed oil painting that hangs beneath one of those wall spotlights, like in a museum.

It's a family portrait, with the four Wayland females all dressed in white; Perry in a black suit. Kirstin is seated front and center with a cherubic blonde baby on her lap, flanked by a pair of miniature versions of herself, right down to the petulant expressions. Looks can be deceiving, but to Barnes, the Wayland twins don't appear to be sweet little girls.

Perry's hand on his wife's shoulder looks as clenched as his smiling jaw. He's handsome in the same way that the Nazis are handsome in Barnes's favorite all-time movie, *Raiders of the Lost Ark*. Clean-shaven and buttoned up, with perfect posture and fair Teutonic features.

"What is it those Valley Girls say? Gag me with a spoon."

"Somehow, you don't seem like the Valley Girl type, Stef."

Kirstin is back, carrying a silver tray that holds three glasses filled with ice and three individual-sized bottles of mineral water. She hands them around, cautioning them to please use coasters. Barnes has spotted those same green bottles in stores lately—not fancy ones, but regular supermarkets and delis where he shops. He's been wondering what kind of New Yorker would shell out money for water in a bottle when the city's drinking supply is abundant and potable. He sips, and finds that the fancy water tastes no different than what he gets for free out of the sink tap.

Kirstin settles on the couch, and Stef goes over the initial report she gave over the phone when she called the precinct. She strikes Barnes as preternaturally unruffled, though it doesn't necessarily mean she knows more than she's telling.

Her full name, she tells them, is Kirstin Billington Wayland.

"Billington—that's your middle name?" Barnes asks, pen poised on his notebook.

"Maiden name. My middle name is Eaton. That's my mother's maiden name. I'm descended from the *Mayflower* on both sides," she adds, answering a question nobody asked.

"*Mayflower*—you mean, the pilgrims?"

"Yes."

"Got that, Detective? *Mayflower*," Stef says, with a hint of smirk she might catch if her eyes weren't fixated on her own reflection in the mirror across the room.

"Got it." Barnes writes it down and underlines it, as if it's as relevant a detail as she seems to think.

"Hey, are you any relation to the Mayflower Madam?" Stef asks her.

"To *whom*?"

"You know—that woman who got busted for running the high-class prostitution ring, two or three years ago."

Barnes jumps in. "Sydney Biddle Barrows. I just saw a preview for a TV movie coming out in a few weeks. Candice Bergen is playing her."

"Oh, yeah? Candice Bergen is a classy dame, too."

Stef may be rough around the edges, but he isn't one to call women dames. Barnes has seen him use the tactic before. He's trying to shake up Kirstin Wayland—that's *Kirstin Eaton Billington Wayland* to them—so that she'll let down her guard.

She stiffly informs them that she is absolutely no relation to the Mayflower Madam, and they move on. She confirms the basic details about Perry. Yes, he's a hedge fund manager. Yes, he's blond and blue eyed. Yes, he's thirty-four. No scars or birthmarks that she knows of, but yes, he does have a distinguishing physical characteristic.

"What's that?" Stef asks.

Kirstin chews her lower lip before answering. "He has a tattoo. Not where anyone would see it, thank God. He got it years ago, when we were at Brown. He knew I'd be upset, so he hid it from me for months. He'd gotten drunk at a frat party, and the next thing he knew . . . It wasn't like him, but I guess we all have our moments. I always tell him to have it removed, but he's not good with pain."

Or maybe he wants to keep the ink. Unlike scars, tattoos are deliberate mementos. Barnes has one himself—*CB* on his right bicep. His father's initials.

"Where's the tattoo?" Stef asks Wayland's wife.

"On his . . . uh . . ." She gestures at her left breast. "Here."

"Chest?" Barnes supplies when Stef fails to come up

with delicate phrasing. Not that Kirstin Wayland has much . . . chest to speak of. She's built like a prepubescent boy. Barnes prefers women with a little more meat on their bones.

"Somewhere around there, yes. I've only seen it a couple of times." Seeing them raise eyebrows, she adds hastily, "You know—in the light."

Stef shoots Barnes a look, as if that revelation has confirmed everything he's ever said—and Barnes has ever assumed—about marital sex.

"What's the tattoo?"

"A pony."

Whatever Barnes was expecting . . . that wasn't it.

"A pony?"

"You know. A little horse."

"Not the same thing," Stef says, as if it matters.

"Does he ride?" Barnes asks Kirstin, who shakes her head. "Do you?"

She seems like the equestrian type, but doesn't ride, either.

Barnes files away the little horse—or pony—aware that the slightest anomaly, like a tattoo on the last man in the world you'd expect to have one, might hold the key to a case.

"How are things between you and your husband, Mrs. Wayland?" Stef asks.

"Are you asking if I think he walked out on me?"

The words clatter into the room and lie there in a brief, awkward silence.

She clears her throat and shifts her position on the couch. "I'm not stupid. I know what you're thinking. But Perry would never leave me. *Never.* Not in a million years."

If there's one statement Barnes has heard so far from every person whose loved one has gone missing, it's that.

He has yet to meet anyone who suspects that their spouse or child willingly walked away, though a good many do. People have dirty little secrets—affairs, drug habits, legal problems, financial problems. They want to escape. Or they're chasing after another woman, another man. Or they're just plain bored.

"Would you say that your marriage is solid, then?" Stef asks. "No problems?"

"Yes, it's solid. No problems. If you're going to talk to my help, then believe me, they'll confirm that. They'll tell you that they've never once heard us argue."

Don't all married couples argue? Maybe not in front of the "help," but no relationship is as perfect as the picture Mrs. Wayland continues to paint. She hands over a stack of photos, interspersing additional biographical details with squirm-inducing memories of breakfasts in bed, foot rubs, pet names.

"He calls me Kirstie, and I call him Perfect Per', because he's perfect, and together we make the perfect pair, you know?"

She and her husband went to neighboring Connecticut boarding schools, and started dating as undergrads at Brown University. They became engaged after he earned his Harvard MBA, and he quickly landed a job at a top Wall Street firm. Following a large Newport wedding and South Pacific honeymoon, they moved to Manhattan. Her father-in-law died before they were married, her mother-in-law just this past summer, "Rest her soul."

"You got along well with her?"

"We adored each other. Perry has always said we were two peas in a pod. I guess most men want to marry a woman like their mother, right?"

Barnes suppresses a shudder.

She tells them about the villa Perry rented in the South

of France for their tenth wedding anniversary in August, and shows off the diamond tennis bracelet encircling her thin wrist. "This was my gift. He loves to spoil me. It's from Cartier."

"Very nice," Barnes dutifully comments.

She looks at Stef. His silence seems to make her uneasy.

"Listen, I know what you're thinking. But you're wrong. Perry and I spent all last Saturday and Sunday house hunting. He wouldn't have done that if he wanted to leave. He hates to waste time."

"You're moving?"

"No, he's wanted a beach house for years. Waterfront, and a sailboat, too. He's going to name it *The Kirstie*."

"So he sails?"

"Yes. Growing up, he summered on Block Island."

"Is that where you were looking for a beach house?"

"*Block Island?* Do you know how remote that is?"

"Never been. Where, then? Down the Jersey shore?"

"God, no!" she says, as if Stef had suggested Iowa. "We were looking in the Hamptons!"

Ah, where else? So, a seaside Hamptons house, sailboat, pricey jewelry, fancy European vacations . . . Perry Wayland obviously enjoys spending his money as much as his wife does.

"What about Monday?" Stef asks.

"Excuse me?"

"Saturday and Sunday, you were house hunting in the Hamptons. Then on Monday, the market bottomed out. Was your husband upset?"

"Who wasn't? But he wouldn't run away because of it."

He tilts his head. "You sure about that? Because—"

"Positive."

"—because I gotta say, Mrs. Wayland, he wouldn't be the first Wall Street guy to, you know, need to take a little step back, or . . ."

Forward. Right off a bridge, or over the edge of a subway platform in front of an oncoming train. Every NYPD cop is aware of the suicide copycat phenomenon, and Black Monday triggered a rash. One person jumps, and others will soon follow. It doesn't just happen here; it happens everywhere. But in New York, daily life is inherently stressful, and potentially lethal skyscrapers, bridges, and rapid transit tracks lurk at every turn. Mentally stable people don't have a bad day and decide on a whim to end it all, but an emotionally disturbed person might—especially when tabloid headlines blast news about someone else's successful escape from this miserable world. An EDP might idly glance out a twentieth-floor window, realize how easy it would be to take a dive, and do it.

Kirstie shakes her head so vigorously that her hair flutters momentarily out of place. "Perry wasn't like that. I mean, he was upset, of course."

"So you talked about that?"

"Not directly. He was stressed. Working late. He had calls from investors at all hours. But other than that, everything was normal. He's been looking forward to this weekend."

"More house hunting?"

"No, my parents are in town, so we're having dinner tonight with them. Tomorrow morning, Perry's taking the twins to FAO Schwarz to buy a birthday gift for their friend Ainsley, and then to her Eloise tea party at the Plaza Hotel in the afternoon. Tomorrow night, we're seeing *Burn This* on Broadway."

"The new Lanford Wilson play."

"You know it?" She raises a dubious eyebrow at Barnes.

"Barnes is a theater buff," Stef says. "Opera, too. Right, Barnes?"

Wrong. But he does enjoy seeing a show now and then, and the play, with its controversial homosexual themes and three-hours-plus running time, has been in the news ever since it opened a few weeks ago.

"I wish Perry were like that," Kirstin says. "But he's not into that sort of thing."

"What sort of thing?"

"Culture. Arts, literature, theater."

"Then why was he looking forward to tomorrow night?"

"Because *I'm* looking forward to tomorrow night. When you love someone, you just want them to be happy."

Barnes weighs a Wall Street businessman who, after the most difficult week of his career, eagerly anticipates a weekend spent dining with the in-laws, sitting through a long theatrical production, toy shopping, and attending a tea party with five-year-old girls.

Kirstin picks up her still-untouched glass of water, and puts it down. Probably worried about the calories.

Stef turns a page of his report. "All right, Mrs. Wayland. You say you last saw your husband yesterday morning?"

"That's the last time he was home, but I didn't see him. I just heard him in his bathroom and dressing room, getting ready for work."

"And you were . . ."

"In bed."

"What time was this?"

"His alarm goes off at five thirty."

"You didn't get up with him?"

"At *five thirty*? No. I was exhausted."

"From . . ."

"The day before."

"Wednesday? What happened then?"

"*Every* day is exhausting. I have *three* children. Two are *twins*."

Picking a hangnail would probably exhaust Kirstin Wayland, if her fingers weren't as impeccably groomed as her toes.

"So you don't know what your husband was wearing when he left?"

"A black wool suit and white shirt, both custom-made. French cuffs, monogrammed cufflinks. Black suspenders, black tie, black wing tips."

Black, black, black . . . and a horse inked on his chest. Johnny Cash fantasy?

"Then you *did* see him?"

"I didn't say that," she tells Stef. "He wears the same thing every day. Well, not the same actual clothing. He has a few dozen suits and white shirts, and they all look exactly alike to me. I tell him to jazz things up a little, maybe a yellow power tie once in a while, but he's not that guy."

"Yeah, me, either," Stef says, as if she might have assumed otherwise.

Thinking of the secret tattoo, Barnes isn't so sure Perry Wayland doesn't have a wild side.

She tells them that her husband usually leaves for work by six thirty, driving himself downtown. His secretary, who's on their short list of people to interview, has already confirmed that her boss spent the day at the office as usual. His Mercedes was in the usual parking garage near his office building yesterday from 7:12 a.m. until 5:44 p.m.

It didn't turn up on the bridge until almost midnight. Where was he in the interim?

Kirstin Wayland says that she didn't speak to her husband during the day, which wasn't unusual.

"Sometimes he calls, but he didn't yesterday."

"Did you worry?"

"I didn't even notice. It was a crazy day. I had a million things going on."

"You were out?"

"I was home."

"Alone?"

"Yes. With my housekeeper, and the nanny."

Alone by her standards.

Still, the concern in her pale blue eyes appears genuine when she asks them what they think might have happened to her husband.

"We can't speculate, Mrs. Wayland."

"There is absolutely no way Perry jumped off the George Washington Bridge last night. Even if he did kill himself—and again, I can assure you that he did not—he'd never do that. He's absolutely terrified of heights."

Barnes glances at the skyline beyond the French doors and terrace.

She follows his gaze. "Perry wouldn't go out there even if I let him."

"If you . . . *let him*?"

"I don't mean it like that. I had all the French doors removed when the twins were born."

Barnes frowns. "But aren't those—"

"Dummy knobs. They're just tall windows now, with shatterproof glass. They don't even open. You hear awful stories about children falling."

"That's what window bars are for," Stef points out.

"Yes, but I don't want to feel like I'm in prison."

Your husband might have.

"You need to check and make sure no one fitting his description is in any of the hospitals."

"First thing we did," Barnes assures her. "But we'll check again."

"Maybe he hit his head and he's wandering around the

city with amnesia." Seeing Stef's expression, she insists, "I'm serious! It happens all the time!"

Yes. It happens all the time . . . in movies, on TV, in books. Seldom does it happen in real life, though it is within the realm of possibility. But in this case?

Barnes's gut is saying that the last time Perry Wayland put on his contaminated shoes and exited this hermetically sealed palace with the white queen and pouty princesses, he knew he wasn't coming back.

He and Stef discuss the theory in the elevator back down.

"I feel like we're hunting down a stray puppy that ran away from the kill shelter," Barnes says.

"If he wanted to leave, he should have done it like a man. Not for his wife's sake. For his kids. I might not be father of the year, but there are some things you don't do. You'll see, some day when you have kids."

Barnes has nothing to say to that.

AMELIA UNLOCKS THE graffiti-covered front door of the yellow brick apartment building on East 125th Street, just off Lexington Avenue. The vestibule has gone dark again. Bulbs never burn out here, or along the corridors and basement laundry room. The building's residents steal them to use in their apartments.

She pauses to check the mailbox, hoping to find a letter from her lost biological family, finding only more bills they can't afford to pay, and useless catalogs filled with items they can't afford to buy. Six flights rise before her in the dim, dank stairwell. She climbs five of them and trudges past a row of doors, behind which babies wail and voices argue as onions fry and soup bubbles on stovetops that give off a faint hint of gas.

At the end of the hall, she lets herself into the silent

apartment. With luck, it will be empty. With three jobs, Calvin is never home . . .

"Dad?" she calls.

"Yeah."

. . . except when she doesn't want him to be.

She adds the mail to the untouched heap collecting dust in a dime-store wicker basket by the door, then drops her backpack on the pullout couch where she's slept for as long as she can remember. Long-unlaundered sheets snake around soda cans, papers and books, and a week's worth of discarded clothing. Bettina had insisted on folding the bed closed every morning and stashing the bedding in the closet.

"Make sure you do that every day while I'm in the hospital," she said last spring, about to walk slowly out the door for the final time.

Voice clogged with emotion, Amelia had promised she would.

Please come back, Mama. Please, please don't leave us.

A futile plea, silently uttered by a stranger, to a stranger.

She turns on the TV. Her two favorite *General Hospital* characters are in the midst of a scene. She sits at the edge of the mattress, inches away from the television, trying to figure out what's going on.

Behind her, Calvin appears in the doorway of the small bedroom, bleary eyed and gray stubbled. He rarely sleeps anymore, even at night, prowling the apartment at all hours. Amelia hears him opening and closing kitchen cabinets, running water, pacing restlessly around her as she feigns slumber so they won't have to talk to each other.

"Aren't you late for work?"

"I'm going."

"Like that?" She eyes his boxer shorts and a too-snug

sleeveless white tee shirt that hugs the rolls of fat around his middle.

"Don't be fresh. How was school?"

"Fine."

"Working hard?"

"All As so far."

He returns to the bedroom. She turns back to the TV and adjusts the rabbit-ear antenna, foil crumpled around the tips because she once read that it helps get a better signal. Cable would be more effective, but Bettina always said it would be a waste of money.

She stares absently at the snowy screen. Tony Jones and Lucy Coc are arguing. Ordinarily, their problems captivate her. Today, she has too many of her own to care.

How could Marceline leave like that? Doesn't she know Amelia was counting on her to help unravel the past?

Maybe she does know. Maybe that's why she left. It sure feels that way.

Calvin is back, wearing dark trousers, buttoning on a light blue uniform.

"This is my last shirt. The laundry has to be done."

One of many household responsibilities that's now become hers—and by far her least favorite. How many times in the last seven months has she lugged a heavy load to the basement community laundry room only to find clothes sudsing and spinning in every working washer and dryer, and a line of impatient neighbors waiting their turn?

"I'll do it later. Too crowded down there right now."

"You checked?"

"I don't have to. This time of day, everyone's doing laundry."

"Well, make sure you do it. And you need to clean up this place, Amelia."

"I will, later."

"Everything with you is later."

"I just need to chill for a few minutes, okay? I had to walk all the way home."

He doesn't ask why; doesn't even seem to hear her. He picks up a framed wedding photo and stares at it.

An almost unrecognizably lanky Calvin wears a skinny tie and dark suit that would never fit him today; Bettina a full-skirted white dress and pillbox hat with a pouf of veil.

When Amelia was a little girl, she loved to look at that faded black-and-white picture. Back then, she didn't notice that the frame wasn't even the right size, or that it was just a square snapshot with a white border. The date is printed on the bottom, September 8, 1956. Bettina told her the church ceremony was simple, and there was no reception.

"Did you walk down the aisle with music?"

"No, child."

"Why not?"

"Because I didn't have a daddy to give me away, and we couldn't afford to pay the organist."

"That's so sad."

"No, it was a happy day. Happiest day of my life."

"What about the day I was born?"

"That, too."

Liar. You weren't even there when I was born.

Amelia had been led to believe she'd entered the world on May 12, 1968, but that was merely the day she'd been abandoned. No wonder Calvin and Bettina never turned it into a celebration with cake and presents. She'd always thought it was because they didn't have time or money for such frivolity. In truth, she didn't get a real birthday because they didn't know when she'd been born.

Calvin blows dust off the frame, sets it back on the table, and goes to the kitchen. She hears him open the fridge and clatter around for the lunch pail containing the second of his daily bologna sandwiches. Bettina sent him off with real suppers to eat on his break—roasted chicken, baked potatoes wrapped in foil, a thermos of homemade vegetable soup . . .

"How about that creamy corn chowder you used to make?" he'd ask, or good-naturedly complain that he liked his potatoes mashed and his chicken fried.

"Well, I like my men alive," his wife would reply, and poke him in the belly.

"Woman, if you want to see *alive*, you make me some sausage gravy and biscuits to go with that chicken and see what happens."

Amelia flops back on the mattress, shoulders landing with a scrunch on a half-eaten bag of Chee-tos—last night's dinner. Sitting up again, she brushes her back and neck, peppering the dingy white sheets with salty orange crumbs.

Bettina would have a heart attack over the mess. She'd worry about stains, bugs, and unexpected company—as if that were likely. Visitors were rare in the little apartment even back when she was alive.

For all her Dixie charm and manners, Bettina never did enjoy entertaining. She'd complain that she had no room to do it properly. No time, either. She worked two jobs. When she had time at home, she wanted to do housework, or just relax. Other than church—which she attended without fail—she left the apartment only to work and run errands.

That didn't stop people from paying their respects after she died. Not just Marceline but neighbors, church

ladies, co-workers . . . more people than Amelia had ever
realized cared about her mother. They trooped through
the door bearing pastries and cookies in white bakery
boxes tied with red string, or flowers from the Korean
market down the street.

More than the forced conversation and never-ending
influx of sickening sweets, Amelia resented those blooms
poking like rainbow ice cream scoops from cones of stiff
cellophane and printed paper. She preferred the muted
blues of Marceline's bouquet.

Bettina would have carefully unwound the thin rubber bands entwining the reedy stems and folded the
paper and cellophane to use later. She'd have added
the granular contents of tea-bag-sized packets bound
with the stems, so that the blossoms wouldn't have
drooped overnight, submerged leaves slimy in scum-
topped water greener than the pickle juice that had
filled the makeshift vase. She wouldn't have liked
Marceline's wayward wildflowers. She wouldn't have
allowed Marceline into the house.

"There's no food. I left twenty dollars on the counter
for groceries," Calvin says. "I'll be home in the morning."

As if she might expect him to do otherwise?

Maybe he's thought of walking out and never coming back to this sorrow-and-anger-drenched place that
seems far smaller for two than it ever did for three. Who
wouldn't consider it? She has.

The door closes. On TV, the credits are rolling. She
missed the end of the program.

If only they had a VCR. Then she could just rewind
and see what she missed.

She'll have to wait until Monday to find out what
happened today, and what happens next.

She sighs and stands up, reaching to turn off the channel. A voice-over stops her.

"All over the world, abandoned children and adoptees have hit a dead end trying find their birth parents. Now, Silas Moss can help. Tonight on 20/20, Barbara Walters will interview a man whose revolutionary research might finally answer the burning question, 'Who am I?'"

PERRY WAYLAND'S OFFICE is located in the financial district, at 195 Broadway. Built in the early 1900s, the ornate twenty-nine-story office building once housed American Telephone and Telegraph, now known as AT&T.

Barnes and Stef learn this fun fact from Gene, a balding, jowly-faced after-hours lobby security guard.

"But that's not the most interesting thing about it."

"No way, there's more?"

Stef's undercurrent of sarcasm escapes the guard, who leans in conspiratorially. "You bet there's more. You hear about that new Michael Douglas movie?"

"Fatal Attraction." Barnes nods. He saw it a few weeks ago at the newly renovated Loew's Victoria on 125th Street. If ever there was a movie that reinforced his intention never to marry, that was it.

"No."

"No?" he echoes, as Gene shakes his shiny head.

"Wall Street. Not out yet."

"If it's not out yet, then how would we know it?" This time, Stef sounds outright prickly. It's late, and it's been a long day. They're waiting for Perry Wayland's secretary, Liz, who was supposed to come down ten minutes ago.

"I'm surprised you haven't heard about it. There's been a lot of buzz."

"Yeah? What's the buzz?" Barnes asks, taking out his cigarettes.

"It was filmed right here." He gestures around the majestic marble lobby, lined with bronze and alabaster chandeliers and towering Doric pillars. "I got a picture with the brother of that guy from *The Breakfast Club*. What's his name—Martin Sheen's son."

"Emilio Estevez? He's in it?"

"No, his brother. The kid from *Platoon*. Charlie Sheen. You ever see—"

He pauses as elevator doors slide open. An attractive brunette steps out, smoking a cigarette. Her panty hose and white sneakers peek out beneath a long tweed dress coat with enormous shoulder pads, and she carries an open leather tote with a pair of high-heeled pumps poking from the top. Her shoulder-length permed hair is nearly as tall as it is long. To Barnes, the tuft of bangs sprayed vertically above her forehead look like something out of Dr. Seuss, despite the *Vogue* magazine cover he glimpsed back at the Waylands' apartment. Anyway, this pleasant-but-plain-faced woman is no Cindy Crawford.

"That's Liz," Gene tells them.

"Sorry I'm late," she calls, her voice echoing in the cavernous space as she hurries toward them. "It's hard to get out of there on a Friday, especially with . . . you know." She glances at Gene, as if wondering whether to mention the reason for their visit.

"They told me about Mr. Wayland," the guard informs her. "I told them I wasn't working last night, so I didn't see him leave. They're going to talk to Ralph. He was here. Maybe he knows something."

Barnes doubts it. Whatever happened with—or to— Perry Wayland likely unfolded after he left the office.

They step out onto the sidewalk teeming with office workers, most of the female commuters carrying their dress shoes and scurrying along in sneakers, like Liz.

"We parked near a diner around the corner. You want to get a cup of coffee?"

"At this hour, I'd rather have Chardonnay."

"Me, too," Stef says, though he's more of a Wild Turkey guy. "But we're on the job, so . . ."

"It's okay. I've got to get home. My son has a game tonight—high school football. I never miss it."

"Where do you live?"

"Staten Island."

"You take the ferry?"

She nods and lifts a sneakered foot. "That's why I wear these. Every night, I walk down to Whitehall. Helps me clear my head."

"We'll walk and talk, then," Stef says. "We can all clear our heads. Come on, Barnes."

As they head south, toward the Staten Island ferry terminal at the foot of Manhattan, Stef asks Liz about her job working for Perry Wayland and discerns that she does everything from answer his phone to order his lunch—same thing every day.

"A Cobb salad and a Coke."

He asks about Perry's demeanor yesterday.

"He was a little agitated, to be honest," she says, exhaling menthol, "but who isn't, with everything that's been going on this week . . ."

"You mean the market?"

She nods.

"So he lost a lot of money?"

"*Lost?* No. Everyone else did, but Perry saw it coming, so he's been preparing. This isn't the first time the market's crashed, you know. It happened in 1929, too."

"So I've heard," Stef says dryly. "So is Wayland psychic, or what?"

"Not psychic. Brilliant. Ever hear of the Elliott wave theory?"

Barnes nods as they stop to wait for the light to change. "Every action is followed by a reaction."

"That's right. The past can predict the future." She tosses her cigarette butt to the sidewalk and grinds it with her rubber sole. "Perry noticed identical patterns to the market leading up to the 1929 crash. A week ago— last Friday—he thought it was shaping up to happen Monday and he said it was going to be cataclysmic."

"How does a person prepare for that?"

"For one thing, you sell." She takes out a pale green box of Salem Slim Lights and focuses on painstakingly removing another cigarette.

"For another thing . . ." Barnes prompts.

She shrugs. "I don't know. I didn't spend the weekend with him. You should ask Kirstie."

"We did," Stef says. "She told us they were house hunting in the Hamptons."

She raises an eyebrow, but says nothing.

"What about that surprises you?" Barnes asks her.

"The Hamptons? Nothing. I mean, a lot of these guys have houses out there." She waves her cigarette hand at the crowd of pedestrians, largely made up of Wall Street types heading toward home or happy hour.

"But . . ."

"I didn't say but."

Barnes tries another tactic as the light changes and they resume walking. "What do you think about the Waylands' marriage?"

"What do *I* think? You should ask—"

"We asked her. Now we're asking you, Liz. Did he seem happy with his wife? I'm not wondering because I have a personal interest, or because I'm nosy. This is an investigation. Your boss is missing. He might be in danger. Did he seem happy?"

She pauses to take a long drag, and offers a slightly strangled, "Not really."

"Was he having an affair, Liz?" Stef asks point-blank.

Barnes anticipates denial, but she shrugs. "I don't know. Maybe. He's been on the phone a lot lately with a woman. She must have called him a thousand times between Monday and when he left yesterday."

"A thousand?"

"A lot," she amends. "She called once or twice last month, and then more often over the past few weeks, but it's been constant since Monday."

"When the market crashed."

"Yes. I mean, the phones were going crazy that day anyway, but she called a lot. And ever since."

"Who is she?"

"Well, he *says* she's an investor . . ."

"You don't believe that."

"Let's just say there's no other investor whose call he takes every time, no matter what he's doing. And there's something . . . I don't know, goofy, about the way he acts when she calls . . ."

"Goofy how?"

"It's like my son, with this cheerleader. He's infatuated with her, and she knows it. I see her seeing the way he looks at her, but she pretends she doesn't."

"So Perry Wayland is . . . infatuated?"

"I didn't say *that*. Just, when he talks to her, he sounds like a teenager who's gaga over some girl. I can't describe it."

"I'd say you just did," Barnes says. "So you hear him talking to her?"

"Not on purpose. It's a small office."

"What does he say?"

She hesitates.

"Again, I'm not being nosy. And I know you aren't, either, if you happen to overhear their private conversations."

"I'm not."

"Right. So if there's anything you've heard him say that makes you think she's not an investor . . ."

"Yeah," she admits. "There are a few things he's said. Like I've heard him tell her he misses her, or that he wished he could see her again but she knew he couldn't. I got the impression they hadn't seen each other in years."

"Anything else?"

"Not really. Just . . . once, I heard him talking to her about a, um, movie they'd seen together."

"Did he say which one?"

"Yeah. It was, um . . ." She shakes her head and looks away. "It was *Deep Throat.*"

Barnes raises an eyebrow. "I'm no hedge fund guy, but I'm going to guess most of them aren't seeing porn flicks with their investors."

"Probably not," Stef agrees. "Did you overhear anything else along those lines, Liz?"

"Along those lines?"

"Or any lines."

She shakes her head.

"This woman . . . does she have a name?"

"I don't know her first name. She's pretty formal. Whenever she calls, she just gives me her last name."

"What is it?"

"White. 'This is Miss White,' she says, and I always put her right through, like he told me."

IT GETS DARK earlier here, 150 miles east of Manhattan. The sky is dusky when Red boards the ferry; pitch-black when it docks on Block Island. The other passengers are met by cars, or friends, or stroll off in pairs toward the brightly lit hotels and restaurants clustered near the landing. Red has a longer walk to a darker place.

What if this is a trap? What if Black found out what happened in the stairwell?

But how? It wasn't in the papers. Red checked them all.

Nobody cares. Derelicts die violent deaths every day in this city. That junkie's murder was insignificant. No reason to worry.

The air is chilly and smells of dank fish and burning leaves. Somewhere out on the lapping water, a night fisherman's boat hums along, headed out to the dark sea.

A familiar landmark appears around a bend in the road. The Plantation restaurant, tucked into a weathered cottage, is open, with a few cars in the parking lot. Bearing no resemblance to a plantation or to the diner back in New York, the place is a throwback to simpler times on the island.

So is the Sandy Oyster next door. The sign advertises *Cottage Vacancies, Weekly Rates, Picnic Grove & Playground, Color TV.* No phones in the rooms, though— not that high-tech. Red spots the pay phone White uses for calls. It shares a weedy patch of grass with a rusting metal swingless swing set, sagging picnic table, cinderblock fire pit, and Dumpster. Ah, the picnic grove and playground.

Gray television light flickers in the small office, and a vending machine hums at its doorstep. Red slips around it to the row of huts, peeling blue paint not faded enough to temper the gaudiness, even in the dark. A few windows are lamp lit with cars parked at the low concrete barriers in front of them. At the far end, an exterior doorknob is tied with a white handkerchief.

Three staccato knocks, a pause to count to four, and a final knock.

The door opens.

It takes Red a moment to recognize the man in jeans and fleece, face masked by at least a day's growth of beard and aviator-framed glasses.

"Come on in," Perry Wayland says. "We've been waiting for you."

Chapter Eight

Amelia never did get around to cleaning up the apartment, doing the laundry, or getting groceries. Nor did she work on a paper that's due Monday. How can she focus when, mere hours after Marceline LeBlanc slipped from her grasp, Barbara Walters is about to interview some old guy who helps people find their birth parents?

She sits on the edge of the pullout mattress as the program begins, with images of a picturesque college town tucked into gorges and rolling hills above a long blue wedge of lake.

"Cornell University professor Silas Moss has made genetic breakthroughs that are bringing long-lost family members home every day."

Cornell? Cornell is in Ithaca.

The camera pans streets lined with stately old homes, quaint shops, and lofty trees dressed in splashy autumn reds and golds. It looks like a movie set. But it's a real place. It could have been Amelia's place. She could have been one of those backpack-wearing students, shuffling along through fallen leaves, laughing beside a bike rack, hanging around on a broad common bumping a hacky sack from knee to knee.

It's been a while since Amelia thought much about Ithaca, or the high school music teacher who'd taken her under her wing. Mrs. Morse had talked Amelia into applying to her alma mater, Ithaca College, and she'd been accepted.

"You're not going!" Bettina said. "You want an education, take business courses at city college. It's free. We can't afford tuition anywhere else."

"But Mrs. Morse said there are grants and scholarships."

"Well, bless her heart," Bettina said. "This Mrs. Morse knows an awful lot about everything, doesn't she. I have a mind to march right on over to that school and ask her what she thinks she's doing, filling my daughter's head with fool nonsense."

"It's not fool nonsense."

And I'm not your daughter.

On television, Barbara Walters strolls along a path with a white-bearded, bespectacled man. Behind them, a clock tower sits high above gabled redbrick buildings and broad greens.

"For decades a fixture on this Ivy League campus, Dr. Silas Moss is a professor of genetics and molecular biology," Barbara says in voice-over. "Back in 1984, he embarked on a pioneering research project with students enrolled in the university's interdepartmental biology and society major. Now, those efforts are coming to fruition."

Cut to an interior office, with Silas Moss seated behind a desk, his shelves lined with books and framed award certificates.

"I've always known I was adopted as an infant," he tells Barbara. "But the mother and father who raised me never wanted to give me any details about it. As far as they were concerned, my life began the minute they brought me home. They were incredible people. They were both scientists with busy careers, married in their forties, lived well into their eighties. I loved them dearly, and they gave me a wonderful childhood. But not a day has gone by that I haven't wondered about my biological parents."

"Did you ever try to find them?"

"Oh, all the time. But where do you begin? Until the past few years, adoptees' birth certificates listed only the adoptive parents' names and adoption records are sealed. They can only be opened by a court order for legal or medical reasons. You have virtually nothing to go on, unless you stumble across some clue or your adoptive family is willing to provide information, which they often don't have and were never given in the first place."

"It seems like trying to find a needle in a haystack."

"Yes. It's just blind, desperate searching, if you can even call it a search."

Amelia thinks of the sea of strangers she's scrutinized since March, and presses a fingertip to the teary corners of her eyes. *Are you my mother?*

"What do you do if you have no hope of finding your birth parents?" Barbara asks the professor.

"Mostly, you wonder. And you let your imagination create a fairy-tale family. In mine, I was the secret love child of Gable and Lombard," he adds with a chuckle. "I watched a lot of old movies with my father, growing up. I had blond hair like Carole, and I loved her screwball sense of humor. My own mother was always very serious."

"Professor, when you say your own mother, and your father, you're referring to your adoptive parents?"

"Of course. They're the only parents I've ever known. And I wouldn't ever have wanted to hurt them. That's why I never got too involved in trying to uncover my roots until after they were gone. They passed away about ten years ago, one right after the other. After they died, I went through every piece of paper in their house, looking for information about my adoption."

"What did you find?"

"Not much. Around the same time, a family moved in next door to me. They have three children. The youngest was a foundling."

"A foundling? Can you explain?"

"The dictionary would define it as 'an infant that has been abandoned by its parents and is discovered and cared for by others.'"

Foundling.

So there's a name for it. A sweet, hopeful name.

That's what I am. I'm a foundling.

"I knew this girl's story long before I got to know her as my neighbor," Silas Moss is saying. "I remembered very well that she'd been found down in the gorge on a cold winter night years earlier. It had been a well-publicized case. Like me, she was fortunate to have been taken in by loving adoptive parents, but she, too, wondered about her roots. She and I bonded over our longing to know, but she had little hope of unlocking her own past. For her, the key didn't lie in sealed written records that might one day be opened. That inspired me to start investigating other kinds of records, if you will."

"Biological ones." Solemn nod from Barbara.

"Yes."

They explain something called DNA, short for deoxyribonucleic acid. Amelia vaguely remembers learning something about it in high school. It's a distinctly patterned chain of genetic material found in every cell of every living organism—broad characteristics shared by many, as well as rare ones unique to that person and their biological relatives.

"DNA testing has been used in paternity suits in recent years and now has the potential to impact our criminal justice system in a very big way," Barbara reports. "This month, at the Florida trial of accused serial rapist Tommy

Lee Andrews, three DNA samples have been presented as evidence in an effort to connect the suspect's semen and blood to a sample taken from the victim. If the state can obtain a conviction based on DNA, we will enter a bold new era in crime investigation and prosecution. But how does this relate to your work, Dr. Moss?"

"A person's DNA is as unique as a fingerprint. There's a one in ten billion chance that two people would share the exact same DNA. But our blood relatives will have similar markers, sharing ancestral origin, physical traits, predisposition to certain diseases, and so on. When comparing a group of samples, we can look for matches among various markers to calculate the possibility or even probability that two people are related."

They discuss a voluntary DNA database Dr. Moss and his students have been compiling over the past few years.

"Where are you getting these samples?"

"Students, friends, local residents—anyone and everyone can be a part of this project," he says. "The more, the merrier, as they say. We put out the call when we started, and more and more people are hearing about us and volunteering."

"How does it work?"

"We get a saliva sample. The cheek swab takes two seconds and is completely painless."

"And then what?"

"And then we map your DNA and use a computer program to compare it to the samples provided from adoptees searching for their roots and birth parents searching for their children."

"Have you solved your young neighbor's mystery?"

"Unfortunately, not yet, but we're hopeful."

"And have you made any matches for others?" Barbara leans forward, hand fisted beneath her chin, wearing a faint smile that says she already knows the answer.

"It's taken a while, but yes. We had our first match last year."

The scene shifts, and Barbara and the professor have been joined by a heavyset woman with a tight bleached-blond perm and a stocky, flannel-clad young man.

"Twenty-six years ago, Dolores Minsk was a pregnant ninth grader who had been sent by her parents to a church-run home for unwed mothers in nearby Buffalo," Barbara's voice-over informs the audience. "When her son was born, nuns whisked him away before she even held him, and she signed the adoption papers without question."

"All the girls did," the woman tells Barbara in a quiet, quaking voice. "Whether they wanted to, or not."

"Did you want to?"

"Not when I got there, no. Not when I started to feel him moving, and started to picture his little face . . ." She takes a deep breath. "But then it started to feel like a nightmare, being stuck there, feeling helpless, and . . . you know. They got to me."

"Who got to you?"

"Everyone. My parents, the nuns, the other girls who were further along . . . they would talk about how they couldn't wait until it was all over, so that they could get their lives back, and pretty soon . . . pretty soon I guess I started to feel the same way, but . . . it wasn't just about me. They kept saying he deserved better. That I had nothing to offer him. And they were right. I had nothing but . . ." She breaks off, overcome, before choking out the last muffled word. *"Love."*

"The scenario was all too common for teenagers back in the 1960s," Barbara's voice informs the audience. "Vulnerable young women in Dolores's circumstances had very few options. Society may never shed the stigma of bearing a child out of wedlock, but *Roe v. Wade* and more widely available access to birth control have changed things dramatically."

Back to Dolores. "After they took him away, I just wanted to get out of there, too. But when I got back home, I just . . . I ached for my son. That's the only way I can describe it. It was a physical ache, more painful than anything I've ever felt."

"Including childbirth?" Barbara asks dramatically.

"God, yes. Yes. Everyone told me to forget about him." The camera zeroes in on Dolores's hand clutching the young man's. "But I just couldn't."

Amelia dabs furiously at her own streaming eyes, fingertips effective as a Q-Tip in a geyser. She reaches blindly behind her and grabs a blanket, using it to wipe away her tears and then—who cares?—to blow her nose.

"You wanted to know what happened to him?" Barbara suggests gently.

"Yes. And I wanted him back. I knew I'd made a mistake. My parents had told me I couldn't come home again if I kept him, and . . . where was I going to go? I still had nothing, and I told myself that at least *he* didn't have nothing, you know? I figured my son had a great life. It made me feel better knowing I'd done the right thing for his sake, even if I was miserable."

"David Kuczowski's life was anything but great," the voice-over continues. "His adoptive parents were abusive, and divorced when he was young. Both remarried and had new families. Young David felt as though he never belonged to anyone, as though he didn't fit in anywhere. Like many lost souls, he turned to drugs and alcohol."

The reporter goes on to tell how he landed in a juvenile detention center, later in jail, and ultimately, in rehab. Now clean and sober, he spotted a flyer early last January about Professor Moss's call for DNA sample volunteers. Always curious about his birth parents, he'd had his cheek swabbed.

Dolores had done the same thing a year earlier, almost to the date.

"That seems like a miraculous coincidence!"

"Not as miraculous as you might think," Professor Moss tells Barbara Walters. "A lot of people, not just adoptees, experience an acute sense of loneliness during the holiday season—a longing for family ties. New Year's is a time for making resolutions, for reassessing the past, and for looking ahead. We get an influx of volunteers every January."

"Not only that," Dolores speaks up, "but David was born in January. Every year on that date, I went to church and prayed that he'd come back to me."

"You never forgot his birthday?"

"A mother never forgets," she tells Barbara with a tremulous smile.

With that, Amelia loses what little grip she had on her emotions and sobs like a baby.

FRIDAY NIGHT WEARS on with no sign of the missing millionaire. According to Homicide, the GWB stairwell murder remains unsolved, as well.

"We can't ignore a murder less than a mile from where Wayland disappeared, around the same time," Stef tells Barnes as they drive back to the Park Avenue penthouse.

"No, but it's not like Perry and Popper traveled in the same circles. What's the connection?"

"What if he was carjacked on the way home from work? Whoever did it got rid of him, went joyriding for a few hours, abandoned the car on the bridge, and took out the junkie on the way back to Manhattan."

"Wayland left the parking garage at 5:44 p.m. You saw

the streets around that building tonight at that hour. A carjacking around there wouldn't go unnoticed. Probably not anywhere on the route from the office to his apartment."

"Maybe he didn't head home. Maybe he had a secret habit and went somewhere more desolate to buy drugs? Or to meet a woman at a trashy motel. And then he was robbed, or carjacked, or whatever."

Barnes nods. "We need to figure out who this Miss White woman is and what she means to Wayland."

"I think we can guess that part. Ever see *Deep Throat*?"

"When did it come out?"

"I think '72, '73 . . . something like that."

He sighs. "I was in grade school, Stef."

A middle-aged man greets them at the Wayland penthouse, wearing rich leather tassel loafers and a blue blazer with a red silk pocket square. Beneath a swoop of silver-blond hair parted on the side, his face is like an overinflated balloon, with the ruddiness of someone who's indulged in a few too many steak dinners and martini lunches over the years. As recently as today, if his potent vodka breath is any indication.

They show their badges and he pumps their hands, introducing himself as Kirstie's father. "Richard Billington, but you can call me . . . Biff." He grins and swaggers a pistol finger at them. "Thought I was going to say Rich, didn't you? I always tell people, that's *what* I am, not *who* I am. Been Biff all my life."

Barnes musters a smile and pretends that it's nice to meet him, feigning commiseration as he complains about the Friday afternoon traffic on the drive in from Boston. Stef does the same, then asks about Kirstie.

"She's soaking in a hot bubble bath. Poor thing is exhausted. So is my wife. She went straight to bed when we got here. I'm manning the phones in case the ransom call comes in. Nothing so far," he adds, as if they'd expected otherwise.

He invites them into the living room. Sure enough, Barnes spies a conical glass that holds an inch of clear liquid, a couple of green olives, and a cocktail onion.

Biff follows his gaze. "Dirty martini?"

"Looks like one to me."

He gifts Barnes's quip with a hearty chuckle. "Quite the detective, young man. But I wasn't asking for a positive ID. I was offering you a cocktail."

"Not on the job, sir, but thanks anyway."

Stef also declines, saying, "We'd like to talk to your daughter, when she's finished with her, uh, bubble bath."

"It might be a while."

"Can you let her know we're here?"

Barnes and Stef settle into the same chairs they occupied this afternoon and Biff disappears, taking his glass with him. When he returns, it's full to the rim, and he sets a bowl of salted cashews on the table.

"Help yourselves. Kirstie will be out soon."

He asks about the investigation as Barnes and Stef make a famished foray into the nut bowl.

"Any suspects?"

"We haven't determined that a crime has been committed," Stef reminds him around a mouthful of nuts. "We've interviewed a number of people."

"Did you find any clues?"

"We're working on it."

Barnes brushes salt from his fingers and takes a pen from his pocket, feeling vaguely like they're Scooby and Shaggy, fresh from the Mystery Machine. Billington could stand in for the ubiquitous ascot-wearing millionaire whose mansion is haunted, though an unscrupulous handyman in a phantom costume isn't likely to hold the key to the Wayland disappearance.

"What can you tell us about your son-in-law, Mr. Billington?"

"Call me Biff. He didn't jump off a bridge."

"You don't think so?"

"I don't *know* so. I mean . . ." With the halting measure of one scrubbing the liquor from his words, he says, "I *do* know so. Perry did not jump off a bridge. He's not that guy."

Not that guy, and not a guy who'd wear a yellow tie. Got it, Barnes thinks. But who *is* he?

"You've met him, right?"

"No. We don't exactly travel in the same circles, Mr.—"

"Biff. Then let's put it this way. If there were a kitten stuck way up high in a tree, my son-in-law wouldn't be the guy you'd ask to rescue it. In fact, he'd *be* the kitten," he adds with a chortle. "Just kidding, just kidding. But Perry is afraid of heights. Doesn't even like to fly."

Stef gestures at the wall of windows, where the skyline glitters beyond the glass. "Why live up here, then?"

"Kirstie fell in love with the view, and the privacy. She wasn't crazy about moving to New York when they got married. She didn't want people on the other side of the wall, or walking around over her head in the middle of the night. So they compromised. That's what marriage is all about, right?"

Watching him take a generous sip of his cocktail, Barnes asks, "Would you say theirs is stable?"

"How stable is anything, these days?"

"Any marriage?"

"The world. We're all going to hell in a handcart, gentlemen. Especially now, with the market going haywire. And Perry missing," he adds—an afterthought.

"If you don't believe he'd take his own life, then what could have happened?"

"He's a wealthy man. Even wealthier now that he's inherited his mother's estate. He was her only heir. Kidnapping makes sense."

"Is that what you think?"

"Kirstie does. Who would know better than his own wife?"

Barnes glances at Stef, thinking of Liz, and of the shadowy Miss White. Reading his mind, Stef gives a slight headshake. He's right. Better not to bring that up now, and risk Biff running back to the bathroom to tell Kirstie before they can. They need to witness her initial reaction, before she goes back to keeping up appearances and professing her husband's perfection.

Biff sips and swirls the contents of his glass and tells them he wants to offer a reward for information on Perry's whereabouts.

"Let's face it, if someone abducted the guy, Kirstie doesn't have a snowball's chance in hell of getting him back in good condition," he says, as if they're discussing a rented tux misplaced in a storm. "And if he wasn't taken or, you know, killed . . . well, let's just say we're not going to want him back anyway. But we can't just move on without giving this thing the old college try, so, fifty thousand dollars. Cash. Oh, there you are, lamb."

Kirstie has appeared in the doorway. She looks frail, wrapped in a turban, silk robe, and slippers—all white, of course.

White.

Ironic, Barnes thinks, that the Other Woman—if that is indeed her role—goes by a name that so perfectly fits the Wonder Bread wife.

"Daddy said you wanted to talk to me."

"Yes. Would you like to speak privately, or . . ." Stef trails off as she settles on the white couch beneath her father's protective arm. Apparently she would not.

"Mrs. Wayland, a few things. First, did your husband own a gun?"

"No! Absolutely not. Perry abhors violence."

It doesn't mean Wayland didn't kill Popper the junkie, but Barnes isn't convinced the two incidents are unrelated. He just isn't sure how the puzzle fits together.

Stef moves on with the questioning. "We spoke with Perry's secretary. She mentioned that he was expecting the market crash. Did you know that?"

"He doesn't talk about work with me."

"He does with me," Biff speaks up. "That's true. He advised me to start selling, fast."

"When?"

"Last week. Good thing, or I'd have taken a big hit."

"Did he ever mention an investor named White? To either of you?"

They shake their heads.

"Or a friend, maybe?" Barnes asks. "An old friend, most likely. A Miss White?"

"*Miss* White?" Kirstie echoes.

"You know her?"

"No, but . . . why are you asking this? Is she a friend, or an investor?"

"Investor," Stef says. "At least, that's what he told his secretary. Liz mentioned that he's had quite a few calls from her this week."

"Really." Kirstie is taut.

Biff pats her shoulder. "Don't you go worrying, sweetheart."

"I'm not. If she called him at the office, I'm sure it was business."

"That's likely. But we haven't been able to identify her or track her down, so we thought maybe you—"

"I've never heard of a Miss White. Sorry. Did you find anything else? Fingerprints in the car, or something?"

"We don't have that information yet. It takes time. We're hoping tomorrow—"

"All right. I'm exhausted. I need to go to bed, if you'll excuse me . . ." Her words and posture are stiff as she rises from the couch. "I still think he was kidnapped, so stay on that."

She leaves the room without niceties.

Biff looks at Barnes and Stef. "Who is this White woman, really?" he asks, with more presence of mind than they'd expect.

"We don't know," Barnes says. "Really."

"You sure?" Gone is the bumbling drunk, and Barnes wonders if it was an act in the first place. "Was my son-in-law having an affair? Did he run off with another woman?"

"We don't know."

Silence. The man tilts his glass, swallowing the rest of his drink.

"Mr. Billington? Do you think . . ."

"I don't know." He gets to his feet. His bloodshot eyes, the same pale shade as his daughter's, are skimmed in frost. "I'd like to turn in now, too. It's been a long day for everyone."

They don't argue.

On the way back to the precinct, Stef shakes his head. "That Kirstie's a chip off the old block. And the old block is a big fat ice cube. For Wayland's sake, I hope Miss White is a hot chick."

"I wouldn't be surprised."

"I wouldn't be surprised if he dove off that bridge, either, to get away from those people."

Back at the precinct, they file for an office search warrant and Wayland's phone records, finish their paperwork, and check in with Ray, their NYPD cohort over at the tow pound. He reports that they're still waiting on the backlogged forensics team to go through Wayland's Mercedes, but there's no obvious evidence of foul play. They arrange to inspect the car first thing in the morning, before interviewing the household staff.

"You want to go get a drink?" Stef asks as they step out onto the street.

"Can't. I'm meeting someone."

His partner grins. "Yeah? Does she have a friend for me?"

Barnes ignores him, walking off into the night.

THIS AFTERNOON, AMELIA had been certain she'd just lost the one person who might help her find out who she is and where she'd come from.

Can Silas Moss take Marceline's place?

She has to find a way to get to Ithaca. Maybe he'll uncover a miraculous DNA match. At the very least, it would be nice to meet someone who knows how it feels to look back and see a gaping hole in your life story. Someone who put a name to who, and what, she is.

A *foundling*.

After learning the truth last spring, she had snooped around the apartment hoping to stumble across some clue about her abandonment and discovery. As expected, she'd found nothing.

At the time, she'd been so consumed by the toxic blur of fury and funeral that she barely remembers the search. Maybe she missed something.

In the small bedroom that now belongs to Calvin alone, she finds the bed unmade, clothing strewn over it and the floor. She steps around a bath towel and his second pair of shoes, scattered facedown, laces frayed, soles nearly worn through.

Though the apartment is small, this room has always been off-limits to her. Calvin and Bettina had their space and Amelia had hers, though it didn't come with a shred of privacy. She's accustomed to it, though in retrospect, she assumes things might be different if she hadn't dropped into their lives without warning nineteen years ago.

Surely they'd have provided more comfortable accommodations for her if they truly considered her their child. If they'd been planning for her, had conceived her . . .

They wouldn't have tossed a biological child into their living room like an overdue library book they'd stumbled across, one that might be snatched away any second. They'd have moved to a bigger place, in a safer neighborhood—a real home.

Instead, their parental existence seemed to have hung in a state of suspended animation, as if they expected her to vanish from their lives as abruptly as she'd appeared.

She glares at the framed black-and-white baby portrait on the bedside table. In it, she's Brillo haired, chubby cheeked and scowling, wearing a limp, tatty-looking knit dress. Bettina had once pointed out a faint stain by the collar, and mentioned that she'd been sick with a stomach flu the day the picture was taken.

"Why didn't you change my clothes?"

"How many dresses do you think you had, child? Santy Claus brought this for you on your first Christmas."

"And it was the only one I had?"

"Mmm-hmm. And no matter how much I scrubbed that spit-up stain, there wasn't enough borax in the world to get rid of it."

"You should 'a waited till I was better to go have my picture taken."

"Child, we didn't *go* anywhere. Back then, a photographer would go door to door in the building. That was just the day he showed up. I still don't know how we even managed to scrape together the money for the sitting fee."

"How old was I?"

"Oh, I don't know. At least seven or eight months, I guess, if it was after Christmas."

Back then, her mother's vague answer didn't set off any alarm bells. Nor did the fact that there were no other baby pictures of her.

"That photographer never came back, so this is all we have," her mother said when she asked.

"I hate it. It's not cute. I look mad."

"You just wouldn't smile that day, no matter what that poor man did. Finally, he gave up, and this is what we got."

Stuck with an ugly picture, just like you were stuck with me.

Amelia turns away from the photo, toward the two simple wooden dressers crammed side by side against the wall opposite the bed. One contains Calvin's belongings, the other Bettina's.

Over the summer, one of the church ladies had come by to see if the Crenshaws could donate Bettina's old clothing to the fall clothing drive. Calvin wasn't home, and Amelia told her they hadn't yet gone through her mother's things.

"It's not good to keep all those reminders around," the church lady said. "I know how hard it is for the husband to part with anything. And maybe even for you. I'm sure you probably want to keep a few sentimental—"

"No," Amelia said. "I don't."

"Then I'd be happy to help you—"

"No, thanks," she said, and all but closed the door in her face.

Calvin heard about it the following Sunday from Pastor Hawke.

"I didn't raise you to be rude," he scolded.

"You didn't raise me to go inviting strangers into the house, either, remember? That's what you said when Miss LeBlanc paid her condolence call."

"That's different. This was a good woman doing charitable work, not—"

"Good woman? She's circling like a vulture, trying to get her claws on Mama's things."

An exaggeration, maybe. Bettina didn't have designer clothes, furs, or jewelry other than her wedding ring and gold cross necklace. She'd worn both daily in life, and continues to do so in death, along with her Sunday dress.

The church lady may not have come here out of greed, but she'd certainly seemed nosy. Marceline LeBlanc had visited out of the goodness of her heart, resulting in a secret friendship Calvin would never have condoned.

Filled with renewed determination to uncover the truth, she opens the top drawer of Bettina's dresser.

If Calvin comes home early, she'll tell him she's decided it's time to start getting rid of things.

After all, it's the truth. She's shed a good deal of the weighty grief for the woman who raised her. Somewhere out there, another woman might be aching for Amelia at this very moment. A woman who, like Dolores Minsk, was told her baby deserved better. Or a woman whose baby was stolen away by someone who believed that was the case, or maybe . . .

Maybe by a couple who'd buried one child and wanted

another so desperately that they'd make up a story about a baby being left in a church.

RED SUCKS IN the cool night air, sweet scented by contrast to the cottage that had smelled as if the carpet had flooded and dried without benefit of disinfectants or open windows. Judging by the stains, that's exactly what happened, probably several seasons ago.

The small room had been overheated and overcrowded—three people shoehorned in with one chair and a double bed covered in a clammy, silky—not in a good way bedspread. Somehow, Wayland, accustomed to luxury, seemed to take it in stride.

Not Wayland. *Black*.

"No names!" White admonished at every slip. There were many. That's what happens when you're overtired.

Not for long, though.

The television light is gone, the office now dark, so Red stops to feed two quarters and a dime into the vending machine. Only one drink isn't sold out, a dark green can of lemon-lime soda that tumbles down the shoot with a deafening clatter.

Teem—wasn't this stuff discontinued a few years back?

Probably. The swig is flat and metallic tasting, but serves its purpose, washing down one of the little white capsules White had provided.

"They'll keep you alert in the days and nights ahead."

"Tylenol?" Red asked, reading the label on the plastic pill bottle.

Black found that hilarious. "Tylenol! How stupid are you?"

"That's what it says! See that? *T-Y-L-*"

Black only laughed harder, and White shushed him, but seemed to be amused, as well. That hurt. A lot.

All because of Black.

"This medicine will help you stay alert," White said. "Just make sure you're careful. It's highly addictive."

"And highly expensive," Black put in. "So don't pop it like M&M's."

"Like you can't afford it?"

"What do you know about what I can afford, you little—"

"It's not about affording it," White cut in. "It's about waste. Red's not going to waste it. Or get wasted. Right, Red?"

"Right."

"Because if you take too much, you're going to get antsy and make a reckless mistake."

"I won't. No mistakes."

Before leaving, Red used the dingy bathroom. There were two toothbrushes in the holder. A cosmetics bag and a shaving kit on the back of the toilet seat. A nightgown and starched shirt draped on the back of the door. Cozy. The two of them holed up here while Red is the one out there risking everything. Why doesn't Wayland— Black—have to get his hands dirty?

This is no longer about sin and immortality. Now it's criminal, snuffing out lives, not in self-defense or revenge, but because White says the women and their children are a threat.

I'm not questioning that. I'll do what has to be done. But if anyone's going to get caught, it's not going to be me.

When Red emerged, the others stopped talking and exchanged a look. Black walked over. "Before you go . . ."

Did he know? How could he know? Did they have a hidden camera in the bathroom?

Standing face-to-face with Perry Wayland, staring into his hard blue eyes, Red flinched at his sudden movement, then realized he was only offering a handshake.

"I forgot to thank you," he said. "For meeting me last night at the garage and for dropping me at Penn Station, and taking my car out to the bridge. I owe you one."

"No, you don't."

"He does," White said, and nudged him. "You do."

Black reached into the pocket of his jeans—the denim too dark, too stiff, too new—and handed over a wad of cash.

"What's this? I already have money for the—"

"It's extra. My way of showing appreciation for what you did for me."

Not for you, jackass.

"How did it go?"

"What?"

"Last night. On the bridge. Any problems?"

"No. No problems."

"Good."

Boarding the ferry back to the mainland, Red is almost certain they don't know about the junkie in the stairwell last night, or the souvenir snatched from the motel bathroom.

Almost.

Chapter Nine

Instead of taking the A train home to Washington
Heights, Barnes gets off at 135th Street. He walks
east toward the Harlem River, past the deli where the
teenagers used to shoplift beer and cigarettes in Barnes's
day. The elderly owner was an easy mark. No one ever
got caught, Gloss included.

He passes the basketball court where at twelve years
old, already over six feet tall, he perfected his jump
shot while his old man coached from a bench, too out
of breath from the two-block walk to join his son on the
court. A little farther down lies the hospital where they
rushed his father in an ambulance after he collapsed on
the kitchen floor. The building's elevator was out of order
again that day, and no one had bothered to fix it. Every
second counted, and the medics lost too many climbing
up and down all those flights. Charles Barnes died of a
massive heart attack at thirty-nine.

His mother draped herself in black and refused to
move away from their crime-plagued low-income building because a storefront fortune-teller convinced her that
her dead husband was still hanging around the apartment. The woman, Madame Esmerelda, would visit and
attempt to channel him on the Other Side.

The séances—and small fortune his mother spent on

them—were the least of Barnes's concerns when the building crimes escalated from robbery and assault to homicide and arson. Barnes persuaded her to leave after a neighbor was killed, and the high-rise has since been torched. Beyond a graffiti-scrawled chain-link-and-plywood construction barrier at the site, a new tower climbs the sky.

His mom now lives in a small Jersey City studio apartment, and has swapped psychics and séances for home shopping shows. She spends her days in front of the TV buying stuff she doesn't need with money she doesn't have and then complaining about the merchandise and her credit card debt in the same breath.

As usual, there's a group of deadbeats on the corner. They eye Barnes as he passes, sizing him up. Guys like that can smell law enforcement from a mile away.

He keeps a steady, casual gaze and gait. He's not alone out here—down the block, he can see what appears to be a heap of rags on the sidewalk in the shadow of a condemned building. If there's trouble, the rags will come to life faster than Kim Cattrall in *Mannequin*.

Undercover cop Eric Connors came up through the academy with Barnes. These days, they cross paths on the mean streets of East Harlem, though Barnes never acknowledges him. It's good to know that Connors and other officers are keeping an eye on things, disguised as hoodlums and vagrants.

Lately, they have their work cut out for them all over the city, but especially here. The old neighborhood slips further every day. Barnes worries about his law enforcement friends working the streets as much as he does about his friends who still live here.

Rounding the corner, he spies a well-kept redbrick three-story building, perched amid squalor like the lilac shrub that blooms every spring amid burned-out tenement ruins around the corner.

Wash lives on the top floor. Barnes stops by the bodega on the first, breathing the familiar scent of coffee, bananas, and the fragrant stargazer lilies bunched in buckets just inside the door.

Alberto Garcia stands behind the register. He has a dark mustache and thick head of black hair despite his eighty-odd years, and is still built, as he likes to say, like a quarter keg with arms and legs. His one good eye lights with recognition and crinkles with a smile, the other covered, as always, by a pirate patch.

"Long time no see! Where have you been all week, *mi amigo?*"

"I came Tuesday about midnight, but you weren't here."

"I'm glad you caught me tonight. I was just getting ready to go upstairs. You want the usual?" he asks, moving over to the deli counter before Barnes even confirms it with a nod. "What's new with you since I saw you last weekend?"

Imminent fatherhood, that's what's new.

Barnes tells him about the Wayland case.

"You think he killed himself?" Alberto asks, slicing the roast pork and layering it onto crusty, mustard-slathered Cuban bread.

"No. Feels staged."

"So he just . . ." He holds up a plastic-gloved hand, wiggling two fingers in a running motion. *"Vamoose?"*

"Most missing persons do." Especially when there's a *Miss White* involved.

"*Loco.* A guy who has everything." Alberto shakes his head, cutting whole pickles lengthwise into paper-thin slices. "Me, I got *nada.* But I will never want to leave Flora and the kids."

"That's why you're the one who has everything."

"The man who has everything, he has everything to lose." The old man crosses himself.

His grandson Tino appears, wearing an apron. He resembles his grandfather, though without the mustache or beer keg belly. He has a young wife, toddler, and newborn whose faint cries filter in from the stairwell until he closes the door.

"I'll take over, Papi. It's time for you to go up to bed now."

"No, I will do it," Alberto says. "You need to work on your *técnica*."

"How much *técnica* does it take to press a couple of sandwiches?"

"It's art, *chiquito*. Watch and learn."

"I've watched. I know how to do it."

"Knowing is not doing. You don't have the patience to—"

"I have patience."

"Not for this. Not for letting a man finish a sentence! You have a short fuse, like your grandmother."

Alberto presses the sandwiches against the hot griddle with the bottom of a cast-iron pan, and his grandson gives Barnes a World Series recount, this time with player perspective.

As a standout high school pitcher, Tino had been scouted by the major leagues before he got his girlfriend pregnant and dropped out to marry her. A different path might have led him to the pitcher's mound at Yankee Stadium across the Harlem River, rather than living here above the store with his grandparents, mother, and an uncle. Eight people, two bedrooms, and no one ever complains.

Five minutes later, Tino is cleaning the griddle, Alberto

has gone to bed, and Barnes has climbed to the third floor, white deli bag in hand.

Frail and unshaven, wrapped in a reed green cardigan, Wash feigns surprise to see him as he does every Friday night. "You really know how to brighten an old fart's day, Stockton. Thanks for coming. But I don't want you doing this anymore. It's getting dangerous here after dark."

"It's been dangerous for years, Wash. How are you feeling?"

"Terrific."

Yeah. Sure.

Wash turns off the TV, where Barbara Walters is interviewing someone, and leads Barnes down a short hallway lined with family portraits. Wash as a child with a trio of doting much-older sisters; with his parents, who lived into their golden years; with his beautiful wife.

He had it all, and lost it. His family is gone, other than nieces and nephews scattered far from New York. When they met, Barnes assumed he was a widower. He and his wife look so happy together in the photos. "No, she ran off with someone else," Wash told him. "And I don't blame her. She wanted to start a family. I was never around. She gave me an ultimatum—her or the job. I chose the job."

"Why?"

"I was on a case. Couldn't walk away. Thought she'd come back when it was over. I was wrong."

"Why do you still have her pictures on the wall?"

"Just because someone leaves doesn't mean you stop loving them, Stockton. She sends me a Christmas card every year. Last one had pictures of her grandkids."

"Doesn't that bother you?"

Wash shrugged and changed the subject. He's good at that.

As always, the tiny, windowless kitchen is cluttered

with plates and bowls, cracker and cereal boxes, orange prescription bottles, and—even now—a couple of full ashtrays.

They sit on rickety chairs at the small table, and Wash raises his brown beer bottle for their weekly toast. "What are we drinking to tonight?"

"You tell me."

"I haven't left this place all week, my friend. But some good must have happened to you out there in the world since I saw you on Tuesday."

"The opposite, actually."

"Uh-oh. What's going on?"

Barnes shakes his head. "Forget it. I don't want to ruin your appetite."

"Fine. The Senate rejected Bork today. We'll drink to that."

Now that he's homebound, Wash spends most days glued to cable news. He's no fan of President Reagan's conservative Supreme Court justice pick, Judge Robert Bork, a vocal opponent to affirmative action. Barnes doesn't like Bork, either, but he'd prefer to toast something more personal. Say, a miraculous cure for his friend's illness.

They clink bottles, and Wash unwraps his sandwich. "Extra pickles?"

"Always."

For a few minutes, they eat in comfortable silence. Barnes washes down his Cuban and plantain chips with gulps of beer, while Wash nibbles and sips, going through the motions. The moment Barnes polishes off his meal, he pushes aside his unfinished food and lights a Marlboro, scowling when Barnes does the same.

"When are you going to quit that filthy habit, Stockton?"

"When you do."

"Too late for me. But it'll kill you." Wash wheezes,

straining to reach the ashtray on the counter. Barnes allows him to try for a moment, to preserve his dignity, then grabs it and plunks it onto the table. "Thanks. What's going on at work these days?"

Barnes tells him about Wayland. Long retired now, Wash is always an avid audience, living vicariously through Barnes's tales from the job and often providing valuable insight.

"You know, your five senses can't pick up on everything, Stockton. Sometimes, you need to rely on your sixth sense."

"Like Madame Esmerelda?"

"Not magical powers. Scientific ones. Biology. Ever seen a mama bear protect a cub?"

"In New York City?"

"You've been to the zoo."

"What does that have to do with this?"

"Every living creature is equipped with natural instinct, Stockton. Listen to yours. What is your gut telling you about Perry Wayland?"

"That he might work for a hedge fund and the market might have bottomed out this week, but he didn't commit suicide. He didn't take a financial hit like some of the others, because he saw it coming."

"Like Madame Esmerelda?"

"No, and not science this time—math. He watches the patterns. He saw that the market was right where it was in the twenties, before the last major crash."

They talk awhile longer about the case before Wash changes the subject in his usual point-blank manner: "You had a bad week. Get some girl into trouble?"

Barnes stares. "Geez, Wash. About those magical powers . . ."

"Plain old common sense. It was only a matter of time,

Stockton, the way you been messing around. You need to borrow some money? I've got some, and I can't take it with me."

"You're not going any—"

"Don't be a fool. We're all going sooner or later. Just take my ashes home from the morgue in a Maxwell House can, Stockton. But don't lug me all the way back uptown. You go downtown, see?"

"Downtown—hey, that Tompkins Square Park is a mess these days, huh?"

Wash ignores the effort to shift the conversation. "And you take the elevator up to the top of the World Trade Center and you go out on the deck and you open that can and let the wind scatter me."

Barnes sighs. "Why there?"

"Twin towers are the tallest buildings in the world."

"I don't know about that."

"In the country, anyway."

"I'm pretty sure the Sears Tower in Chicago is taller."

"Well, I don't want to be scattered over Chicago. New York is my home, my heart, my blood. You understand, Stockton? This is where I want to be. You make sure."

"And you want . . ." Hoarse, he tries again. "You want *me* to be the one?"

"You're my family."

"Why are we even talking about this? It's a long ways—"

"No, Stockton. It isn't, and you know it as well as I do."

Barnes bows his head.

"Listen, I can handle this, and so can you. I'm not young. There are tragedies in this world, but what's happening to me isn't one of them. My mother always said that if you dance, you'd better be prepared to pay the fiddler. Oh, how I've danced, Stockton. And so have you.

So, getting back to that . . . I'll give you the money to take care of it. However much you need. A hundred, two hundred? There's a clinic—"

"Oh! I thought you meant take *care* of it. You know— the *kid*. Not . . . I mean, even if she—it's too late for that. She's due soon."

"And you're finally getting around to telling me? You going to marry her?"

"I just found out about it myself, and I don't even know her! She's a complete stranger!"

Wash levels a look at him.

"I mean, we were, uh, together one night, but . . . I haven't seen her since. For all I know, this is some kind of scam. Maybe she's not even pregnant. If she is, maybe it's not mine. A shady lady like that—"

"I thought you didn't know her."

"I don't."

"Then how do you know what kind of woman she is?"

"Not too hard to figure out." Sometimes, his old bad-ass self sneaks back in, filtering the world and everyone in it through a disparaging, spiteful lens. "Look, I just feel like she might be lying about the pregnancy. Or trying to nail me with child support for someone else's kid."

"Because she's shady?"

"Right."

"And she's shady because she slept with you on the first date?"

"Not a date. I just picked her up in some bar."

"What does that make you?"

A real douche bag. That's what you are, Gloss.

Wash sighs. "Tell me what you're going to do."

"I'm not going to marry her, if that's what you were hoping. I guess I should . . . uh, talk to her lawyer."

"Screw the lawyer. Talk to *her*."

"The lawyer's the one who sent the letter."

"This isn't about paper. It's about people. And about perspective. Ask yourself who you are, Stockton. Better yet, who you want to be. Because trust me, someday when you look back—"

"Screw someday, Wash. I have no idea who I am right now. But I know for damned sure who I can never be."

Wash digests that. Nods. "Don't be weak, Stockton. Do the right thing."

"Sure, yeah, no problem." Barnes thrums his knuckles against the table. "What *is* the right thing?"

"What did your father do?"

"That's different. He and my mother weren't . . . like this."

"You sure about that?"

Barnes stops thrumming. "Do you know something about it?"

"What I know is that your daddy was younger than you are when you came along, and he did whatever he had to do to make it right."

"You mean marry my mother?"

"I mean a lot of things. He stepped up and he made sure he managed to support you, even though . . ." He shakes his head.

"Even though what?"

"It wasn't always easy, Stockton. He tried to do the right thing, though. If you didn't know that, I'm telling you now."

In all the years of their friendship, Barnes has never asked how Wash met his dad, but it's not hard to figure out. Wash was a cop. According to his grandmother and his mother, too, his father had a wild streak in his younger days. They didn't elaborate, and Barnes didn't ask for more information.

Better to remember the great things about his dad than speculate over the few youthful missteps he'd made before he settled down. It never occurred to him that his father might have considered Barnes himself one of those mistakes, or that the missteps might have continued after he was born.

"This isn't helping me, Wash. What am I supposed to do?"

"You don't need me to tell you that."

"Maybe I do."

"A man stands up to his responsibilities." Wash peers at him, rolling an unlit cigarette between his fingers. "But you don't want to hear that."

Barnes says nothing.

"You're playing it out in your head, Stockton, aren't you? Imagining how things will turn out if you do this, do that. But right now, you don't have the right perspective. Later, you can look backward and forward and see things differently. Even yourself."

"Why do you keep talking about later? This is about right now."

"That's what you think. But you make a choice, and someday you're either going to regret it, or congratulate yourself that it was the right one."

"There is no choice. I'm not going to help raise a kid, period. It'll be better off without me."

"Were you better off without your father?"

"Hell, no. It's the same thing, whether you drop dead on your kids, or take off because the stock market crashed, or because their mother is a pain in the ass, or because you're not cut out for being a dad and you never wanted kids in the first place. The kid gets hurt in the end."

"So . . . it's better to hurt them in the beginning, is that what you're saying?"

"Yeah, it is," Barnes mutters. "It's exactly what I'm saying."

WHEN AMELIA LOOKED into Bettina's dresser after she died, she gave it only a cursory search. Tonight, she's more thorough, moving the neat stacks of white nylon underwear, bras, and slips from the top drawer to the bed.

She lifts the yellowed newspaper liner at the bottom. Empty.

She replaces the lingerie one garment at a time, shaking each piece and hoping to see some clue—her birth parents' names and addresses, maybe?—drop to the floor. It doesn't happen.

She isn't sure what she's expecting to find. But that television program had filled her with doubt about the Crenshaws' story, and newfound urgency to learn about her past.

She moves on to the next drawer, filled with socks and nightgowns, and finds herself ensnared by the familiar scent of Shower to Shower talcum powder. It lassos her to the past, to the day everything changed. The day Amelia glimpsed the truth in Bettina's medical file. The day Bettina drew her last breath, alone.

Calvin will never forgive Amelia for that.

She'll never forgive him for a lot of things.

She looks over her shoulder toward the living room, almost expecting to see him there watching her. Or maybe her mother's ghost, wearing an accusatory expression.

I know what you're up to, child. Don't you lie about why you're goin' through my things.

The doorway is vacant. Calvin won't be home from his overnight shift for hours.

Amelia moves on to his dresser. Nothing there is folded. The top drawer contains a few pairs of rumpled boxer shorts and stray socks and sleeveless white tee shirts gone gray since she took over laundry duties. Most of his things are in the hamper or scattered on the floor around it.

If she were a good daughter—his *real* daughter—she wouldn't let the dirty clothes pile up this way. She might even gather it all up and haul it down to the laundry room right now, waiting her turn with the other women who will either ignore her or ask her questions, equally unappealing scenarios.

They always want to know how she is, how her father is.

"We're good," she'll lie, same as always.

Finished with Calvin's dresser, she moves over to the closet. The rod is thick with hanging garments, the floor with dusty shoes, a suitcase, a folding step stool, and a plastic bin stuffed with Bettina's summer clothes. She rotated them into her overcrowded dresser every spring and filled the bin with the sweaters, hats, and gloves that still fill her drawers from last winter. Her last winter.

Amelia swipes at another unexpected wave of tears for the woman she'd thought was her mother; the woman she'd mourned and then tried to forget, if not forgive.

There are two shelves in the closet: one just above the hanging bar, the other too high to reach. She starts with the lower shelf, peeking into a trio of round hatboxes bearing old-fashioned-looking labels of stores she's never heard of. Her father's fedora occupies the first. She tried to talk him into giving it to her last year, when she wanted to dress up like Boy George for a Halloween costume party, but he refused.

"I can't have you getting it all crushed and dirty. That's my good hat."

"You never wear it."

"I do when I go someplace special."

"Like where? It's out of style."

"Then why is Boy George wearing it?"

At the time, she might have laughed. Now the memory irks her. Selfish of him, not letting her borrow some stupid old hat that's just been collecting dust on a shelf.

"You can wear one of my church hats to the party," her mother offered.

"And go as who? Princess Diana? In case you haven't noticed, I'm not blonde. Or white."

Replete with bows, feathers, and blusher veils, her mother's hats did look like something British royalty might wear. There had been nothing fancy or sophisticated about Bettina, with her roly-poly figure and homespun, shabby wardrobe. But on Sunday mornings, when she put on her good dress and angled one of these headpieces over her dark hair, she sometimes looked almost elegant.

I never told her that, though, did I? Not since I was little.

Amelia thrusts aside regret with the hatboxes and reaches up to the shelf again.

She pulls down a cardboard banker's box filled with financial documents, household bills, tax returns. She'll go through it some other day, in case something of interest might be tucked among the innocuous papers. But it doesn't seem likely.

She unfolds and refolds an afghan Calvin's grandmother had made for him and Bettina when they got married. It's crocheted of wool so prickly that Amelia opted to shiver through many a drafty night instead of itching and scratching beneath it. She shudders, seeing that bugs have gnawed holes in the lacy pattern. Her parents should have taken better care to store a family heirloom.

Their *family, not mine.*

Her mother's quilted sewing box is the only other thing on that shelf. It holds an array of notions, spools of colored threads, and a length of leftover orange rickrack that brings back a harsh memory.

Bettina used this zigzag trim to encircle the uneven hem of a hand-sewn dress that was supposed to look like one Amelia had coveted in a store window. They couldn't afford to buy it, so Bettina attempted to re-create it using an outdated Butterick pattern and ugly pastel pink fabric from the remnant bin. One sleeve was noticeably shorter than the other, both gathered with elastic that left puckery red rings around Amelia's wrist and forearm. She wore that awful dress to school once, and refused to wear it again, preferring her mother's disappointed tears to her classmates' cruel taunts.

"I'm sorry," Bettina said later. "I should 'a known better. My mother and aunts made all my clothes. I always wished I could just once have something store-bought."

Swallowing a twinge of remorse, Amelia unfolds the low stepladder and climbs up to investigate the top shelf.

She doesn't bother to look at the envelope from the photographer who took the senior yearbook portraits at her high school. She looks halfway decent in the pictures, wearing the studio's sophisticated black shoulder drape and fake pearls, but every shot has the word *PROOF* stamped across it. Her mother claimed they couldn't afford to order anything, but one day, they would.

Yeah. Sure you will.

Nor does she reexamine a pair of old photo albums, relics from her parents' childhoods. They've dragged them out and gone through them plenty of times over the years. She feigned interest as they pored over milky photos of family members she's never met, whom she now knows aren't even related to her.

She sets the albums on the floor, along with a collection of her old report cards stuffed into a frayed brown envelope. Boring, boring.

Wrapped in dry cleaner's plastic, a large, tightly woven basket sits wedged high atop a stack of boxes. She tugs it forward, careful not to tilt it and spill the contents. But it's empty. She tosses it onto the floor, shaking her head. What a waste of precious storage space. And why wrap a stupid old basket in plastic when the heirloom afghan sits unprotected and moth-eaten a shelf below?

She pulls out the large white cardboard box that sat beneath it and lifts the lid. Under a layer of tissue paper lies the white taffeta dress Bettina had worn when she got married.

She takes it out and holds it up, a wisp of soft fabric fluttering against her cheek. Pressing the tops of the sleeves to her shoulders, she faces her reflection in the full-length mirror on the other side of the closet door.

It couldn't have been considered a wedding gown, even on Bettina. The hem would have fallen just below her knee; it rides a few inches above Amelia's. The neckline is a simple circle; the bodice unadorned by lace or sequins; the skirt by flounces or bows.

I look like her. It's a strange thought, because of course she doesn't, and why would she?

Bettina was short, squat, and dark skinned; Amelia is tall, thin, and light skinned.

And yet . . .

There were times, over the years . . .

Before she knew she didn't share her mother's blood or—what is it called? DNA?

There were times when Amelia would laugh, and someone would say, *"Oh, you look just like your mother when you smile."*

She'd never seen it back then.

Why now?

She sure isn't smiling.

She yanks the closet door open again, thrusts the dress back into the box, and crams on the lid. Then, overtaken by guilt, she removes it and smooths the fabric, folding it. The dress may not be meaningful to Amelia, but Bettina did make an effort to preserve at least this family heirloom.

As she tucks it back into the tissue paper, she realizes that there's something more in the box. Her mother's wedding headpiece, she assumes, reaching for the scrap of lace.

But it's not connected to a hat. It must be a nice wedding handkerchief, or . . .

No, it's a doll's tiny, ruffled dress, made of delicate pastel fabric.

Amelia had a rag doll once, but not one that would have worn this dress. Her mother must have. But why would she preserve doll clothes in a box with her wedding dress?

She holds it closer, and notices a label sewn into the back collar. It's hard to read, but she makes out "Best & Co." . . .

That used to be a fancy department store here in New York. They could never have afforded to shop there, and anyway, Bettina had been raised down south.

The label contains another word. Is it . . .

She frowns, remembering the film she'd seen last year, *My Beautiful Laundrette*. What the heck . . .

No. It's not *Laundrette*. It's *Layette*.

Layette means it's not a doll's dress—it's for a newborn baby.

A store-bought and expensive dress couldn't have belonged to Bettina, but it mattered enough for her to pack it away in a special place, just as she'd kept the tiny gold ring with the sapphires.

Amelia's breath catches in her throat.

It must have been mine. And it's blue.

Chapter Ten

October 24, 1987
Boston, Massachusetts

just died in your arms . . ."

Tara sings along with the cassette playing on the stereo as she walks Jake Kilpatrick to the door. Earlier, her favorite band, Cutting Crew, had performed the hit power ballad live on the *Tonight Show*.

"How many times are you going to rewind that after I leave?" Jake isn't a fan of new wave music like she is.

"Till I get sick of it."

"How can you not? It's got the same lyrics over and over."

"That's why I love it! I think it should be our song."

"If I say yes, can I stay?"

"No."

"Come on, we're both consenting adults."

"I have an eighteen-year-old daughter."

"So do I."

"Yours lives in Medford with her mother. She isn't sneaking out at all hours to meet her boyfriend."

"She might be."

"Well if she is, he's not twenty-five."

"Liam's not that old."

"He's twenty-four, then. Last night, she went to bed at nine o'clock and I thought she might be sick so I went up later to check on her, and she had her giant teddy bear in her bed under the covers so I'd think it was her, asleep. Anyway, now she's grounded, and I have to set a good example." She turns the dead bolt, slides the chain, and opens the door for him. "Get home safely."

"I always do. Lock up after me."

"I always do."

He turns up the collar on his jacket, gives a wave, and disappears into the dark drizzle.

She watches him go, a faint smile playing at her lips.

Before Jake, she'd only ever had a handful of awkward dates. She was too busy raising her daughter and helping her aging aunt and uncle keep the tumbledown Victorian's mansard roof over all their heads.

In August, she let a friend talk her into answering a personal ad in the *Phoenix*. It didn't say, *"Soon-to-be-laid-off Southie boiler room engineer, father of four with angry ex, seeks hard-knocks, soon-to-be-homeless diner waitress—single mom of troubled teen preferred."*

Yeah, she and Jake were a match made in heaven—or in a Bon Jovi song.

Their first date was at Murph's Bar and Grill across East Broadway, neon lit now in a row of low Victorian homes that have seen better days.

Locals have been predicting that the neighborhood will be on the upswing when—not *if*—the yuppies start moving in. It's hard to envision the Brooks Brothers and BMW crowd settling here amid sagging steps, peeling paint, and missing shutters.

The neighborhood was different when she visited as a little girl. They'd take Amtrak up from Brooklyn every March to visit Aunt Patsy and Uncle Tommy. The famed Southie Saint Patrick's Day Parade marched right past the door.

Still does. But Tara makes sure to get out of town every year on that day.

She can't bear the memories of that final parade in 1968. She was a house guest here then, visiting with her parents, little sisters, and Lucky, the orphaned kitten they'd adopted the week before.

"Black cats are bad luck!" Uncle Tommy said when he saw Tara cuddling the tiny creature on the porch.

"Blarney, just look at the Irish eyes on this little guy. They're greener than any of ours!" Aunt Patsy said. "Come on in, everyone. You, too, Lucky. Come in, come in."

She ruled this ramshackle roost, just as she'd ruled Grandma's old Bay Ridge apartment when she and Tara's mom were growing up in Brooklyn, and now rules her new Daytona Beach retirement condo. She and Uncle Tommy are letting Tara and Emily stay on here rent-free through the end of the year. They can't afford to keep the house and she can't afford to buy it, so she should be looking for a new place. But she doesn't want to move at all. It's been home ever since . . .

"Don't let it in, lamb." She hears Aunt Patsy in her head. *"Think about something happy."*

Happy . . .

Saint Patrick's Day 1968 stands out as the last happy day of her life. East Broadway was awash in a sea of green jubilation, and Tara herself was full-to-bursting with rich, raisin-studded soda bread and the excitement of seeing Bobby Kennedy in person.

"There he goes!" Daddy told her as they marched past. "He's going to be the next president of the United States! You just wait and see!"

"Which one? Which one is he?"

"The one on the left."

RFK looked dignified striding alongside his brother Teddy, younger and full of swagger in a brash green tie.

Slurring on a tide of Guinness, Uncle Tom correctly predicted she'd never forget this day, as Aunt Patsy and Mom bickered good-naturedly over which of the famous siblings was more handsome. They agreed that oldest brother, Jack, had been the true star of the family.

"Such a shame," Mom said, and crossed herself as she always did when someone brought up the late president. On the November day he was assassinated, school was dismissed early. Tara arrived home from seventh grade to find her mother huddled on the couch in front of the TV, sobbing as if JFK had been a personal friend.

"This is the worst tragedy ever," she wailed.

Mom didn't live to watch his younger brother Bobby meet the same fate. Less than a week after the Saint Patrick's Day parade, the Brooklyn Butcher murdered them all in their sleep—Mom, Dad, Linda, and Kimmy.

Tara moved to Boston to live with Aunt Patsy and Uncle Tom. They said Lucky the kitten could come with her.

"I don't have him anymore. Black cats are bad luck."

She'd thrust him outside the day she came home from the hospital, and expected him to scamper into the bushes. Instead, he stayed on the doorstep mewing, watching her through the windows with sad green eyes that had seen everything that happened in her bedroom that terrifying night.

Back in the living room, she turns off the stereo and ejects the cassette tape. She puts it back into her Walkman, and attaches it to the high, pleated waistband of her new acid-washed Lees that set her back a whopping thirty-two dollars at Filene's.

"For *jeans*?" her friend Cindy said on the phone earlier. "You can get two pairs for that."

"Not like these. There's a jean jacket to match. It has shoulder pads. I put it on layaway."

"Are you crazy? You can't afford to throw all this money around! What if Emily decides to go to college or something?"

"She can get a loan like everyone else."

Tara places the Walkman headset in the teased hair riding high above her forehead, presses Rewind, and then Play.

"I just died in your arms . . ." She gathers the empty Sam Adams bottles from the attic steamer trunk now serving as a makeshift coffee table. Her aunt and uncle moved most of their furniture to Florida, leaving shadowy patches floating like phantoms on sun-faded rugs and wallpaper.

For the second time in her life, she has no idea where she's going to live next. The first, in the hospital, she pretended to be asleep while her grandmother and Aunt Patsy argued at her bedside. They'd just come from the quadruple funeral. Nana wanted Tara to live with her—until they discovered she'd conceived the rapist's child. Aunt Patsy saw her through that miserable pregnancy, and made arrangements through the church for the baby's adoption long before she was born. Tara assumed it would be like putting the kitten out on the step, but when she held her tiny daughter, an unexpected tide of maternal love swept her. She'd lost everything, and then found this tiny person, fragile and unspoiled, gazing up at her with wide blue eyes.

In that moment, Tara was certain she and Emily belonged to each other.

In this one, her daughter seems like a stranger.

Her friend Cindy, the mother of Emily's best friend, always reminds her that temperamental and even sneaky behavior is normal in teenaged girls. But she doesn't know the truth about Tara's past, or her secret fear that Emily inherited some dark, violent paternal gene from *him*.

She testified at the trial, carrying sixty pounds of post pregnancy weight, with breast milk leaking under her sweater. She kept her chin up as Uncle Tom hustled her past shouting reporters at the courthouse, and did her part to make sure that her family's murderer would be imprisoned for life. For her, that was closure. She shed the past like the extra weight and her old last name, taking her uncle's name to hide the truth from the friends she later found in Boston. Even Emily doesn't know the whole story. She's aware that Tara's family had been killed, but not that it was murder. She doesn't know Tara had been raped, or that she'd been born out of a lethal crime. In their stoic Irish Catholic household, certain things were not discussed, certain questions weren't asked, and certain emotions were kept to oneself.

The song ends, and she presses Stop on her Walkman to rewind it. As the tape whirs, she hears a thump overhead. It came from the back of the house, where Emily's bedroom windows face the flat roof of the back service porch, an old trellis serving as sturdy, if wisteria-entangled, ladder rungs.

She wouldn't dare defy Tara by sneaking out again, but what if her deadbeat boyfriend is sneaking in?

Her gaze falls on the magnet-held refrigerator gallery of Emily's artwork. The papers are yellowed now, and curling at the edges, but Aunt Patsy could never bear to take any of them down.

"I'll leave that to you," she told Tara when she left in May.

Tara managed to remove a couple of crayoned drawings—stick figures, puffy green trees studded with red dots—no, not apples, first-grade Emily had explained, long ago. They were her favorite cinnamon candies.

"Candy doesn't grow on trees, honey," Tara said.

"It does in my picture, Mama."

Sweet, sweet Emily. Whatever happened to that pig-tailed little angel?

She heads up the carved mahogany staircase.

She's not a kid anymore. She thinks she's in love with this dirtbag.

That last winter in Brooklyn, Tara, too, had an inappropriate boyfriend. She was only a year younger than Emily when she snuck off to the free clinic to get birth control pills. Her boyfriend dumped her that February, but she'd kept taking the pills, certain they'd get back together. She shouldn't have been able to get pregnant the night she was raped, and yet there she was.

At the top of the stairs, Tara walks past her own door, down the hall to Emily's room. She pushes the headphones back and knocks on the door. "Em? You awake?"

Silence, other than the song faintly audible through the headphone speaker buds resting somewhere around her collarbone.

I just died in your arms . . .

She turns the knob.

The bedside lamp is on, and someone is in bed.

She's relieved to see that it isn't a teddy bear this time. That's her daughter's blond hair on the pillow, teased high and cemented with dippity-do.

"Em?"

No response.

"Em!"

Stinker. She's pretending to be asleep.

"I know you can hear me. I want to talk to you. Come on, sit up."

Still, she doesn't stir. Tara hurries over to the bed, yanks back the covers . . .

And shrieks.

Emily is drenched in blood, blue eyes staring vacantly at the ceiling.

A hand clamps around Tara's mouth, smothering her agonized scream. A strong grasp wrestles her back, away from the bed, holding her as a blade slices her throat.

The last thing Tara hears is her own dying breath and her favorite song, muffled as a tide of blood washes over the headphones.

I just died . . .

AFTER LEAVING WASH, Barnes stops at one of his old Harlem haunts for a couple of drinks. It's not the kind of place he tends to frequent these days. Bottom shelf booze, seedy clientele, restrooms so filthy he chooses to use the back alley as a urinal instead, with evidence that he's not the first. He'd walked in needing to forget that his old friend's days are dwindling and the paternity mess is waiting for him at home. He walks out hoping the cheap whiskey has done the trick, and stops on the way home to pick up a pint of Jack.

Stepping into his small apartment, he's hard-pressed to recall why he was so excited to move in here a few months ago. Somehow, a high floor, white walls, and minimalist décor don't hold the same allure they did at the Waylands' Park Avenue penthouse.

No designer furniture, marble floors, or skylights here, though. Just plastic milk crates and curbside castoffs; beat-up parquets and two air shaft windows covered in plastic venetian blinds that refuse to stay open or closed. No matter how he fiddles with the cord, the narrow slats settle into a position insufficient for letting in sunlight or keeping out voyeurs from across the way.

He crosses over to the kitchenette and flips a wall switch. The overhead fixture illuminates Connie scurrying away from last night's meatball sub, abandoned in its deli bag on the countertop alongside the lawyer's letter.

He ignores it and the cockroach and looks for a glass. They're all in the sink, dirty. He dumps the Jack into a Yankee Stadium freebie cup emblazoned with Don Mattingly's number, tosses the bottle into the garbage, and takes a room-temperature sip. He still hasn't gotten around to buying ice cube trays, though if he had, he'd probably have forgotten to fill them.

Perry Wayland's fridge has an automatic ice maker. He has a sparkling row of Baccarat rocks glasses and a bar stocked with the finest single malt Scotch money can buy—Barnes had read the labels in awe.

I still don't blame you for walking out of there, man. Sometimes you have got to just save yourself. I hope Miss White is more deserving and appreciative than your wife is.

He pictures Wayland floating on a yacht in a sun-splashed sea, shirtless, maybe even tanned, his horse tattoo slick with Bain de Soleil. He tosses his wedding ring overboard to sink like an untethered anchor. It must be nice to have extracted himself from the four demanding females in his life.

Barnes takes a long sip of whiskey, relishing the heated descent to his gut. It boomerangs to his head, swaddling edgy thoughts in a haze.

Is Kirstin lying awake right now, wondering if she misjudged her husband? Wondering about his market crash prediction and the mysterious old friend who's been calling him at the office? At least Stef didn't mention *Deep Throat* to her. If he had, Barnes figures, she'd be wishing that her husband had indeed dove off a bridge.

He's meeting Stef at seven to head over to the tow pound.

Seven . . .

Damn, that's early. Better get a head start.

He takes out the Maxwell House coffee can, thinking

about Wash. One . . . two . . . three sloppy scoops, scattering black grit over the counter, including the lawyer's letter.

"This isn't about paper. It's about people."

Barnes considers that as he sets up the coffeemaker for tomorrow morning and finishes his cigarette.

Maybe Wash was right. Maybe he should try talking to Delia, instead of negotiating with some money-hungry attorney . . .

If he decides to deal with it at all.

If he ignores the whole damned thing, it might just go away, like the cockroach that disappeared into some dark crevice.

Don't be weak, Stockton.

Sorry, Wash. I tried to do the right thing, but it's not like I know where she is.

No? Isn't that what you do for a living? Find people?

Well, it's not like he can just call Delia. He doesn't have her number. According to her lawyer, she doesn't live there anymore, and how does a homeless person afford a lawyer, anyway?

Don't be weak . . .

If Delia were a missing person, where would he begin? With what he does know about her, which is . . .

Not where she lives. Not even where she works, if it's true that she lost her job after becoming pregnant. But he knows where she worked back in March.

He plunks down his glass, picks up the phone, and dials 555-1212.

"Directory assistance, how may I help you?"

"Yeah, Charley O's in Manhattan, please."

"Which one?"

He pauses, thinking back to that night. "Is there one on Eighth Avenue in the west forties?"

There is. He scribbles down the number, and then dials

it. The female voice that answers is harried, music and chatter blasting in the background.

"I'm looking for Delia," he says. "Is she there?"

"Delia who?"

"She's a waitress there."

"Delia Montague? She's not here anymore, sorry. Goodb—"

"Wait, do you know where I can reach her? I need to talk to her. Life and death."

"Oh, come on."

"It's the truth."

The baby. Wash. Life. Death.

"Is this Bobby?"

"Yeah." *Sure. Why not.*

"It's about time you came back around. Jesus."

"Where is she?"

"Staying with Alma out in Bed-Stuy last I heard."

"Got the number?"

"Hang on. I got a lot of customers here." She drops the phone with a clatter.

Barnes paces as far as the phone cord will let him go. At least three, maybe five minutes go by before the woman returns.

"Don't you go telling her I gave you the number. I don't know if she wants to hear from you after everything, you know what I'm sayin'?"

I don't even know who you are.

"Don't worry. I won't tell her."

Barnes writes down the number, hangs up, and looks at it. The area code is that new one, 718 for Brooklyn, Queens, and Staten Island. Bed-Stuy—Bedford Stuyvesant—is in Brooklyn.

He dials. A woman snatches up the phone on the first ring, sounding breathless.

"Hello?"

"Delia?"

"Doctor Herndon?"

He hesitates, hearing a high-pitched moan in the background. "No, it's . . ."

"Then I can't tie up the line! We're waiting for the doctor to call back. Breathe, Dee. Just breathe," she calls, then asks, "Who is this?"

"Wrong number," Barnes says, and hangs up.

"Do the right thing," Wash says in his head, not even wheezing.

If Barnes doesn't, Wash will go to his grave thinking he's weak.

Are you?

No. Gloss was weak.

And Gloss is gone.

AMELIA PUTS EVERYTHING back into the closet the way she found it—all except the little blue dress from Best & Co.

She sits on the edge of the bed clasping the delicate fabric against her mouth and nose, breathing it in search of her long-lost mother's scent. She smells only her not-mother: Bettina's Shower to Shower lingering in the air, or maybe just in Amelia's memory.

She can see Bettina packing away this dress like an heirloom, and for what? Had she been saving it, like the ring, for a special occasion? Maybe she meant for Amelia's own daughter to wear in the far-off future. Had she intended to tell the truth one day, when Amelia was grown and gone from this house?

All she really cares about is what happened *before* Calvin heard her forlorn cries in the empty church—and whether that is, indeed, a true story.

This fancy store-bought dress is her first clue.

"Just an itty-bitty baby, lying there like Moses in a basket . . ."

Basket?

Heart pounding, she hurries back to the closet, drags out the stepladder, and climbs up on it so hastily that it teeters beneath her.

Familiar with the biblical tale of newborn Moses floating along in the tall reeds, she hadn't considered that Calvin might be referring to a real basket. But a literal interpretation of his comment might explain the empty one Bettina had painstakingly preserved in dry cleaner's plastic.

Before, Amelia had tossed it aside without even looking at it. Now she takes it down, unwraps it, and studies it.

This isn't cheap dime-store wicker like the one that holds the mail in the living room.

It's made of tightly coiled straw bands in patterned shades of brown and cream. The style is unusual, and yet this isn't the first time she's seen it. The basket is strikingly similar to one she saw . . .

Was it today? Where?

She closes her eyes and thinks back, searching her weary, cluttered brain. At school, maybe? She hasn't been anywhere else. School, the subway, and—

The answer comes to her, and her jaw drops.

Marceline LeBlanc was carrying an almost identical basket when she rode away on the bus.

Chapter Eleven

arlier, from the porch roof outside Emily's open bedroom window, Red had seen the girl lying on her bed, feet propped on the wall, one hand twirling the long cord of her pink princess phone like a jump rope. She was having a long telephone conversation with someone—a boyfriend, it became apparent. Red heard most of it, despite the pattering rain and music coming from the tape deck.

"No, I mean it. You can't come over tonight . . . She's downstairs, but . . . No, I know she won't see you, but I need some space . . . No, not because of her, she's . . . All right, yeah. It is. It's because of my mom, and she . . . Yeah, she did, for a month this time, but—oh, please. Where am I supposed to go?" A pause, and she chuckled softly. "Yeah, it would be nice, but this isn't some old Beach Boys song, Liam. This is my life, and I'm stuck here for now . . . No. No! Come on, you know . . . Because if she catches you here this time, she'll . . ."

The conversation dragged on. Red stayed flattened against the wall outside the window, trying to stay dry beneath the narrow third-floor ledge overhead.

"Wait, are you breaking up with me? No, it's not the same thing. A break is—okay, fine! Fine! Fine!"

Emily slammed the phone down with a sob. When Red dared to peek again, she was close enough to touch, holding a lit match to the tip of a cigarette. No wonder the window had been open on a cool, rainy night.

Red leapt back into the shadows, heart racing.

"Liam?" she called softly into the night. "I told you not to come over!"

"I had to see you." The rain must have muffled any vocal unfamiliarity in the whisper, because Emily sighed and opened the window all the way.

Heart pounding, Red climbed through and found her with her back turned, arms folded in resignation. One push, and she tumbled onto the bed. One slash with the blade, and her giggle was lost in a gurgle of blood. She wasn't even cold before Tara walked into the room.

Five, maybe ten minutes after slitting her throat, Red was cruising south on Interstate 93. Now the Rhode Island State Line is in the rearview mirror. It would be fun to return to the Sandy Oyster and share the good news with White: *"Two down."*

"Already?" White will say, violet eyes wide with appreciation and admiration. *"Just like that?"*

"Just like that." The comment should be accompanied by a casual gesture, like clap-brushing one palm against the other to emphasize how easy it was.

"That's amazing," White will say. *"Six more to go, and—"*

And only five accounted for.

Anyway, there will be no ferry at this hour, and even if there was, Black is there. By now, he might have gone into the bathroom and figured out that something's missing.

The wipers make a scraping sound on the dry windshield. The rain has stopped at last, replaced with fog that creeps over the landscape and into Red's brain.

Coffee. Coffee would help.

At a Connecticut McDonald's teeming with truckers, Red dumps the tainted slicker and gloves into a parking lot garbage can and uses the restroom before going to the counter. The line is long, the place short staffed. It takes almost ten minutes to get to the register.

Red orders a Happy Meal, a couple of Egg McMuffins, hash browns, and two cups of coffee, and adds, "Family road trip." So very clever.

"Mmm," says the girl behind the counter, counting out change.

"Yeah, they're waiting in the car. Starving."

The cashier doesn't acknowledge that, but a trucker waiting for his order asks, "You heading northbound or southbound?"

"South."

"That's good. There's an accident on the northbound side by New Haven. Car hit a deer. Took me a half hour to get through there. Watch out for them. I've had two run out in front of me in the last hour."

"Thanks for the tip, buddy." Red grabs the white paper bag and all but runs out the door.

The parking lot is quiet. No witnesses to note that there is no starving family waiting in the car.

But that was close. Nothing like teetering on the fine line between deflecting suspicion and overengaging.

Under cover of the dense mist shrouding a dark, wooded stretch of highway, Red hurtles the food one piece at a time out the passenger's side window, unwrapped for scavengers who will eliminate the evidence. The wrappers are tossed a few miles later, along with the Happy Meal box and toy. The bag stays, a handy carryall.

And the coffee, to wash down another pill.

Welcome to Westchester County, New York.

Seeing the green sign, Red remembers something.

Christina Myers's son lives around here with his adoptive family. Having spent some time last month learning

his routine, Red knows where to find him at this hour—
and he isn't tucked in bed behind locked doors.

AMELIA TURNS HER college backpack upside down,
dumps the contents onto the floor, and peers inside. It
might be able to hold a toothbrush, pair of jeans, and
maybe a sweater. She supposes she can leave everything
else behind, but then she'd have to come back.

She returns to the bedroom and finds the suitcase she
spotted earlier in the closet. It's unexpectedly heavy.
Opening it, she sees that it's still filled with the clothes
Bettina had packed on the day she was admitted, as if
she expected to be up and about, wearing something
other than a hospital gown. When the bag came home
without its owner, Calvin must have shoved it right into
the closet.

Amelia eyes the folded stack of clothing inside. No
time to put it all away now. She pulls out a plastic drawer
from the cheap unit that serves as her own dresser, tosses
her clothing onto the floor, and replaces it with Bettina's
from the suitcase. She crams it all in, wadded into the
corners, heedless of wrinkles. It's not as if anyone is
ever going to wear these things—certainly not until the
church lady comes around for next summer's clothing
drive.

Who cares? I'll be long gone.

Though there's no telling where she'll be by then, she's
made up her mind where tomorrow will find her.

She rewraps the basket in dry cleaner's plastic, then
attempts to put it into the empty suitcase. A hair too
wide, the basket might fit if she forced it, but if it's what
she thinks it is, she's not willing to risk denting it. She
returns it to the high closet shelf.

But she does place the little blue dress into the suitcase
before filling it with her own undergarments, jeans, leg-

gings, and sweaters. She adds toiletries, then eyes the textbooks, notebooks, pencils, and pens scattered across the floor, thinking about the paper she's supposed to be writing and the studying she should be doing.

After a moment's hesitation, she packs everything into the book bag again, save a pen and a mostly empty notebook. She takes them to the kitchen, tears out a page, and writes a quick note.

Went to visit a friend.

She pauses. Does he realize she no longer has friends? Maybe he'll assume it's Marceline. Let him. He won't know she's gone.

She closes the note with his own parting words, the ones she hadn't been certain he meant. Maybe she doesn't, either.

I'll be back.

She puts the note on the counter, pocketing the twenty-dollar bill he'd left there for groceries. She just hopes it's enough to get her to Ithaca, New York.

She lugs the heavy suitcase to the door, thinking of Marceline LeBlanc, with her weighty satchel and that unusual basket so similar to the one in the closet.

Maybe the coincidence means nothing—or at least, has nothing to do with Amelia's past. Maybe Miss LeBlanc and Bettina bought the baskets in the same local store, or from the same street vendor. Maybe she jumped to conclusions, thinking she was found in a basket.

Calvin might answer that question, if she were willing to stick around and ask it.

She is not.

She turns and takes a last look around, feeling around

in her soul for nostalgia, or regret, or something, anything, that might make her want to stay here.

She hears her father's voice, the day of the funeral, as he sat at the kitchen table with his face buried in his hands.

"I don't want to talk about this anymore, Amelia."

"Well, I do. Don't I count?"

"Now is not the time. I just lost your mother. I'm not—"

"So did I! *Again*. I've lost *two* mothers. I want the truth! You owe me the truth!"

"I told you the truth."

"You didn't tell me anything."

"You know everything I know. That's all there is."

"But—"

He slammed his hands on the table and rose to glare at her. "I don't want to hear about this ever again! Ever!"

Her gaze falls on the note she left for him on the counter. She snatches it up, crumples it, and buries it in the trash can.

Then she walks out the door, and this time, she doesn't look back.

BARNES TAKES THREE subways and a gypsy cab to reach the hospital in Queens, just over the border from Brooklyn, not far from JFK Airport and Stef's neighborhood, Howard Beach. The eastern sky above the flat roof is tinged pink.

Typical Saturday, predawn—three ambulances are parked in front of the ER doors, lights flashing, medical personnel scrambling to help victims of what was probably a car accident in one case, and a street fight in another.

He makes his way past the commotion to the main entrance, hoping it won't be locked. This area is crawling with troublemakers and protestors these days, some of them violent. And hospital security has been a hot-button topic following a rash of newborn abductions, including an unsolved one he investigated on a Harlem maternity ward in August, and a doctor recently gunned down at nearby Kings County Hospital.

But Barnes is able to walk right in, past the vacant front desk, and follow signs to a bank of elevators. He pauses to scan the wall directory.

"Excuse me! Where do you think you're going?"

He turns to see a uniformed security guard coming out of the men's room down the hall, still pulling up his fly. Nice.

"Labor and Delivery."

"You can't just go strolling in there, kid."

Kid? Who does this guy think he is, Stef? He even looks like him—white, middle-aged, flaccid and florid.

"Come on, move it. Get out 'a here."

Barnes reaches into his pocket.

"Hands in the air, now!" the guard barks.

"I wasn't going for a weapon!" Barnes shouts. "It's just my badge! I'm NYPD!"

"I *said*, hands in the air!"

Barnes lifts them. "My badge is in my pocket," he says through clenched teeth. "See for yourself."

The guy reaches in, pulls it out, peers at it, and hands it back to Barnes. "Sorry, Detective. But you can't be too careful."

He mutters that it's okay and turns back to the elevators, jabbing the up button.

As the elevator ascends, he checks his watch, then closes his eyes, massaging his temples with his thumb and forefinger. He's meeting Stef in a few short hours. He should be home in bed.

After polishing off the Jack Daniel's, he fell onto his

futon fully clothed, so weary he failed to muster the energy to turn off the lamp. But there's a difference between sheer exhaustion and actual sleepiness on a night when the woman who claims to be having your baby is actually . . . having your baby. Somebody's baby, anyway. Or so she says.

It sure sounded like it, judging by the agonizing moans in the background and the fact that they were waiting for a doctor callback.

Or so they said.

Wondering whether it was an elaborate setup, he finally got up, turned on the coffeemaker, and did some good old-fashioned detective work—unrelated to Perry Wayland. He again called directory assistance and located an obstetrician named Wilfred Herndon, based in Bedford-Stuyvesant. He collected the numbers for every hospital in the area. Then, he started calling them, asking the main switchboards to connect him to Labor and Delivery. From there, he claimed to be a neonatal specialist and asked whether Doctor Herndon could be paged.

"Who?" the staff asked at the first four hospitals.

At the fifth, the voice on the other end said, "He's on his way in, but I don't think he's here yet. Can you hang on while I check?"

As soon as she put Barnes on hold, he hung up and headed for the door, not stopping to ask himself why he felt compelled to be there.

If you still haven't figured that out, you can be damned sure that it's not the best idea you've ever had.

The doors open on the Labor and Delivery floor. Barnes forces himself to step out. The nurses' station is right in front of him. He makes his way toward it, past giant, framed photos of babies. Somewhere down the hall, he can hear a newborn's thin, high-pitched staccato cries. An orderly pushes past with a disheveled, bathrobed young woman in a wheelchair, fixated on the swaddled bundle in her arms.

Babies, babies everywhere.

Why isn't that getting to him? Somehow, he's immune to the reality of what's unfolding here—fragile new lives beginning all around him.

Usually, it's the opposite. He remembers back to when he was a rookie cop, on the scene at his first homicide. He'd anticipated an adverse reaction to the macabre crime, or perhaps a flood of emotion for the poor dead person and his family.

The shooting was gang related and the victim was young, just a kid. He died a painful, grisly death. Somehow, Barnes managed to detach his emotions and focus on the job at hand. He kept squeamishness at bay despite the gaping abdominal gunshot wound and blood-spattered walls. Even the smell didn't get to him—he'd taken a more seasoned officer's advice and dabbed cologne under his nostrils before venturing into the building.

"Careful," an officer said, when Barnes mentioned that he was surprised at how well he was handling it. "It hits you when you least expect it."

He was right. That day, Barnes came undone when he saw the medical examiner jab a needle into the corpse's eyeball to extract fluid for testing.

A woman behind the desk looks up from a cup of instant noodles and flashes a pleasant smile. She's wearing a yellow smock printed with little birds. Swans, maybe.

"Can I help you?"

"Yes, I'm looking for a patient, Delia Montague. Is she here?"

She consults a clipboard.

Those aren't swans on her apron, he realizes. They're storks.

For some reason, for Barnes, those storks are the damned eyeball needle today. Dozens of happy little storks, winging a big fat bundle of nausea and emotion from his gut to his throat. He manages to stay rooted, waiting for the nurse to respond.

Maybe he was wrong—about the doctor, the hospital, all of it. Please, please let him have been wrong. Let him get out of this place without having to—

"Yep, she's here. Are you . . . ?"

Ask yourself who you are, Stockton. Or better yet, who you want to be.

Get out of my head, Wash. I'm doing this my way.

Oh, yeah? You mean, not at all? You going to take off now? Is that it? Without even—

"Sir?" The nurse is waiting for him to fill in the blank. Is he . . . ?

A doctor?

A cop?

"I'm the father."

SQUATTING ON THE corner of Eighth Avenue and Forty-Second Street, the Port Authority Bus Terminal is one of those places your mother warns you about. Bettina would have, if she'd ever imagined that Amelia might find herself here at this hour. In her whole life, she's only visited the enormous building a handful of times for church outings. That was always in broad daylight, accompanied by a large group.

Now everything is closed. It hadn't occurred to her that she'd have to wait until morning to catch an Ithaca-bound bus.

"Lost, sweetheart?" A toothless man who reeks of BO,

long hair caked in grease, falls into step beside her as she hefts her heavy bag away from the closed Trailways ticket window. "Need someplace to go?"

No gullible, fresh-faced fool just off the bus from the heartland, she avoids eye contact as Bettina had taught her years ago, fixating on an enormous sign for Maxell VHS tapes.

"Child, anyone bothers you, you just ignore him."

"What if he doesn't ignore me, Mama?"

"You shout for help."

"What if there's no help around?"

"Then you be fierce."

The disgusting stranger dogs her. "Come on, how about a little—"

"Get away from me!"

He persists until another man, well dressed and groomed, steps in.

"Get lost, dirtbag!" he orders, and the dirtbag slinks off into the shadows.

Amelia thanks him.

"No problem. You need a place to stay? Because you can't spend the night in here. They'll eat you alive. Come on, I'll help you."

The words are kind, but his eyes are hard.

Be fierce.

"Get lost, dirtbag!" Amelia barks with far more mettle than she feels, but it does the trick. Bettina would be pleased.

Filled with a sudden longing for her mother, and home, she remembers that Bettina is gone, and home holds little comfort or familiarity now. No going back. Only forward.

Forward, however, is in a holding pattern.

She's stuck in the terminal overnight, like the pigeons

darting in the rafters and the few unfortunate commuters for whom TGIF had dragged on too long. Having missed the last bus home to Jersey or Rockland, they slump on filthy benches with briefcase pillows and trench coat blankets.

Amelia doesn't dare make herself so comfortable—or vulnerable. She huddles in a dark corner on a bench where she can keep her back to the wall and an eye on the ticket window.

Panhandlers jangle change in paper cups, madmen rant, and Holy Rollers preach over microphones that echo threats of Armageddon that seems to have come early to this cavernous place. It's populated by multitudes of lost souls, toting remnants of ruined lives along dim corridors that ricochet with shrieks and moans, running footsteps, catcalls, threats, profanity, and voices arguing in every language.

Pimps, prostitutes, and drug dealers grin and prowl like sharks, emboldened by the recent appeals court ruling that the police can no longer arrest them for loitering. Beat cops, few and far between, don't give them a second glance as the night wears on. Nor do they bother with Amelia, perhaps assuming she, too, is depraved, criminal, or homeless.

She's cold and cramped from sitting upright, feet planted on her suitcase like an ottoman. A couple of vagrants eye the bag, and she knows that if anyone tries to grab it, she will risk her life to save that little blue dress.

Be fierce.

She thinks about Bettina and Calvin. And about Marceline, wondering where she is, and why she left, and when—whether—she's coming back. She wants to deny that there was a finality to her parting; wants to think that if she herself returns to the neighborhood, Marceline will be there, same as always.

She'd always been intrigued by her, but now . . .

The old woman is a friend. Maybe the only one she has left in the world.

She could have helped me. She knew something.

Chapter Twelve

Dawn is a few hours off and high school basketball season more than a month away, but Kevin Donaldson's alarm clock jangles at 4:45 a.m. Ever since school started Labor Day week, he's been getting up to work out for three hours every morning, weekends included. There's a lot riding on his senior year performance on the court—college acceptances, scholarship money, and a chance to claim the captainship.

Coach Harding had moved him up to varsity halfway through his freshman JV season, and he's been the star forward ever since. Thanks to him, the team made the play-offs for the first time in a decade. Thanks to him, they won the championship.

Last season, Coach gave a big speech about all the qualities he looks for in a captain—leadership, skill, positive attitude, team player, good grades . . .

Kevin, sitting in the bleachers, was prepared to stand, certain Coach was describing him. But then he said, "Dale Stokes."

Dale Stokes? Not even a senior?

It was a slap in the face.

"Jack Harding's always been a fair guy. Did you do something to piss him off?" Dad asked that night.

"Nope."

"Are your grades slipping?"

"Better than ever," Kevin assured him, not mentioning

that Amy Morrison was tutoring him after school. That meant she did his assignments while he pretended to be listening to what she was saying about logarithms, chemical formulas, and herself. All boring topics, but she's the smartest girl he knows who's not too smart to let him cheat off her in the classroom and carry his workload outside of it.

"Dale Stokes scored a lot of points last season," his mother pointed out.

"Nowhere near as many as I did. And he's got the personality of a wet towel. And then there's that butt-ugly mole on his cheek—"

His mother frowned.

"What? It's true."

"Maybe the coach thinks you're a little too full of yourself."

"Maybe the coach is full of sh—"

Mom cut him off there. She doesn't like foul language. Kevin usually doesn't use it around her, but it was all so unfair.

Coach can't bypass him this season, though. Dale tore his meniscus on the baseball field last spring, and his high school sports career is over. The only decent junior player is one F paper or bong hit away from flunking out of school or winding up in jail. There's no way Kevin won't be named captain.

He leaves his brother, Eddie, sleeping in the tiny bedroom they've shared for seventeen years now. Twin beds, though they're not twin brothers. Most people assume they are, since they're both seniors.

He goes across the hall to the tiny bathroom. Old pipes groan as he turns on the water. No hope of hot at this desolate hour, unless you let it run. But you can't, because the sink has a clog and will overflow, and Dad can't afford to get it fixed.

"Become a plumber," he said when Kevin complained the other day. "Or an electrician. That's where the money is. You can be an apprentice next year, and—"

"I want to go to college."

"Like your brother. I know," he said, as if Kevin is just blindly doing whatever Eddie does, when in fact, he's older by five months.

Mom and Dad tried for years to have a baby before they scraped together enough money to adopt. She once let it slip that she'd found out she was pregnant with Eddie the day after they brought newborn Kevin home.

What would have happened if she'd found out the day before, instead? Would they still have wanted him? Probably not. They could afford one child on his father's machinist income. They had room in this tiny ranch house, and in their hearts, for one child. They got stuck with two.

He splashes cold water over his face, dries it with a threadbare towel still damp from last night, and looks into the mirror. He sure doesn't look like the rest of the family. They're stocky and fair with round, smiley faces; he's lanky and dark, with angular features that are . . . not sulky, exactly, though that's what his mother's been saying for as long as he can remember.

"Stop sulking, Kev."

"I'm not. Just because I don't go around grinning like a village idiot doesn't mean—"

"Well, you should. You have a lot to be happy about."

He knows what she's thinking whenever she says that, or when she tells him to count his blessings, or consider those less fortunate.

All right, so he's lucky they plucked him from his real mother's arms in a Yonkers home for unwed teens back in the winter of 1969.

He grabs his toothbrush from the four that dangle in

the rectangular porcelain holder built into the 1950s pink-and-black tile backsplash Mom is always talking about replacing.

"If you wait long enough, it'll be back in style," his father tells her.

"That'll be the day. I'd love a pretty blue, with Laura Ashley drapes to match."

"What is this, *Knots Landing*? You know we don't have the money for all that."

Money. Everything, his whole life, his future, is always about money.

Teeth brushed, Kevin returns to his room. He throws on the sweatshirt, running shorts, and sneakers he'd left on top of his dresser last night and fumbles for his Walkman on the desk he and Eddie share.

"Quiet!" His brother turns over with a rustle and huff.

"You be quiet!"

"Hey, I'm not the one who—"

Kevin leaves the room, closing the door behind him as loudly as he dares at this hour. It would take a full-blown slam to wake his father, but his mother is a light sleeper. Sometimes she comes out of the bedroom when she hears him stirring. Back in September when the sun came up as he was leaving, she'd just tell him to be careful. But now that it's dark for the duration of his workout, she freaks out. Yesterday, she tried to stop him from going.

"You could be hit by a car, running on the dark streets."

"I stay on the sidewalk," he lied. "And my sneakers have DayGlo strips. You can see me from miles away."

"So you're a target! Someone could jump out of the bushes and mug you."

"It's Westchester, Gloria, not the South Bronx," his father called from the bedroom. "Come back to bed. Nothing's going to happen to him. Leave him be."

"I don't like this one bit."

"Then get me a membership to Bally Total Fitness."

"With what money?" His father appeared in his boxer shorts, groggy and grizzled with beard and irritation. "We're saving for college, remember? Why don't you get yourself a paper route to help out a little, since you like to get up and roam the neighborhood so early?"

Tables turned. Mom shifted gears to defend him. "He doesn't need a paper route, Chaz. I don't want him out there in all kinds of weather."

"He's out there anyway."

Kevin presses Play on his Walkman, and Richie Sambora's talkbox strains of "Livin' on a Prayer" blast into his ears. It's enough to drown out his parents' voices in his head as he makes his way through the quiet house. They're always nit-picking each other. Sometimes he wonders if he might have been better off with . . .

But that's crazy. What happened between his birth parents was a hell of a lot worse than stupid bickering. He's seen his adoption records. He's the product of a violent rape.

In the kitchen, he takes an egg from the fridge and cracks it into a glass. He holds his nose and gulps it down, like Stallone in *Rocky*. Only Sly's mother wasn't going to yell about all her eggs disappearing, and how is she supposed to make his brother's favorite macaroni salad for lunch now, and doesn't he know he's going to get botulism or whatever disease it is that people get from drinking raw yolks?

Kevin opens the back door. The cat is waiting. It hates him, even though he's the one who lets it in every damned morning.

It'll purr and cozy up to everyone else in the house, even Dad, who hates cats and wishes Eddie had never insisted on adopting the stray. But the creature always gives Kevin a wide berth, tail twitching.

He opens the storm door.

"Go on in."

The fat tabby just stares at him.

"No, I'm not going to feed you. You can wait. Stupid cat."

It scurries past him and disappears into the shadowy kitchen.

Kevin steps out into the early-morning chill. Fog drifts in the air, dank with the scent of the river and moldering leaves. He heads down the steps and around the house to the driveway, where the Buick is parked.

When Kevin turned sixteen, he begged his father for a learner's permit.

"Why? You won't have a car."

"I can drive yours when you're not using it."

"That's when your mother takes it to do the shopping."

"Not every day. When you're not using it and she's not using it, I can—"

"What about your brother?"

"He's not even sixteen."

"He will be in a few months, and I don't want to listen to the two of you fighting over the car every day. You want a permit, get a job and earn the money to buy your own car."

"I can't do that with basketball."

"Then you'll have to wait till there's no basketball."

"There's always going to be basketball!"

"Then there's your answer."

When Eddie turned sixteen, he had no interest in learning to drive. Kevin thought his parents might see the light now that there would only be three people vying for the Buick instead of four, but his mother said, "Eddie's right. You boys can wait a few more years."

"He *said* that?"

"Yes. Driving is too dangerous at your age."

"Dangerous! That's crazy!"

"No means no," his father said.

For almost two years now, every time Kevin sees the car just sitting there, he wants to scream.

Instead, he runs—fast and far away, Walkman volume turned as high as it can go.

His feet hit the pavement with satisfying slaps in time to the music as he heads down the block lined with houses identical and puny as Monopoly game pieces. He stays in the middle of the street, well away from parked cars and piles of wet leaves spilling from curbs to gutters. There's no traffic at this hour on the side streets, and very little on the main drag when he crosses it toward the uphill stretch closer to the Hudson River.

"Whoa . . . we're halfway there," Bon Jovi sings in his ear.

He turns up one narrow block after another, same route every day.

There's a car behind him. He didn't hear it approach over the music, but headlights illuminate the misty street rising ahead of him. He jogs toward the right shoulder to let it pass, but it doesn't. Turning into the glare of high beams, he wonders why the car is just sitting there, swaddled in fog, idling in the middle of the road a few yards back.

Maybe it's a cop. Maybe he thinks Kevin committed some crime and is running away. Maybe he's shouting at Kevin out the window, telling him to stop. He pulls the headphones from his ears just in time to hear the engine race as the car barrels at him.

He jumps toward the curb to get out of the way. Too

late. The last thing he sees is a blinding flash of head-lights before thc world goes black.

"THIS YOUR FIRST?"

Barnes looks up from the foam cup of coffee he's just pulled from the vending machine in the lounge across from the nurses' station.

"Second," he tells the stranger who just dropped into an uncomfortable vinyl-upholstered chair. "I think. Or maybe my third. Guess I lost count."

"You lost count? *Day-um*, brother. That's cold."

"Yeah, it's not great—in fact, it pretty much sucks," he adds, after pausing to take a sip of brew that's more lukewarm than cold. "So if you were thinking of trying it . . ."

"Oh, I'm past the thinkin' and moved onto the doin'. Where were you nine months ago when my ladyfriend and everyone else was telling me how great it was gonna be?"

"Nine months . . ." Barnes breaks into a grin, holding up his white cup. "We're not talking about this, are we."

"Huh?"

"I thought you were asking me about the coffee. I've had three cups—pretty sure it's three—and yeah, it sucks and it's cold. But you were talking about kids."

The guy laughs, hard. Slaps his knee. He's wearing wire-framed glasses, gold chains, an oversized hooded sweatshirt that reads *Public Enemy*, and . . .

"Are those Nike Air Max?" Barnes asks, admiring the red, white, and gray sneakers as the guy crosses a foot over his knee.

"Hell, yeah, brother. So this is your first one?"

"It's . . . yeah."

"Same here." The guy extends a hand. "Name's Rob."

"First or last?"

"Neither. Just a reminder of something that happened. Something I never want to happen again. You?"

"Barnes."

"First or last?"

"Only one I use." He settles into a chair, tapping his dwindling pack of cigarettes on his knee and glaring at the No Smoking sign on the wall.

"They've got a lotta nerve," he tells Rob. "If there's any place a guy should be able to light up, this is it. You a smoker?"

"Just weed. And stogies. Check these out." He pulls a packet out of his sweatshirt pocket and shows Barnes a dozen cigars. Half of them have blue *It's a Boy* bands, half pink *It's a Girl*.

"You having twins?"

"Lord, I hope not. But I figured I better cover all my bases, you know what I'm sayin'? I wasn't ready for this. I thought she was using protection. How about you?"

"I thought the same thing," Barnes admits, and it occurs to him that they might both be talking about Delia.

"This was some splurge, I'm tellin' you," the guy goes on, talking about the cigars. "They're Cubans. Got them in Havana, man."

"You went to Havana? How'd you get there?"

"The long way. But I had to see it, you know? I got Cuban blood."

"Me, too." Barnes's paternal grandmother had left before Castro's regime. Abuela couldn't revisit her homeland in her lifetime, and died hoping her grandson might visit in his.

Rob puts away his cigars. "Hey, you notice we're the only two people in here? That's 'cause those other fools, they're all down the hall listening to that screamin' and cursin'. Now that's not for me. She wanted me in there with her, but I said, 'girl, I ain't no Florence Nightgown,' you know what I'm sayin'?"

Barnes nods, pretty sure he does. "Nightingale."

"Yeah, I ain't no nightingale, I ain't no nurse, I ain't no doctor. I told her I don't want to see no blood, I don't want to cut no cord. You just push the damn thing out and when it's all cleaned up nice, you tell someone to come and get me. You hear me, brother?"

"I hear you. Is your ladyfriend's name Delia, by any chance?"

"No, why?"

"Mine is," he says, as if he'd been expecting a coincidence.

Rob takes that in stride. "She try to get you in there, too?"

"No, she has a friend in there with her."

Beyond the plate glass window, the sky goes from pink to gray to pale blue as he and his new friend talk about everything but fatherhood. Rob's hundred-dollar sneakers, fast food, subway woes, music . . .

Rob works for a record label. Barnes is impressed.

"What do you do?"

"NYPD. I'm a detective."

"Hey, I was only foolin' about the weed, you know. I didn't—"

"Don't worry." Barnes grins. "Your secrets are safe with me."

"Cool. You got a badge and shit? You got a gun?"

"Mr. Barnes?"

He looks up to see a nurse in the doorway, surgical mask dangling around her neck.

"Would you like to meet your daughter?"

THE PORT AUTHORITY failed to eat Amelia alive as her cold-eyed friend had predicted. Having made it through the night—without sleep, but still—she has to endure only twenty more minutes until the ticket window opens. The first bus to Ithaca leaves in an hour, and she's going to be on it.

She stands and stretches, and a painfully full bladder makes itself known. She didn't dare venture into the ladies' room in the night, watching a steady parade of unsavory characters—male and female—pass through the doors. Now she has no choice.

She hauls her suitcase into the bathroom. It's filthy, and a thick stench hangs over the place—no surprise there. Toilets have overflowed to soak the garbage strewn on the floors. There's no soap, no running water at the sinks, and several stalls have no doors.

Amelia waits for one that does, shifting her weight from one foot to the other, on a line that could pass for a police lineup of seedy suspects. Streetwalkers in blue eye shadow, short shorts, and platform heels, disheveled bag ladies, teenaged junkies, a tiny, vacant-eyed woman who repeats everything everyone else says, and a good-natured transvestite in gold lamé from chic veiled chapeau to pointy stilettos. She—he?—knows many of the others by name, calls Amelia "Doll," compliments her on her jacket, and asks if her—his?—eye makeup is smcared.

"No, it looks good," she says, grateful to have finally met a decent human being in this hellhole.

"Looks good," parrots the tiny woman.

"Thanks, doll."

"Thanks, doll."

Amelia is reluctant to say anything else, but manners are manners, so she mutters a quick, "You're welcome."

The tiny woman's "You're welcome" is just as clenched. It might have struck Amelia as funny at some other time, in some other place, but she doubts anything could amuse her right now.

At last, she makes it to the head of the line, and a stall door opens.

"I'll watch your bag," an emaciated teenaged girl says, a few spots behind Amelia, "and then you can watch mine."

Hers is a torn Duane Reade shopping bag filled with what appears to be nothing more than additional crumpled plastic bags.

"Don't do it, doll. Leave her alone, Gloria."

"Mind your own business, Ronnette," the girl shoots back, and the drag queen rolls his—her?—eyes.

Jaw set, Amelia drags her suitcase across the filthy tile to the stall, making a mental note to wipe down the bag as soon as she gets to a place where there are paper towels and water and—oh, Lord, disinfectant. She herself should bathe in it, after this experience.

She wrestles the bag inside and with some maneuvering manages to close the door, not sure, and not caring, how she's going to make her exit.

No toilet paper. No surprise.

Fishing for a tissue in her backpack, she drops a pen on the floor. It rolls on into the next stall. She doesn't necessarily want it back. Then again, it's the only pen she has, and when she meets Silas Moss, she might want to write something down.

Hoping the pen landed on a relatively clean patch of tile, she stoops and sees that it did not. No longer interested in retrieving it, she sees Ronnette's gilded stilettos facing the toilet a few stalls down, and just beyond, another familiar pair of shoes. Her heart stops.

"Marceline?"

A toilet flushes. The red leather booties shuffle and exit the stall.

"Marceline, wait! It's Amelia! I need to talk to you! I'm going to Ithaca to meet Silas Moss, and he—"

"You all right, doll?" Ronnette calls from her stall.

Frantic to catch her friend, she fumbles with the tissue, fumbles with her jeans, fumbles with her suitcase and the door. By the time she wedges herself from the stall, there's no sign of the red booties or the woman attached to them.

"Did you see her?" she asks the others on the line. "The woman who just walked out of that stall? The one in red shoes?"

No response, other than a, "Yo, you tripping?"

She pushes past them, out the door. The terminal is stirring to life as employees and travelers trickle in, and she scans the area for Marceline.

No sign of her, nor of anyone wearing red shoes, but that doesn't mean she wasn't there. Corridors branch in every direction. She could have disappeared down any one of them.

Maybe she didn't hear you calling her.
Maybe it wasn't even her.
Maybe you dreamed the whole thing.

She shuffles to her seat by the ticket window.

No. Marceline was here, and now she's vanished in a mystical *poof*, like the spirits she talks about.

The ticket window opens with a snap of the shade.

Amelia thrusts Marceline from her thoughts and steps forward, hoping she has enough money for a ticket out of this place.

The young female clerk looks at her without greeting, mere seconds into her workday and already burdened by on-the-job boredom.

"Um, how much is a ticket to Ithaca?"

"You a student?"

"You mean . . . *there*?"

"Anywhere."

"I go to Hunter."

"Eight one way, sixteen round-trip."

Amelia pulls Calvin's twenty out of her pocket and puts it in the grooved slot beneath the window.

"Round-trip?"

She hesitates and then shakes her head.

"No. One way."

BACK IN NEW YORK City before dawn, Red hands two dollars to the too-friendly man in the Whitestone Bridge tollbooth.

"How are you this morning?"

"Fine."

"Everything okay?" He seems to be peering into the car.

Why would he do that? Why would he ask that question? Did someone tip him off? White would never, but Black? What if he found out about the—

No. Even if he realized it was missing, he wouldn't have put two and two together so quickly.

Ignoring the attendant's question, Red drives on, following a string of taillights crawling through the fog across the span and then south on the Van Wyck.

"Leave the rental car at JFK in the long-term lot," White had said last night. "That way, it'll be nearby when you need it. But not so close that if anyone finds it, they'll find you."

"Anyone . . . like who?"

"Who do you think? If the cops look for the car and find it at an airport, they'll assume you hopped a plane."

Uneasy, Red asked, "Why would they be looking for it?"

"They won't if you do your job right," Wayland—Black—had to butt in as usual.

"Don't worry. It's just a precaution," White said. "To throw them off your trail in case anyone sees anything."

The only people who'd seen anything in Boston or Westchester are gone from this earth. It might be days before anyone finds Tara and Emily. The first person to drive by Kevin Donaldson's broken body is going to call the cops for sure, but they'll assume it was an accident, or a random hit and run. That's why Red had resisted the impulse to jump out with the knife after running over the kid. It would have felt good to jab him a few times, just to make sure he was dead. Just to experience, one more time, the seductive thrust of rigid blade into soft flesh.

It hadn't been nearly as satisfying to back up and run him over again for good measure.

In retrospect that wasn't a good move. If the police take a good look at the tire tracks, they might figure out that it wasn't an accident.

Relax. It's still not going to lead anyone to you.

Red pockets the rental car key alongside the knife and lighter, grabs the McDonald's bag, and gets out of the car.

Oh.

Oh, no.

That's why the toll-taker was concerned. The whole front end is dented. There are smears of blood in the crumpled metal.

It's okay. He probably thought you hit a deer.

Shaken, Red bolts for the Pan Am arrivals terminal and finds a line of yellow cabs waiting.

"Where to?" the ebony-skinned driver, wearing a da-shiki and woven Muslim prayer kufi, asks in accented English. The bulletproof safety partition between the seats is open.

"Manhattan. Corner of Ninth Avenue and Forty-Sixth Street."

"No luggage?"

"Lost."

"That's too bad." He sets the meter and steers away from the curb. "Hope the trip was worth it?"

"Yeah."

"Where'd you go?"

"Timbuktu."

The driver glances over his shoulder in surprise. "I am from Mali! The capitol city, Bamako. It is only one thousand kilometers away from Timbuktu!"

What are the odds? What are the freaking odds?

Pretty damned high, perhaps, given the African garb and accent.

You should have been paying attention. You shouldn't just blurt things without thinking. If the cops ever come looking for you, questioning cab drivers . . . and toll attendants . . .

"Before I come to America last year, I fight there, in the Christmas War on the Agacher Strip, not far from Timbuktu. You were there last week when Sankara was assassinated in Burkina Faso coup d'etat, yes?"

What the hell is he talking about?

"No."

"No?"

"No."

Blessed silence for a few moments. Then, "I miss Bamako so very much. You flew from there?"

"No."

"Then how you—"

"I need to rest. I've been up for days."

Red pulls the safety partition closed, cutting off the driver's disappointed apology.

Believe me, it's better for both of us if we cut this conversation short right now.

Feigning sleep, Red thinks about Kevin Donaldson's body. By now, they must have found it. They might even be canvassing the neighborhood to see if anyone saw what had happened.

No one had. The suburban side streets had been deserted, just like in Boston. Not a witness in sight.

Not a witness anywhere—until now.

Timbuktu.

That homesick chatty cabbie doesn't know how lucky he is to be on the other side of that safety partition.

Chatty cabbie . . .

Jesus.

"THERE SHE IS," the nurse tells Barnes, stopping in front of the glass-walled nursery. "Front and center."

Yes. Oh, yes.

There she is.

Wrapped in a delicate white blanket and crowned by a pink beanie, she's lying in a transparent cradle like a tiny, perfect princess.

Clutching the pink-banded Cuban his new pal Rob gave him, along with a hearty congratulatory handshake, Barnes edges closer on wobbly legs.

"Isn't she precious?" the nurse asks from far, far away.

Mesmerized, Barnes nods. She is precious. The most precious thing he's ever seen in his life.

"Awwwww . . . here you go." The nurse pulls something from her stork-printed apron pocket and hands it to him. "I always have tissues. There are a lot of happy tears around here."

Not mine.

Barnes bows his head and wipes his eyes, struggling to hold back a heaving, sorrowful sob because now that he's seen this child, he knows he'll do anything within his power to protect her from all the horrible things in this world that might hurt her . . .

That includes your old man.

His tiny, perfect daughter will never even know he was here today. She won't know who he is, or where he is, or that there was a moment—fleeting, crazy—when he saw her and thought maybe, just maybe . . .

But no. No way.

This is the unselfish thing he's doing for her. *Not* being there. Not pretending, not trying, not considering . . .

Barnes aches for his father every day of his life. For what his mother might have been, if tragedy hadn't struck. Now for Wash, slipping from his grasp.

Every day, he meets people who are desperate to find lost loved ones. It doesn't matter to them if the person left willingly. In the end, it's the same. If someone was there, and then gone, you miss them. You look for them. For the rest of your life.

You can't miss what you never had.

The nurse escorts him back down the hall, leaving him at Delia's room.

The woman lying in bed bears no resemblance to the one he met back in March. The blood vessels around her eyes have burst. Her hair is matted. She's huge. Swollen legs and feet poke from beneath the blanket on one end, swollen face on the other, with a hump rising between.

She looks up to see him gazing at that stomach, wondering if there might be some mistake.

Nearly nine months, papers from a lawyer, a precious pink girl down the hall, and she says . . .

"Fluid."

"Huh?"

"I still look pregnant. They said it'll go down. You can sit." She gestures at the chair by the bed. "Did you see Shareese?"

"Who?"

"The kid."

"Shareese?"

"She's named after Alma's sister. She died in August."

"Alma?"

"Shareese! The first Shareese. Alma's *here*. Downstairs,

getting something to eat. Long night. You like it? The name?"

No, he doesn't like it. Not that he has a say.

"Yeah. It's nice."

"Yeah." A pause. "You never called."

A stronger man, a weaker man, a different man—might apologize.

She isn't the first woman to tell Barnes he never called. But she's the first one who gets more than a shrug and a *"What'd you expect?"*

"I didn't know."

"You didn't get the messages?"

"I got them. I mean I didn't know why you were calling."

A sound escapes her fleshy throat—something between a laugh, a snort, and a sob—and she looks at the concrete wall opposite the window.

Just like Barnes's apartment. This city is full of walls, and people trapped behind them. People who stare out bleakly and can never escape. And people who do, and it's his job to find them. He has to get back to work, dammit.

"If you knew I was pregnant, you'd have called me back. No, wait. I know. You'd have gotten on your white horse and rescued me. You'd have gotten down on your damned knee and given me a diamond ring."

"Is that what you—"

"Hell no! I don't want to marry your ass." She makes eye contact at last. "I just want you to own your mistake."

"My . . ." He thinks of the tiny pink princess down the hall. "Don't call her that."

"Isn't that what you're thinking? You made a mistake, did a stupid thing, and now you have to pay for it? You're an officer of the law. You know how it works. You do the crime, you serve the time."

"So you're punishing me?"

"I just want what's mine. I want . . . I just want you to

help me." Tears spill into the angry scars around her angry eyes. "I don't want to get all up in your business, and I don't want you all up in mine. I just need to make sure Shareese has everything she needs. You understand?"

He nods. But understanding what she's asking doesn't mean he's capable of following through. How is he supposed to come up with the money to support another person—two, from the sounds of it—when he can't even support himself?

He plucks some tissues from the box on the bedside table and hands them to her.

She wipes her eyes and blows her nose, hard. "I got nothing. No job. No money. No—"

"No money? You hired a lawyer."

"He's just Alma's cousin, doing me a favor." She resumes counting off on her fingers. "No insurance. Nowhere to live. No husband. Bobby said—"

"Wait . . . Bobby? He's your husband?"

Delia nods. "Ain't seen him since New Year's. I been staying with Alma."

"I'm sorry for what you've been through. And I'm going to do everything I can to make this right."

On the way back down the hall, Barnes stops to take another look at his daughter in the nursery. This time, he notices the card taped to her transparent cradle.

Wait a minute. Her name isn't *Shareese*. It's *Charisse*. That spelling changes everything. *C-h-a-r* . . .

The first four letters of his father's name. Delia had no way of knowing that.

"Hey, Charisse, you've got a guardian angel," he whispers, adding as he walks away, "And, baby girl, you're going to need one."

RED CRACKS AN eyelid and surveys the familiar stretch of Ninth Avenue beyond the cab's open back window.

Bathed in a neon-muting early-morning sunlight, Hell's Kitchen is a shade less seamy than usual, its ubiquitous layer of grit rain-washed into gutters and storm drains. The depraved characters who prowl the neighborhood at most hours have retreated into their subterranean tunnels, or wherever night creatures go when the rest of the world stirs to life.

Red shifts on the uncomfortable seat and fights a yawn. The second pill has worn off, drowsiness slinking in like a silken temptress.

The cabbie, silent for the duration of the ride in from Queens, stops at a light and dares to speak, calling out to be heard through the plastic partition. "One more block. East side of the avenue, or west?"

Red hesitates. Home is to the east, coffee shop to the west. Exhaustion wages a fierce battle with hunger. When you've gone twenty-four hours without food and twice as long without sleep, which craving is more pressing?

"West."

"Near corner, or across Forty—"

"Near!"

Questions, questions . . .

"All right. I'm just trying to do my job. Get you to where you want to go."

Red says nothing, clenching the hidden knife handle. It would be so easy to just slide the window open again and reach out and . . .

The light changes. The cab tears along the final block as if the driver can't wait to be rid of his passenger.

Don't worry. It's mutual.

The meter reads $20.85. Red pulls a twenty from the wad of cash Wayland handed over and hunts for smaller bills, coming up with three dollars and a ten. One is too little, the other too much.

"Need change?" the driver asks as Red thrusts the

twenty and ten into the slotted compartment between the seats.

It's one thing to have given Barb an excessive tip. But for a random taxi driver, that would be just as memorable as a measly one.

"Five back."

An agonizing wait as the cabbie digs it out in ones. ". . . four, and five. There you go. Need a receipt?"

Red bolts from the cab, shoving the money into the pocket that contains the knife and cursing when the blade slices tender flesh. The good riddance is mutual, the taxi barreling on south toward the next intersection. Wincing, Red pauses outside the coffee shop to examine the bleeding thumb tip.

"Coming in?" A police officer holds the door open, then spots the open wound. "Hey, you okay there?"

"Yeah, I just . . . Guess I cut myself on the edge of the door when I got out of that cab."

"Might want to get some antibiotic ointment on it right away so you don't get an infection."

"Will do. Thanks, Officer." Red steps past him, into the vestibule, sucking blood from the throbbing wound. It tastes of rust and salt.

Had Tara and Emily and Kevin tasted their own blood in their last moments? Had Mother? If this small cut stings so, they must have died in agony.

Caught between after-hours drunks and early-morning regulars, the place is quiet. A few solo diners sit along the counter, where pie wedges rotate in their glass dome. Someone is vacuuming in back, by the booths.

A napkin dispenser sits beside the register and a row of cans with slit plastic tops, labeled with every charity known to man. Coalition for the Homeless, Famine Relief, AIDS . . .

Don't they know it's too late?

Scowling, Red plucks a napkin and wraps it around the cut, watching a cockroach saunter along a row of gumball machines.

"What's new, pussycat?"

Barb is smiling, her eyes and mouth radiating a network of fine trenches etched by years of cigarettes and laughter. She's wearing her blue uniform with tan panty hose and thick-soled white rubber shoes, her dyed yellow hair pulled back in the usual stubby ponytail.

"Hey . . . what is this, BYOB day?"

"What?"

"Bring your own breakfast." She gestures at the McDonald's bag that conceals Red's napkin-wrapped thumb.

So much for unobtrusive.

"Oh. No." Red searches for further explanation—why? *I don't owe her anything.*

She leads the way to a booth without further comment, though not without further questioning. "You must have exciting plans to be out of bed this early on a Saturday. What's on the agenda?"

"Chores, errands . . . maybe a nap." Red smothers a yawn.

"That's what Saturdays are—Oh! Did you cut yourself?"

"It's nothing."

"Looks like something to me. We have a first aid kit somewhere out back. I'll go see if anyone knows where it is. Need a menu, or having the usual?"

"The usual."

"I always ask. You never know when someone's going to shake things up."

"I like things the same."

"Me, too." Barb points her index finger. "Apple pie, warmed not hot, coffee with a little milk, not cream, and three sugars, coming right up."

"You always get it right."

"I make it my business to remember everything about my customers, pussycat."

That could be a big mistake.

Half an hour later, back in the apartment with a belly full of apple pie and coffee, Red tosses the morning papers on the table and waters the spider plant drooping in its plastic container on the windowsill.

"And it was said unto them that they should not hurt the grass of the earth, neither any green thing, neither any tree, but only such men as have not the seal of God on their foreheads."

Revelations. One of the first passages White had shared last spring, after they'd been reunited.

"Only the chosen few have the seal. You do, Red. That's why I had to find you again, after all these years."

"To save me."

"Yes. Time is running out."

"How long do we have? Hours? Days? Weeks?"

"If I could tell you, I would. When it happens, we need to be ready. That's why we need to destroy these outliers."

As it turned out, *we* means Red.

Still no sign of the stairwell murder in the tabloids, but Perry Wayland's disappearance is front page news.

The *Post* headline, Might as Well Jump, is a nod to the Van Halen song. It's printed above a photo of the George Washington Bridge.

Billionaire Boys Suicide Club, screams the *Daily News*. The article about Perry Wayland's disappearance is accompanied by sidebars about a despondent broker who'd jumped in front of the number 5 train at Wall Street yesterday afternoon, and another so-called stock market suicide earlier in the week. The tabloids are prone to exaggeration.

Not according to *Newsday*. There, he's a mere Missing Millionaire, grim-faced in a family photo, surrounded by his wife and three daughters—all blonde, beautiful, and smiling like they don't have a care in the world.

"They won't even miss me," Black had said when they discussed the bridge ruse White had conceived after following Red to the top of the World Trade Center. "Kirstin's life will go on as usual. Shopping, Jazzercise, lunching at Maxim's. I'm just a meal ticket."

"Not to me. You're a prophet."

Noting Black's prompt satisfaction, Red felt a prickle of misgiving. *White is proficient at telling him whatever he wants—needs—to hear.*

But it's not that way with me. We go way back. We were there for each other in our darkest days. We love each other. White said so.

Red tosses the papers onto the coffee table, thumb throbbing, dark splotches staining the beige bandage Barb had insisted on providing back at the diner. In the kitchen, Red peels it back and washes the wound beneath the faucet, wincing at the sting of soap. The cut is open and oozing, sending a river of pink coursing over the porcelain sink.

Blood . . .

Kevin Donaldson had flown into the air and hit his head on the pavement. He'd most likely been knocked unconscious, perhaps even died on impact. But what agony did Tara and Emily experience? Their cuts were deep, severing their carotid arteries, as White had instructed.

"Do that first, and then live it up. Have a little fun with the knife. Just make sure your first cut is the deepest."

"Yeah, like the song," Black said. "Rod Stewart."

"No, Cat Stevens."

"I don't think he sang—"

"He did. In 1967." White was curt, unappreciative of contradiction. "Trust me, I know."

"How?"

"Because it was my father's favorite song, okay?"

"Okay. Sorry."

Remembering Black's chagrin, Red smiles and opens the bedroom nightstand drawer, where the square metal tin of Band-Aids resides along with a loaded revolver, Vietnam dog tags on a beaded metal chain, and a Bible with a corner page folded to Revelations 6:3–4. Red opens it.

> *When the Lamb opened the second seal, I heard the second living creature say, "Come and see!" Then another horse came out, a fiery red one. Its rider was given power to take peace from the earth and to make men slay each other. To him was given a large sword.*

More like a switchblade, but . . .

Everyone has a purpose, White said long ago.

White . . .

Red flips back to 6:1–8.

> *And there before me was a white horse! Its rider held a bow, and he was given a crown, and he rode out as a conqueror bent on conquest.*

And 6:5–6.

> *There before me was a black horse! Its rider was holding a pair of scales in his hand. Then I heard what sounded like a voice among the four living creatures, saying, "A quart of wheat for a day's wages, and three quarts of barley for a day's wages, and do not damage the oil and the wine!"*

Finally, 6:7–8.

There before me was a pale horse! Its rider was named Death, and Hades was following close behind him. They were given power over a fourth of the earth to kill by sword, famine, and plague, and by the wild beasts of the earth.

Spelled out neatly here, all so easy to grasp.
Red, White, Black . . .

"Why don't you call him 'Pale'?" Red had asked White, early on. "Why do you call him by his real name?"

"Because in ancient Aramaic, the name Oran means pale. That's why he's powerful, and we need to serve him and carry out his orders. He was born to be the first horseman."

Chapter Thirteen

Barnes stops at the coffee cart near the precinct and greets the Pakistani vendor who's there seven mornings a week, always polite, always smiling, rain or shine.

"Good morning, good morning! Breakfast special?"

"Yep." Barnes hands over two dollars in exchange for a plastic-wrapped buttered Kaiser roll, a small regular coffee, and two quarters in change. He detours to the pay phone on the corner outside Duane Reade, anxious to call Wash to tell him about the baby without being overheard by anyone at work. A beefy man is already parked in the phone kiosk, holding a roll of quarters. Clearly he's going to be a while.

At the precinct, Barnes finds Stef on the phone giving a press statement about the Wayland case. He gestures that he'll be off in a few minutes. Barnes finishes his coffee, chucks the cup into the garbage, and goes to the kitchenette, a brightly lit nook tucked into a corner by the restrooms.

Marsha is there, pressing buttons on the microwave. "Morning," she says.

"So I hear."

"You want coffee?"

"Need is more like it."

"You sure?" She picks up a grimy glass coffeepot that's nearly boiled away on the hot burner, and sets it down again. "Looks more like molasses today than motor oil. I'll pass."

"Not me." Barnes fills a white foam cup with the treacly muck, takes a sip, and wrinkles his nose.

"Rough night?"

"They don't come much rougher."

"Good for you, lover boy."

He should tell her that it wasn't like that, but then she'll want to know what it *was*.

Instead, he asks what she's working on. She tells him about a drug bust; he tells her about the Wayland case.

"Yeah, I saw that in the papers. He went to Brown. Andrea did, too, around the same time."

Marsha talks even more frequently about her roommate than she does about her dog.

The microwave dings, and she removes an oversized, steamy muffin. "Want half?"

"Is it chocolate?"

"Fat free oat bran."

"God, no. Can you ask Andrea if she knows Perry Wayland? Maybe she can shed some light on his past."

"She's at work. I can page her, but she might not call me back till later, and she probably won't know him. Do you know how many people there are at Brown? It's not small."

"I know, but maybe she knows his wife. She went to Brown, too. Her name is—"

"Kirstin Eaton Billington Wayland, of the *Mayflower* Billingtons," she says, peeling away the muffin's fluted wrapper.

"How do you know that?"

"It was in the *Daily News*. I wonder if she knows—"

"The Mayflower Madam?" Barnes cuts in, grinning. "Says she doesn't."

"Bet she's lying. Andrea says all those blue bloods are

all intertwined one way or another. And maybe she did know the Waylands at Brown, since they're all rich WASPs, Andrea included."

"Really? I'd have expected a strong, proud black woman like you to have a strong, proud, black . . . *friend*."

"Trust me, I have plenty of strong, black, proud *friends*, lover boy." Marsha smiles and exits the kitchen.

Barnes carries his coffee back through the bustle and maze of desks. Still on the phone, Stef holds up an index finger, and he sits down to wait, rubbing his tired eyes and trying to get his head back into the case. Right now, it doesn't feel like a priority. Perry Wayland's life is likely not in danger. Barnes can't even remember what the guy looks like, or why anyone gives a damn where he is. Rich SOB.

Off the phone, Stef gives him a once-over. "You look like hell. Where have you been?"

"Sorry. Family emergency."

"Everything okay now?"

"Yep."

"Good. Guess who that was on the phone?"

Ordinarily, Barnes would make a wiseass guess. Today, he can't even come up with a legitimate one.

"Wayland's father-in-law, Biff Billington. Said Daddy's Little Girl cried all night and he can't stand to see her so upset." Stef rolls his eyes. "So he's doubling the reward. Just like that, the guy antes up a hundred grand."

"So . . . what, you don't think a father should do everything in his power to help his daughter?"

"You feeling all right, Barnes?"

"That money's a drop in the bucket to a guy like him. Who are we to judge?"

"I'd judge a lot less if we could claim it ourselves. I could really use it right about now."

"Same."

"Oh, yeah? What would you do with it, kid?"

"You know, the usual. Food, rent, pay down my mother's credit card debt . . ." *Provide for my newborn daughter.* "How about you?"

"Food, rent . . . OTB."

"So . . . the usual."

"Always." Grinning, Stef grabs his keys and pulls on a brown tweed sport coat that wouldn't close over his stomach if he ever bothered with buttons. "You ready to go?"

Barnes nods, though he's forgotten where they're going. He knew on the way over here, but the detail seems to have flitted from his weary brain. Sleep deprivation impairs cognition, and he's exhausted, with an endless day ahead.

"Ray was expecting us an hour ago. You know how he gets."

Ray. Right. Over at the tow pound. They're going to check out Wayland's impounded Mercedes.

"You see the papers today?"

"No."

Stef grabs a stack of morning tabloids from his desk. "Get caught up on the way over."

Traffic is light along the West Side Highway. Barnes barely has time to scan the *Daily News* coverage of the case before they reach West Thirty-Eighth Street. Billionaire Boys Suicide Club might sell papers, but there's no more evidence that Wayland had any personal connection to the subway jumpers than there is hard evidence that he dove over that railing.

Staged suicide—classic for a guy like that. By now, he's reinventing himself with his friend Miss White, hundreds or thousands of miles away from the ice princess he married.

That's a challenging task for most people—tough to disappear without a trace on a shoestring budget. A vast stash of cash makes it a whole lot easier to get out of town, even buy yourself a whole new identity. Who hasn't dreamed about doing that?

They've reached their destination, Pier 76 on the Hudson River. Barnes tucks the newspapers under the front seat as Stef pulls into a spot designated for NYPD.

Open twenty-four hours, the tow pound is busy even at the ungodliest. You'd be hard-pressed to find another place in the city—other than Central Booking—filled with more irritated New Yorkers who aren't about to admit having done anything wrong.

A few dozen scowling people wait in a long line at the window, outraged about having to pay a couple of hundred dollars to reclaim their own vehicles. Several others sit on chairs filling out clipboard paperwork, grumbling to themselves and each other. Many are looking in their pockets for cash, some are looking for loopholes, and at least one is looking for trouble.

"I swear it's my car!" shouts the man at the front of the line. He has a fake tan and frothy, lemon-colored hair, and sports a muscle tee shirt, neckerchief, tight denim cutoffs, and tube socks with clogs.

"Then where's the documentation?" the clerk asks calmly, tucked behind bulletproof glass.

"I gave you—"

"And I'm giving it back, because it's useless."

"Come on, lady, what do you want from me, blood?"

"Something more than a Polaroid would be a good start. Come back when you have paperwork. Next!"

He trudges away, crossing paths with Stef and Barnes, and pauses to hold the snapshot alongside his face. "See this? I'm sitting in my car. You can see the plates and everything."

They glance at the shot of Lemonhead behind the wheel of a red Mustang.

"Nice try," Stef says.

"What, you don't think that's me?"

"Oh, it's you. I may have lousy eyesight, but I'd know that yellow bouffant anywhere."

"If you want to start something with me, Chubs—"

"He doesn't." Barnes nudges his bristling partner. "Come on, Ray's waiting."

They find Ray in the cavernous indoor parking area reserved for vehicles that are part of a crime scene investigation. He's taking notes on a clipboard beside a shiny red Alfa Romeo Milano missing all four tires.

Barnes whistles. "Someone had a bad night."

"You don't know the half of it. Car was double-parked on Avenue A, stripped clean by the time we got it. Owner was shot in the head."

"For double-parking?"

"What? No! That would be crazy! It was a drug deal gone wrong," he explains earnestly.

Stef likes to say Ray isn't the sharpest tool in the shed. Barnes thinks he's just young and has yet to develop the jaded character that allows more seasoned cops to make grim jokes on the job.

Stef leans into the windshield, hands cupped above his eyebrows. "They even took the bloodstains, huh?"

"He wasn't shot in there. Happened over in Tompkins Square."

Ah, the so-called shadiest park in town, a description that has nothing to do with trees.

"Heard it was a war zone down there overnight," Barnes says. "More than usual."

"Yeah, all hell broke loose after the shooting. They rounded up at least two dozen derelicts. Anyway . . . you're here about that Mercedes from the GWB, right?"

"Yeah, much as I wouldn't mind test-driving that white Jag." Stef gestures at the Alfa's cordoned-off neighbor.

"Sorry, not allowed."

"I know, Ray. Wow, fully loaded. I bet the tow driver couldn't wait to pounce on this one. Where'd they find it? Sutton Place?"

"Upper East Side. Kilo of coke under the seat. Owner's a sixteen-year-old preppie. Come on, the Mercedes is back there."

Ray leads them along the row of cars. The vast space echoes with rumbling, beeping tow trucks maneuvering vehicles into empty spots. A couple are banged up, and most are stripped, like the Alfa. These days, you can't leave a car for more than five minutes in certain neighborhoods without sacrificing hubcaps and more. But they find Perry Wayland's black Mercedes intact.

All three men pull on gloves. Ray takes a plastic bag from his pocket, removes a key, and turns it in the driver's side door lock. "Key was left in the ignition."

"Happens all the time in bridge cases," Stef says, opening the door and reaching across the front seats to pull the passenger's side lock button for Barnes. "Not much use for it at the bottom of the river."

"Or on some remote tropical island," Barnes adds, leaning in. He pictures Kirstin Wayland sitting here in the passenger's seat just days ago, driving out to Long Island to hunt for her dream house. The Mercedes smells like new leather and cologne. He opens the console—empty—then lifts the plush floor mat.

"Already looked under there," Ray says. "Thought maybe I'd find a bobby pin, loose change . . ."

"Or a couple of hundred-dollar bills, right?" Stef asks.

"Thousand-dollar bills, with this guy. Wait, do they even make thousand-dollar bills?"

"Hell if I know. This car looks like it just rolled off the dealer lot. If he was abducted, then it happened without a struggle."

"Forensics dusted for prints."

Barnes closes the door and steps back. "I doubt they'll turn up anything. Wayland's probably on a beach by now—warm turquoise water, amazing women, bottomless mai tais . . ."

"Bottomless women and amazing mai tais would be even better," Stef says.

"If Wayland's on the beach, I bet the water's cold and gray."

"Why's that, Ray?"

"I've never been to Minnesota, but it's not exactly tropical."

Stef scowls. "What the hell are you talking about?"

"I found a clipping in the car about Minnesota."

"You think he's at the World Series?"

"No. That's the weird thing." He produces a plastic evidence bag that contains a piece of newsprint. It's torn on two sides; straight-edged on the others.

"Someone cut this out of the paper with scissors," Barnes notes. "There isn't enough border outside the text on the right-angle edges to be the corner of a page."

"You're right. Those cuts aren't factory made. They're a little jagged," Stef agrees. "So that means Wayland—or someone he knows, or someone who was in this car— clipped this from a paper because he wanted to save it, or it meant something to him."

Less than a column's width and about two inches long, the piece is missing most of a headline and key pieces of information, but there's enough for the gist of the article. Barnes shakes his head. "Wayland didn't go to Minnesota, Ray. At least, not to Lake Wobegon."

"How do you know?"

"Because it isn't a real place. This article is about Garrison Keillor, the author who does that public radio show, *A Prairie Home Companion*. It was a big deal when it went off the air a few months ago."

NPR, though? Kirstie had said Wayland wasn't into culture. With a gloved hand, Barnes turns over the plastic-shrouded newsprint. The reverse side is a true crime retrospective. Looks like it marks the anniversary of the Manson murders, or . . .

No, not the Manson case. A similar one, much closer to home. Barnes turns to Stef and Ray.

"Either Wayland was a closeted Garrison Keillor fan, or he had some morbid fascination with the Brooklyn Butcher."

AMELIA DOZED OFF before the bus left the Port Authority. She'd been looking forward to seeing the countryside beyond the urban area where she's spent her entire life, but she slept her way through the Hudson Valley, across the Catskills, and north through farmland to the fringes of the Finger Lakes.

She awakens to disembark on Seneca Street in downtown Ithaca like Dorothy stepping into a technicolor Oz. Cayuga Lake gleams in the distance, electric blue as the sky framing the Cornell clock tower on the northeast hillside and Ithaca College campus in the southeast. Golden midday sun shimmers like a waterfall over lush hillside foliage in splashy citrus shades.

Starved, she spots a restaurant awning down the block and heads in that direction, passing quaint, small town storefronts and a smattering of pedestrians. According to a sign on the awning, it marks not just a restaurant, but the *DeWitt Mall*. Having seldom ventured beyond the five boroughs, Amelia has never been to an actual shopping mall, but she's seen plenty on TV. They're always vast, brightly lit modern buildings with escalators, chain stores, and food courts.

This old-fashioned brick-and-stone façade looks more like a school and is occupied by locally owned businesses: a guitar store, bookstore, antiques store, and the restaurant, called Moosewood. It doesn't look like a fancy place. She has plenty of leftover money from the bus ticket, and she'll order something cheap and simple.

A waitress greets Amelia with a friendly smile. She has long gray braids and granny glasses, and she's wearing jeans and clogs beneath an apron.

Amelia sits at a table by the window with her bag by her feet, one strap around her ankle, and searches the menu for something she can afford. And likes. Or even recognizes.

"Need more time?" the waitress asks, poised with an order pad and pen.

"I was just looking for . . . a hot dog, maybe?"

"Sorry, sweetie. This is a vegetarian restaurant. You must be new in town. Where are you from?"

"New York . . . City," she adds, remembering that Ithaca is also in New York State. It just feels like another state. Or country. World.

"I should have guessed. Street smarts." She gestures at the bag strap wrapped around Amelia's leg under her chair. "I used to do that, too, back in the day. New York is my hometown, but I came up here for college thirty years ago and never left. Now, what can I get for you?"

"I should probably . . ." Amelia pushes back her chair. "Is there, maybe, a McDonald's around here or something?"

"Hold on. If you're in the mood for a burger, you can get one right here."

"But I thought—"

"It's a tofu burger. Try it. I'm an owner—it's a coop- erative—so I might be biased when I tell you the food is great, but you'll love it. I promise."

Turns out she's wrong about that. But Amelia—no stranger to broken promises—takes it in stride. Not wanting to hurt the waitress/owner's feelings, she hides the unappetizing brownish-gray patty under a ruffle of verdant lettuce that bears no resemblance to the anemic heads of iceberg back home. It's served not on a ketchup-smeared white bun, but on thick wheat toast spread with thousand island dressing. There are French fries on the side, but they're made from sweet potatoes. Amelia pokes at them until the waitress shows up with a smoothie "on the house."

At last, something Amelia can stomach. It's fresh and vibrant as the foliage beyond the window, and she drains the glass.

"Are you here looking at colleges?"

"No, I'm looking . . . for someone. Dr. Silas Moss?" she adds, on the off chance that the waitress knows him.

The name is promptly met with a smile and nod.

"Si's one of our regulars. Not a fan of tofu, either. Does he know you're coming?"

"No, I . . . I guess I should have made an appointment. Maybe I should go back to New York and call him at his office next—"

"See, that's the thing about should-haves. They're always too late. I don't believe in regrets. What's your name?"

"Amelia Crenshaw."

"I'm Aline. Listen, Amelia, I'm guessing that you went to an awful lot of trouble and expense to get here today. See it through."

"But . . . I mean, I didn't think about . . ." *Anything. I just ran.* "I didn't see any cabs, and—"

"Cabs? Oh, city girl." Aline chortles. "Silas lives around the corner. Ten-minute walk, tops. Go out the door, hang a right onto North Cayuga Street, and keep going till you see a three-story yellow Victorian with a big wraparound porch and maroon shutters—on the left, in the middle of the block right after the park. You can't miss it."

"I . . ."

"You're going."

Amelia smiles. "I'm going. Thank you. Can I have the check, please?"

"Someone already took care of that, sweetie."

"What? Oh! You didn't have to—"

"Not me, I swear. And they wanted to be anonymous, so that's all I'm saying."

Flabbergasted, she looks around the crowded restaurant filled with strangers. "But . . . why would anyone pay my bill?"

"Someday, when you come across someone who looks like they need a friend, or a favor . . . you'll do the same for them."

Tears welling, Amelia ventures back out into the cool sunshine and hangs a right up North Cayuga Street.

Chapter Fourteen

Margaret Costello's child doesn't seem to exist.

Red has spent hours searching for an overlooked clue in painstakingly labeled folders that hold a stash of microfiche printouts, photographs, press clippings, stolen documents, and medical records dating back to 1967, the year before the Brooklyn Butcher murders. Nothing.

Red yawns and shifts in the uncomfortable wooden chair, restless.

Too much adrenaline. Too much to do. Too much caffeine. Too much . . .

The Tylenol bottle sits like a centerpiece amid the books and papers spread across the table.

No, not nearly enough of that.

White had said to use the pills sparingly because they're addictive. Who cares about that now, though? Judgment Day is coming. Afterward, mortal problems will cease to exist for the chosen few.

Chosen *four*.

That's two too many.

Red snatches up the bottle, dumps out a couple of pills, and swallows them without water. They burn going down, leaving a chemical aftertaste, but it doesn't matter. Nothing matters but finding that girl.

Back to studying a pair of images in the Costello file, just in case . . .

One is a newspaper clipping showing the Costello house on Sixty-Fourth Street in Bensonhurst, the morning after the crimes. It looks almost exactly the same today, captured in a glossy print Red had snapped on September 3, 1987, according to the date stamped in the lower right corner. The two-story house has a flat roof and unadorned yellow brick façade. Two windows upstairs and two down, with a door between them. Margaret's room was upstairs in the back, according to another clipping that details the crimes and speculates how the killer might have gotten into the house.

Back when the article had been written, the police and press didn't know that Oran had a key. They suspected a mob hit, because the parents and grandmother had emigrated from Sicily. But Joe Costello had no known mafia ties. Besides, a hitman wouldn't have been so sloppy, and wouldn't have left witnesses alive.

Margaret's boyfriend had been questioned and released. Later, so had Tara Sheeran's and Christina Myers's. Theoretically, a young woman could have snuck her lover into the house while her family slept. It was even possible that he'd gone into a murderous rage.

But repeatedly?

Not unless all the teenaged rape victims were protecting the same secret lover. The police had searched in vain for a link among the girls—something more relevant than age, general geographic location, religion. All were Catholic, which wasn't unusual in those Brooklyn neighborhoods at that time.

The authorities had missed the one key thing the girls had in common. Not surprising. In those days, birth control clinic visits were closely guarded secrets. Today, no one would bat an eye.

A droplet of fresh blood splashes onto the photo.

"Dammit!" Red goes to the bathroom, peels off the oozing bandage, and stares into the mirror.

No sleep, too much caffeine, stale skin in staler clothing, all that medication on an almost empty stomach . . .

Recipe for recklessness.

You need a shower, and some food.

Early on weekday mornings, the water runs from hot to lukewarm to ice-cold within a minute of stepping into the shower. Today, it's at least five. Long enough for Red to shake the lethargy and wonder what will happen if by chance White is wrong about what lies ahead. What if there is no Judgment Day? What if the world goes on turning? What if all of this is for nothing?

Wrapped in a towel, Red goes into the kitchen. The refrigerator shelves are empty, but as always, the crisper is filled with apples. Macouns, Cortlands, McIntosh, Golden Delicious . . .

The fresh bandage mottles with blood as Red works the paring knife over the fruit, then rinses the blade, just like on that long-ago day in the trailer when Mother lay dead on the floor. Sweet white flesh and shreds of skin swirl in the sink and are trapped in the strainer.

Red carries the apple slices to the living area, turns on the television, and takes a bite. A bit too tart. Needs a sprinkle of cinnamon sugar, but the cabinets are as bare as the fridge.

"Waste is sinful. Buy only as much food as you need to last a few days at a time," White instructed.

Until today, Red never had an inkling of misgiving about that command or any other.

"Do you trust me?" White asked that first night, over coffee after the World Trade Center.

"Yes. I trust you."

And now?

I don't know. But I don't trust Black.

The noon newscast has begun, with stories about war brewing in the Middle East; nuclear testing in France; President Reagan's upcoming arms control address. On the heels of a segment about continued financial fallout from Black Monday, a familiar face appears onscreen.

"Coming up next, what happened to Manhattan tycoon Perry Wayland? Police are asking for your help, and his family is offering a reward."

The photo is gone, replaced by a Shower to Shower commercial with a cloying jingle. "Just a sprinkle a day . . ."

A sprinkle a day . . .

A sprinkle of cinnamon sugar . . .

An apple a day keeps—

No. Red forces down a mouthful of sour green Granny Smith and crams in more, chewing and swallowing, tamping Mother and the doctor into dark places.

Perry Wayland reappears on TV. The camera pans out to include his wife and children. It's the same photo from this morning's newspaper.

"Hedge Fund manager Perry Wayland remains missing at this hour, his car towed from the George Washington Bridge. Authorities have not ruled out suicide, though a search of the Hudson River and adjacent shoreline recovered no evidence of remains. Police say that isn't unusual, but they're continuing to follow other leads. Wayland lives with his wife and children on the Upper East Side, where neighbors described him as a quiet family man who keeps to himself. He was last seen leaving his office at 195 Broadway on Thursday evening. Kirstin Wayland is offering a substantial reward for information leading to her husband's whereabouts."

As the reporter gives the missing persons hotline information, Red imagines calling it.

I know where you can find Perry Wayland. He's on Block Island with—

"Tragedy in Yonkers today," the anchorwoman says, against a graphic of a chalk-outlined body, "when a star high school athlete was killed in a predawn hit and run. Seventeen-year-old Kevin Donaldson was struck early this morning while jogging alone on this quiet side street. The area was covered in dense fog at the time, and the driver likely failed to see him. There were no witnesses. A neighbor walking her dog came upon the victim just after seven o'clock . . ."

Red stares at the televised image of a familiar sloping road lined with small houses. Rescue vehicles flash red lights in the street, and neighbors congregate on the sidewalk behind police barricades.

What if Christina Myers is watching the same newscast and realizes Kevin Donaldson is her lost child?

"Authorities are asking anyone with any information on the tragedy to come forward. When we come back, the Cardinals are set to face off against the Twins in Game Six of the World Series in Minneap—"

Red jabs the button to the right of the screen, and the television goes dark and silent.

The Donaldsons and Yonkers police aren't offering a substantial reward like the Waylands are, but if someone saw Kevin Donaldson mowed down not once, but twice . . .

Even if a witness had been lurking and noticed the car, though, he or she wouldn't have gotten a good look at the driver. Red had been cloaked in the raincoat, hood pulled up. But if someone did see, and the police release a description of the car and someone else—say, the toll clerk on the Whitestone Bridge—remembers seeing it early this morning, dented and covered in blood . . .

They still won't track it to you.

Not even if they find it in long-term parking at JFK.

But if they start asking around . . .

Red thinks of the taxi driver and Timbuktu, of the cop on the sidewalk, of Barb . . .

Paranoia takes hold.

Christina might have been in touch with her son's adoptive family all along, if not with the boy himself. Or she could have been keeping tabs on him from afar, as Red had done.

If she finds out he's been killed, she'll go up to Westchester. If his adoptive parents were unaware of his connection to the Brooklyn Butcher case, she'll tell them. And even if she thinks Kevin's death was a tragic accident, if—*when*—she hears about the Sheeran double murder, she'll become suspicious, go to the police . . .

Her Sheepshead Bay address is scribbled on a sheet of notebook paper at the front of the folder that bears her name. There's an envelope of surveillance photos taken last month, and notes chronicling Christina's routine and those of her neighbors. Further back in the file, black-and-white crime scene photographs from 1968 clearly show the exterior and interior layout, complete with bloodstains spattered on the floors and walls.

You can wash the gory remnants from nonporous surfaces like porcelain and stainless steel, but no amount of scrubbing will erase them from floorboards and plaster. Even if you bleach them away, mask them in wood stain or paint over them, the scars remain.

Nobody knows that better than me.

Red goes to the bedroom, opens the drawer, and takes out the gun.

SILAS MOSS'S HOUSE is yellow, all right. Not pale and buttery, or a tawny historical shade, but more like . . . rubber ducky yellow. It's also enormous, far bigger than the Victorian homes on Striver's Row back in Harlem. It has a wraparound porch, and rises three turreted stories into autumn maple boughs that almost, but not quite, matches the maroon trim and the mansard roof's fish-scale shingles. A cold breeze rustles the foliage and creaks one of the shutters. If not for the bright-colored paint, this place would remind Amelia of every haunted house in every scary movie she's ever seen.

She scuffles through dry leaves littering the walk and climbs the steps. Off to one side, a couple of fat pump-kins and a pot of orange mums should clash with each other and the paint job, but somehow, it all coordinates.

She reaches for the doorbell, then sees a hand-lettered index card taped above it.

Bell Out of Order. Please Knock. (Loudly!)

She hesitates, then knocks.

After a moment, she knocks harder, and the door opens.

"There, that's more like it!"

She's heard that people on television look different when you see them in real life, but white-bearded, be-spectacled Silas Moss looks exactly the same. Maybe that's because he's not an actor, just a regular person. He's wearing suede slippers with his brown corduroy slacks and tan cardigan sweater.

"You're not Jessie," he informs her. "You must be Amelia."

"How did you . . ."

He leans forward and whispers, "Magic."

"Really?"

He chuckles and holds the door open, gestures for her to step over the threshold.

Thrown off that he knew her name, she stands rooted

to the rubber doormat, her so-called street smarts belatedly kicking in.

I don't like you talking to strangers, Bettina counsels from beyond the grave.

If Amelia had heeded that warning, she would never have gotten to know Marceline, who does believe in magic. Practices it, even. It's too late to count on her for help, but Silas Moss is right here.

"Coming in?" he asks.

She gives a decisive nod and steps over the threshold, wincing when he slams the door behind her.

"Sorry. Wind caught it. Can I take your coat? And your bag?"

She hesitates, not wanting to part with the tiny dress even for a few minutes. But she does hand over her coat.

He opens a closet door, and a plastic bag topples out. It appears to be full of other plastic bags. The professor quickly hangs her coat—on top of another coat, she notices—then scoops the bag from the entryway's mosaic tile floor and crams it back onto the packed closet shelf, where it's sure to fall out again the next time he opens the door.

In the foyer beyond the vestibule, a crystal chandelier hangs from a high ceiling, and a grand staircase of carved wood curves along two walls with a wide, windowed landing halfway up. The floors are polished wood and the wallpaper is a rich bronze swirly pattern. Through an archway, she sees a living room filled with fancy dark wood furniture, framed oil paintings, and shelves filled with books. Not paperback novels like Bettina used to read, but thick leather-and-clothbound volumes that look like the ones they keep in a glass case at the library, well beyond the grasp of ordinary patrons.

The place looks and feels like the history museum Amelia once visited with her elementary school class, except it's not clean or orderly. Every surface is cluttered with stacks of books and papers. A heap of clothing is draped over the newel post at the foot of the stairway, and a small laundry basket and several pairs of shoes line the lower steps, tripping hazards waiting to be carried up. The furniture is dusty. Dry leaves tracked inside are scattered well beyond the door.

"Come on into the kitchen. I was just making some lunch. You'll eat again, even though you've already had yours, won't you?"

"I . . . How did you know . . . *magic* again?" Seeing his expression, she answers her own question with a smile.

The kitchen is surprisingly small for a house this size, though it would be large by New York standards. Several of the narrow, dark wood cupboard doors are ajar, the wide white porcelain sink is heaped with dishes, and the old-fashioned six-burner stove is grease spattered.

On the speckled countertop, she sees a loaf of Wonder Bread, a jar of dill pickles, a white-paper-wrapped package of deli ham, and a jar of mustard. It's not the fancy or spicy variety, but the bright yellow kind that matches the house. He gestures at two plates, each of which holds two pieces of bread as if he'd been expecting her.

"I'm making you a sandwich, Amelia. I promise there's no tofu involved."

The light dawns, and she grins. "Did Aline call you?"

"You don't believe in magic?"

She thinks of Marceline. "Sometimes."

"Good for you. So do I. Because if you believe in science, you believe in magic."

"What do you mean?"

"'Any sufficiently advanced technology is indistinguishable from magic.' You've heard that, right?"

"No."

"Haven't you read anything by Arthur C. Clarke?"

"No," she says again. She's never even heard of him.

"Hang on a second." He disappears into the next room, leaving Amelia to ponder her embarrassing lack of intellectual sophistication until he returns to hand her a book. "Here you go. Read it."

"Um . . . *now?*"

He laughs. "Did you take Evelyn Wood?"

"What?"

"The speed-reading course."

Oh, right. She's seen the commercials with Steve Allen.

"It's a first edition. Take it with you, and return it whenever you have a chance."

"I can't—I'm just visiting. I don't know when I'd be able to return it."

"Anytime is fine. You have to read it."

She looks at the cover. *Profiles of the Future: An Inquiry into the Limits of the Possible.*

"Now, do you like cheese?"

"Cheese?"

"On your sandwich. I don't, but my friend Jessie does, so I have some."

"You don't have to make me a sandwich. I just wanted to ask you a couple of quick questions, and then I can get out of your way."

"You're not in my way. I hate eating alone, and Jessie is running late."

"Oh—I don't want to eat his lunch."

"First, there's plenty of food. Second, Jessie isn't a he, she's the girl next door, about your age. I keep an eye on her when her parents are out of town. So, cheese?"

"No, thank you."

"Mustard?"

"Yes, please."

"And you're here because . . ." he asks, as if it's part of the sandwich preferences.

"I, um—I watched *20/20* last night. I want to see if you can help me find my birth parents by checking my . . . is it DMA?"

"DNA. It stands for deoxyribonucleic acid."

"Do you think you can help me?"

"That depends on a lot of different factors. Why don't you tell me your story."

Amelia shares a condensed version as he constructs a pair of simple sandwiches, pours two glasses of apple cider, and gestures for her to sit down.

"That's all I know," she concludes, sliding into a rickety wooden chair at the small round table. "I mean, it's all I was told. There might be more to it."

"There usually is. I'm sorry for the loss of your adoptive mother."

"Thank you."

"As someone who's been blindsided by such a dramatic personal past, you've suffered terrible losses, my dear. Not least of all, your very identity."

Even Marceline had never seemed to grasp the stark reality of her life.

"Thank you," she says again, this time in a whisper. "Thank you for getting that. Me."

He picks up his sandwich with two hands. Before he can take a bite, the front door opens and a voice calls, "Si? Sorry I'm late! I had to finish doing my Cinderella chores. You should see the list they left me."

"Jessie," Silas informs Amelia.

Breezing into the room, she's hardly the girl next door type. With the exception of her fuchsia lipstick, she's wearing black from her oversized plastic earrings to her combat boots. Her hair, sleek and short on the sides and long on top, falls in a side-parted swoop above her big dark eyes. Pert meets punk—a brunette version of Mary Stuart Masterson in *Some Kind of Wonderful*, the movie

Amelia saw at the Beekman with the guy from her psych class—back when Bettina was still alive, and still her mother, and Amelia herself was still . . .

Me. I was me.

Until the professor put it into words, she hadn't quite understood that she'd lost her identity. She's an imposter, and so are the people who'd raised her.

No wonder she needed to come here. She isn't just trying to find her birth parents. She's trying to find herself.

Jessie stops short, seeing Amelia. "Oh. Hey."

"Hi."

"Jessamine McCall, this is Amelia . . ." Silas shakes his head and looks at her.

"Crenshaw." She stands, the way Bettina taught her, and offers a hand to the girl.

For a moment, she just looks at it. Then she reaches out her own hand. She's wearing silver rings on every finger and a stack of black rubber bracelets. Her nails are stubs that look bitten, polished black.

"Everyone calls me Jessie," she says. "Except Si, when he's being all proper."

"As opposed to improper." Silas shuffles to the counter. "I'll make you a sandwich, Jessie, while you two girls get acquainted."

"I can make my own sandwich." Jessie is already opening a cupboard and grabbing a plate.

Silas takes it out of her hands. "I know you can, but today, I'm going to make it for you, because I think you're going to be interested in what Amelia has to say."

"Why?" Jessie looks from him to Amelia, clearly not the kind of girl who wants to sit around listening to a stranger's sob story.

"Because she's a lot like you."

"Oh, yeah?" She turns from Silas to Amelia, looking like a little kid whose mother just made her hand over the sandbox shovel to the new kid. "Are you failing English lit? Do you love the Ramones? Are you allergic to dogs? Does your college essay suck?"

"Uh . . . no?"

Jessie turns back to Silas. "You're right. We have *so* much in common."

"You do." Calmly layering ham slices on white bread, he adds, "Amelia is a foundling, too."

HEADING UP FDR Drive, Barnes and Stef mull the scrap of newspaper found in Perry Wayland's car.

"Now I'm rethinking that dead junkie on the bridge," Barnes admits. "Before, I'd have said Wayland wasn't capable of murder. Now I'm not so sure."

"A lot of people have macabre interests, though," Stef points out. "People research old crimes all the time. And serial killers have groupies. Even Ted Bundy got married in jail a few years ago."

"Divorced last year. Saw it on the news. Stef, you were around for the Brooklyn Butcher case. Do you remember it?"

"Not the kind of thing you forget. It was part of the reason the brass made a big push to get the new centralized communications center up and running that summer. Even the patrol officers got portable radios, and we started using 911 for emergencies."

"Did you work the case?"

"Not directly. I was Missing Persons even then, and all of those victims were accounted for, dead in their beds."

"Not the teenaged daughters, though. I mean, they weren't dead. He raped them, but they lived, right?"

"They all lived, and they were all pregnant. Boy, do I remember that. It was right around the time Judy talked me into trying for a girl. I thought it would be nice, you know, after three sons—but it didn't happen. She thought it was my fault. Like I wasn't trying hard enough. 'Even the Brooklyn Butcher is four for four,' she said one time. Nice, huh?"

"Four for four?"

"Four families murdered. Four teenaged girls raped. All four pregnant."

"I don't think I knew that part."

"Not all of them admitted it in the press, but . . ." Stef shrugs. "Four for four. And there I was, shooting blanks, according to Judy."

"Four rapes, four pregnancies. What are the odds?"

"Not good, statistically, but it turned out it wasn't random luck, remember? Wait a minute, you don't, do you? Were you even born in '68?"

"Yeah, I was born!" Barnes scowls. "I'm not a teenager."

"So what were you back then? In nursery school?"

"Kindergarten!"

"Oh, kindergarten. Sorry. So while I was chasing serial killers around, you were coloring with Cray-Pas."

"I thought you didn't work the case."

"Not directly, but you've got a psycho working his way across the city slaughtering families in their beds, everyone's on high alert."

If Barnes was in kindergarten in '68, Wayland would have been fourteen, maybe fifteen, sequestered at a tony Connecticut boarding school.

"Why the fascination with a twenty-year-old serial murder case? It's not like he ever lived in Brooklyn."

"I think you're reading too much into it. Maybe he wanted to read the Minnesota thing on the flip side. Maybe someone else dropped it in the car, or it was stuck to his shoe, or . . . who knows? It could have come from anywhere."

"You're right, it might not mean anything. But my gut tells me it does."

"Mine doesn't. Don't fixate on a hunch. File it away for now, because you might miss something more important."

It's the opposite of what Wash told him about a detective's intuition, but worthwhile advice. For now, Barnes decides to take it.

"This is your hood, right?" Stef asks as they exit onto East 125th Street.

Hood. Barnes cringes.

"You mean Harlem? Yeah, I used to live up here, and I have friends who still do."

"Good thing one of us knows his way around here. I don't want to get shot up trying to find the cleaning ladies."

"Housekeeper and nanny."

"Whatever. Just tell me where to go, kid."

Barnes would love to tell him exactly where to go, but refrains. "It's not that hard. Streets are a grid, just like midtown."

"Midtown's different."

"Different how?"

"Nicer. Cleaner. Safer. Better. No offense. That's just the way it is."

"Are you talking about the socioeconomic disadvantages people have up here? Or the color of their skin?"

"I'm talking about what I see with my own eyes. And about crime statistics. You want me to show you some? Because if you think I'm making it up, then—"

"No, believe me, I've seen them."

"Good. Then you be sure to watch your own ass when you're slumming up here."

Silence falls between them. Barnes chews his lower lip to keep further comment from spilling out, and consults the address Kirstin Wayland gave them yesterday.

"Turn right . . ."

Stef turns in silence.

"Up two blocks."

"Then what?"

"Then left—no, not there . . . yeah, here. . . ."

A few minutes later, they're knocking on the door of a decrepit three-story brownstone. Graffiti-covered rolling aluminum gates cover the adjoining storefronts. Jaunty Latin music plays inside, two different songs on two different speakers coming from two different parts of the house. Voices chatter above the music, and a baby wails. The door opens, and a delicious, savory aroma tumbles out, mingling with the carbon tinge of burnt toast.

Barnes and Stef flash their badges at the middle-aged man who answers.

He doesn't smile. *"Por qué estás aquí?"*

"Dónde están Maria y Milagros Ruiz?" Barnes asks, and the man shakes his head.

"Nunca he escuchado de ellos."

"What's he saying?" Stef asks.

"He's never heard of them."

"That's bullshit. Tell him—"

"I've got this, Stef. Okay?"

"Papi!" A little girl too old to be wearing a diaper— especially *only* a diaper—darts into the hall and wraps her arms around the older man's legs, peering out at Barnes and Stef with enormous dark eyes.

Barnes crouches and leans toward her. *"Hola! Dónde están María y Milagros?"*

She turns and shouts into the house, "Millie! Millie!"

The man shushes her, and she scoots away. Behind the man, a tiny, dark-haired woman pokes her head through a doorway. Seeing Barnes and Stef, her eyes widen in fear.

"It's okay," Barnes tells her quickly, and repeats in Spanish, *"Está bien."*

He confirms that she's Millie, and asks whether Maria

is here. Told she isn't, he asks if they can come in and speak for a few minutes.

Millie nods, but the man holds up a hand to stop them. *"Mantenerse fuera!"*

"Yes, we'll stay outside. That's fine," Barnes says.

Millie steps out, closing the door behind her. She's wearing only a thin polyester blouse patterned in green and orange palm trees. A brisk wind kicks a smattering of dry leaves along the cracked concrete, and she hugs herself.

"Tell her to go get a sweater or something," Stef tells Barnes.

He translates the command to a polite question, and she shakes her head.

"Are you sure? It's freezing out here."

"I don't have sweater," she says in broken, but precise English.

"Where is your sister?" Barnes asks. "Or is she your cousin?"

"Maria? She is *tia*—aunt. I am older. She is at her Saturday job. You are here about Señor Wayland?"

Stef looks surprised. "So you know . . ."

"Si. I know. I am not stupid."

"Who said you are?" It's a rhetorical question on his partner's part, Barnes knows, but the young woman answers it.

"Señora Wayland thinks we are stupid." She peers at them. "She told you that?"

"Nah, she thinks we're stupid, too," Barnes tells her with a smile, and sees it reflected in her dark eyes. "What do you know about Señor Wayland?"

She doesn't answer.

"Miss Ruiz, if you know something, you need to tell us," Stef says.

"Mrs."

"Mrs. Wayland told you something?"

"No . . ." She glances at Barnes in confusion. *"No soy señorita."*

"Ah, *Señora* Ruiz?"

"Sí."

Smiling faintly, he turns to Stef. "She's married. She wants you to call her Mrs. Ruiz. Not Miss."

"Where's your husband?"

"He is home in Fajardo, with my daughter."

"That must be tough," Barnes comments. "Taking care of someone else's little girls when you have one of your own."

"It is . . ." She seems to search for the word, but settles on pressing a fist to her heart, tight-lipped.

"What about Perry Wayland?" Stef prods. "What do you know about him?"

"He is gone." Her gaze is as shuttered as the check-cashing place next door.

"How do you know that?"

"Because he is not there."

Barnes speaks up before Stef can blurt something sarcastic. "What does Señora Wayland say about it?"

"To me, she says nothing. But she is angry."

"Angry?" Barnes echoes. "Not sad, or worried?"

Stef adds, "Angry means—"

"Angry! I know angry!" She gives an exaggerated scowl and wags her index finger in mock ire.

"You do know angry. Did you hear them arguing, then, before he disappeared?"

"No, I sleep here, at my room." She gestures at the upstairs windows behind her. "When I get to their home in the morning, he is gone to work."

"Every morning?"

"Sí."

"But you see him sometimes? And you've heard them arguing lately?"

"*Si*."

"About what?"

She shrugs.

"Why do you think he left?"

She throws up her hands. "How can I know?"

"Did he have a gun?" Barnes asks. "Do you think he hurt himself?"

"No. No *cojones*. He is . . . how do you say in English? Chickenshit."

Barnes bites back a smile. "So he'd be afraid to jump off a bridge, then, is that what you're saying?"

"*Si*. He make me kill spider in bathroom. Afraid of this, afraid of that. And the *señora* . . ."

"She's chickenshit, too?"

She laughs. "No! He is afraid of her, too! That is why I think he just . . . go away."

"Do you think he had someplace in mind, *señora*?" Barnes asks. "Someone to go with? Or to?"

She frowns, as if she doesn't understand—or doesn't want to say.

Stef gets right to the point. "Did he have a girlfriend?"

Millie looks down.

"Miss—Mrs. Ruiz? Did you ever hear of a Miss White? Señorita White?"

"No."

"It's important that you tell us everything you know."

"I don't know Señorita White."

"What *do* you know?"

"One night, I stay because the baby, she is sick, and Señora Wayland needs sleep. I hear *señor* on the phone, very late."

"What was he saying?"

"He say, 'I will see you when it's time, but not yet . . .' You know. Things like that."

"Who was he talking to?"

She shrugs.

"By any chance do you remember when this was?"

"*Si*. My birthday. My uncle, he makes a cake, and I miss the party."

"I'm sorry. When is your birthday?"

"On *10 de octubre*."

"About two weeks ago." Barnes looks at Stef.

Two weeks ago, Wayland was missing an old female friend and saying he couldn't see her.

Apparently, he'd since changed his mind . . . right around the same time he foretold the stock market crash.

AMELIA STARES AT Jessamine McCall.

Foundling?

Last night on TV, Silas Moss had mentioned that the young girl who moved in next door to him years ago had inspired his interest in DNA research.

"You were abandoned, too? When?" Jessie asks.

"1968. I was a baby, a few weeks old. That's what they told me, anyway."

"Who?"

"My par—the people who found me. Or so they say."

Never have Bettina and Calvin seemed further from being her parents. Mouth too dry to form words, she reaches a trembling hand toward her glass and sips the cider.

"Amelia's story is a little different than yours," Silas tells Jessie. "She doesn't have anything more to go on than her adoptive parents' word. It wasn't made public."

"So *your* life wasn't blasted all over the news? Want to trade places?"

"I . . ."

"Don't mind Jessie, Amelia. She's a little bitter." Silas says it with a smile, but gives the girl a stern side glance as he sets her sandwich and a glass of cider on the table.

Jessie plunks herself down. "Who wouldn't be bitter, having to grow up with the whole world knowing you were the baby nobody wanted?"

"That must have been hard. It wasn't much fun for me, either, finding out at my age, which . . . I mean, I don't even know how old I am. All my life, I've thought my birthday was May 12."

May, when the air is soft with the promise of summer, fragrant with lilacs blooming in the vacant lot. May. Mother's Day.

She swallows hard. "But that's just the day they found me. No wonder I never had a birthday cake. It shouldn't matter so much, right? But to me, it's just one more thing I lost. My *real* birthday. It's not just that I'm older than I always thought I was—maybe a lot older, or maybe just a few weeks, and I know that doesn't sound like a big deal, but . . ."

In the grand scheme of things, a cake and a day on the calendar mean so little—and so much. She studies her sandwich.

Jessie touches her hand. "Hey, it's a big deal. Stuff like that is a really big deal. Other people take birthdays for granted, you know? They just don't get us."

Us.

Amelia looks up with a grateful smile.

"So you never knew your parents weren't your parents until . . ."

"March," she tells Jessie. "I found out by accident. At my mother's deathbed."

"She died?"

"Yeah."

No polite sympathy from Jessie. "That sucks. She was

going to go to her grave without bothering to tell you the truth?"

"She did. She never knew I'd found out. How about you? You always knew?"

"Oh, yeah. Diane and Al are big believers in brutal honesty. Like, before they left this morning, Diane told me that she wishes I hadn't gotten my new wave haircut before I had my senior portrait taken, because she thinks I should have a more classic, timeless look. Do you believe that bullshit?"

"You call your parents by their first names?"

"*Adoptive* parents. Not to their faces, or when they can hear me, but they're up in New England looking at colleges with my brother. He's a senior, like me. They're seeing Harvard today, Yale tomorrow."

"Other way around," Silas tells her. "Your mom gave me the itinerary and phone numbers of where they'll be. She was disappointed you wouldn't go with them, by the way. Thought you might change your mind at the last minute."

"Why? Michael's a freaking genius. The colleges he wants to see are so far out of my reach that they might as well be on Beta Pictoris."

"On . . . what?"

"Star in Pictor," she explains—sort of—around a mouthful of sandwich.

"Pictor is a constellation," Silas tells Amelia, "and Michael isn't the only genius in the McCall family."

"Yeah, my sister, Michelle, is even smarter. She's a senior at Dartmouth."

"You seem pretty smart, too."

"My grades are in the toilet," she informs Amelia cheerfully, "except for the stuff I like. I have straight As in science. Too bad it's not on the SATs. I'll be lucky if I can get into community college with my scores."

"There's nothing wrong with community college."

"There is if your parents are Ivy League professors. Oh, wait. They're not my parents."

The brand of sarcasm is familiar, though Amelia tends to keep her own snide commentary to herself. Marceline is her only confidante these days, and irony isn't her strong suit.

"What are you, a freshman?" Jessie asks.

"Sophomore."

"Cornell?"

"No, I go to college back home in New York. I've never even been to Ithaca until today."

Jessie turns to Silas. "You didn't tell me she was just visiting! I thought she was one of your students."

"Is that why you're being so prickly?"

"You mean jealous? Sorry, Amelia. I can be a little competitive." Deep, adorable dimples appear on either side of her broad grin. "But I'm a real sweetheart when you get to know me. Aren't I, Si?"

"When you want to be."

Amelia can't decide whether to like Jessie, or not. One moment, she has an edge, the next, she seems vulnerable. Still . . .

If anyone's going to give her a pass, it should be me.

For the first time since she found out the truth, her foundling secret isn't isolating her; rather, the opposite. Sitting at Silas Moss's kitchen table, she feels as though she's stumbled into an exclusive club meeting and been welcomed with open arms.

"Can you help me?" she asks the professor. "If I give you my DNA, I mean?"

"I can take your sample and enter it into my database. If your birth parents, or even a close blood relative, are in the system, then we might get a match for you."

"Do you think there's a good chance you will?"

"A *good* chance? The database is growing larger every day. But it's nowhere near encompassing a wide swath of the local population, let alone New York City, where you were found."

Jessie adds, "And someone would have to be looking for you in order for you to find them."

Amelia's heart sinks, though it isn't really news to her. Deep down she knew, before she even came here, that the professor wasn't going to wave a magic wand and produce her birth mother waiting to embrace her.

A mother never forgets.

She so wanted to believe that it could happen, wanted to believe . . .

In magic.

If you believe in science . . .

She thinks of Bettina's doctor, who'd convinced her that modern medicine would cure her. Amelia herself had read through the medical paperwork, yet she, too, had been optimistic.

She's had her fill of false hope.

"Never mind, Professor. I'm sorry I bothered you. I don't—"

"Bothered me? Not at all. This just isn't something that's going to happen overnight, Amelia. It's a long process. It might take years. You'll have to have patience and keep in mind that your chances of a match will get higher as time goes on and more people enter my database and others."

"There are others?"

"Yes. I'll tell you more about everything. But for now, I'll go get the paperwork so that we can get a head start." He gets up and shuffles into the next room, calling back, "First thing Monday, we'll go to the lab and take the sample."

"Monday? But I . . ."

Was going to leave before then?

And go where? Back to Harlem, and Calvin?

"We can hang out over the weekend if you want," Jessie says. "Where are you staying?"

She bows her head, eyes swimming in tears, fumbling on the table for her paper napkin. It's bad enough that there's no hope of finding her mother anytime soon. Now she's stranded far from home, and . . . home isn't even home anymore.

After a moment, someone gently presses a soft, folded tissue into her hand. She tries to dry her eyes, but the tears keep coming.

"Hey, don't cry. Diane and Al are gone until Monday. You can totally stay with me, okay?"

Amelia looks up to see Jessie's dimples on full display.

"Okay," she says gratefully.

Chapter Fifteen

Biff Billington, dressed for tennis, doesn't seem thrilled to see Stef and Barnes again so soon.

Stef asks the obvious question. "Going somewhere, Mr. Billington?"

"Just down to Racquet and Tennis."

"Isn't that a private club?" Barnes is familiar with the exclusive Park Avenue males-only bastion that made headlines a few months ago for refusing to admit top-ranked female champion Evelyn David.

"Yes. I belong there."

Certain that's true in every way, Barnes watches Biff's face as Stef tells him there's been a development and they need to speak with him and Kirstie.

"How long will it take, do you think? I have a court reserved and I'm meeting someone," he tells them. "Did you find Perry?"

"Not yet."

But shouldn't he have asked that immediately? It's always a red flag when a family member fails to ask the obvious question—at least, in the expected priority—or seems to presume the missing loved one isn't coming home. But in this case, Barnes's gut tells him that Billington is guilty only of self-absorption.

At least he wastes no time today in rounding up Kirstie, along with her mother, Helen, a svelte older version of her daughter, with well-coiffed silvery hair. Seated together on the sofa, Kirstie and her mother are wearing white, too, but not for tennis. They're in silk blouses and pearls. The rich really are different. If Barnes is home on a Saturday morning, which is rare, he's in his rattiest sweatpants. "Mrs. Wayland," Stef says, "did Perry ever mention the Brooklyn Butcher?"

"The Brooklyn Butcher?" Kirstie echoes. "What are you talking about?"

Her blank reaction appears genuine. Her parents, too, appear taken aback.

"The Brooklyn Butcher . . . do you mean those murders back in the sixties?" Biff asks Stef. "Why would you ask about that?"

"What about Garrison Keillor, Mrs. Wayland?"

"The writer? What about him?"

"Ever read his stuff? Are you a fan?"

"Never read him. He's too . . . you know. White bread. I'm not into the wholesome, goody-goody Midwestern thing. I like literature with more of a sophisticated edge."

"Like . . ."

"Like . . . I don't know. Sidney Sheldon." Kirstie's pale brows furrow. "What does any of this have to do with anything?"

"That's what we're trying to figure out. Do you think Mr. Wayland read Garrison Keillor? Or listened to the radio show on NPR, maybe?"

"NPR? *Perry?*" Helen Billington emits a grim little laugh.

"That's a no, Mrs. Wayland?" Barnes asks, focused on Kirstie.

"That's definitely a no."

"What does any of this have to do with anything?" Biff asks impatiently, and Stef holds up a finger, asking his daughter if anyone besides her husband drives the Mercedes.

"No, I have my own. Why?"

They explain about the newspaper clipping found in Perry's abandoned car, and ask if Kirstie or her parents have any idea how it got there. They do not, and seem disturbed by it—even Biff, who has ceased checking his watch.

"Did you get any tips on the hotline yet?" he asks Stef.

"Not yet. It should be on the radio, and our local television affiliates are airing it on the noon broadcasts."

"Good. I hope it works."

Fifteen minutes later, Barnes and Stef are back in the car, listening to a 1010WINS report about Wayland's disappearance and the reward.

"Think we're really going to get anything out of that?" Barnes asks.

"Other than wild-goose chases? With a reward this size, we're going to hear from every nutjob in the city. Amazing, how low some people will stoop to get their hands on that kind of money. Or any kind of money."

Barnes finds himself thinking of his own father, remembering something Wash said last night.

"He stepped up and he made sure he managed to support you, even though . . ."

Even though what? he wonders again.

"You know he tried to do the right thing" . . .

Wash's phrasing—*tried*—implies that his father hadn't always been successful at integrity.

He remembers a distant day in the park.

"I don't ever want you taking something that doesn't belong to you, son," Charles Barnes said as they watched one cop handcuff a purse snatcher and another console the weeping near-victim. "You promise?"

"I promise."

"Good. I learned that the hard way. Don't make the same mistakes I did."

"You stole something, Daddy?"

"Once. Maybe twice."

"Did you go to jail?"

His father changed the subject. Or maybe Barnes did, seeing the look on his face and not wanting to hear the answer. He never forgot that moment or his promise, but that didn't mean he kept it. Not after his dad was gone. Not while he was Gloss.

Stef jars him from the memory. "Are you hungry, kid?"

"No. Why?"

"Bet you didn't eat breakfast."

"Bet you're wrong."

"Bet you're hungry again anyway."

Stef's right. That buttered roll did little to fill the gnawing emptiness Barnes would like to think is simply hunger.

Braked at a light on Broadway, Stef gestures down the block at their favorite lunch haunt, where the aging waitress flirts with Stef and gives Barnes extra scoops of ice cream on his pie a la mode. "We can stop at the coffee shop."

"No, that would take too long," he says, though his empty stomach rumbles in protest. "We need to get back to work."

Again, his thoughts drift to the past, and his father.

"You stole something, Daddy?"

"Once. Maybe twice" . . .

How did Wash meet his father?

Probably the same way he met Barnes. Only his father, by Barnes's calculations, was already married with a child when he and Wash crossed paths. If he stole something, maybe there was a reason.

How far would a man go to put food in his son's mouth and keep a roof over his head?

The light changes and Stef drives on. "You okay, kid?"

"Yeah." Barnes hesitates. "Yeah." Then, "No. But I don't want to talk about it."

"I lied. Maybe I can help."

"Got a spare hundred grand lying around?"

"Who'm I, Biff Billington?"

"Too bad we don't get the reward if we solve the case."

"Tell me about it. Do you know how many times that's crossed my mind?"

They park near the precinct. Out on the sidewalk, Barnes gestures at a food cart down the block.

"I'm going to grab a hot dog. You want anything?"

"Thought you weren't hungry."

"I lied."

Stef grins and reaches for his wallet. "Two dogs with onions and sauerkraut, and a knish. Make it two. Extra mustard on everything."

"Got it. It's my treat."

"For all that? Who're you, Biff Billington?"

Barnes holds a grin until his partner disappears into the building. His life would be a lot less complicated if he were a millionaire, that's for sure.

He turns and walks down the block toward—and then past—the hot dog vendor. This time, the pay phone is available. He fishes two quarters from his pocket, feeds one into the slot, and dials Wash's number.

His friend used to answer on the first ring. These days, it takes him so long to get to the phone that you'd think the apartment is a mansion, or that it has only one extension. There are three—the wall phone in the kitchen, and handsets in both the living room and bedroom, a Father's Day gift from Barnes. He wanted to buy him an answering machine, too, but Wash refused.

"Don't waste your money. These days, I'm always home. And if I'm going to be gone for any length of time, I'll make sure you know where to find me."

Barnes listens to the phone ring, and ring. He's about to hang up when he hears a click. "Hello?"

"There you are!"

"Here I am," Wash agrees, wheezing on the other end.

"How are you feeling?"

"Great!"

Guess everyone's lying today.

"What kind of trouble are you in?"

"What makes you think I'm in trouble?"

"Come on, Stockton. What's going on? Don't waste your dime."

"Quarter. Went up two or three years ago."

"For a phone call? Highway robbery. Tell me what you need."

"I don't need anything. I just wanted to tell you . . ." He breaks off, emotion distorting his voice like helium.

He clears his throat, pushes his register back down where it belongs. "I, uh, wanted to tell you about . . . the baby."

"Ah, the baby. Did you speak to the young woman's attorney?"

"I spoke to the, uh—I actually *saw* her. Delia."

"Well, that's a step in the right—"

"Wash, she was born this morning! I was there. Well, not in the room. But at the hospital."

"Well, well. Congratulations, son. A little girl?"

"A little girl."

For a moment, neither of them speaks. Barnes because he's again trying to shove the sappy frog from his throat; Wash because he's coughing and wheezing.

"Sorry. Happens sometimes."

"Maybe you should tell the doctor. Maybe—"

"He knows, Stockton. Nothing he can do. Now tell me about your daughter."

"She's tiny. Pink. Pretty. Her name is Charisse."

After my dad. But I'm the only one who knows that.

"You take some pictures to show me?"

Barnes is panged by the question, with its implication that he was there with a camera, like . . .

Well, like a real dad. A proud one, cigars and *It's a Girl* balloon in hand, with a snug, happy home waiting for the newborn.

"Stockton?"

"Sorry . . . my time's about to run out and I've got to get back to work."

"Wayland case is all over the news. Any breaks?"

"Maybe. We're looking into a possible connection to the Brooklyn Butcher. Remember that?"

"Remember it? I worked it. I was at the courthouse the day they convicted Oran Matthews. Listen, it's funny you should bring that up, because I was just watching the news, and—"

"Please deposit twenty-five cents," a robotic NYNEX operator interrupts.

Barnes curses and shoves the second quarter into the slot. So much for checking in with the hospital.

Wash is coughing again. Barnes waits for him to finish.

"Sorry."

"It's okay. What were you saying about the news?"

"One of the girls who survived those attacks back in '67 was killed last night, and her daughter, too, up in Boston."

AT THE TURN of the century, Sheepshead Bay was a seaside resort for the rich and famous. Even 1967 photographs depicted a picturesque New England–style fishing village. Now it's decidedly urban, with fast-food restaurants, vacant lots, and condo construction. Crime is on the rise here, as in much of the city. Broken glass and graffiti dot the landscape, car alarms yowl, and vagrants nap in doorways or push shopping carts.

The Myerses' block, once primarily Italian and Irish, has been transformed by an influx of Eastern European immigrants. Little has changed about the family's residence, a beige brick duplex where they occupied the first floor twenty years ago. But the backdrop, compared to the old photos in the case file, is almost unrecognizable.

Slavic tongues lace conversation. Russian Orthodox onion domes have replaced Roman Catholic steeple crosses. Storefronts have Cyrillic signs. It's easier to find a restaurant serving borscht and pirozhki than spaghetti. At the neighborhood pastry shop, cases once lined with trays of cannoli display *vatrushka* and *sochniki*. The corner bar serves more varieties of vodka than beer.

"Excuse me! Excuse me!" A young woman steps into Red's path, shaking a red-and-white can. The plastic top is slit, like the ones beside the cash register back at the diner. "I'm collecting for the Humane Society. Can you help?"

"No." Is everyone in New York City looking for a handout?

"Even just a nickel, or penn—"

"I said *no*!"

"Hey, you don't have to push me!"

Short-tempered, limping along on blisters, Red ignores her shout, thinking of the gun and relieved when she doesn't force further confrontation. Sheer exhaustion can cause even an ordinary person to do crazy things. For someone under tremendous pressure, racing against the clock to rid the world of false prophets . . . well, it would be dangerous to go on without taking precautionary measures.

Time for another pill.

Red detours into a small Ukrainian grocery. Here, too, slit-topped donation containers sit beside the cash register, begging spare change for charity. Don't those would-be do-gooders know it's too late to save themselves, or anyone else?

Too late, too late . . .

The blonde woman behind the counter has a broad, pretty face.

"I can help you find something?" she asks in a thick accent.

"Bandages."

"Sorry. I do not have. Goodbye."

Her wideset blue eyes are vigilant as Red searches the beverage case for at least one recognizable brand among the unfamiliar bottles with foreign labels.

"What else you are finding?"

"You mean *not* finding." Irritation crackles along Red's pulse points. "I'm *trying* to find Coke, something like that. I just need to take some medicine, and—"

"Not here! No drugs!"

"No, not *drugs*. I meant—"

"Go!" She waves toward the door as if shooing a gnat. "Goodbye! Goodbye!"

"It's just Tylenol, lady!" Red gropes for the bottle to show her. "I need—"

"Get out!"

Red stands motionless, facing the refrigerated case, pulse raging. Her reflection in the glass reveals a rigid, narrowed stare. Red's hand burrows into the jacket pocket, not for the bottle or knife, but for the gun. There are no other customers here. The door and windows are closed. Show her the weapon, grab the cash in the drawer so that it looks like a robbery, and something to swallow the damned pill . . .

And then you shoot her, and you're out. Fast.

Yeah, and later, when they find Christina Myers's body up the street, they'll think the motive for her murder was robbery, too. They'll blame escalating neighborhood crime, and never connect it to—

"Mama?"

A child's delicate voice pierces the roar in Red's ears.

A small boy peeks around the end of an aisle, holding a stuffed animal so beat-up that its species is not discernible. The kid clutches it close to his heart like it's the most precious, delicate thing in the world. Like it's his only friend. Like it's magical. He says something playful to the woman in their language. She answers with unmistakable affection, while keeping a watchful eye on Red, moving toward the door.

Stupid kid.

Back out on the street, Red dumps a white pill from the bottle and swallows it without water, just like earlier, back at home. Anything to banish dangerous exhaustion. Again, the pill leaves an acrid chemical burn. Again, Red ignores it, resuming the brisk stride toward the Myers house.

At the dry cleaner's, two men are loading plastic-wrapped garments into a van parked at the curb, leaving the small storefront empty. Beyond the glass, several collection cans line the counter. Inspiration strikes, and Red opens the door as though this were the intended destination.

"I'll be in to help you in a second," one of the men calls. "Take your time!"

Moments later, the man hurries in from the street as Red is heading back out. "Sorry about that. Are you here to pick up?"

"Yeah, but I forgot my item receipts. I'll come back."

"You don't need them." He takes a spiral-bound notebook from beneath the counter and flips through the pages. "What's the name, and when did you drop off? I can look you up in the—"

"That's okay, I wanted to clean a few other things. I'll go home and get them. Be right back!"

Red is out the door, carrying the golden ticket that will ensure admittance into Christina Myers's home.

Chapter Sixteen

Even now, Christina Myers finds herself listening for wedding bells.

For years, they chimed every Saturday afternoon at this hour in the steeple at Saint Paul's down the block, signaling the end to a wedding mass and the beginning of another happy couple's lives together.

Mom sometimes allowed Christina and her little sister, Allison, to walk over to Saint Paul's to watch the wedding party leave the church.

"I need you right back here, though," she'd say. "Don't get in the way, and don't wander. As soon as you get your look at the bride, you come home."

Christina would stand, holding her little sister's hand, on the curb opposite the old redbrick church, Allie bouncing from foot to jittery foot, waiting for the fairy tale to unfold. From their post, they could hear snatches of music from the ancient pipe organ. At the opening strains of Mendelssohn's recessional, the big wooden doors would open and out they'd spill—pretty bridesmaids in matching dresses clutching handsome ushers' arms, a dazzling bride floating along on a cloud of white lace and tulle, a groom who couldn't take his eyes off her.

Christina and Allie always stayed until the newlyweds had ducked through a shower of rice thrown by gleeful families and friends who lined the steps. Then they headed home, leaving behind laughter, car engines starting, tin cans tied to the bumpers rattling over the streets. Through it all, the bells pealed high overhead to celebrate another happily ever after.

"When you marry Billy, can I be your maid of honor and wear a pink dress and carry roses?" Allie asked one Saturday, close to the end. It was January, the church engulfed in snow globe flurries. Christmas wreaths still hung on the front doors and carpeted the slushy steps with dry needles. That day, the bridesmaids wore velvet; the bride a white fur cape.

"You're too young. Carolyn's going to be my maid of honor," Christina said, thinking that her best friend would look nice in blue velvet that matched her eyes.

"What about me?"

"You can be my flower girl."

"I'm ten! That's too old for a flower girl!"

"Well, it's too young for a maid of honor."

"Well, sixteen is too young for a bride. By the time you're old enough to get married—"

"Billy's going to propose as soon as I graduate. We'll have a summer wedding, and then we'll go abroad."

"For a honeymoon?"

"No, to live. We're going to backpack through Europe. London, Paris, Rome . . ."

"Forever?"

"For a while. And then we'll probably come back and settle down and have babies."

"Can I be the godmother, Christy? I'll be old enough by then."

"Billy's sister will be older," she said—cruelly, it seems, whenever she looks back. If only she'd known that Allie wouldn't be around forever. That she was about to lose everyone she loved—even Billy.

He was at her side on the cold February day when she followed the row of caskets out of Saint Paul's. Hearing the clanging high overhead, Christina realized there must be two sets of bells in the tower—one for mournful, measured funeral tolls; the other for glorious wedding chimes.

In the car on the way to the cemetery, she mentioned that to Billy.

"No, they're all the same bells, Christina. We played up there when I was an altar boy."

"But . . . they can't be! They sound so different than all those wedding days!"

"No, they don't. It's you. You feel different today, so they sound different."

Everything was different, that day, and forever after.

Billy stayed with her at the cemetery, and held her while the coffins were lowered into the ground. But the police were waiting to take him away.

"They think I did it, Christina! Tell them I didn't!" he shouted at her as they led him to the patrol car.

She couldn't find her voice until after they drove off.

"He didn't do it!" she whimpered to herself. "I know who did, but . . . I can't remember."

The man who'd killed her family and then raped her had worn a mask. She was there and yet not, lying beneath him in the dark, hearing his grunts and Allie's dying moans in the other bed. At one point, there was something—a whiff of fragrance in his hair, or maybe some note of familiarity in his voice when he told her to shut up and stop crying . . .

Clarity broke through the merciful haze and for that instant, she thought she might know him.

But she lost consciousness before it was over, and later, she couldn't recapture the fleeting recognition.

She knew only that it hadn't been Billy.

The police questioned him for a long time, and when they let him go, he came back. Once, twice, a handful of times. But his parents didn't want him around her, and he no longer seemed to trust her. She was alone.

Sister Anthony came to stay. She was Mom's aunt, and she lived in a convent upstate. They'd never seen much of her, but after the murders, she became Christina's guardian. Pious and unsmiling, Sister Anthony told her there was nothing to do but pray. So she did. She prayed for her family to come back, prayed for Billy to love her again, for *someone* to love her, someday, for the school year to end and when it did, for a way not to go back in the fall.

When she realized she was pregnant, she believed that her prayers had been answered. She needed that baby; needed to believe it was Billy's child, and not . . .

Sister Anthony sent her upstate to a home for expectant unwed mothers. There, she made friends with other pregnant young women, watched her belly grow, and thought about what she wanted for her child. Hers and Billy's. He would come back, and they would be a family, and she would be a bride at Saint Paul's.

Her son was born on Christmas, like Jesus, and she believed the child was meant to be her savior. Exhausted from the grueling delivery and drugs that numbed the excruciating pain along with her brain, she allowed the nurses to whisk him away, not realizing she'd never see him again.

"It's better that way," Sister Anthony told her later, after she'd signed the adoption papers. "He was conceived in sin and violence. You could never love him."

"But—"

She couldn't bring herself to tell Sister Anthony that he might have been Billy's son. It didn't matter. It wouldn't have changed anything. Guilt-ravaged and grief-stricken, she could never have wholly loved that baby, or anyone, ever again. She was meant to be alone.

That was her punishment for a sin so shameful that she had never managed to utter it in the confessional. And so a wrathful God had taken matters into His own hands with an agonizing penance.

At fifteen, she'd lost her virginity—not even to Billy, but to a senior who told her she was pretty. It happened at a party her parents had forbidden her to attend, but she lied about babysitting and went anyway, and drank forbidden vodka, and smoked grass. When the boy led her to a dark bedroom, she went willingly. The encounter was painful and awkward. Afterward, terrified of pregnancy, she swore to God that if she could just get her period, she would never do it again, until her wedding night.

Then Billy came along.

She not only broke her promise to God, but she went against the teachings of the church, visited the clinic and obtained birth control pills.

No wonder God was so angry. No wonder He had destroyed her life, robbing her of everyone close to her.

For almost twenty years, she's lived surrounded by reminders of what happens when you stray off the path.

The house is as it was back then, full of their belongings, and memories. Every day, she's forced to think of the people she'd loved and lost—her parents, her sister, Billy, her boy, and the life that was supposed to be hers.

She'll never have a child of her own, and so she nurtures lost, gentle souls at the animal hospital.

She'll never marry, but listens for the echo of long-ago wedding bells, though Saint Paul's was torn down a few years back.

She sits on the burnt orange sofa in the living room, the mantel clock clicking in time with her knitting needles. A ball of red yarn bobs alongside her as she pulls the strand. Christmas is two months away, and she's making mittens for St. Jude Children's Research Hospital, as she has every year for at least a decade. Before that, when she still knew all the neighbors, she made mittens for them.

During the bleak upstate autumn while she was waiting to give birth, one of the nuns, Sister Helen, taught her how to knit. It seems cruel, now, that they encouraged her and the other girls to make little booties and knit caps for the babies they were carrying, knowing they would never get to dress them, cradle them, love them. The clothes went with the newborns to their new homes, along with letters the nuns had the girls write to their children's new families.

"I don't know what to say," Christina wailed, still sore and bleeding from delivery, yet forced by Sister Helen to hold a pen over a sheet of blank stationery.

"Say whatever is in your heart."

She scribbled in black ink, so hard that the paper tore. She wadded it up and threw it at the elderly woman, who deposited it into the wastebasket and handed Christina a fresh sheet of paper. "Would you like me to help you?"

"I would like not to do this."

"Dear Sir and Madam . . ."

"Sir and Madam? Don't I even get to know their names?"

"Dear Sir and Madam, thank you for accepting this infant into your loving home. I am grateful to you for providing him with all the things I cannot—"

"That's not true! I can give him a home, too. And food, and love . . ."

Sister Helen got her way in the end. Christina wrote the letter and sent it, and the little white cap and booties, away with the little boy she never saw again.

She's never forgotten that day. Nor has she ever forgotten how knitting had soothed her during those awful months. She couldn't bear to make more baby booties, but she learned how to make a scarf. She used bright orange yarn, Billy's favorite color. She'd heard that he'd gone to college for a semester and then dropped out. By the time the scarf was finished, it was summer. And when she finally worked up the nerve to knock on his door, it was too late.

"Billy's gone," his sister said, glaring at her, and at the tissue-paper-wrapped package in her hands.

"Gone where?"

"Overseas."

"To Europe?" She was stunned, for some reason, that he'd taken their backpacking trip without her, even though everything had changed.

"To Vietnam."

Billy never came home. She later thought of him every time she heard the song "Billy, Don't Be a Hero."

He wasn't, she'd think. *Not mine, anyway.*

The orange scarf is still wrapped in tissue paper, tucked in a drawer upstairs. She never made another one. But she learned to knit mittens for all the neighbors, and a little sweater for the landlord's poodle, and a larger sweater for his Irish Lab. The neighbors were grateful and so were the animals, nuzzling Christina and offering unconditional love. Someone suggested she volunteer at the animal shelter, and at last, she found her salvation.

Her vet tech job barely pays the bills, but she spends her days nurturing forsaken creatures. Nights are harder. There's too much time to think. Too much time to listen, not for phantom bells, but for creaks and footsteps.

She never heard him coming on that awful night. Slept soundly through her parents' massacre down the hall, and even her little sister's slaughter in the bed across the room. The nightmare blindsided her.

Long after he was arrested and sent to jail—after she

knew he could never come back for her—she maintained a restless, prayerful, round-the-clock vigil. She told herself it was good training for the sleepless nights that lay ahead after the baby was born, yet unaware that some other woman would be stirred awake by her son's wee-hour cries.

Home alone at last, she listened for the baby that never cried, footsteps that failed to fall, wedding bells that—

A blast of doorbell shatters the hush.

Startled, she sets aside the needles and yarn and goes to the door. A human shadow waits beyond the frosted glass. Probably someone looking for the couple upstairs, who are away for the weekend.

Christina stands on tiptoe to remove the dead bolt key hidden above the narrow door molding, inserts it into the lock, and opens the door.

"Hi, I'm collecting for the Humane Society." A stranger shakes a coin-filled red-and-white can identical to the one she'd seen the other day while picking up her threadbare coat at the dry cleaner's.

Christina has nothing to give, but her heart softens as always, confronted by the reminder that one way or another, many are worse off than she is.

"Care to contribute for food and shelter for stray cats and dogs this winter?"

"I actually just donated to them."

"That's wonderful. Every dollar helps."

"If I could give more, I would, but—"

"Even nickels add up. And pennies. Whatever you can spare, ma'am."

Pennies? Fair enough. Some spare change might have fallen through a hole in her coat pocket lining she couldn't afford to have replaced. And she's seen first-hand the ravaged animals on the street.

"All right. Hang on. I'll see what I can find." She turns

away, looking around for her coat. There it is, draped over the back of a chair.

The Pendleton wool overcoat was her father's. Judd Nelson wears a similar one in *The Breakfast Club*. After she saw the movie a year or two ago, she went to the master bedroom closet, pushed aside guilt and her mother's clothes, and culled vintage menswear from her father's 1960s wardrobe. Now, even the hand-me-downs are threadbare.

Reaching into the pocket, she pokes her index finger through the hole in the lining, fishing around to find a dime and pennies that slipped through the other day.

"Sorry," she calls, glancing toward the door, "I'll be right—"

A hand claps over her mouth, another yanks her head back by the hair, and she sees a knife cut a glinting swath toward her neck the moment before it makes contact.

She drops to the floor, blindsided . . . again.

"HAVE FUN AND be good, girls," Silas calls after Jessie and Amelia as they head down his front steps.

"Don't contradict yourself, Si," Jessie calls back with a laugh, and Amelia wonders what she's gotten herself into as Silas closes his own door with a final wave.

Jessie points next door at the three-story white Victorian with a gingerbread porch, dormers and bay windows. "That's my house. We'll go there first and dump your bag."

"First? What's after that?"

"Fun," she says simply, and leads the way down the walk and over to the one next door.

"It looks a lot like the professor's house," Amelia observes, "except it's not yellow."

"Diane had a conniption when Si painted his place. When we moved in, it was a gaudy turquoise-blue color, so she was thrilled when he told her he was going to paint it. I think she was thinking white. You should have seen her face when she saw the yellow!"

"Why did he choose that?"

"He says it was because the paint was on sale, but I think he secretly wanted to piss off Diane because of the way she treats me."

"She's not nice to you?"

"No," she says flatly as they climb the steps.

"Who did all these decorations?" Amelia asks, gesturing at the pumpkins and pots of bright fall flowers on the steps. The doormat imprinted with a grinning jack-o'-lantern and reads *Happy Halloween*.

"Diane. Aren't they the cheesiest?"

"I think they're nice."

"Oh, please. You do not."

"Is she really that bad?"

"Yes. I mean, other people might think she's okay, and, like, Si is always telling me to lighten up about her, but I think he's just trying to get me to deal because he hasn't been able to find my real mom. The second he does, he knows I'm out of here." She steps back and gestures at the front door. "After you."

"Isn't it locked?"

"Around here? Are you kidding?"

Amelia turns the knob and steps over the threshold, expecting another cluttered, museum-like mansion, but this house is clean and much more orderly. There's wall-to-wall carpeting throughout, and the wallpaper and furniture are modern, in pastel stripes and pretty Laura Ashley floral prints. Instead of old paintings, there are photographs in old-fashioned gilt frames. Even at a glance, Amelia can see that Jessie is in most of them—solo school portraits, or posing with her two siblings, or with her whole family.

There are dolls everywhere—old-fashioned dolls in old-fashioned toy carriages, vintage dolls Amelia remembers from TV commercials, tiny, fragile-looking porcelain dolls smiling behind a glass cabinet door, and even a Cabbage Patch doll, so rare a few years ago that people rioted trying to get their hands on one.

"Are these all yours?"

"No. Diane collects them. Do you want to change before we go?"

"Go where?"

"Wherever. We'll cruise around town. Maybe see some people."

"Who?"

"Whoever's around. So if you want to change or freshen up or something . . ."

"No, thanks."

"You sure?"

Amelia nods and follows her toward the back of the house. The layout is similar to the one next door, but here, the wall between the dining room and kitchen has been replaced by an island with painted stools and a wooden butcher-block countertop. Everything is blue and white, from the wallpaper to the speckled pottery displayed on a shelf above the lace curtained windows. A framed cross-stitch design reads *Welcome to Our Country Kitchen.* The air wafts with a faint savory smell, and there's a big basket of apples on the counter, some with leaves still attached to the stems.

The refrigerator is covered with magnet-pinned post-cards, business cards, photos, and children's artwork.

She leans closer to examine a picture of Jessie wearing a black drape and pearls—her senior portrait. The word *PROOF* is stamped across the front, just like Amelia's back in her parents' closet. But this one has a canceled check for fifty dollars paper-clipped to it, along with a receipt saying the order will arrive in November.

Her gaze shifts to a faded drawing of two smiling female stick figures connected by ten carefully aligned fingers. Wobbly crayon letters spell out *To Mommy Love Jessie.*

"Hey, Amelia, let's go!"

She turns away and follows Jessie into a small mudroom and across another Happy Halloween doormat. Jessie grabs a key ring from a row of hooks beside the back door and they step outside.

Sunlight filters through high branches, glinting on golden leaves that dance toward a foliage-drifted lawn fringed by a dazzling red shrub border and colorful fall flowerbeds. Amelia takes in the swing set by the garage and the basketball hoop suspended above the door, thinking of the crack-dealer-infested playground by her apartment back home.

Jessie opens the driver's-side door of a Horizon hatchback parked in the driveway.

"You're . . . driving?"

"Unless you want to?" She dangles the keys toward Amelia.

"No, I don't . . . I mean, I can't . . ." She just shakes her head and climbs into the passenger's seat. When Jessie said they were going to cruise around town, Amelia had assumed she meant on foot. Back home, no one she knows has a car, and certainly no one her age has a driver's license.

"Do you like U2?" Jessie asks, ejecting a cassette from the tape deck, and pops in another.

"Um . . . yeah, sure."

"I figured you would. We have a lot in common, you know?"

Not nearly as much as she thought. They were both

abandoned, but only Jessie was rescued in the truest sense of the word. She grew up in this lovely home with a real family, while Amelia was raised in urban poverty, isolated by rules and lies.

"Bet I can guess your favorite song on *Joshua Tree*."

"Bet you can't," Amelia responds, because that's what you say, and she can't admit that she's never heard the whole album. There's no tape deck at home. She doesn't even have a Walkman.

"Here, I'll play it for you." She presses a button and a low, familiar rhythmic guitar intro comes from the speaker.

As it builds to the opening lyric about climbing the highest mountain, Amelia is relieved that at least it's one she knows.

"Was I right? Is this your favorite song?"

Amelia asks, "You mean because of the choir?"

"Choir?"

"The Harlem Gospel Choir just performed this a few weeks ago with U2 at Madison Square Garden. I know a few people in it."

"You know *Bono* and the *Edge*?"

"No! I know people in the Harlem Gospel Choir." Well, one person—a cousin of a friend who'd worked with her at the ice cream shop last summer.

"Amelia! No way! This is totally unbelievable!"

"Well, I live in Harlem, so it really isn't. Why did you think this was my favorite song if you didn't know about the choir?"

"Listen to the words!"

Jessie barrels backward out of the driveway and slams the brakes at the curb as a redheaded kid whizzes past on a bike, inches from the bumper. Jolted, Amelia braces herself against the dashboard. She's ridden in cabs a few times, but it never occurred to her to check for a seatbelt. She buckles herself in now, hoping Jessie won't be insulted.

Jessie doesn't seem to have noticed. "This is us, Amelia! We still haven't found what we're looking for!"

Amelia grins. Yeah. "I Still Haven't Found What I'm Looking For" is definitely her favorite s—

What in the . . . ?

She gapes at the familiar figure on the sidewalk opposite Jessie's house.

"Wait! Stop!"

Jessie doesn't hear her above the music or her own voice singing. As they tear off down the street, Amelia swivels to look through the back window, heart racing. How can it be?

It can't be. And it isn't.

The sidewalk is empty. No sign of her now.

But Amelia would swear she'd just glimpsed Marceline LeBlanc standing in the shadows of an overgrown shrub, the red satchel and woven basket at her feet.

"Okay, thanks. I'll fax you the pictures in a few minutes." Heart racing, and not from the twenty-five or so cups of coffee he's had today, Barnes disconnects his call with Boston Homicide.

Seated at the adjacent desk with his own phone pressed against his ear, Stef shoots him a questioning look.

He nods and mouths *Got it.*

"Something just came up. I'll call you back in a few minutes." Stef hangs up and looks at Barnes.

"It's true. Tara Sheeran and her daughter, Emily, were murdered sometime overnight, and her boyfriend is in custody."

"Mother's boyfriend, or daughter's?"

Barnes flips back through his notes. "Must be the daughter's, based on his age. His name is Liam Smith. He was sneaking into the house through an upstairs bedroom window when he saw the victims."

"Sneaking in? What the hell?" Stef rubs his mustache with his thumb and forefinger.

"Yeah. He ran down to the corner bar and told them to call the police. But it sounds like he's got a strong alibi leading up to that. They're looking into it."

"It'll check out, if history repeats. Back in '68, a lot of guys on the force were sure Christina Myers's boyfriend killed her family."

"They were the Butcher's first victims?"

"Right. His parents swore he was home in bed, and he was cleared, but not everyone was convinced he hadn't snuck over there in the night. Month or so later, it happened again—that was the Sheeran case. They hauled in her boyfriend, too."

"Alibi?"

"Home in bed, just like the first kid, and the next two," Stef says. "All four girls had boyfriends. There were crazy theories that they were in cahoots."

"The boyfriends? You mean with each other?"

"Yeah, or the girls with each other, or the couples."

"For what possible motive?"

"You name it. I don't think anyone was convinced at least one of them wasn't an inside job till they nailed Matthews after the fourth killing."

Barnes frowns. "Is there any chance they arrested the wrong—"

"Not a chance. Oran Matthews was a psycho religious freak. Thought he was the second coming."

"Like Charles Manson."

"Right. Manson might have been inspired by the Butcher murders when he went on that killing spree a year later."

"Only he got his followers to do the killing. What about Matthews?"

"Not a cult thing, just him. Confessed, convicted, sentenced to death, but in '72, when the Supreme Court decided capital punishment was unconstitutional, that was converted to life without parole. While you were on the phone, I confirmed that he hasn't escaped Sing Sing."

"They don't call it that anymore, do they?"

"I do." Stef shrugs. "Anyway, he didn't go back to finish off Tara Sheeran nineteen years after the fact. So who did?"

"Did Matthews have followers, like Manson?"

"You're thinking Wayland?"

"You're not?"

"He was just a kid in '68. What about the boyfriend in Boston?"

"He's a little younger than me." Barnes consults his notes again. "Twenty-four."

Stef spares him a joke about his age, asking, "What about the girl, Tara's daughter—she's how old?"

"Eighteen. Her name is—*was*—Emily."

"Then she's the kid who came from the rape. Oran Matthews's biological daughter."

"I didn't put that together. You're right." He pauses, thinking about the murdered young woman.

The Butcher's Daughter . . .

She entered this world because of a violent act, and she left it the same way.

He thinks of his own daughter, born not of rape, but reckless indifference.

The Heartless SOB's Daughter.

"Barnes?"

"Yeah. Sorry. I just . . ." He shakes his head, lights a cigarette, takes a deep drag, and goes back to his notes. "Tara and her daughter were going by the last name Kelly. The cops had no idea of the connection to the

Butcher case until they started digging to reach next of kin. Sounds like the boyfriend didn't know, either."

"Did anyone?"

"I get the impression that they've been living under the radar in Southie all these years."

"Bub had cousins up there. Not a great neighborhood. Maybe it was a random thing. Armed robber breaks in, mother and daughter get in the way. Maybe it had nothing to do with their past."

"Or with Wayland going missing Thursday?"

"I've seen bigger coincidences. Tell me about the crime scene."

"They found a set of muddy footprints to and from the bedroom window. Forensics is checking them out to see if they can match the boyfriend. Victims were side by side on the bed. Stabbed. Not shot. With a gun, you can take out two victims almost simultaneously—bam, bam—no one has a chance to get away. But with a knife? Crime scene should've been a mess."

"It wasn't?"

"'No sign of a struggle,'" Barnes reads from his notes, and takes another deep drag on his cigarette. "Maybe because they knew the attacker, and they didn't die at the same time. Could have been spaced out. Guy sneaks into the daughter's bedroom, kills her, waits around for the mother to show up, kills her, too."

"So it would have been premeditated, and the motive's not robbery."

"Right. But what is it?"

"Finish what the Butcher started twenty years ago," Stef says. "And that means the other three girls need to be notified."

"The ones who survived?"

"Yeah. I pulled this list together while you were on the phone." He hands over a sheet of paper.

Barnes scans the names, places, and dates.

> *Myers Family, February 13th, Sheepshead Bay—*
> *survivor: daughter Christina, 16*
> *Sheeran Family, March 22nd, Bay Ridge—survivor:*
> *daughter Tara, 17*
> *Costello Family, May 10th, Bensonhurst—survivor:*
> *daughter Margaret, 17*
> *DiMeo Family, June 6th, Dyker Heights—survivor:*
> *daughter Bernadette, 17*

Barnes taps his cigarette into the silty remains of his coffee, and looks up at Stef. "Where are the other three now? We need to find them and let them know they might be in danger. And what about their kids? If Tara's daughter was targeted, the others might be, too."

"Yeah, no kidding. I'm already on it."

Stef gets back to it, and Barnes goes through the pictures Kirstie Wayland gave them yesterday. He's going to fax some to Boston Homicide in case anyone's seen Perry in the area, maybe with a female accomplice. A variety of images would be ideal, but he looks virtually the same in all of them—wedding day, holding newborn twins, corporate headshot. Posed, poised, wearing his signature dark suit and a smile that never seems to reach his pale blue eyes, even when he was young and presumably in love with his bride-to-be. In fact . . .

Barnes takes a closer look at a candid shot Kirstie said had been taken at the annual Brown University Campus Dance in 1972. Unlike the rest of the crowd, Perry and Kirstie weren't feeling groovy. No bell bottoms and piped, ruffled placket cascading between wide lapels for him, no psychedelic miniskirt and plunging décolletage for her.

Maybe that's why he's looking past her, at a woman

standing off to the side. Her go-go boots, bare legs, big blue eyes, false eyelashes, and cascading black hair are a stark contrast to Kirstie's knee-length white taffeta and ballerina bun. She's wearing a cinched purple suede thigh-length coat with fake fur trim and appears to be on her way out, as if she has better things to do than drink spiked punch with preppy Ivy Leaguers.

Back in those days, Barnes watched *Soul Train* on TV with his father. In that outfit, oozing sexy attitude, the girl in the purple coat would have fit right in on the glittering dance floor.

Except, she's white.

White . . .

Barnes grabs a magnifying glass and leans in for a closer look.

Wayland is definitely looking at her. She isn't returning the favor, but her body language—coy posture, and the hint of a smile at her lips—seem to indicate an awareness of the man.

He's infatuated with her, and she knows it. I see her seeing the way he looks at her, but she pretends she doesn't.

Liz had been describing Perry Wayland's attitude toward Miss White, not the woman in this photo. Unless . . .

What if they're the same person?

Chapter seventeen

O n a high after Sheepshead Bay, Red takes the subway back to Manhattan.

Only one other New Yorker seems to grasp the
telltale signs that Judgment Day looms. A wild-eyed man
boards the downtown local. Barefoot, wearing ragged
trousers and a tattered army coat that reeks of sweat, he
looks like a panhandler. But he isn't asking people for
money. He's warning them.

"Repent! Repent, ye sinners, for the end is nigh!"

The other passengers ignore him, staring vacantly at
the graffiti-painted ceiling or burying their noses in the
New York Post, the *Daily News,* and *Newsday.* Ironic,
since the tabloids are crammed with stories about war-
ships in the Persian Gulf, unprecedented drought and
famine, the freak hurricane in England that took dozens
of lives, the mysterious epidemic that's killed tens of
thousands, primarily homosexuals and junkies—and
the pivotal event, Monday's catastrophic stock market
crash.

It was just as foretold in Revelations: *"Woe! Woe to
you, great city, where all who had ships on the sea became rich through her wealth! In one hour she has been
brought to ruin!"*

Preparing to disembark in the East Village Red offers
the subway prophet a couple of fifty-dollar bills and a bit

of advice, with a nod at the other passengers. "You can't help them. They're not believers."

"Do *you* believe?"

"I do."

"Have you repented?"

"I have, my brother."

They wish each other peace and shake hands. The prophet's is crusted with filth, Red's with dried blood.

The gloves! You forgot to wear the gloves!

The doors slide closed between them. Red watches the dark tunnel swallow the train, then heads out into daylight toward Alphabet City, where seedy gives way to disturbing.

Bent in rigor mortis, a young woman's needle-tracked bare arm rises from the puke-splashed sidewalk. A herd of bleary club kids step around and over her, faces smeared with ennui and eyeliner. Perched on the hood of what's left of a Ford Fiesta, a strung out street poet narrates an expletive-laced missive about zebras and marigolds. The car's hubcaps and innards are long gone, a parking ticket wiper-pinned to the brick-broken windshield and an antitheft device clamping the steering wheel like a condom on a corpse.

"Help me? Please?" A bedraggled panhandler in grimy fatigues and a black bandana do-rag shakes a change-filled paper cup.

Red stops short with a curse.

"Hey! What'd you call me?"

"Not you! I just remembered something." It's not just the gloves—Red left the collection can behind at the Myers house.

"I remember something every day!" the bum shouts. "No matter how much I want to forget, I remember a nightmare."

"Makes two of us."

He waves that off with a grimy hand. "You weren't in Nam."

"You were?"

"Got shot up good."

There's a dog tag around the man's neck. Something twitches in Red's soul.

Daddy had been part of the 173rd Infantry Brigade. He was mortally wounded in a Vietcong ambush near Saigon in November 1965. The news of his death didn't reach home until the following month.

Yeah. Merry Christmas.

"Help a wounded vet buy a hot meal. Please? I'm starv—"

"Here." Red hands him several of Perry Wayland's fifty-dollar bills.

"Thank you! God bless you! Bless you!" He scurries away.

The street poet breaks off his rambling recitation to say, "He got shot up over there, and now he shoots up over here."

"So?"

"So he's just gonna buy crack with your money."

"Not my money."

"Well, if you're handing it out—"

"I'm not."

Red moves on and settles in to watch Margaret's building, back to worrying about Sheepshead Bay.

How could you have forgotten the gloves? And left that damned collection can behind?

Come on, you know how. Because you were flying high on amphetamines—way too high, and you got reckless.

At least you closed and locked the door behind you when you left, right?

You did, didn't you?

Those damned pills are making everything a blur.

Beyond this nook, the block writhes with depravity. Rats scuttle around a ripped bag of fetid garbage. Junkies shoot up, trip out, pass out. Crack whores turn tricks in an adjacent alley. On the stoop next door, a drug dealer haggles with a pair of kids fresh from the suburbs. They're trying to play it cool in their acid-washed designer jeans and vibrant-hued Benetton sweaters with crisp button-down collars poking out, mullets combed just so. But they're in way over their moussed, blow-dried heads.

"We can pay!" One waves a wad of cash at the dealer.

The other, alarmed, says, "Put that away, Todd!"

Too late. The dealer whips out a switchblade and demands the money.

"What about the coke, man?"

"First, you pay."

"Give it to him, Todd!"

He does. The dealer grabs the cash, slashes him in the face, and takes off toward Avenue D.

"Oh, my God! Noooooo! I've been stabbed!"

The taller kid pulls a white handkerchief—for real?—from his pocket and hands it to his friend, who waves it around, shouting for help.

"Shut the hell up!" someone calls from an open window above the street.

A pair of young women, nostrils pierced and long hair spiked in Mohawks, stroll past, laughing.

"Stabbed? Yeah, right. Imagine what happens when he stubs his toe."

"Bet he really screams bloody murder."

Bloody murder.

Across the street, a grimy-looking man exits Margaret's building. Platinum hair cut in a gravity-defying shag, he looks like Billy Idol, in black leather, chains, and eye makeup.

Red steps out of the shadows and crosses the street.

The man has paused to light a cigarette. He looks up warily from the lighter.

"Do you live there?" Red asks.

"Why?"

"I'm looking for someone."

Silent, the guy blows a smokescreen between them.

"Margaret Costello. Do you know her?"

"No."

"How about Peggy?" That's the name Margaret uses sometimes.

"How come?"

"Is she here?"

"You a cop? Because—"

"I'm not a cop." Red pulls out folded bills. "I owe her some money."

"She's not here. I'll give it to her."

"I don't think so. Know where I can find her?"

"Not anytime soon."

"How do you know that?"

The guy hesitates and looks at the cash. "Fifty bucks, and I'll tell you."

Red shrugs, peels off a bill, and hands it over.

Another pause. The money came so easily he clearly wishes he'd asked for more.

"Come on, I don't have all day." Red thrusts another of Wayland's fifties into the guy's hand to speed things along. "Where's Peggy?"

The extra cash does the trick. "There was a Tompkins Square sweep overnight. They grabbed her with a bunch of other people. She's in jail."

As FAR AS Barnes can tell, nearly all the tip line callers are either nutjobs or people who, upon further questioning, have zero helpful information about Perry Wayland. Some are well-meaning; most, money-hungry.

Predictably, no one reported seeing Wayland jump from the bridge, but a number of witnesses said they'd passed the Mercedes pulled off in the right-hand lane on the bridge before roadside assistance arrived on the scene. Most said it was empty, though a few thought they'd seen a driver silhouetted behind the wheel and assumed he was waiting for a tow truck.

A truck driver, however, claimed to have seen Wayland get out of the car and climb onto the northern walkway now open to cyclists. He said he'd broadcast it on his CB radio—a heads-up to truckers behind him. A broken-down car on a bridge means delays.

"I just can't believe someone with a fear of heights would walk along that open span a couple hundred feet above the water," Barnes tells Stef. "I think someone followed him across and he got into her car. If we find her, I bet we find Wayland."

"Miss White, right? Only no one saw a second car pull up."

"True. But someone at the plaza in Fort Lee would probably have noticed a guy coming off the bridge, and no one saw that, either. He didn't evaporate."

"Wayland seem like a Jersey guy to you, though? What if he walked back to Manhattan? And when he climbed down that stairway, he ran into our friend Popper, who tried to mug him, and . . ." Stef points an imaginary gun and makes a shooting sound.

"Wayland seem like a badass vigilante to you?"

"No," Stef admits.

"He had an accomplice. That make sense. Look at this picture. See the way he's staring at her?"

"Who wouldn't be? She looks like a brunette Brigitte Bardot. That doesn't mean she's Miss White."

"See, here's the thing about that. We know Wayland and Miss White go way back. Far enough to have seen

Deep Throat together, anyway. That movie came out in 1972. Which is when this photo was taken. So the timing is right, and—"

"That doesn't mean this random girl in the background is Miss White, kid. Just because he's looking at her—"

"No, let me finish. It's the *way* he's looking at her. And the way she *knows* it. She seems . . . I don't know . . . smug. Like she's the one in control. Like she knows she has him whipped."

"If anyone has him whipped, it's his wife."

Barnes shakes his head. "Not like this. Look at his body language. He's stiff, turned away from Kirstie. Turned *toward* the fine woman in the purple coat. See?"

Stef looks it over. "I do. Maybe you're right."

"My gut says I am. I just faxed the photo over to someone who might be able to ID her."

"Who's that?"

"Friend of Marsha's who works at Sloan Kettering. She went to Brown around the same time as the Waylands. How about you?"

"Me? I didn't go to Brown. I'm a Harvard man."

"Hardy-har-har-Harvard." He points at the manila envelope in Stef's hand. "I meant, what'd you find out about the girls?"

"I got addresses and phone numbers for Christina Myers and Bernadette DiMeo. They're both local. Still looking for Margaret Costello."

"What about their kids?"

"DiMeo never had one. Lost it before it was born. Christina Myers gave up hers for adoption. Margaret Costello was photographed leaving the hospital with a newborn in '69, but who knows what happened to her?"

"Margaret, or the baby?"

"Both. There's not a whole lot of—" He breaks off as the phone rings on Barnes's desk. "Get that, kid. I'll go back to digging around at Records."

He walks off to track down more information about the Butcher's victims and their offspring as Barnes answers the phone. It's Marsha's friend Andrea.

"Oh, hey, thanks for calling. I faxed over that photo a few minutes ag—"

"I know, I got it."

Ah, modern technology. "That was fast. Did you recognize—"

"I'm working, so I can't really talk right now. I just wanted to let you know that I definitely recognize the girl in the purple coat. I'm off in an hour if you want to meet so that I can tell you what I know."

"Yeah, I can come right up to the hospital." Barnes grabs a pad and pen. "You're at York and what?"

"Sixty-Seventh Street. I'll meet you outside by the main entrance. For now, let me give you her name so that you can start looking into it."

"I'd appreciate that. What is it?"

In the background, someone is talking to Andrea. "I know, I am," she tells whoever it is, and then, "Gypsy Colt."

Barnes taps the pen anxiously, waiting for her to finish the other conversation.

"Hello?" she says.

"Yeah, I'm still here."

"Okay, I have to go, so—"

"Wait, you said you'd give me the name?"

"I just did. Gypsy Colt."

"Oh! I thought you were talking to . . . Never mind. So, the name is *Gypsy* . . ." He writes it down. "Did you say *Colt*?"

"Yes, it's—" Again, the background voice. "I know!

I'm coming right now! Stockton, I really do have to run. I'll see you in an hour."

With a click, she's gone.

Barnes reexamines the photograph of the woman in the purple coat. He's not surprised she'd have a crazy hippie name.

Gypsy Colt.

She might look like a gypsy, with her exotic beauty and colorful clothing, but if *Colt* is after the weapon, it doesn't fit the era's peace and love vibe.

"Who was that, kid?"

He looks up to see Stef standing over him. "Marsha's girlfriend."

"*Girlfriend?* So Marsha really is one of those, uh . . ."

Barnes remains silent.

"Never mind," Stef mutters. "What'd she tell you?"

"I got a name for her." He points to the girl in the picture. "But it can't be her real one. It's Gypsy Colt."

"Like the movie?"

"Movie?"

"Yeah, called *Gypsy Colt*. Judy dragged me to it when we were dating. I told you she was a nut over Westerns."

"So this was when, back in the fifties?"

"Fifty-four. We met at a New Year's Eve party. Judy was pregnant with Frankie Junior by the Fourth of July, we got married two months later. Want to know what I did on my wedding night?"

"I'm sure I can guess."

"I'm sure you can't. We listened to the last episode of the *Lone Ranger*."

"You mean watched?"

"No, the radio series. We couldn't afford a TV till the sixties. So there we were, parked outside a motel in

Niagara Falls with the radio on, and my bride was more interested in riding a fake horse than—"

"Horse!"

"Silver." Stef nods. " 'Hi-yo, Silver, away'—that's what the Lone Ranger used to—"

"No, I know, I mean . . . you're saying *Gypsy Colt*— the movie—it's a Western? So there's a horse in it?"

"What, are you kidding me? In the movie, Gypsy Colt *is* a horse. That's its name. What—oh." His eyes widen. He, too, remembers the slight anomaly Barnes filed away as a potential clue.

"Exactly, Stef. Perry Wayland has a horse tattoo."

NOTHING AMELIA HAS ever experienced can compare to this glorious afternoon. For the rest of her life, she will remember riding along in a fast car with a girl her own age at the wheel, wind blowing their hair through the open windows, music blasting, singing about how they still haven't found what they're looking for.

Except maybe Amelia has. Part of it, anyway.

Jessie has driven her around town and well beyond, along the inclined shore of the boat-dotted lake. They cruised past a couple of stately looking fraternity houses in Cayuga Heights, where Jessie claims to have "partied," and back down through Collegetown, a neighborhood filled with bars and restaurants.

Now they're on Cornell's stately campus. Jessie parks by a large brick building called Stocking Hall and takes her inside to the Dairy Bar, run by the Agriculture School and Food Sciences Department.

Treating Amelia to surprisingly affordable—and generously portioned—ice cream, she promises that it's going to be the best she's ever tasted. "There's nothing better in the world. You'll see."

"Isn't chocolate ice cream, chocolate ice cream?"

"Not here."

No, not here. Never has Amelia tasted such rich, creamy decadence.

"Wow, you were right. Why is it so good?"

Jessie smiles. "I'm always right. Everything is fresh. They have their own cows, and the students come up with the flavors. They're always changing."

Licking their cones, they stroll along walkways and broad greens. Jessie points out the stone building on the Arts Quadrangle where both her parents have offices and the brick one that's home to Silas Moss and the lab. Amelia doesn't want to think about why she's here, or what lies ahead, or behind her. She doesn't want to wonder whether Marceline LeBlanc—or maybe her ghost?—might be lurking nearby. The scenarios strike her as equally preposterous, leaving only the unsettling possibility that even though she made up for some lost sleep on that long bus ride, she's seeing things, imagining things.

"Hey, Jessie . . . is Ithaca College around here?"

"Of course! It's Ithaca, isn't it? You want to see it?"

She hesitates. "Yes."

They're off again, driving back through town, past the Commons, a blocks-long brick-paved pedestrian mall along State Street, and south along Route 96 to another campus. This one is more compact but equally scenic, tucked on South Hill overlooking the town and the lake beyond. There's no need to talk in the car with the music blasting at top volume, but when they reach campus, Amelia reaches out to turn it down.

"Hey! This is our song!"

"Sorry, I know, I just wanted to tell you something. I wanted to study music and theater here, and they admitted me, but . . . my mother said no."

Jessie's response is a predictable, "That sucks."

"Yeah."

"But it's not too late. Transfer here next semester. It's not like she can stop you anymore."

"My father can."

"You're eighteen, right?"

"Nineteen. I think. For all I know, I'm twenty."

"Then you can do whatever you want."

"Legally, maybe, but I'm so broke I can barely afford a bus ticket home."

"So you'll get loans, scholarships, a job . . . that's what people do."

It's what Amelia has done.

She doesn't argue when Jessie suggests they check out the Admissions Open House that's going on today. They find a parking spot up by the football stadium and fall into step behind a student-led campus tour. Noticing them, the handsome young guide introduces himself as Brody.

"I'm Jessie, and this is Mimi."

"Are you guys prospective students?"

"Mimi is."

"That's great. What are you planning to study?"

"Um . . . well . . . musical theater, maybe, but . . ."

"That's great. The performing arts building is our next stop."

It's impressive. Amelia can almost see herself on that stage, or singing scales in one of the practice rooms. Not that it's going to happen. But it's fun to imagine.

From there, they move on to see the landmark fountains, the new campus center that opened just two weeks ago, and the apartment-style residence hall now under construction.

Amelia thinks of her chaotic daily commute from Harlem to Hunter. What would it be like to meander instead from a brick dormitory across the tree-lined green to class in one of these modern academic buildings?

The tour winds back toward the admissions building, and Brody says they'll all go inside for hot cider and more information.

"Time to go," Amelia whispers to Jessie.

"No way! You can find out about transferring in January."

"I didn't say I wanted to do that," she hisses.

"Yes, you did."

"No, you said that I *could*, and I was just agreeing with you. It doesn't mean—"

"It can't hurt to just see what your options are."

Amelia wants to tell her that in this life, everything can hurt. That she has no options. That she has to go back home, back to her sad, unsatisfying life.

I still . . . haven't found . . . what I'm looking for.

The song echoes in her head, and rich, sweet ice cream lingers on her tongue. Maybe Jessie is right about this, too.

WAITING OUTSIDE MEMORIAL Sloan Kettering hospital, Barnes watches a man help a feeble woman from a wheelchair into a cab at the curb. He's wearing a tan Burberry trench coat that whips in the chilly breeze; she's bundled in a coat and blanket and wearing a head scarf. At a glance Barnes mistook them for mother and son, but he now sees that they're a couple, probably in their thirties. Her withered frame is ravaged by disease, sunken face devoid of brows and lashes and emotion.

"I'm not young," Wash had said. *"There are plenty of tragedies in this world"* . . .

They're playing out here at York Avenue and Sixty-

Seventh Street—people fighting for their lives, or worse, for their children's. How do they bear it?

"Detective Barnes?"

He looks up to see a slender, attractive woman pushing through the glass doors. Her shoulder-length blond hair is permed, with a puff of bangs teased high above a pretty face. She's wearing a jean jacket over scrubs and white Nikes—regular ones, not hundred-dollar Air Max.

"Sorry I'm late. I can never get out of here on time. And sorry I'm eating in front of you," she adds, taking a bite of an apple, "but this is breakfast and lunch, and I'm starved. Do you mind walking and talking? I have to get home to the dog or—"

"He'll eat a shoe? Poop on the bed?"

"I see you've met Krypto."

"Not in person, but Marsha talks about him all the time. You, too. You, more," he adds, as they head toward the uptown corner.

"I never know what she tells anyone at work. We try to be discreet about our personal lives, because people can be . . . intolerant."

"It's nobody's business who anyone goes home to."

What if someone—say, his daughter, and her mother—were to move in with Barnes? Not as a family, of course, because a family consists of a married man and woman and their children. A family isn't, say, two women and an enormous dog, or a man and a woman he once slept with and her—*their*—baby. But what if he lets Delia stay with him, instead of with her friend? Just while they figure out how to go forward as . . . some kind of cozy, untraditional, non-family?

No. No way. It's a bad idea. Head back in the game, Barnes.

He hands Andrea the original photo. She stops walking to examine it.

"Wow. There's a blast from the past. I haven't seen her since I graduated in '72."

"Kind of unusual that in a school that size, a senior would remember a freshman."

"She seemed older. Older than me. Older than everyone." She hands back the photo, and they resume their uptown stride. "Trust me, she was pretty unforgettable."

"Because she was so beautiful?"

"A lot of people are beautiful in one way or another, right? I mean, beauty is subjective. But Gypsy had a worldly way about her. This larger-than-life magnetism that made her . . ."

"Popular."

She shakes her head. "*Memorable*. Like I said. I mean, cheerleaders are *popular*, the girls who are class officers and in all the clubs. She wasn't any of those things. Not like them. Not wholesome, or cliquish . . . she'd wander, always on the fringes."

"Wander. Like a gypsy."

"Exactly."

"So it's a nickname? Not her real name?"

"I have no idea."

"Where was she from?"

"Somewhere down this way, I think—New York, New Jersey, maybe. I didn't know her very well. We hung out one night. It was . . ."

"Memorable?"

"Very." She smiles and takes a bite of her apple.

"When you say she wasn't wholesome, do you mean she got into trouble?"

"It's not like she was ever arrested or kicked out of school, but she sure didn't worry about rules or laws or what anyone thought. She smoked whatever she felt like smoking whenever and wherever she felt like doing it. Cigarettes, pot, God knows what else. And she didn't drink beer or mixed drinks like the rest of us. She drank Scotch."

"*Scotch*?" Barnes thinks of Perry Wayland's penthouse bar, with its row of high-end single malt bottles.

"The good stuff. Straight up. She never seemed drunk, though, or stoned. Gypsy was always in control, keeping an eye on things. On *people*. There were always a lot of guys around her. Women, too. I had a little crush on her myself, and I got the feeling it was reciprocated."

"So she was . . ."

"Bisexual? I heard rumors."

"College campus, the seventies . . . free love, right?"

"There was nothing that impulsive or whimsical about it. She was calculating. She knew exactly what— and whom—she wanted, and she always got it—him, her . . ."

"So if she'd wanted Perry Wayland, even though he had a girlfriend . . ."

"Oh, please. I knew his girlfriend. Wife, now. Those two were perfect for each other."

She waves her half-eaten apple toward the bins of produce along the sidewalk at a Korean market. "They were both bland as those bananas. Now, it looks like they've been fruitful and multiplied into a whole bunch. I saw their family picture in the paper this morning. Perry, Kirstie, and three tiny Kirsties. You're wondering if he ran off with Gypsy Colt, right?"

Barnes nods. "Do you know if they ever got together in college?"

"People talked. Perry wasn't really her type, so everyone wondered what she saw in him. No woman likes a blah guy—or girl, for that matter—unless she's pretty blah herself."

"Like Kirstie Billington?"

"Right. Gypsy couldn't have been as interested in bananas as she was in . . ."

"Apples?"

She grins and takes another bite of hers. "Exactly. There were plenty of interesting people around that campus at that time. Perry Wayland wasn't one of them. He was smart, but everyone was. Came from big money, but a lot of us did. But you could be in a room with him for an hour and you'd never notice him unless he stepped on your hand. That's actually how I met him."

"He stepped on—you mean your foot, right?"

"No, my hand. It was a crazy party. Not my usual scene, but a friend dragged me there. Not Perry's scene, either, he said. He wanted to go back to the dorm to study, but he said Gypsy wanted him to stay."

"So he stayed." Barnes nods. That sounds familiar. Even then, women were bossing Wayland around.

"Gypsy got him to loosen up, though. She talked him into trying a hit of acid."

"Why?"

"I don't know. For kicks, I guess."

"And he did it?"

"Yep. Then she got him to drive everyone out to the Cape in his car to watch the sun come up. He had this big black Cadillac convertible, and we all packed in. We went skinny-dipping at the beach. Gypsy was the first one in. It was September. She was tan with no bathing suit lines. We all noticed. Obviously, not her first time skinny-dipping."

"How about Perry? Did he do it?"

"He kind of had to. But he was the last one in."

"Did you notice whether he had a tattoo?"

"A tattoo?" She laughs. "No way. He was a pale, scrawny little thing, complaining about the cold water and worrying about sharks. Anyway, no one lasted long in there. We left and went to breakfast—Gypsy's idea. Perry paid—also her idea."

"So she used him for his car and his cash?"

"There were other guys with cars and cash. Way better looking, way sexier guys. But they probably weren't so compliant."

"Did Kirstie know about Perry and Gypsy?"

"If she did, she probably didn't feel threatened. She had the pedigree. Perry would have been disinherited if he tried to marry a girl like Gypsy Colt."

"How do you know?"

She turns to look at him. "Because I grew up the same way. And I didn't marry a Perry Wayland."

"Your parents disinherited you?"

"So they say. They're still alive and kicking, so time will tell. But if they did, it's worth it." She flashes a small smile. "Sometimes, a fortune comes with more baggage than you're capable of carrying for the rest of your life."

Before they part ways at the subway station, Andrea promises to put him in touch with someone at Brown who can share specifics about Gypsy Colt. Barnes thanks her, and she wishes him luck.

He eyes the subway. Downtown, or up? If this case were just about a runaway millionaire, he might go up to Harlem to check on Wash. Or all the way down to Brooklyn, and his newborn daughter. But what if Wayland had something to do with those two dead women in Boston?

At least Margaret Costello's not in danger. She'd turned

up in police custody, arrested for possession and disorderly conduct in last night's Tompkins Square Park raid. Right now, the Butcher copycat is the least of her worries.

Barnes spots a phone booth outside a deli, and he heads in that direction. His empty stomach is queasy from all the caffeine, but he buys a cup of coffee and gets two quarters in change. Outside, he feeds one into the phone and calls Wash. He'll be watching cable news, and may even have an update on the Boston case before it reaches Barnes through official channels. And he might have contacts who can provide information on the Butcher's surviving rape victims and their offspring.

The line rings, rings, rings . . .

"These days, I'm always home. And if I'm going to be gone for any length of time, I'll make sure you know where to find me."

Barnes hangs up and retrieves the quarter that clatters into the coin return. Consulting the number scribbled on a note in his pocket, he pushes the coin back into the slot and dials the neonatal ward.

"Hi, this is Stockton Barnes, and I'm calling to check on my daughter." Somehow, the word rolls off his tongue, unexpected fluency in a foreign language.

"What's her name?"

"Charisse Barnes."

"Charisse Barnes . . ."

"Sorry! Slip of the tongue. I meant Montague."

"Montague Barnes?"

"Charisse Montague." So much for fluency.

A pause. "I don't see any patients here by that name."

"Oh, you need the patient's name? Delia Montague."

"She's the mother?"

"Yes. And I'm the father."

"You said." Another pause. He can hear bustle in the background, and phone lines ringing. "There's no phone extension in the room, so I can't—"

"That's okay, I don't need to talk to her. I just wanted to know how the baby is doing."

"I can't release that information over the phone."

"What? Did something happen?"

"Sir, for all I know you might be anyone, and I can't—"

"I'm not *anyone*! I'm the father!"

"That very well might be the case, but—"

"It *is* the case. Look, just tell me if there was some kind of emergency with my daughter . . . She was just born this morning, and she was early."

Her tone softens slightly. "I understand your worry. I wasn't implying that there was an emergency, just that I'm not supposed to give out information about patients' conditions over the phone because there have been a few kidnappings in area hospitals."

"I know that. Can you just let me talk to Delia, then?"

"We're very busy here. If you'll hold, I'll find someone to go see if Ms. Montague can speak to you directly."

"Hold for how long? I'm on a pay phone."

"It'll be a few minutes. Five, maybe ten . . ."

He closes his eyes briefly, face tipped skyward. "Okay. I'll call back. I just . . . I wanted to make sure Charisse is hanging in there."

He pauses, hoping for reassurance.

"All right, then, goodbye." She hangs up, and his own words echo back loud and clear.

"I'm not anyone."

Barnes uses the other quarter to call Stef at the precinct.

"Where the hell are you?"

"Uptown chasing a lead on Gypsy Colt. She's—"

"Boston Homicide called. They found a cufflink at the scene. It was monogrammed PAW."

Perry Archibald Wayland.

Chapter Eighteen

Bernadette DiMeo-Anderson goes to church every weekday morning before heading to the lab where she works as a research scientist, and seven times every weekend: three masses on Saturdays and four on Sundays, including the six o'clock evening service.

That one always feels anticlimactic, populated by people who have better things to do on Saturdays, sleep in on Sundays, yet drag themselves here out of good old-fashioned Catholic guilt inflicted by a spouse, a parent, or maybe themselves. Bernadette used to be shocked to see the younger crowd wearing jeans at that mass. Father Joe, the older of the two priests, liked to comment on that. Father Dennis, the younger one, said he was just glad everyone showed up.

The old rules seem to be loosening up a bit, but Bernadette can imagine what her parents would have said about jeans at mass. Or about Father Dennis, who wears them himself when he's off. Bernadette sees him around the neighborhood sometimes, and he looks just like anyone else. He always smiles and stops to chat with her.

Father Joe never does.

That's because he knows.

She told him years ago, in the confessional.

Back then, tormented by the secrets and by familiar urges, she believed it was the right thing to do. As soon as she'd uttered her sins aloud, though, she knew it was a mistake. She could feel the judgment oozing through the mesh screen that separated her dark little booth from his; could hear it in his voice when he told her he could not absolve her sins unless she went forward and owned up to what she'd done. According to him, she had to make it right with the rest of the world, not just with him, and with God.

"Are you going to tell?" she'd asked him, alone in the dark, clutching her rosary beads so hard her diamond dug into her palm. She was still married then, and always turned her ring around when she left the apartment, so that no one would see the large gemstone and mug her.

"I can't reveal what you've told me. I can only offer counsel and guidance to help you do the right thing."

Bernadette had thought the right thing was going to confession. She hadn't realized there was more to it.

Someday, she prays, Father Joe—or God—will absolve her. Going to early mass every morning before work and all weekend, every weekend, may or may not help. Her divorce definitely did not.

When she left Doug, she hoped to have the marriage annulled.

"On what grounds?" Father Joe asked, and proceeded to run through the possibilities. Fraud, bigamy, willful exclusion of children . . .

Nothing applied. Not even that. Doug had never wanted children, and she couldn't have them. Not anymore.

Not since she was seventeen, when she'd perforated her uterus with a wire coat hanger.

Doug never knew about that. He just thought she was a feminist. That's why she's hyphenated her name. But it's not why she never had a baby.

Father Joe knows about the coat hanger. Knows the rest, too.

He never quite meets her eye when she files past him with the rest of the parishioners after mass.

"Enjoy your weekend," he tells everyone, standing in the doorway shaking hands. "See you next week. Enjoy your weekend . . ."

He says the same thing to her now. He said it earlier, too, after four o'clock mass, and knows he'll say it again tonight after the seven o'clock and another four times tomorrow.

"Enjoy your weekend," he tells her, grasping her warm hand in his cool, bony one, and staring at a spot beyond her left ear. "See you next week."

Does it count as a lie? He knows he won't see her next week. He'll see her in a couple of hours, unless something happens to one of them in the interim.

She descends the steps to the street, buttoning her old wool dress coat. It's warm—much warmer than the one she had on the night that she . . .

But she doesn't like to think about that, even now. So she thinks about the coat, wishing it were more fashionable. These days, everyone is wearing a straight cut, ankle-length dress coat with shoulder pads, or an oversized menswear look. Her coat is hopelessly outdated, knee-length and flared, with a belt and wide lapels. Fashion shouldn't matter when you're barely making ends meet as a single woman in the city. But it would be nice, she thinks, to have something new for a change.

She hurries down Eleventh Avenue, past meandering tourists browsing restaurants for a pretheater dinner. They should have made reservations, but nobody ever seems to plan ahead.

Nobody but Bernadette.

That's why she stops at the corner deli to get a paper cup of Italian wedding soup and half a ham sandwich for dinner. She's not hungry now, but she will be after the final mass of the evening, and this deli closes early.

"Want chips, Bernie?" asks the young man behind the register, and she shakes her head.

"Not tonight, but thanks, Andy." She takes the brown paper bag and heads wearily back out to the street.

The weather is changing. The zippers on her cold-weather skirts are a little tight. If she can't afford new clothes, then she can't afford to gain any weight.

Always thinking ahead . . .

The landlord is raising her rent on January first.

Her friend Sally, who lives in the apartment next door, is already planning to move full-time to her boyfriend's place in the Catskills. She spends every weekend up there as it is. Bernadette feeds her cat while she's gone, and she returns the favor whenever Bernadette leaves town for a conference. She's going to miss Sally.

"How about you, Bernie? How are you going to stay here?" Sally asked.

"I can't, unless I take a second job."

"I saw a sign in Macy's the other day. They're hiring weekend cashiers for the holidays."

"I'll check it out," Bernadette murmured, knowing it's out of the question.

Her Saturdays and Sundays are encompassed by church. Seven masses on weekends and five during the week might not preserve the roof over her head, or keep her from burning in hell for what she did nineteen years ago, but what other hope does she have for salvation?

THE CUFFLINK CHANGED everything.

Until it turned up at the Boston murder scene, Barnes wasn't convinced Wayland's disappearance was connected to the murders. The newspaper clipping found in the Mercedes could have been a fluke. And the timing?

Wayland goes missing, and women start turning up dead. So what? How many other people have vanished this week? Are they all suspects?

But now . . .

"It just doesn't make sense," Barnes tells Stef, finishing his cigarette as they cruise the Sheepshead Bay neighborhood, looking for a place to park. "How does Perry Wayland live his whole life as an upstanding citizen and then one day, just pick up and leave his family—"

"Happens all the time."

"I know, but it's the rest of it. Killing the girl a serial killer left behind twenty years ago? *And* her kid?"

Stef shrugs. "You never know what people are hiding."

"If Wayland did something like that to his own wife, I'd understand."

"Yeah, she's a real—"

"No, just . . . it happens. Crime of passion. But how's he connected to Tara and Emily? What does he have to do with the Brooklyn Butcher case? What triggered him to revisit it now?"

"Stock market crashed."

"Except, he saw it coming and protected himself. So if Black Monday was the trigger, it's for another reason. And the cufflink feels off. Any other random belonging dropped at the scene—anything, loose change, a key, a glove—those things aren't going to point to Wayland right away. But something engraved with his initials?"

"You're right. It seems too pat. So you think someone's trying to frame him. Hey, there's a spot." He brakes and backs up.

"That's too small. You can't park this tank in there."

"Watch me."

With guidance from Barnes on the curb, and considerable maneuvering, Stef does manage to wedge the sedan between a delivery truck and a Plymouth Volaré. He climbs out of the car huffing as if he's just run a marathon, and points at a pair of striking young women talking to a man on a nearby stoop.

"Is that the Polish chick who was just on the cover of *Playboy*?"

"You mean Paulina Porizkova?" Barnes peers at the taller of the two, her long hair flowing, long limbs bared despite the chill. "She's Czechoslovakian, by the way."

"Same difference."

"No, it's not the same dif—"

"Whatever. That's her."

"No, it's not!"

Stef turns to look at him. "You never got that hot dog, kid."

"What?"

"You skipped lunch. Low blood sugar. It makes you crabby."

"I'm not—"

"Go in there and get yourself a bag of chips." He points to a small Ukrainian grocery on the corner. "Make it two—I want barbecue—and a Diet Coke. I'll wait here." He leans against the car hood, facing the two young women.

Not hungry, but glad for a momentary reprieve, Barnes heads into the store.

A blonde woman greets him somewhat warily from behind the counter. A little boy kneels on the floor nearby. He shares her high cheekbones and coloring but not her reticence, impishly brandishing a ragged stuffed animal with a mock-ferocious roar.

"Uh-oh, buddy. Looks like a fierce . . . what is he, a bear?" Barnes asks the child.

The mother is beside them in a flash, with a protective hand on the boy's shoulder.

"What you need finding, mister?"

"Just a snack, and a Diet Coke."

The word has triggered something in her. She shakes her head rapidly and steps between Barnes and the boy, casting a nervous glance toward the street. "Not here."

"That's all right, I just need . . ." He pauses, unnerved by the distress in her wide-set blue eyes. "Is everything all right, ma'am?"

"Who sent you?"

"Who sent me? No one sent me, I just . . ." He reaches into his pocket, wanting to reassure her, but succeeds only in terrifying her further.

She cries out—then sees the badge in his hand.

"I am sorry. I think you have gun, like before. Like . . . evil here—before. Today."

"I'm a police officer. Did someone rob you? Or try to hurt you?"

"No, because I say . . ." Her voice becomes loud and sharp. "*Get out! Go away!* And then . . ." She points to the door and waggles two fingers to indicate the culprit running off down the street. "Goes away."

"Good for you." Barnes nods at her and flashes a smile at the undaunted little boy. "Your mom is pretty fierce, too, buddy."

Back out on the street, Stef is looking impatient, and the young women have disappeared. Barnes hands him a small bag and a plastic bottle, both with foreign labels.

"What the hell is this?"

"Cherry juice and fried bacon skins."

"Don't they have any American food in there?"

"American food, Ukrainian food . . . same difference."

"Wiseass. Let's go." Stef thrusts the snacks back at him. "What happened to your friend Paulina?"

"It wasn't her. Just some kid going door to door collecting for UNICEF."

"No way, really?"

Barnes crunches his way through a bag of salty greasy goodness as they head down the street past a bakery, a pub, and a dry cleaner, all doing a brisk business as the day winds down.

There it is—the house where the Myers family was massacred in 1968.

They ascend the steps and Stef presses the bell.

After a wait, he presses it again.

It looks like Christina isn't home.

Stef knocks on the door, then leans into the glass pane, hands cupped above his eyebrows.

"What the—" He jumps back and looks at Barnes, eyes wide. "Call for backup. We're too damned late. He got her."

"THIS IS CRAZY," Amelia tells Jessie as they follow Brody up the steps to the admissions building. "Why are we doing this?"

"Because you wanted to come here."

"No, I didn't."

"Then why did you apply?"

"My high school music teacher told me I should."

Brody and the tour disappear into the admissions building. Amelia holds back, grabbing Jessie's arm.

"I don't think I can do this."

"You can't say that about something you're already doing." Jessie pushes open the door and holds it for her. "Come on, Mimi."

"Mimi?"

"Doesn't anyone call you that?"

"Never."

"Well, I do."

They step over the threshold.

Inside, they find several information tables staffed by

students and faculty. Jessie propels her toward the nearest one.

"This is crazy."

"I love doing crazy things, don't you?"

"No! I never do crazy things."

"So running away today wasn't—"

"I didn't run away from anything."

"No?"

"No. I . . . ran *to* something."

"Exactly. You ran here."

"To Silas Moss. Not—"

"Hello, ladies. Can I help you?" asks the woman seated at the table.

Amelia shakes her head, but Jessie says, "I'm looking for information about transferring here for the spring semester."

"Wonderful. Go right over there and speak to the man in the blue sweater vest."

Jessie thanks her and drags Amelia toward him.

"Let's get out of here! I don't want to speak to anyone," she hisses.

"I know, that's why I'm doing it for you. We're a good team. I'll talk, you listen."

That's exactly what happens. The man tells Jessie that she doesn't have to apply again to gain admission next semester. She just has to fill out paperwork to reactivate her status and send her transcripts. And she has to do it in the next few days if she wants to come here in January.

"Don't worry, I will," Jessie says cheerfully.

Ten minutes later, they're back in the car with transfer student pamphlets, release forms, and a thick financial aid department packet.

"See? You're all set."

"For what?"

"For moving to Ithaca in January."

Jessie pulls back out onto the highway. Amelia flips through the pamphlet. She really could do this if she wanted to . . .

Do I?

"Amelia?"

"Yeah?"

"There's one last stop on my tour," Jessie tells her. "Ready to see my suicide bridge?"

BARNES STANDS BACK by the door as the forensics team photographs what remains of Christina Myers.

Rigor mortis has yet to set in, indicating that she was murdered within the past few hours. Stef is out front with a couple of the homicide detectives, calling around to track down Bernadette DiMeo and Margaret Costello.

Christina wasn't just stabbed, but viciously mutilated, her face beyond recognition. Trying to envision Perry Wayland inflicting those brutal wounds in a knife-thrusting rage, Barnes flinches at the gore and turns away, bacon rinds and cherry juice churning in his gut.

There was no indication of forced entry. The house has been ransacked, but it's impossible to tell if anything is missing, and it doesn't look like a break-in. The front door was unlocked, the key protruding from the interior dead bolt.

Something catches his eye, sitting on a table just inside the door.

Frowning, he leans over to examine the charity collection can. He'd noticed several similar ones on the counter in the Ukrainian grocery store. He thinks of the young clerk, rattled by an "evil" would-be robber who'd run off toward the Myers house this afternoon. Of the young girls down the block, collecting door-to-door for UNICEF.

"Detective?" he calls to the lead investigator. "I think I know how the perp got in."

Five minutes later, he and Stef duck under the yellow crime scene tape surrounding the Myers home and stride down the street, past the lineup of vehicles with flashing lights and a throng of curious neighbors.

"Bet Margaret Costello never thought getting hauled into jail would be the luckiest thing that ever happened to her," Stef comments. "I just hope they get to Bernadette DiMeo in time."

She lives in Chelsea, and still isn't answering her phone. A couple of officers are on their way to check on her.

This time, the young blonde woman smiles when Barnes comes through the door of the Ukrainian market.

"Hello! You are liking treats from my country? You want to buy more?"

"They were great, thanks, but we're here on an investigation." He and Stef flash their badges and introduce themselves.

The woman's name is Anna Oliynyk. She and her son live above the store with her father, who owns it.

"We need to ask you some questions about the attempted robbery, ma'am," Stef says.

"Not robbery."

She shoots a worried glance over her shoulder. Barnes spots the little boy curled up in a playpen, asleep, hugging his stuffed animal close to his chubby chin. Kids are really something. Pure and innocent in a world that's anything but.

"Tell us what happened, Anna," he says. "About the evil man."

"No, not evil man."

Stef looks at Barnes. "What's going on?"

Like he knows.

"Ms. Oliynyk, when I was in here before, you said that

a bad man was here with a gun, and you had a feeling . . ." She's still shaking her head. "So that didn't happen? The evil—"

"Yes, happened! I know evil. I get very bad feeling here." She pats her head. "Crazy eyes. On drugs."

Stef shows her a missing persons flyer with the close-up of Perry Wayland.

"Is this your crazy, evil man?"

She barely glances at it. "Not *mine*! Not—"

"Oh, for the love of . . ." Stef glares. "Fine. Not yours. Is this *the* crazy, evil man?"

Anna glares back. "Not *man*. She was *woman*."

Chapter Nineteen

I s this your bridge?" Amelia asks Jessie as they get out
of the car on Thurston Avenue, alongside a stone span.
It stretches high above a deep, wooded gorge with a
waterfall spilling over rocks far below.

"No. Mine's up there, in the woods."

Hands shoved in her jacket pockets, head down, she
leads Amelia on a silent trek up a steep trail toward the
span. The air is thick with damp must, alive with drifting
leaves and rushing water. They pass a couple of hikers,
and an older man with a big dog straining to get off his
leash. The animal's eager movements rain clumps of dirt
and pebbly showers over the edge in a way that makes
Amelia shudder.

"That's it," Jessie says, pointing at a narrow, rickety-
looking pedestrian span up ahead.

"It's beautiful. We're not going across it, are we?"

"What's wrong? You can't be afraid of heights. You live
in New York City, with, like, the Empire State Building
and everything."

"It's not like I've ever been up there."

"Are you kidding?"

"Tourists do that."

"So you've never been in a skyscraper?"

"Yes, but . . ." She stares at the bridge. "That isn't a
skyscraper. It's wide open. And if you fell, you'd die."

"No kidding. That's why it's the Suicide Bridge."

"That's the name of it?"

"It's what I call it, because people—students, mostly—have been killing themselves here for over a century. It's kind of our thing here in Ithaca."

"It happens in New York, too. People jump from bridges. And buildings. In front of the subway, too," she adds, remembering how she had to walk all the way home from school—wow. Was that really only yesterday?

"That's disgusting and gory. I would never jump in front of a train. Not even back when I wanted to kill myself," Jessie says matter-of-factly.

"You wanted to *kill yourself*?"

She gives a vigorous nod. "No one knows about it but Si, and now you. He says I didn't really want to die. He thinks I was just angry and upset. But how would he know? He's not that kind of doctor. He's a scientist, not a shrink. Did you ever think about killing yourself?"

"Never."

"Well, sometimes, when you're really miserable, you just want the pain to end."

After a moment of uncomfortable silence, Amelia asks her why she was so miserable, pretty sure she can guess.

The answer surprises her. "My boyfriend broke up with me. Out of nowhere. After three months of going out. He, like, called me up one night and said he didn't want to go out with me anymore."

"So you were . . . ?"

"Suicidal. Yeah."

"And it didn't have anything to do with being . . . you know . . . a foundling?"

Jessie's laugh is bitterly cavalier. "Not everything does, you know. Not for me, anyway."

Amelia isn't entirely sure she believes that.

"Anyway, after Ryan dumped me, I'd come out here and think about throwing myself over the edge. I would have done it right over there." She points to the middle of the bridge. "The exact spot where I was abandoned."

And that has nothing to do with being a foundling, huh?

"If you stare down at the waterfall long enough, you feel like you just want to be a part of it. So powerful, you know? Just rushing away . . ."

Jessie falls silent for a long moment. Then she grabs Amelia's hand and tugs her toward the bridge. "Come on, Mimi. You made it this far. I have to show you the spot."

"Is THIS THE woman who was here?" Barnes asks, showing Anna Oliynyk the photo of Gypsy Colt.

She dismisses it as quickly as she did Perry Wayland. "No."

"Not so fast!" Stef's voice, loud and gruff, triggers a rustling in the playpen.

The little boy sits up, rubbing his eyes and emitting a wail. His mother promptly reaches for him.

"Ms. Oliynyk! We need you to take a closer look at the picture."

"Stef, will you let her pick up the baby?"

"You need to tell her that this isn't a current picture. She's not going to look the same."

"Anna?"

She turns back to them, the little boy resting his head against her shoulder, sucking his thumb.

"Can you please take a closer look? This woman would be older now. In her thirties."

She obliges and shakes her head. "Not her."

"You're sure?" Stef asks.

"Yes!"

So much for Barnes's theory that Gypsy Colt and Miss White are the same person—if it was, indeed, Miss White who came in here earlier. There's a chance that the incident wasn't connected with Christina's murder, but Anna's description makes him think otherwise. The carnage down the block is nothing if not *evil*.

"Can you please describe the woman?" he asks, pen poised on his notepad. "How old was she?"

"Like me."

"Your age. Twenty-two? Are you sure? Not older?"

"Maybe twenty-three, twenty-four . . ."

"Not in her thirties, or older?"

"Not older."

As decisive about this as about the rest, she'd be a perfect witness if not for the language barrier. When he asks for a physical description, it comes gradually, with fumbling and gestures, but it's concise. She tells him the woman was white, about five-four, had a stocky build, short dark hair, and gray eyes. With more effort, Anna relates that the suspect had a bandage on her thumb, and wore jeans, a jean jacket, and white sneakers. But she's still trying to convey something else, something important.

"She have . . . How you say?" Anna points to her face. "Red."

"Makeup? Blush?" Barnes suggests.

"No, no, not . . ." She frowns, still pointing. "Red!"

"Pimples? Acne? A rash?"

"No!"

"What the hell is she trying to say, Barnes?"

"I don't know. Just let her talk!"

"She's not saying anything!"

Equally frustrated, Anna is searching for the right word. "Red. Big hurt. Old hurt."

"Old hurt . . ." Barnes turns to Stef. "Show her your gut!"

"What?"

"Where you were knifed! Show her!"

The light dawns. Stef opens his jacket and pulls up his shirt.

"Like that, Anna?" Barnes points at the gash in the roll of fatty gut.

"Yes! Yes, like that! But right here!" She touches her face with her thumb and forefinger to indicate the size and location of the large red scar on the suspect's right cheek.

TURNING ONTO WEST Twenty-Ninth Street, Bernadette thinks of how good it would feel to change into sweatpants and curl up with her supper, her cat, and whatever's on TV. Instead, she'll take a break, and then head back out to church. She's been thinking about that job at Macy's, wondering if it might be time to ease up on her weekend mass schedule. She'd still go, of course—as often as possible. But if she doesn't find a part-time job, she's going to wind up homeless.

Unless she pays a finder's fee, she'll never find monthly rent cheaper than what she pays for her small top-floor apartment in this six-story redbrick apartment building.

"Ma'am, are you Bernadette DiMeo?" A pair of uniformed police officers step from the shadows beneath the fire escape. Both are young, one an attractive Hispanic woman, the other a rugged-jawed guy with a sandy crew cut.

"DiMeo-Anderson. Yes. Did something happen?"

"We're making sure you're all right, ma'am. There have been a couple of incidents . . ." The male looks to the female officer.

"What kind of incidents? Was there a break-in in the building?"

"No, not in the building. But violent crimes have been committed against three women you have ties to."

"What? Who?" She thinks of Sally, and her colleagues at the lab.

"Christina Myers, Tara Sheeran, and her daughter, Emily."

Bernadette reaches out to clasp the cold metal railing with her shaking hand. "What . . . what happened to them?"

"They are deceased, ma'am. I'm sorry."

"Deceased? You mean . . . murdered?"

Both officers nod.

"What about Margaret Costello?" Bernadette hadn't really known the others, but Margaret . . .

"She's unharmed and in custody."

"Are you taking me into protective custody, too?"

They look at each other and shake their heads.

"She isn't in protective custody," the female officer explains. "She just happened to be picked up last night in a raid."

Probably not for the first time, Bernadette guesses.

"Who killed the others?"

"The suspect is still at large, but we do have a description." They ask her about a stocky brunette who has a red scar on her right cheek.

"I've never seen her, no. I have no idea who that is."

"We're keeping an eye out for her."

"That's why you're here? You think she's coming?" Wide-eyed, she looks from one to the other.

"If she does, we'll be here. One of us will keep the building's exterior under surveillance, and the other will be posted right outside your door."

"What about . . . am I allowed to leave?"

"We wouldn't advise it. Why? Do you have someplace to go?"

She thinks of mass. Just this once, she has good reason to skip it.

"No," she tells them. "I'll stay home."

AFTER ISSUING AN APB for the female suspect, Barnes and Stef learn that Anna Oliynyk isn't the only Sheepshead Bay witness to have had a run-in with her.

A dry cleaner up the street had called the police earlier to claim that a woman fitting her description had stolen his Humane Society collection can. He'd reportedly apologized for bothering them with what seemed at the time like a petty crime. He, too, saw her head up the block toward the Myers house.

The NYPD is staking out both Margaret Costello's apartment in the East Village and Bernadette DiMeo's apartment in Chelsea. The media has blasted out a BOLO—*be on the lookout*—for the female suspect, stressing the most identifiable characteristic—the red scar on her cheek.

With a description like that, it's only a matter of time before someone spots her. Or she'll turn up at Costello's or DiMeo's place, and the uniforms will arrest her.

Meanwhile, the reward hotline has brought a fresh onslaught of tips, with a couple of credible sightings. "We're looking at a long night," Barnes tells Stef as they get out of the car back at the precinct. "I'm going to grab those hot dogs. You want two? And a knish? Extra mustard on all?"

"Nah, you might bring back some weird ethnic knish instead."

"A knish *is* ethnic."

"Kid! Relax! I was just joshing you. I'm not hungry, but go get yourself some food. You're getting crabby again."

At the food cart, Barnes orders three hot dogs and

then wolfs them down as he waits for an elderly woman to get off the pay phone. It can't take long; she's just calling a car service to pick her up. Several shopping bags from Alexander's sit on the sidewalk beside her lug-soled black old lady shoes.

A fire engine comes screaming down the avenue. It barely misses a taxi, which swerves out of the way and in turn almost hits a jaywalking pedestrian.

The cabbie leans on the horn and screams out the window, "What the hell's the matta wichu?"

"Pedestrians got the rightaway, you jerk!"

"Firetrucks got the rightaway, you—"

The cabbie's profanity-laced snarl disappears into a cacophony of honks from surrounding traffic and a rattling construction jackhammer and the old lady shouting into the phone, "No! Eighth Avenue! Eighth!"

Barnes eyes the subway entrance at the end of the block, longing to escape uptown, to check on Wash, or downtown, to check on the baby. But he's not going anywhere anytime soon unless it involves Perry Wayland.

Running footsteps join the ruckus and Barnes turns back just in time to see a scruffy-looking kid about to make a grab for the old lady's shopping bags.

He throws himself in the mugger's path and whips out his badge. The kid does a skidding about-face, and disappears.

Shaken, the intended victim hangs up the phone and thanks Barnes, tears rimming her weathered eyes. "Do you know what's in those bags? A new black dress and shoes to wear to my husband's funeral on Monday."

"I'm sorry for your loss, ma'am."

"He always took care of me. Now I'm alone, and the city is so dangerous now . . . What am I going to do without him?"

Barnes pats her shoulder and reassures her she'll be all right. Reassured by the lie, she digs around in her big vinyl purse, producing a lace handkerchief to wipe her eyes, and a crumpled dollar, which she tries to give to him.

"Thank you, ma'am, but I can't."

"I insist. You poor police officers put your lives on the line every day. They don't pay you anywhere near what you're worth."

"I appreciate the thought, but it's illegal."

"Nonsense. I always tip the nice young traffic policeman who helps me cross the avenue in front of my building."

Barnes considers asking her where she lives. But what's he going to do, report a fellow officer for pocketing a buck now and then from a grateful old lady?

Code of silence.

He waits with her until the car service appears, helps her into the backseat, loads her shopping bags into the trunk, and once again extends his sympathy.

"God bless you and keep you safe, Detective Barnes."

Your lips to His ears, he thinks, returning to the pay phone. Even if Wash went out earlier, he's got to be home by now. It's getting dark out, and he just warned Barnes last night about the dangerous streets. Yet he still isn't picking up.

Barnes calls directory assistance, gets the number for the bodega, and dials it. No answer there, either.

All right, that makes no sense. The place is open twenty-four hours. He must have dialed wrong. Rather than waste another quarter or more time now, he calls the hospital, prepared to argue his way to information on his daughter.

This time, however, when he explains who he is and what he wants, a nurse tells him to hold.

After the longest few minutes of his life, he hears, "Stockton?"

"Delia!"

"They said you called. I thought you'd come, or call back. I couldn't even get in touch with you." She's woozily accusatory. Fair enough.

"What's going on? Is the baby . . ."

"She's okay now, but . . ."

His heart clenches. "What happened?"

"She had some troubles, so they took her upstairs."

"Upstairs where? What kind of troubles?"

"Something with her breathing."

"*Something?* Something what? She couldn't breathe?" Neither can he, the air suctioned from his lungs as he thinks of that fragile, precious infant, alone in a glass cradle, struggling . . .

"They gave her some medicine through a tube. They're going to keep her in the ICU."

"For how long? Did they say?"

"I hope not long. You're gonna have to pay for this, and if she needs expensive medicine—"

"Don't worry about that right now," he snaps. "Just make sure they do whatever they have to do for her."

Silence for a moment. And then, "Oh, don't you worry yourself, either. I will. And I'll make sure you get the bill."

"Listen, I didn't mean—"

She hangs up on him.

With a curse, Barnes slams down the phone so hard the surrounding shelter rattles.

He lights a cigarette and smokes it fiercely as he walks back to the precinct and the case of the missing, possibly murderous, millionaire. It's not productive to waste energy resenting Perry Wayland, but damn, it's satisfying.

"Barnes! Where've you been?" Stef jumps up from his chair and grabs his suit jacket.

"I told you. I went to get hot d—"

"Where, Nathan's in Coney Island? Come on, we're driving out to Long Island. Wayland was spotted out there Thursday night, getting off the train in Montauk."

Chapter Twenty

The female cop, Officer Vazquez, stands poised beside Bernadette as she unlocks the door to her apartment. She finds it dark and still. Flipping on a light, she sees that everything is just as she left it—even Chappy, her cat, who was sleeping on the couch when she headed out earlier.

He usually barrels toward the door when he hears the key. This time, he saunters over after she opens the door and rubs against her legs, purring, instead of ferociously head-butting her.

"Everything look okay?"

"Yes, other than the fact that my cat isn't dying of starvation for a change. He's probably on his best behavior because you're here." Bernadette picks up the cat and pets him, not sure what's supposed to happen next. "Do you, um, want to come in?"

"That's not necessary, as long as you don't see anything out of the ordinary?"

"No." The whole apartment—living room, kitchenette, bedroom, and bathroom—is visible from where they stand, just inside the door. The policewoman does check the windows in the living room and bedroom, confirming that they're locked, and scanning the fire escape beyond.

"All right, then. I'll be here in the hall, just in case . . ." Seeing Bernadette's expression, she adds, "It's a formality, really. Officer Dwyer won't let anyone get past him outside."

Closing the door after her, Bernadette hesitates before locking it and sliding the chain. It seems superfluous with an armed cop on the other side, but she's seen movies where the killer sneaks up and kills the guard. She can't bear to think of anything happening to the nice lady in the hall, and she seems capable of defending herself, especially against another woman. But Bernadette feels better knowing there's an extra measure of security between her and the rest of the world.

She leaves her own dinner on the counter and sets out a bowl of food for Chappy. He pokes at it and strolls away, uninterested.

"Did you catch another mouse? Is that it?"

The only other time Bernadette came home to find that Chappy wasn't frantic for food, she'd quickly discovered the reason: a mostly devoured mouse by the heat register in the bathroom.

She goes in there now, bracing herself for rodent remains, but there's nothing. She scrubs her hands with soap and hot water, as she always does when she comes home, but this time, she keeps glancing at the closed vinyl shower curtain.

You'd think Officer Vasquez would have checked behind it, just to make sure . . .

But why would she? There's no reason to believe that someone got in while Bernadette was out. The door was double locked, the windows were locked . . .

It's fine. Everything is fine. There's no one hiding behind the shower curtain, unless . . .

Unless someone is hiding behind the shower curtain.

She turns off the water and dries her hands, staring at it. Then she holds her breath and counts, one, two—

On three, she yanks the curtain aside.

The tub is empty. Of course it's empty. No stocky murderess with an angry red scar on her cheek.

Why kill the others after all these years?

Is it like when that Manson's follower, Squeaky Fromme, tried to assassinate President Ford back in the '70s? Is this killer trying to protest Oran's imprisonment?

More likely, she's just some kook looking for attention. Even notorious killers John Wayne Gacy and Ted Bundy have their creepy bands of devotees. Bernadette has encountered her share of Brooklyn Butcher–obsessed freaks over the years. But this one has done the unthinkable.

Bernadette tries to muster sorrow for the dead women, but feels nothing other than shock, of course, and maybe a macabre fascination. She's lost her ability to feel.

She goes to the bedroom and sheds the too-tight skirt and pantyhose, feeling guiltier over that than for her grief deficiency.

She dons elastic-waisted sweatpants, exactly as she'd longed to do when she was walking home and facing the prospect of heading back out to another mass. But she didn't choose to skip church. The officers ordered her to do so, right? Well, not ordered, exactly. If she'd insisted on going to church, Officer Vasquez probably would have accompanied her. But it's not easy, dragging herself up and down the avenue in all kinds of weather to hear the same sermon over and over and over . . .

Nor was it easy to destroy the embryo planted in her womb by the lunatic who murdered her family.

Nothing has been easy since that terrifying June night in Dyker Heights.

Not a day went by after that when she didn't wish that she, too, had been slaughtered in her bed. When she found out that she was pregnant, she truly intended to take her own life, but . . .

You were a coward. You couldn't do it. Not then.

On a hot August night, she ended the pregnancy alone in the bathroom of the apartment where her family had died. Her grandmother, who spoke only Italian and had moved in as her legal guardian, found her hemorrhaging on the floor and called an ambulance. Two days later, Bernadette found out she would never bear children. The following week, she went off to Cornell University. Her parents would have wanted her to go.

That fall, she lived one life at school and another when she made the journey back to testify at the trial. There, she met the other girls. Tara Sheeran and Christina Myers bonded over their pregnancies. Despite the circumstances, Bernadette sensed an unimaginable flurry of anticipation whenever she saw them. They actually seemed to want their babies.

Margaret Costello was pregnant, too, but she was different. She kept to herself. There was nothing giddy about her.

She wasn't brave, or stoic, or even just resigned, Bernadette later realized. Just in shock, and maybe stoned sometimes, too.

She didn't want the baby. She didn't necessarily want to be alive, either. But she didn't seem capable of doing anything about it.

That's why Bernadette decided to help her after her daughter was born.

Sometimes, she thinks about what she did and she

sees herself as a savior. Other times, she wonders if Satan himself entered her body that night and made her do what she did.

She returns to the living room, shoos Chappy off the couch cushion, and reaches beneath it. Hidden there is the one thing she wouldn't want Sally to see if she decides to snoop sometime while feeding the cat.

She pulls out a large brown envelope, opens the metal fastener, and removes a stack of yellowed *Ithaca Journal* clippings from January 1969.

"Baby Rescued in Gorge," Jessie tells Amelia as they stand halfway across the suspension bridge, staring down at the gushing white waters of Fall Creek. "That's what the headline said the day I was found."

"How do you know?"

"One of the nurses at the hospital cut out the newspaper article. I'll show you. There are pictures of police officers holding me, and the bridge, and the girl who found me. The nurse thought I'd want to know about it someday, so she cut out everything that was in the papers after I was found, and she made a scrapbook. She gave it to my parents when they adopted me."

Amelia digests that. The person who'd found Jessie had called the police. Jessie had been taken to the hospital. A kindly nurse had given her a tremendous gift. And then she'd been legally adopted into a stable, loving family. Everyone involved seems to have done everything right.

Not in Amelia's case. All she has is a stupid little dress that was probably made for a doll, and a basket that may not even mean anything, and a story that for all she knows is entirely made up.

Wind gusts, and the bridge sways. She grabs the low

rail and looks up at the darkening sky so that she won't have to look down at that rushing water that can sweep you away . . .

"Are you okay, Mimi?"

"Yeah. I just . . . I can't believe someone carried a little baby out here."

"I know, and in the dead of night, in January. It was two degrees out. *Two.* Whoever did it just left me there to freeze to death."

Whoever did it . . .

Her mother?

"I used to think the girl who found me was my actual birth mother. Like, maybe she secretly had me, but she couldn't keep me because she was only twenty, you know? She was a pre-med student at Cornell. Really smart. She didn't want to just leave me somewhere, so she pretended she found me in the gorge."

"That's possible."

"No, it isn't."

"How do you know?"

"Because I found her last year and she said she wasn't my mother."

"Maybe she was lying."

"Maybe I just wanted to believe my mother wasn't someone who would leave a tiny baby all alone to freeze to death on the coldest night of the year!" Jessie snaps back at her. "But that doesn't make it true."

"Well, maybe your mother wasn't the one who left you. Maybe you were kidnaped."

Jessie smiles a sad smile. "Bet you want to believe the same thing, right? That you had a wonderful, happy home and some stranger broke in and stole you in the dead of night and left you somewhere."

"It could happen."

"But people don't kidnap babies for kicks. They have a reason. Like, ransom. Or they couldn't have a baby and they wanted one."

Amelia thinks of Calvin and Bettina.

"So anyway . . ." Jessie sighs. "This is my bridge. And that's my sad story."

"At least it has a happy ending."

"Yeah, right."

"Jessie, you live *here*. In this beautiful town. In a real house, with a sister and brother and parents who take you to look at colleges and pay for things and don't believe in lies. I don't have that."

Jessie stares at her, and she braces herself for a sarcastic comment.

It doesn't come.

"I'm so sorry this happened to you," she says softly, wrapping her arms around Amelia. "But we're going to find our moms, you know? We are. And Si's going to help us."

Our.

We.

Us.

"Let's make a pact, Mimi. If you find your mom before I find mine—or the other way around—we won't just move on and forget each other. We'll still help each other look, okay?"

"I could never forget."

"Neither could I, but maybe if life gets normal for you and you have your mom back . . . you know. It might happen. So we have to promise."

"I promise," Amelia says as they shake on it. "I promise I'll help you if you help me."

"WE LUCKED OUT, kid," Stef says, driving east on the Long Island Expressway. "Try coming out here during rush hour, or on a summer weekend, and traffic would be crawling. It would take you five, six hours to get out to the Hamptons. Ever been out there?"

Barnes shakes his head, lighting a cigarette and staring out at suburban neighborhoods. Lamplight, chimney smoke, minivans.

"Barnes?"

"No. Never. You?"

"No. Heard it's nice, though."

"Yeah?"

"Yeah."

The conversation lags.

"Why are you so quiet?" Stef asks after a minute.

"Just thinking about the case."

He has been wondering what Wayland has to do with that homicidal Scarface back in New York, and if he really did take a train to Montauk Thursday night, but mostly, he's worrying about his daughter.

How much money will it take to make sure she has the care she needs?

More than Barnes can possibly earn or borrow, that's for damned sure. What the hell is he going to do?

Stef interrupts his thoughts again.

"Something's eating you, kid. Everything okay with your family?"

"Yeah."

"Because this morning, you said—"

"Turned out fine. Nothing to worry about."

"Good. Hey, you want to know what's eating me?"

He does not, but Stef is going to tell him.

"Missing game six."

The World Series. After all that's happened today, Stef is thinking about a baseball game?

To be fair, it's just another day on the job for him. He's jaded enough after all these years not to be thrown by

Christina Myers's brutalized corpse. He isn't losing an old friend. He doesn't have a newborn in the ICU. He isn't trying to come up with . . .

How much?

"Listen, I like to bust your chops, kid," Stef says. "But that doesn't mean I wouldn't help you if something's wrong."

"Weren't we talking about baseball?"

"*I* was talking. To myself."

"I told you. The case—"

"Yeah, the case. The case can wait for a second. You and me, we got each other's backs. You know that, right? You're not alone. You got family."

Stef isn't talking about Wash, or the baby.

He's talking about the job.

"Thanks. That's good to know."

"Good. So let's get this done and get back to the city so you can . . . do whatever you have to do. Take some time off if you need it. Maybe a leave—"

"Thanks, Stef, but I don't need a leave. I just need to keep working."

Keep getting paid.

But it's never going to be enough.

BERNADETTE REMEMBERS THE cold more than anything else.

The January wind whipped through the gorge so that she could feel the bridge tremor and sway beneath her thin leather loafers. She'd grown out of last season's snow boots, and the wool car coat that had carried her through Brooklyn winters was no match for the harsh Ithaca climate. Her hands were so numb in knit gloves that she couldn't feel the handle of the baby's carrier as she lugged it onto the span.

It was slippery. She skidded more than once, nearly losing her footing close to the edge.

But that was the whole point, wasn't it?

She *wanted* to make the death plunge into the gorge. She was planning to die. And she wasn't going to do it alone.

"Where are you taking her?" Margaret had asked when she handed over her tiny daughter, wearing a pink snowsuit. But she didn't seem to care very much. She was ready to forget the nightmare and the child she'd been forced to bear.

"Don't worry. I'm giving her to someone who deserves her."

Margaret gave a resolute nod. Maybe she suspected the truth. Maybe not, because she gave Bernadette a few formula-filled bottles, some cloth diapers and safety pins, and two spare outfits, all she had. She was surrounded by boxes, preparing to leave the apartment where her family had been murdered. Free to make a fresh start unencumbered, she had rented a studio apartment in Manhattan.

"What should I tell people?"

"You mean family? Friends?"

Margaret shook her head and explained that she was a first generation American; her relatives were strangers in Italy. She'd had few friends before it happened, and had distanced herself from them in the months since.

"Then who are you worried about?"

"The press knows I had a baby."

Just as they knew Bernadette had not—though they weren't aware of the true reason.

"This is going to fade now that the trial is over. They're not going to keep tabs on you forever. Especially if you're moving out of here. No one needs to know where you went. You can disappear."

That, essentially, is what Margaret had done, swallowed by the city and a drug habit that might have been inevitable even before the tragedy.

That day, as Bernadette was walking away with her baby, Margaret chased her down, calling, "Wait!"

She turned back, certain the other girl had changed her mind. But she was holding something out.

"Here, this should go with her."

"What is it?"

"One of the nurses at the hospital left it under my pillow for me."

"You mean, when you had the baby?"

"No, not then. Last May. When I was . . . recovering. After . . . you know."

"Oh."

"They were really nice to me there. One day, they left me a cross made of palm fronds, and another day, they left this. It was too small for me, though, so I might as well give it to her."

Bernadette took the packet and left her standing there. As she walked toward the subway, she looked back once, certain she'd see Margaret wistfully watching them go.

She was wrong. She'd already gone back inside and closed the door.

Bernadette boarded an Ithaca-bound bus crowded with students heading back for the new semester. None gave her a second glance, and the tiny girl slept quietly the whole way.

Back on campus, she smuggled the baby into her empty dorm room. Her roommate was from California and wouldn't be back until the next evening. That would give Bernadette plenty of time to write a suicide note. She'd been composing it in her head for a month, ever since she'd failed one final and barely passed the rest before returning to Brooklyn for Christmas in an empty apartment.

But who would find the note? The roommate she'd met a few months ago? They weren't even friends, really. She'd probably be glad to find herself living alone in a double room this semester.

Instead of writing the note, she unwrapped the packet Margaret had given her.

It contained a little gold necklace.

She put it on the baby, then changed and fed her. Not because she had a nurturing bone in her body, but because she was wet and hungry and starting to fuss. An infant's wails would bring curious co-eds to her door.

To this day, Bernadette is certain things would have been different if her bus had arrived after dark and she'd gone straight to the gorge. Without time for second thoughts—time to take a good look at the baby and wonder if she really was pure evil.

How could she not be? She'd been conceived in a heinous act and her father was Satan himself, hell-bent on a mission to populate the earth with his disciples. If she was allowed to live, she would grow up to do terrible things.

Yet she seemed so sweet, cooing softly and staring up at Bernadette with big dark eyes that looked so like Margaret's.

Looking to her Bible for answers, Bernadette found them in John 8:44. *"You belong to your father, the devil, and you want to carry out your father's desires."*

She waited until after midnight to leave the dorm, carrying the baby inside her coat. That was a mistake.

She wanted to hide her from prying eyes, not . . .

The child's warmth enveloped her, and her sweet scent infiltrated every breath. She was a reminder of what Bernadette might have had, if she hadn't ended her own pregnancy. She contemplated living—keeping Margaret's child; raising her as her own, even as she stood on the bridge, staring out into the black chasm.

The baby whimpered.

"It's okay," Bernadette whispered, teeth chattering. "It'll be over soon, and it won't even be that scary. I'll be with you."

And I'm terrified.

Not just of the fall, but of what lay beyond.

Before she'd decided to take her own life, she'd thought she might have a chance at going to heaven. Abortion wasn't murder if you were killing the devil's spawn, was it? Tossing this child into the precipice would be the same thing, wouldn't it? But if she went over, too, it was a sin. No gray area with suicide.

As she stood wrestling with that, she heard footsteps crunching down the snowy path. Someone was coming.

Her first instinct was to flee, and take the baby with her. But if she wasn't going to take her own life, she wasn't going to take the child's.

She laid the baby on the snowy ground. As she ran into the frigid darkness, she heard thin little wails piercing the night, and then sirens.

She followed the saga in the newspapers, keeping all these clippings in case Margaret ever came back into her life and wanted to know what had happened to her baby.

They did cross paths a few times, years ago. But Margaret was vacant, brain fried, too dead inside to care what had happened to the daughter she hadn't wanted, or about Bernadette, or herself. Now—

A shadow falls over the page.

Startled, Bernadette looks up.

A woman is standing in front of her. She has a bright red scar on her right cheek . . . and a gun in her hand.

SITTING AT THE counter island, Amelia turns the pages of Jessie's scrapbook as her friend bustles around the kitchen. Claiming to be a great cook, she'd stopped at a huge, beautiful modern supermarket and bought groceries for dinner using her parents' credit card.

"They just let you use it to buy stuff?"

"Within reason."

"What's it like to be rich?"

"We're not rich. We're just regular."

"Not where I come from."

Busy at the stove, Jessie wants dinner to be ready before her favorite television show, *My Sister Sam*, airs.

"I can't believe you don't watch it," she tells Amelia as she sautés mushrooms in butter to make the kitchen smell as homey as it looks. "You'd love it. It's so real. Like, last week, the teenaged sister, Patti, was thinking she should lose her virginity. Have you?"

"Have I what?"

"Lost it."

"Oh. No." Nowhere near.

"I lost mine to Ryan. That's why I was so upset when he broke up with me. He was my first."

Her first. Have there been more?

Jessie falls silent, perhaps pondering her lost love as she stirs the mushrooms.

Amelia might be the city girl, but she's nowhere near as worldly as her small town new friend.

After the supermarket, Jessie had stopped at a liquor store and bought a jug of wine with a fake ID.

"Aren't you afraid of getting arrested?"

"It wouldn't be the worst thing that ever happened to me."

No. It would not.

Amelia goes back to the scrapbook, reading an article that includes a statement from the female student who came across an infant girl abandoned on the bridge before dawn that frigid winter morning. The baby was lying on the ground, bundled in a pink snowsuit.

"I still don't get what would she be doing out there in the middle of the night," Amelia muses.

"Cutting through to get back to her dorm."

"All alone? At that hour?"

"There's a fraternity house right there. She probably got together with some guy."

"He could have walked her home."

"Yeah, well . . . frat guys," Jessie says, as if she knows something about it.

Amelia studies the photographs in the scrapbook, grainy on the age-darkened newsprint, with captions. There's the baby with the police and hospital staff, and a long shot of the bridge. The backdrop is snowy, the pristine blanket trampled along the span.

"I wonder if the police tried to follow footprints to track the person who left you there?"

"The way the wind blows up there, they'd be covered right away." Jessie splashes wine into a simmering pan. "I'm lucky I wasn't buried alive before someone found me. But maybe that's what she wanted. Or worse."

She pours more wine into two large plastic tumblers and offers one to Amelia.

"No, thanks."

"Why not?"

"I don't drink."

"Why not?"

"It's illegal, for one thing." For another, teetotaler Bettina drilled the evils of alcohol into her head.

"Only as of a few years ago. When Michelle turned eighteen, Diane and Al bought her a bottle of champagne because they thought it was unfair that the drinking age had been raised to twenty-one. They'd never do that now, for me. Everything goes her way."

"Your sister's?"

"And my brother's, too."

"I thought he was younger than you."

"Michael? He is. But everything goes his way, too." She pauses to swig some wine from the glass. "Diane and Al can't do enough for him and my sister—their real kids, you know? They're both geniuses, they never get into any trouble, they look like each other and like Diane and Al . . . I mean, come on. Their names even match. Michelle and Michael. Michael and Michelle. Guess who's the odd man out around here? I'm like Cinderella. That's what I tell Si. They should have named me that."

"Cinderella?"

"Cindy for short. I always liked that name. Instead they named me after a stupid necklace."

"There's a necklace named Jessamine?"

"Nobody calls me that. I just go by my nickname. And Diane thought Jessie sounded like a Western name, you know? Like a cowgirl."

"Why would she want you to be a cowgirl? Because of the Dairy Barn?"

"No!" She laughs, gulps more wine from her plastic glass and offers the other one to Amelia.

This time, she takes it, sips cautiously, and swallows. It's room temperature, and kind of bitter, and she hates it—until it slides down to warm her from the inside out. Hmm. Not so bad, after all.

"My name has nothing to do with the Dairy Barn."

"Then why did they want you to be a cowgirl?"

"Here, I'll show you." Jessie leans toward her, un-buttoning the top two buttons of her shirt. For a weird, awkward moment, Amelia thinks she's going to make a drunken pass.

"When they found me, I was wearing this charm, see?" She pulls out a gold chain fastened around her neck. "I wear it every single day. I used to think my real mother might see it and know it was me. Yeah. She'd come up and be like, 'Hey, where'd you get that little gold horse? Because I gave the exact same one to my baby girl.'"

RELISHING BERNADETTE DIMEO's look of stunned terror, Red watches the paper she was holding slip from her slack hand and flutter to the floor.

She'd thought she was safe here, barricaded in her little apartment with a police officer outside the door. She'd never dreamed that she'd locked herself inside with her executioner.

She opens her mouth to scream.

Red cocks the pistol. "Make one sound, and I will kill you right here, right now."

Bernadette closes her mouth.

Fool. Doesn't she realize it's going to happen anyway? Does she really think Red is here to talk to her, and walk away?

Red can see the wheels turning. She's wondering how Red got in. It never even occurred to her that someone might have been waiting for her. Watching her apartment—for a while now.

Someone who could see everything from the roof next door—including the neighbor who used the key to let herself in and out of the apartment to feed the cat one day when Bernadette was out of town. A neighbor who conveniently leaves town herself on weekends. Sally won't know until late tomorrow night that someone broke her window, crawled into her apartment, and borrowed the key to the apartment next door. By then, it will be over.

Red had been hiding under the bed when Bernadette arrived with that police officer, but they hadn't bothered to look under there.

If they had, I'd have shot them both on the spot.

Killing a cop isn't part of the plan, but you do what you have to do.

Like the stairwell junkie.

Like the cufflink, tossed like a breadcrumb on the bedroom floor up in Boston, meant to lead the cops to Wayland. Just in case White is wrong about what's going to happen. In case the world is going to keep on turning after all.

Red looks down at the newspaper clipping on the floor. The word *baby* jumps out from a headline.

Bernadette's boot-clad foot comes up off the floor and kicks, hard. Red starts to fall backward, catching herself on the table.

The woman is up off the couch, moving to the door.

Red chases her down, gun in one hand, grasping with the other. Her fingers clutch and then lose a wisp of Bernadette's hair. She's almost made it to the door, lunging toward the lock.

Red would waste precious moments reaching for the knife. Nothing to do but squeeze the trigger.

The bullet zips past and lodges in the wall. "Help!" Bernadette shrieks.

Hearing a commotion in the hall, Red takes aim.

This time, the bullet reaches its target.

Bernadette drops to the floor, blood splattered across the white walls.

Any second, the cop is going to burst through the door. Red turns back, racing toward the couch. She twists the lock on the window behind it, throws it open, and remembers to grab the paper-clipped newspaper articles before she climbs out.

Chapter Twenty-One

Yeah, I'm one thousand percent sure that's the guy," the Montauk cab driver tells Stef and Barnes with a nod at Perry Wayland's photo. "He had a baseball cap pulled down low over his face, but I got a good look at him."

"From where?" Stef asks, and the man gestures at a row of parking spots near the platform.

"I was waiting right there, same as always, when the train pulled in around midnight. This is the last stop. He got off with a handful of locals. Summertime, you got all kinds of people coming out from the city, and they double, triple up in my cab. This time of year, fares are hit-and-miss. I thought for sure that guy would need a ride, so I asked him, but he ignored me. Just kept on walking."

"He wasn't with a woman, was he?"

"Nope, alone."

"Have you ever seen her?" Barnes shows him the photo of Gypsy Colt.

"Good-looking. No. Her, I'd remember."

"So you say he kept walking . . . Did you notice which direction, by any chance?"

"Sure did. He went up that road." He points to the north, toward the water.

"What's there?"

"Just a boatyard, but it's closed at that hour. Deserted at this time of year. Thought it was kind of strange."

Barnes and Stef look at each other, and then thank the driver.

"I get the reward, right? If you find him?"

"Don't worry. If we find him, we know how to find you."

They get back into the car.

"You thinking what I'm thinking?" Stef asks as he starts the engine.

"Someone—probably his gal pal—picked him up by boat."

"Yep. By now he's probably out of the country."

They drive up the short lane to the boatyard. It's deserted tonight, too, the small building closed and dark. A sign on the window lists the off-season hours and a number to call for fishing charters and day trips to the North Fork, Shelter Island, and Block Island.

"Wayland spent his childhood summers on Block Island," Barnes says.

"Yeah. I'll call the number. And the precinct, too, for updates." Stef heads over to the pay phone.

Barnes waits in the car, his thoughts going back to his daughter, and the money, but not for long. Stef comes bounding back.

"Tip came in from a woman out on Block Island, Barnes—right across the sound. Wayland is holed up at a cottage there with a woman."

DARTING ACROSS THE flat roof of the building next door to Bernadette DiMeo's, Red hears sirens.

New York City. There are always sirens.

But this time, they're coming for me.

She peers over the low ledge at the street below. So far, this block of West Twenty-Ninth remains quiet. Any second, though, squad cars and rescue vehicles will show up and officers will fan out searching for the gunman.

She goes to the back of the roof, where a second fire escape descends to a small alleyway between this building and the one behind it on West Twenty-Eighth Street. Light spills from several windows facing the steep, rickety iron staircase. Earlier, she crept up past them.

Now there's no time for stealth. Her feet clatter on the fire escape as she descends to the alley. Twenty-Eighth Street is business as usual at a glance—a few pedestrians and dog walkers along the sidewalks, one-way east-bound traffic crawling along toward Eleventh Avenue.

Red runs in the opposite direction, toward the West Side Highway and a sea of northbound yellow cabs. She raises her arm, and a driver promptly pulls over in front of a fenced construction site. They're working back there behind the plywood and chain-link fence, using noisy equipment that mingles with the approaching sirens. Red hops into the backseat as traffic whips past.

"Where to?" the cabbie shouts above the din, turning off the dome light and setting the meter.

Good question.

Not home.

Not Block Island.

The pills that were supposed to help have left Red edgy—not in a sharp and ready for anything way but in an overly irritable, tense way.

Breathing hard, she opens the spiral-bound album in her hands. On the first page, she sees an article dated January 1969, about an abandoned baby. Her eyes widen.

"Lady?"

"Ithaca."

"Huh?"

"I need to go to Ithaca!"

"I can't take you to—"

She lifts the gun, aims at his head, and pulls the trigger. He slumps over.

She jumps out of the backseat and into the front. Shoving the driver out of the way, she shifts into gear and barrels north. She has no idea how to get to Ithaca. For now, she just needs to get out of New York.

The Lincoln Tunnel is only a few blocks away.

Ten minutes later, she's in New Jersey. She makes a series of turns off the highway and abandons the bloody cab on the quietest side street she can find, grabbing the driver's wallet and cash. She strides up one block and down another until she spots a shaggy-haired young man about to get into a beat-up old Volkswagen Beetle.

"Excuse me! Can you tell me where, uh, Ithaca Street is?" she calls.

He turns, standing beside the open car door, head tilted as he thinks about it. "Ithaca Street? Is it off the Boulevard?"

"I'm not sure. Probably." Still walking toward him, she scans the block. There's no one around. It's a clear shot from here to the corner, where a sign indicates that the highway is to the right.

"What are you trying to find? A house?"

"Yes." She keeps an eye on the car keys in his hand, her own in her pocket, holding the gun. "I have an address . . . here, let me show you."

She pulls out the gun, aims, and pulls the trigger.

He drops to the ground.

She plucks the keys from his hand, jumps into the car, and barrels toward the highway.

AMELIA SITS CROSS-LEGGED beside Jessie on the couch in the McCalls' pretty living room. *My Sister Sam* is on TV. Their plates—and the wine jug—are almost empty.

"You were right, Jessie."

"I'm always right." She hiccups. "About what?"

"You're a great cook."

"I know, right? That's Diane's recipe, but even she says I make it better. You want some more?"

"No, thanks. I'm full." Of chicken marsala, and plain old marsala.

"I hope you saved room for dessert, because it's special."

"Is it chocolate ice cream from . . . what's that place again?"

"The Dairy Bar? No! It's better."

"You said there's nothing better."

"I was wrong." She picks up both plates.

"You said you're always right!"

"I was wrong about that, too!"

That strikes Amelia as hilarious. Jessie laughs, too, and heads toward the kitchen, leaving their forks and knives behind. Amelia reaches for the silverware, starting to get up, but Jessie calls, "Don't come in here!"

"I was going to help. You forgot the—"

"I'll get it later. Just chill!"

"All right. I'm chilling!"

Amelia's gaze falls on the doll sitting next to her on the couch, familiar from Saturday morning television commercials of her childhood.

"Hey, I know who you are! Chatty Cathy, right? I wanted you so badly when I was a kid. Every little girl in the world had you, except me. Can you talk?"

Finding a ring in the doll's back, she pulls the cord and hears a high-pitched electronic, *"May I have a cookie?"*

"Maybe, if that's what Jessie's bringing us for dessert." Amelia giggles, and pulls again.

"Nice Mommy."

"Yeah, Jessie has one, doesn't she? She just doesn't know it."

She sighs, sets the doll aside, and leans back against a mauve, heart-shaped cross-stitch pillow embroidered *Home Is Where the Heart Is.* It's signed with the initials *DM.*

She envisions Diane McCall sitting with an embroidery hoop in this cozy room, while her husband, Al— the musician in the family, according to Jessie—plays the upright piano. There's open sheet music propped above the keyboard.

The song is "Lean On Me."

It plays in her head as she allows her eyes to close.

When you're not strong . . .

Right now, she feels anything but. The travel, the emotion, the wine . . .

"Surprise!"

She opens her eyes to see that the room has gone dark, and Jessie is back, smiling in candlelight glowing on . . .

Is that a *cake*?

"Happy birthday to you," Jessie sings. *"Happy birthday to you. Happy birthday dear Mimi . . ."*

Tears roll down Amelia's cheeks.

WITH THE FUEL gauge edging dangerously close to empty, Red drives the stolen VW north out of New Jersey, where all the gas stations are full service.

For all she knows, she's spattered in blood. Even if she's not, she's better off avoiding contact with people who might ask questions—at least until the pills wear off.

If you take too much, you're going to get antsy and make a reckless mistake.

She's made more than one. Every time she pulled that damned trigger, she increased her odds of being caught.

Past the Delaware Water Gap and over the state line in New York, she exits the highway onto a lonely rural road. Pulling onto the shoulder not far from the ramp, she opens the door to illuminate the interior and checks her reflection in the rearview mirror. No blood from the neck up. Very little from there down, either, but there are a few spatters on her jean jacket. She takes it off, empties the pockets onto the passenger's seat, wads the jacket into a ball, and tosses it out into the night.

The engine is running and she's going to run out of gas any second now, but she needs to find out whether the idea that took hold when she saw that headline could possibly be correct. Otherwise, she's on a wild-goose chase to Ithaca.

She flips through the yellowed newspaper clippings.

The first is dated January 1969, when a baby girl was abandoned in Ithaca, New York.

If she isn't Margaret Costello's missing child, then she's Bernadette DiMeo's. Either way, the girl's father is Oran Matthews, and her half sister is Gypsy Colt.

And either way, they—Pale and White—are waiting for Red to eliminate her.

The last article was published later that spring, with the headline "Happy Ending for Baby Doe."

By then, the foundling had a name.

Jessamine McCall.

HALF AN HOUR after getting the new tip, Barnes and Stef are shivering on a small boat that bounces across the dark water toward Block Island. The captain, Dewey, reminds Barnes of Alberto Garcia's grandson, Tino. He, too, is dark, handsome, good-natured, and married despite being in his early twenties.

He knew nothing about Wayland and hadn't seen him around the boatyard. He was willing to shuttle Barnes and Stef out to the island, but warned that it wouldn't be a pleasant ride, and he was right.

Wayland is reportedly holed up at the Sandy Oyster, a cottage colony not far from the ferry landing. A clerk there had seen his story on the news and called the tip line to say he'd showed up a day or two ago, and is staying with a woman who'd been there all week. The clerk hadn't checked her in or gotten a look at her, and said she didn't want housekeeping.

If she's Miss White, Barnes wonders, then who's the crazy killer with the scar on her face?

With a storm brewing, Rhode Island law enforcement isn't particularly concerned about a missing Manhattan millionaire being sighted on the island. They said they'll send an officer to check it out and meet Barnes and Stef at a restaurant adjacent to the Sandy Oyster.

The boat hits a rough patch. Stef curses, and Barnes clings to the wet rail to avoid being pitched into the sea.

"Sorry!" Dewey shouts, gripping the wheel. "Almost there!"

Barnes stares at the gold ring on his left hand.

What if I married Delia?

No. He doesn't love her. He doesn't even like her.

The wedding band, though, reminds him of the tiny gold ring he keeps on his key chain as a reminder that his father is with him. He found it in March . . .

Wait a minute. Was that the night . . .

He thinks back. Wash in the hospital. Bub's retirement party. Delia.

Yes. He'd found the ring the night his daughter was conceived.

The island looms dark in the sea, with a yellowish haze of lights clustered around the harbor and smattering of pinpricks beyond. Dewey ties up at a small marina near the ferry landing.

"Weather's going to turn, Detectives. How long do you think you'll be?"

"Could be ten minutes," Barnes says. "Could be longer. Depends on what we find."

"I'll wait around to take you back, or you'll be stuck out here for a while."

"Might not be such a bad thing." Stef eyes a couple of quaint hotels and restaurants. "Not much peace and quiet in Howard Beach these days."

"Well, I've got to get back. And I need to make a quick phone call before we leave the marina," Barnes says, and Stef trails him toward a bank of phone kiosks at the deserted ferry parking lot.

"I'll call the precinct while you're at it."

"And I'll be waiting for you guys in there." Dewey heads for a pub with a wave.

Barnes dials Wash and is relieved when he answers. "I've been trying to call you for hours! I thought something happened to you! Where have you been?"

"I've been trying to call you, too, Stockton. Where are you?"

"Block Island, on the case. Why were you calling me?"

A pause. "I've been at the hospital."

"Again? What—"

"Something happened. Not to me."

Wash takes as deep a breath as is possible for a man in his condition, and Barnes braces himself for whatever is coming.

IN THE MOUNTAINS, Red finds a service station off the exit and shivers without the jean jacket as she pumps her own gas. Exactly five dollars' worth, to minimize contact with the cashier in the glass booth. She hands over the bill to a young woman who doesn't bother to look up from a *People* magazine article about Glenn Close and Michael Douglas.

Black had bragged about meeting the actor, who's working on a new film shooting in his office building. Red got the sense that he was trying to impress White, but she seemed bored by the story. Maybe she'd heard it before. More likely, she just doesn't care about Hollywood. Maybe not about Black, either.

They'd met at Brown University back in the early '70s. Perry's version of the story is that they'd fallen madly in love. White never said that.

"Do you love him?" Red asked her last summer. They were alone together, just like the old days back in Rockland, in their shared bedroom in the foster home.

White laughed. "I think you're jealous."

"Do you love him?" Red persisted.

"I love *you*. Why do you think I found you after all these years?"

Because you loved me?

Because I'm chosen?

Because you knew what I did to my mother?

And you knew I'd do anything for you?

One thing is certain. White needs Black. His money, anyway. None of this would be possible without it.

Yet he's rubbed Red the wrong way, from the moment they met last summer. Aware that Red had just gotten the tattoo, he bragged that he's had his for years. But then White gave him a look, and he shifted gears, like he did in the cottage, offering the handshake and gratitude and cash. The first time, it had been fake concern for any physical discomfort the tattoo might have caused.

"I know how much it hurts," he said. "I remember the pain. It was excruciating."

"Not at all," Red said. Nothing hurt as badly as the hot iron Mother pressed to her cheek that awful night, or what the so-called doctor did to her behind closed doors in his examining room in the worst part of town.

White also has a horse tattooed over her heart.

"Does Oran have one, too?" Red asked.

"Yes. His was there long before he went to prison. But you need to call him Pale, remember? No real names."

"Except mine," Red agreed, though it's just a nickname.

The other kids called her Red at school—cruelly, because of the angry scar on her face. She came home crying to her mother, who in a lucid moment took her to a so-called doctor to see if he could do anything about it. As if he were a plastic surgeon, and not just some quack who'd lost his license, a convicted pedophile in another state.

"Come on, now, be a big girl."

"Please stay with me, Mommy. Please!"

"The doctor wants me in the waiting room. Go on, now. Go!"

"Don't worry, little lady. This won't hurt a bit . . ."

The scar on Red's face was nothing compared to the new, invisible ones. But he convinced Mother that it had faded due to his "treatment," and that she had to return, again and again . . .

Didn't Mother know there was something wrong with him? She may have. But you don't bring a battered child to the most upstanding pediatrician in town. Even back then, doctors were on the lookout for child abuse.

For a long time, Red had told herself that Mother didn't mean to hurt her. She was just so sad, and so angry, about George . . .

Red's father had been killed in Saigon in November 1965, when the wall calendar froze. If that hadn't happened, none of the rest would have, either. If he had lived, her mother would have, too. There would have been no scar. No doctor.

Red wouldn't have had to kill anyone.

But this girl, Margaret's daughter . . . she'll be the last one. When she's gone, Red will finally be free.

She gets into the car, pops another pill, and speeds on toward Ithaca. Salvation is so close she can taste it, sweet as an apple.

HANGING UP THE phone, Barnes turns to find Stef waiting for him.

"Looks like we've got an ID on the woman with the scar, but she's—hey, is everything okay? I'd say you're white as a ghost, but . . ." Stef grins.

Barnes bows his head and swipes a hand at his eyes.

"Are you *crying*? Just because I made a little joke? Sorry, kid, but . . . you'd better grow a thick skin, or—"

"I have a thick skin! Thick, and black! And I'm not *crying* over some idiot remark you made. I just lost a friend, okay?"

Stef's eyes widen. "I'm sorry. Geez. I'm so sorry. I am. What happened?"

"He was . . ." He stops, clears his throat. Tries again. "He was shot resisting a holdup."

"Where?"

"His family's store. In my old neighborhood." Just minutes before Wash broke the news, Barnes had been thinking about Tino Garcia. And now . . .

"It's dangerous up there."

"It's dangerous everywhere, Stef. *Everywhere.*"

A pause.

"Listen, I just found out that Bernadette DiMeo . . . she's been killed. The suspect slipped past the guards. She's like Catwoman or something. Stealthy. But there's a good lead from a patrol officer who saw her get out of a cab this morning and go into a coffee shop in Hell's Kitchen. The waitress there says she's a regular and hasn't missed a day."

"Where is she now?"

"On the run in a stolen car, with another couple of DOAs to her name."

"What *is* her name?"

"Last name is Skaggs. First is . . ." He consults his notes. "Enid. But everyone called her Red."

Chapter Twenty-Two

Funny thing about wine.

Amelia's initial impression: bad.

Then: good.

Now, after they've polished off the last of the jug . . .

Bad. Really bad. Blech.

"Are you okay?" Jessie asks.

"I'm really . . ." She frowns. Yawns. "I'm a little queasy. Maybe I shouldn't have had two pieces of cake, but it was so good. Thank you so much for giving me a birthday."

"You're welcome so much. Now you can't say you never had one."

"No. Maybe this is the day I should celebrate it from now on. October . . . What is it?"

"Twenty-fourth. But not for much longer." Jessie yawns. "Time for bed. You can choose any bedroom you want. Al and Diane's, or my sister's, or even my brother's, if you don't mind sharing it with a pet lizard."

"No, thanks."

"Or you can stay in my room. I have a futon."

"Me, too!" All this time, she's been envying Jessie, thinking her life is a lot more perfect than she lets on. That if she had the kind of mother Jessie has— adoptive, or not; legal, or not—she'd never complain.

But if Jessie sleeps on a futon, too, maybe they really do treat her like Cinderella.

She opens her mouth to speak, but a hiccup falls out.

Jessie laughs. Her dimples are so nice. Amelia wishes she had them. Dimples, and Jessie's life. That would be good.

"Come on, Mimi. Time to go upstairs. I'll give you the bed, and I'll take the futon."

"Wait . . . you have both?"

"Yeah."

"In your bedroom? A bed *and* a futon?"

"I had a lot of sleepovers when I was younger, and I don't like sharing my bed, so Diane thought it would be a good idea to get a futon for when my friends were here."

A bed, and a futon, and a room, all to herself.

And a mother.

Thoughts swim in Amelia's head against a marsala current and one spills from her lips. "Why are you even looking?"

"What?"

"For your mother who left you alone in the cold on a suicide bridge. I don't get it. Why do you want to find her?"

"Same reason you want to find yours. Because she's my real mother."

"But you *have* a mother. Diane raised you, and she gave you—" She flops her hand around. "Everything."

"This isn't everything, Mimi. Believe me. And you had a mother who raised you, too."

"She didn't give me everything. Or anything. Not even close. And she's gone, so . . ." She shrugs. "It doesn't matter anyway."

"She didn't choose to leave you, though. She got sick. You know that, right?"

"Of course I know that! I was there! You weren't."

"Okay, well, you weren't *here*, either. You don't know how I felt, growing up always knowing—"

"It's better than never knowing!"

"Is it?"

They stare at each other.

Jessie scowls and sways toward the stairs. "Let's go to bed. This is stupid. We're tired and drunk."

"I'm not drunk."

"Yeah, you are. Come on."

"I'll sleep here, on the couch."

"Fine. Good night."

"Good night."

Jessie goes upstairs and closes a door with finality.

This *is* stupid. Amelia should leave. Yep, that's what she's going to do. She's going to leave and go . . .

Where?

Even if it were a good idea to show up on Silas's doorstep in the middle of the night in this condition, she's so dizzy she can barely fumble her way across the room to the couch.

The doll is in the way. She tosses it toward a wing chair. She misses, and the doll falls onto the rug.

"Sorry," Amelia tells her, as she pulls the afghan over her and sinks her head onto the heart-shaped pillow that reads *Home Is Where the Heart Is.*

Chatty Cathy is silent, staring up at her with plastic eyes.

RED WAS EXPECTING to drive into a sleepy little village, but Ithaca is a college town, alive even at this hour. Driving past a minimarket, she spots a phone booth with the local directory in a black binder attached to the interior wall.

She makes an impulsive U-turn and belatedly checks for cops. She's in luck—this time. But the VW must have been reported stolen by now. She parks it outside the store, takes her stuff, and locks the car.

She'll have to figure out another mode of transportation from here.

She throws away the keys and old newspaper clippings in a garbage can that smells like puke. After a furtive check to make sure no one is watching, she breaks a stick from a shrub and uses it to push the evidence deeper into the foul can than anyone would ever be willing to dig.

Then she goes to the phone book, opens the directory, and scrolls through the *M*'s until she finds a name that matches the one in the article.

McCall, Allen

The door opens and a trio of young men emerge into the parking lot, laughing loudly and carrying a quarter keg.

"Excuse me," Red calls. "Where's North Cayuga Street?"

"That way." Hands full, one of them gestures with his head. "Right up the hill."

It looks steep. Red is chilly, and exhausted. This is the homestretch. She'd better take another pill—two, for good measure.

When this is over, she'll find someplace to sleep for a while before she drives back to Rhode Island to tell White the good news.

IN SILENCE, BARNES and Stef make the short, dark, wet walk to the Plantation restaurant, with its neon billboard advertising live televised sports, karaoke Tuesdays, and stuffed quahogs. The bar area is full of sports fans, as are all the booths with the best view of the TV, where sportscasters are analyzing the Twins' win and the outlook for Game Seven tomorrow. There's no sign of Wayland, nor of the promised local law enforcement.

Stef isn't surprised. "They weren't in any rush. Let's

get something to eat while we wait. My treat. Anything you want."

"What is this, a night out on the town? We have to get back."

"So . . . what, you want to just forget about Wayland?"

"Of course I don't—"

"Then sorry, kid, but we're stuck while we're stuck. If he's out here, he's not going anywhere tonight, and it looks like he didn't kill anyone in Boston or New York, either. Disappearing with your mistress isn't a crime."

"The cufflink—"

"You said yourself it's too obvious. This woman, whoever she is, must be framing him. God knows why. But we're here. We have to wait for the locals. I'm hungry. You're crabby. Might as well eat."

They sit in a back booth, where the sightline to the bar television is partially blocked by a life-sized, moth-eaten scarecrow tied to a pillar. Barnes takes in the other half-assed Halloween decorations, the butt-filled ashtray on the table, and, beside it, salt and pepper shakers that appear to have been licked by a toddler.

"Hey, fellas. I'm Kim." The waitress has a broad, freckled face and a friendly smile. "What can I get for you?"

"Another spot for that scarecrow would be good," Stef says. "We can't see the sports highlights."

"Sorry, but the boss would kill me. His wife made it."

Barnes sees Stef open his mouth and curtails whatever he's going to say by asking the waitress how the game played out. Not that he cares.

"Twins were down by three runs going into the bottom of the fifth, but they scored four runs, and then Hrbek hit a grand slam in the bottom of the sixth, and—"

"Really? Hrbek can't hit."

"That's what everyone thought. Twins won, 11–5. Now, what do you want to eat?"

Barnes orders a grilled cheese and fries. This isn't the kind of place where you ask about the specials, much less the soup of the day. But Stef does, and orders it, even after Kim goes back to the kitchen to see if there's any left. "It's either beef vegetable, or lentil. I'm not sure which," she reports.

"Either is fine. I'll have a bowl."

"There's barely enough for a cup. I'll make it on the house."

She disappears, and returns to drop off two fountain sodas and a cup of mushy brown liquid. Stef tastes it with a filmy spoon.

"Well? Is it beef vegetable, or lentil?"

"You got me."

"Is it edible?"

"If you're not the galloping gourmet."

Watching Kim head back to the kitchen, Barnes realizes they should have shown her the photos of Wayland and Gypsy Colt. He was too preoccupied with Tino to give it a thought.

Stef reaches for the salt and pepper shakers and tries to sprinkle his soup. The tops appear to be clogged—with toddler spit, most likely. He knocks them both against the table and liberally douses his soup with some of each before asking, "You doing all right, kid?"

"Not really."

"Sucks to lose a friend."

"Yeah."

Barnes slides the ashtray closer and reaches into his pocket for his cigarettes. As he pulls them out, something falls to the floor under the table. He starts to bend.

"It hit my foot. I got it," Stef says, and reaches down. When he lifts his hand, it's holding a cigar.

A Cuban.

With a pink band that reads *It's a Girl*.

He looks at it, and then at Barnes. "What the hell? Where'd you get this?"

It would be so easy to lie. Say he found it. A friend gave it to him. Anything but the truth.

But when Barnes opens his mouth, that's what falls out.

PEERING IN A ground-floor window of the big Victorian house on North Cayuga Street, Red spots someone asleep on the couch. She can't make out a face, just a lump under an afghan, but it has to be her. It *has* to be.

Heart racing, she steals around the side of the house to see if anyone else is in there, awake. Lights are on, but the other rooms appear empty.

Now she just has to figure out how to get in. There's a mudroom, with windows on three sides and a back door with a Welcome mat. She tentatively turns the doorknob, certain it's locked.

It isn't. Maybe because there's nothing in here worth stealing—just a broom, a trash can, and some coats hanging on a hook. The inside door is locked, though.

She lifts the mat.

No key.

But a quick search reveals a key ring hanging on a hook beside the door, half buried in the folds of a black jacket. Certain none of the keys on it will open the back door, she tries one. No.

Another. No.

A third—

The lock turns.

Just like at Bernadette's apartment.

Red breaks into a grin.

She opens the door quietly and creeps into a huge kitchen, lit by a light under the stove hood. In its glow, Red spots a gorgeous wicker basket heaped with freshly picked apples, waiting on the counter like a welcome gift.

She isn't hungry. She's far too worked up to eat. Yet she can't resist. It's been so long . . . too long . . .

She snatches a crisp red Cortland and takes an enormous bite.

It's good, so good, like the ones she ate every day when she was a kid.

It brings back memories, though. Some are nice—before they found out Daddy was never coming home, and Mommy threw away the medicine that kept her "fits" at bay, and the hot iron left its indelible mark, and Georgy Girl stopped talking, like Zechariah in the Bible.

Red had learned about him at Sunday school, and again many years later, in one of White's so-called bedtime stories at the foster home. Back then, Red was allowed to call her by her real name, Gypsy. She was six years older, and she liked to treat Red like a little sister. Red liked that almost as much as she liked when they were alone in the dark, cuddled in one of the twin beds.

"I have been sent to speak to you and to tell you this good news," Gypsy read from the book of Luke one night. *"And now you will be silent and not able to speak until the day this happens, because you did not believe my words, which will come true at their appointed time."*

She looked up at Red. "Do you understand?"

"I . . . I think so."

"And you believe it, right?"

"With all my heart."

Now Gypsy's prophecies have come true.

Red finishes the apple and throws the core into the garbage, resisting the urge to take another. You can't have too much of a certain food without someone thinking there's something wrong with you.

If your foster parents decide you're eating too much of one thing, they'll tell the social worker who will alert psychiatrists who will put you through all kinds of tests to see if you're crazy.

"Why do you eat so many apples?" they'll ask, and when you shrug and say you just like them, and ask what's wrong with that, they'll say nothing's wrong with liking something, as long as you're not obsessed.

"I'm not obsessed! I'm keeping the doctor away!"

"What?"

"An apple a day! An apple a day!"

If you shout at them and bury your head in your lap rocking and sobbing and trying, trying, trying not to remember the doctor, the doctor will barge in anyway—into your head, into the room. He won't be the same doctor who tormented you while your mother—your insane, abusive mother—sat in the waiting room pretending she believed he was erasing the angry scar on your face. But you will shrink in terror when you see the white coat, because you know what men like him can do to you.

This doctor will give you a shot and the screams and terror will go away for a while. You won't return to the foster home, and Gypsy. You'll be sent to a hospital, the kind where they don't hurt you with their hands and tools and prods and probes, but with questions that make you remember all the things you want to forget, need to forget . . .

"An apple a day." That's what Mother always said. *"An apple a day . . ."*

You do what you have to do to keep the doctor away.

Red tries to swallow, forcing the apple down into her gut with the white pills and the memories. It threatens to come churning back up. She rushes to the sink. She scoops cold water into her mouth with trembling hands.

The girl on the couch must be a sound sleeper. Lucky her. She doesn't have to cower in bed, listening for footsteps, and Mommy.

Red pauses to steady herself, pressing a jittery hand against the refrigerator.

There, she sees another sign.

Like a treasure map *X*, a red apple-shaped magnet sits on top of Margaret Costello's portrait, the one in the black drape and pearls. Only this one says PROOF across the front. Her hair isn't teased high and flipped up at the ends. It's shorter now, swooped across her forehead, hiding her widow's peak.

But that's her smile for sure. The dimples are unmistakable.

She's here. I've found her.

Red slips toward the front of the house, careful not to make a sound.

In the living room, she moves toward the figure under the afghan. She's almost there when she spots something lying on the floor in her path and a gasp escapes her.

It can't be!

Georgy Girl.

"HAPPY BIRTHDAY, DEAR Mimi . . ." Jessie sings, and hands Amelia a gift-wrapped box.

"I'm not Mimi."

"Yes, you are! Open your present! You're going to love it! It's the one thing you want. The thing you've been looking for!"

"But it can't be. The box is so small, and all I'm looking for is—"

"Don't you believe in magic, Mimi?" Silas asks, and poof! There's Marceline, with the basket. There's a baby in it, and she looks like Amelia, and she's wearing a blue dress trimmed in white lace.

Mimi . . .
I'm not Mimi!
I'm not me . . .
Me.
I'm looking for me. And there I am!

She reaches for the baby, but it's just a doll. Plastic. Fake. If you pull the ring in her back, she says, *"I love y—"*

Amelia opens her eyes to see a stranger standing a few feet away.

She's holding the doll—and a gun.

GEORGY GIRL—HERE. After all these years.

Soaked in cold sweat, Red juggles the gun with a trembling hand, needing to hear the words at last. She fumbles for the plastic ring and pulls the cord. Not hard enough. The doll makes an odd little groan.

"Stop that! Talk! Say *'I love you'*!"

She yanks the cord.

"Nice Mommy."

"No! She wasn't! She hurt me! She didn't love me. You did. Tell me. Tell me!"

"Nice Mommy."

Red hurtles Georgy Girl across the room. She smashes into the wall behind the couch, and the couch . . .

The girl is sitting up now with her feet on the floor as if she'd been poised to escape.

She isn't Margaret's daughter, or Bernadette's. Nor can she be Oran's. There's nothing pale about her. Nothing white. She's black.

Black.

It's a sign.

Red aims the gun, hand shaking violently.

If you take too much, you're going to get antsy.

The girl, too, is trembling.

"Don't move," Red tells her. "Where is she?"

"Who?"

"The baby!"

Something dawns in her eyes. She knows. She knows exactly what Red is talking about.

"She isn't here."

"Don't lie to me." Red moves toward her, chest aching. Her heart is broken. It broke twenty-two years ago when her father was killed in Vietnam and her mother turned into a scary monster and handed her over to an even more terrifying one.

She raises the gun and slides her thumb to cock the weapon, but it won't settle the way it should. It's jerking all over the place, even though she learned to shoot ten years ago at a range where she took aim at targets, pretending they were the doctor's head.

Through the roar in her ears, she hears the gun cock, and now she can pull the trigger if she can just find it and squeeze.

She finds it.

Squ—

AFTER FINISHING THEIR food, Barnes and Stef used a pay phone at the Plantation to check with local law enforcement. They're tied up, shorthanded, and can't get here anytime soon. Barnes and Stef are going to check out the Sandy Oyster on their own, and call for backup if they need it, which isn't looking likely.

"I meant to take a leak before we left the restaurant," Stef says as they pick their way across the gravel lot toward the cottage development. "But you got me all worked up with your story about the kid, kid."

Barnes shakes his head. "You can't call me a kid when I've got one."

Telling his partner about the baby may not have been

a warm and fuzzy experience, but it's better that way. Stef was his gruff self, so there was no need for Barnes to scour raw emotions. He's the last person who'd pass judgment on the fact that Barnes hadn't even gotten past a one-night stand with the child's mother. Having stuck around for his kids long after he'd stopped loving his wife, he wasn't going to tell Barnes to get married, or run away, or even do the right thing.

"Listen, one last thing about this, and then we can drop it. I'm not going to give you advice, because you and me don't have much in common. I don't know what you need to do or how you need to do it. But if I can help you, I will. That's it."

"I appreciate that. I . . ." Stupid emotions. Barnes attempts to cover them with a joke. "I'll take a million in cash. Big bills are fine."

"If I had it to spare—or at all—I'd give it to you, kid." Stef gives him an awkward little punch on the arm, then gestures at the small office, where a television screen is flickering. "Guessing there's no restroom in there. Go find our clerk. Her name is Mandy. I'll be right in." Stef heads toward an overgrown area with a swing set, unzipping his fly.

Barnes steps inside. A drab, pudgy man in a stained Patriots sweatshirt looks up from a tabletop television. The room smells of BO and the Doritos he's eating from a jumbo-sized bag.

Showing his badge, Barnes tells him he's looking for Mandy.

"Me, too. She's not here."

"Do you know where she is?"

"Called in sick tonight. She in trouble with the law?"

"No, I just need to ask her a few questions about a case. Are you the manager?"

He's the owner, and informs Barnes that he was *sup-*

posed to be at a sports bar on the mainland today to watch Game Six with his buddies. Instead, he's stuck out here overnight with this dinky set, which gets bad reception even with the rabbit ears. To make matters worse, he's a Cardinals fan.

"There's always tomorrow," Barnes tells him, wondering where Stef is as he pulls out the photos of Perry Wayland and Gypsy Colt. "Have you seen either of these people?"

"Seen them where?"

"Here? Or . . . anywhere on the island?"

"No."

"How many guests do you have here tonight?"

"A few."

"Mind if I take a look at the records and see who's staying here?"

"I wouldn't mind, if I could find the records." He gestures around the cluttered office.

"Why don't we look for them?"

Barnes does most of the looking. Five minutes later, there's still no sign of the registration book, or Stef.

"Thanks for the look," Barnes says. "I'm going to go outside and talk to my partner."

Looking happy to be rid of him, the owner settles back at the table, adjusts the antenna, and reaches into the bag of chips.

Barnes steps out. There's Stef, looking anxious, over by what can only be the playground and picnic grove.

"I was just coming in to get you, kid."

"Get me for what?"

"We can go. I used that phone over there to call the precinct. Figured I'd better tell the captain the locals didn't show and we're on our own. Turns out Mandy isn't coming."

"No kidding. She called in sick."

"She's sick, all right. She called the tip line to say she made it all up."

"What?"

"Yeah. Said she never saw Wayland. It was a scam. She sent us chasing out here for no reason."

His words don't ring true. Barnes peers at him. His face is masked in shadows. "Are you sure about that?"

"Positive. Call the precinct yourself. They'll tell you."

On a day like this, it's not surprising that Barnes's instincts are off. He shrugs. "I don't need to call anyone. Let's get out of here before we're stranded."

SOMEONE SCREAMS, AND Amelia whirls to see Jessie at the foot of the stairs, barefoot and looking like a little girl who awakened from a nightmare . . . to a nightmare.

"Who is that? Oh, my God! Did you stab her?"

She looks down again, at the unconscious woman on the floor. A steak knife protrudes from her arm. It's the one Amelia had used earlier to cut into her chicken marsala. The one Jessie had forgotten to clear from the coffee table. The one Amelia had somehow found the courage to grab, and use, when she realized the lunatic was about to shoot her.

"Is she dead?"

"No! Please, Jessie. Please, call for help." Amelia sinks to the floor, staring at the gun that dropped from the woman's hand when she lunged at her with the knife.

"I'm calling Si." Jessie is panting, hall phone in hand, dialing.

"No, call the police, and an ambulance."

"Si will do it. I can't! It's ringing." She rakes a hand through her hair. It sticks up, a natural center part rising from a point high on her forehead. "God, Mimi, how did this . . . What happened?"

"I don't know! I woke up, and she was here, trying to kill me."

"But why? Who is she?"

"I think . . . oh, Jessie, I think she might be your mother."

"STOCKTON."

Barnes looks over at Stef, behind the wheel. He never calls him by his first name.

"Yeah?"

Stef says nothing, staring hard at the highway beyond the windshield wipers.

Rain started falling as Dewey guided the boat back across the choppy sound back to Montauk. Now it's sleet, and the salt trucks are out, rumbling up and down the Long Island Expressway.

Stef takes a deep breath like he's going to say something, but doesn't.

"What?"

His partner takes one hand off the steering wheel, reaches into the pocket of his suit coat, takes out a bulky envelope, and passes it to Barnes.

"What's this?"

"Open it."

"But—"

"Just do it."

Barnes does. "What . . . what is this?"

"Cash. All in hundreds. Not a million bucks, but a lot. Enough, I think."

"For what?"

"Your daughter."

Barnes stares at the money for a long time. "You got this from Perry Wayland. He was there?"

Stef nods.

"But—"

"I said I was going to help you."

"I didn't ask you to!"

"Did you ask me to save your life a few weeks ago? You're not stupid, kid. You know it's what we do."

Barnes stares at the envelope. "I don't understand. You asked Wayland for money to help your partner's sick baby, and he did?"

"It didn't go like that."

"How did it go?"

"I didn't ask. He offered. And it wasn't all for you. I'm not stupid, either."

So he kept some. Terrific.

"You lied."

"I didn't lie. I didn't know he was there. I saw him out back when I went to take a leak, and he saw me. Knew right away I was a cop."

"But . . . I thought you said Mandy lied."

"I said she *said* she lied, when she called the precinct. She really did call."

"But not because she was trying to pull a scam?"

"No. When Mandy called the hotline, she'd really seen him. I guess she took back her story when she realized she could do better than Biff's reward by going straight to Wayland."

"Why did he leave his family?"

"Why do most people leave? He's sick of his life. He just wants to chill out and—"

"Chill out?"

"That's how he put it. Look, kid, things are complicated when you're married. You don't know. You don't *want* to know. You said it yourself. But you have a daughter—"

"This is not," Barnes bites out, "about my daughter."

After a long silence, Stef says, "He's with his old girlfriend. Gypsy Colt. Miss White. Same person. You were right about her. Good instincts, kid."

Barnes closes his eyes and tilts his head back, listening to the rest.

About how Perry was unhappily married, and still in love with his old sweetheart. He gave her an engagement ring. They're leaving the country by boat before dawn, going where no one will ever find them. Everyone will be better off. His wife is set for life, and so are his daughters. They won't have to worry about a thing, financially.

Head still back, eyes still closed, jaw still set, Barnes makes up his mind. He puts the money in his pocket.

Neither will mine.

WHY, AMELIA WONDERS, don't hospitals have comfortable benches?

This one, in the waiting area outside the ER, is worse than the one she and Calvin shared at Morningside Memorial back in March, after Bettina died.

Maybe they want you to get used to suffering while you're here, because that's what you'll do when you go back to your life. A hospital visit never leads to anything good.

Unless you're at the maternity ward.

Not a thought Amelia is emotionally equipped to entertain right now.

Jessie is beside her, half leaning, maybe dozing. At least she stopped crying.

Too stunned to cry, too shell-shocked to sleep, Amelia goes over and over what happened. Waking up to see the stranger with a hideous, disfigured face. Grabbing the knife. Trying to save Jessie.

"Si!" Jessie sits up abruptly.

So she wasn't asleep. She's looking at Silas, walking

toward them. He's wearing the cardigan sweater he'd thrown on over blue flannel pajama bottoms and slippers when he rushed next door earlier, hearing the sirens.

When he reaches the bench, he wastes no time in telling them what's going on. "She didn't make it."

Amelia gasps. "Did I—"

"You didn't kill her, Amelia. That wound was superficial. They said she had a heart attack."

"But—that's not—how old was she? Forty?"

"No. Only twenty-seven."

Amelia closes her eyes, seeing the scar. She asks Silas if the police told him how she got it.

"No, but . . . it sounds like she had a hard life. Terrible things happened to her, and . . . she did some terrible things."

"If she was twenty-seven . . ." Jessie says in a small, un-Jessie-like voice.

Amelia turns to look at her, the light dawning.

"You're eighteen! She couldn't be your mother."

"Absolutely not." Silas pats Jessie's shoulder. "You might never find your mom, but that person . . . that wasn't her."

She's crying again. "I don't need to find my mom. I think Amelia was right. I already know where she is."

Amelia hugs her, wishing she could say the same thing. Through her own tears, she sees Silas looking at her. He gives a little nod, as if to remind her of what he said earlier.

It's not going to happen overnight.

It might never happen.

But maybe someday . . .

"Can we get out of here?" Jessie asks Silas.

"Not yet. The police have more questions, and reports to fill out." Seeing her expression, he adds, "Don't worry, it's routine. They spend hours on paperwork after something like this."

"Hours? Can I call my parents first?" Jessie asks.

"I already did. Reached them at their hotel in New Haven. They're on their way home. But Amelia, I think you should call your dad."

Her dad? And say what?

She forces a small smile, a nod . . .

And a lie.

"I already did."

Chapter Twenty-Three

Sunday, October 25
Block Island

Kim carries the coffeepot toward the booth in the back, wondering about the woman who's been sitting there for hours. She's nothing special at a glance, but close-up, she looks like Elizabeth Taylor. Younger, with big violet eyes and strands of dark hair falling beneath a fashionable fedora. Every guy in the place would be all over her if she hadn't disguised her beauty in that getup and sat with her back to them all, facing the wall, her pretty face hidden even from the two guys in the next booth.

They weren't locals, nor were they tourists. Detectives, maybe, wearing suits. The handsome young black one seemed caught up in some drama of his own, and the dumpy old guy kept complaining about not being able to see the TV, slurped his soup, and dribbled it down his shirt without noticing. She wished she'd doctored it up a little in the kitchen after she saw the tip he'd left her.

The jolly Twins fans had stuck around to celebrate long after the game ended. The woman stayed, too. Earlier, she'd told Kim she's spending the weekend on the island with her boyfriend, and he's getting on her nerves.

"I just need a place to chill out. Do you mind if I hang out, take one of those booths for a while?"

"Not if you don't mind that it won't have a view of the game."

"Game?"

"World Series. Game Six. Guess you're not a sports fan."

"Not baseball. But I used to be into horses."

"Riding?"

"Riding, jumping, racing, being," she said with a sly smile, and Kim felt like she'd missed a joke. She was too busy then to figure it out.

She still can't, though things have slowed down now that the regulars have shuffled off to their beds.

"Can I get you a warm-up, hon?"

The woman doesn't seem to hear her, staring at the pitiful scarecrow lassoed to the pillar like a bad guy in a spaghetti Western. He's slumping forward, as though even he is ashamed of his decrepit state.

Kim notices a huge, expensive-looking engagement ring on the woman's left hand. Wow. She should have been friendlier, tried to sell her some pie. She might have gotten a nice tip to make up for the cheapskate cop.

"Hon? Can I get you some more coffee?"

This time, she blinks and looks up. "No. Thanks."

"You sure?"

"Positive. Do you know what time it is?"

"Just past midnight. My little one will be up bouncing around before daybreak."

"You have a child?"

"Yes. A little girl."

"I bet you'll do anything for her, right?"

"Anything in the world."

The woman nods, as if that's what she expected.

"Do you have kids?" Kim asks.

"Me? God, no. Never. That's not my scene. I'll take the check, please. I have to be someplace."

"Everything around here's closed at this hour."

"I'm going boating."

"Night fishing?"

The woman nods, as if that suggestion will do. Maybe she's stoned or something.

"Coastal storm in the forecast. You're not going out on the water alone, are you, hon? Because that would be dangerous."

"No, with my boyfriend."

"You mean, fiancé?" Kim gestures at the ring.

"Oh. Yeah."

"Not getting on your nerves anymore?"

"Now that I've had a chance to chill out, I'm over it."

"That's good." Kim goes to fetch the check, totaling a dollar. She'll be lucky to get a quarter tip.

The beautiful woman evaporates into the night while Kim's back is turned. But she left a crisp fifty-dollar bill on the table.

Brooklyn

BACK AT THE precinct, Barnes had allowed Stef to fill out the case paperwork with the glaring omission. He called the hospital and made sure his daughter is stable. Then he went through the motions of completing work duties, thinking about Wayland's choices and his own, Andrea's words ringing ominously in his ears.

"Sometimes, a fortune comes with more baggage than you're capable of carrying for the rest of your life."

But not having money to save someone you love comes with even more.

He did feel a small sense of closure upon learning that Enid Skaggs had died up in Ithaca. At least the strange, scarred woman can't hurt anyone else. That part is over, though the case will continue to be unraveled in the days ahead.

It's not clear why she was fixated on the Brooklyn Butcher case, though as Stef pointed out, she's hardly the only one. He believes her attempt to connect Perry Wayland to the killing spree was opportunistic. That she heard about the missing millionaire and fixated on that, as well.

"It didn't hit the papers till Saturday," Barnes pointed out. "The Sheerans were killed Friday night."

"He went missing Thursday. She lives in New York. She heard about it, or she had some connection to him. Who the hell knows? Maybe she ran into him somewhere. Maybe she cleans his office building."

"How'd she get the cufflink?"

"We'll find out. Maybe she stole it. Or he lost it, and she found it."

Like the little gold ring engraved with a blue *C*.

They're back out in the storm now, Stef navigating the slick roadways in Brooklyn. He's dropping Barnes at the hospital on his way home.

The radio crackles with activity. Number-coded dramas are playing out all over town. There are a couple of 10–52s—*domestic disputes*—though only one is coded *F* to indicate a *firearm* involved.

Countless 10–10s—*narcotics sales*.

One 10–33—*explosive device*—in Tompkins Square Park. Update: unfounded.

So far, there's been only one 10–65—*missing persons*,

accompanied by a BOLO for light-skinned black female, aged nineteen, five-foot-nine, 120 pounds. Last seen Friday at home on Lexington Avenue in Harlem, reported by the father. If Wayland's case were officially wrapped up, Barnes and Stef might have been assigned to this one, but it's not going to happen today. Not any time soon.

Stef stops the car in front of the hospital. "Just the way it is, Barnes. The way it has to be. You know that, right?"

Barnes is silent.

Beyond the windshield, the rain has turned to a wet snow.

Wash, in his head: *"Nothing like that first snowfall. Scrubs away the grime, makes everything fresh and pretty . . . It's all about the timing . . . whether it's welcome depends on when it shows up and whether you're ready."*

Barnes pats his pocket to make sure the envelope is there, and his key chain holding the little gold ring.

C . . . for *Charles.*

And for *Charisse.*

He already has Dad's initials tattooed on his arm. He'll give his daughter the ring. One day, maybe it can remind her of him.

If, going forward, he could be half the man his father was—half the man Wash is . . .

But I don't know. I just don't know.

"Thanks, Stef," he says, opening the door. "For . . . the ride."

"You're welcome for the ride. For *everything.*"

Barnes gets out of the car and walks toward the hospital, toward his baby girl, leaving Stef alone in the car with the radio crackling about Amelia Crenshaw, the missing girl in Harlem.

Manhattan

AT LAST, GREGORY Devlin spots the Port Authority looming beyond the bus windshield wipers.

His day started before dawn on Saturday, driving the first morning shift that takes him from the city up through the Hudson Valley and then northwest into the Catskills. The bus always starts off full, but starts to empty out when they reach the college towns—Poughkeepsie, Binghamton, Ithaca . . .

It fills up again in Rochester with folks riding to the last stop, Buffalo. Before embarking on the return trip, Gregory gets to take a decent break. It's too short for a nap, but long enough to order some chicken wings at the Anchor Bar. He's a regular there now.

"You get the same thing every week," the pretty young waitress commented today, setting down his double order of medium wings. "Don't you ever want to change it up?"

"I would if I could get wings down in Queens, where I live, but no one's ever heard of them there."

"I'll come visit you and bring you some," she said with a flirty smile.

He changed the subject to the Bills-Miami game, thinking of his pregnant wife at home. She'll be sound asleep by the time he gets there, and he won't stir three hours later when she rolls her roly-poly self out of bed to go to her job as a Key Food cashier. Sometimes, he worries about what's going to happen when the baby comes and she can't work for a few weeks.

"We'll get by," she told him just yesterday and patted his hand, as if that were a plan and not an empty reassurance.

Yawning, Gregory guides the bus along the network

of tunnels and ramps leading into the terminal, the headlights catching more than a few scuttling rats of the furry and human variety. This place is a dump at any hour, but especially overnight, when the most degenerate population segment takes over and the cops seem to turn a blind eye. Sometimes, he worries that certain passengers won't make it out of here in one piece.

Tonight, he's concerned about a pockmarked, bespectacled high school kid who boarded in Rochester with a viola case.

At least there are no little old ladies this trip. Not frail ones, anyway. Just the same no-nonsense broad who boarded last minute Saturday morning and sat solo in the front row seat reserved for disabled passengers. He could see her in the rearview mirror, quietly facing forward, basket perched on her lap. She disembarked up in Ithaca. When he stopped there for the evening run back to New York, there she was again. The bus was crowded, and she had to sit somewhere in back.

She reminds Gregory of his Auntie Ruth, who before she lost her marbles was also a sassy black woman. She looked a lot like this one—attractive for her advanced age, with a thick coil of salt-and-pepper braids.

"Port Authority," he calls, flicking on the overhead light and pulling into the gate. "Last stop, Port Authority."

The passengers stir to action, some waking from a sound sleep. He steps out and opens the luggage compartment, handing over their bags as they file past him. The old lady is taking her sweet time moving down the aisle to the door.

Gregory wills her along, looking for tokens in his pocket and thinking about food, home, and bed. Maybe he'll jump off the subway three stops before his own and pick up a couple of slices from his favorite pizza joint on Queens Boulevard.

He finds two brass tokens mixed with the loose change and drops one as he sorts it from the quarters. It rolls under the bus. Gregory drops to his knees on the filthy pavement and strains to reach it with his hand, not wanting to go belly down in his white shirt. Almost . . . almost . . .

Got it.

"Child, what you doin' down there?"

Recognizing the accent, he turns, expecting to find himself face to feet with orthopedic shoes and saggy stockings. Instead, he sees a pair of lace-up booties in the same red leather as the satchel she's waiting to claim.

She's shed her coat, now wearing a gaudy fringed shawl, and her coiled braids are hidden beneath a bright watermelon-colored headdress. She slings the handle of her cloth-covered woven basket over her arm and holds out a brown hand for her satchel.

"It's been a long day. Let me carry it for you, ma'am."

She shakes her head and says something.

It takes him a moment to translate: "Where I'm going, you're not." Probably true, unless she's in the mood for pizza.

"Are you taking a cab? The subway?"

"Neither."

"Well, is someone waiting for you? Because the weather is getting—"

"I not be gwine till dayclean. T'night, I stay here."

He looks at her in dismay. "You can't do that. You have no idea what this place is like at night."

"I do. I stayed last night in the terminal after the bus was canceled, and—"

"They didn't cancel any Ithaca buses last night."

"Not to Ithaca."

"So you spent the night in this hellhole and then you got on the wrong bus?"

"No." She shakes her head. "I changed my plan, for a friend."

"A friend in Ithaca?"

She nods. "But she's okay now, so I can go home on the bus in dayclean."

"Sure I can't help you with that bag?"

"No, t'engky."

"Get home safely, ma'am, wherever it is," he calls as she shuffles through the door.

She gives a muffled reply as it closes behind her.

Gregory catches only one word.

Island.

Ithaca

IN A SMALL, windowless office, Amelia sits across from two police detectives asking her countless questions. There are some she can't answer, and a few she'd prefer not to. Like about why she came to Ithaca to find Silas. And whether her father knows she's here.

For a split second, she considers lying, as she had when she told Silas she'd called Calvin. But you don't lie to the police. She admits she'd left home without telling him where she was going, though at her age, that's not such a big deal, is it?

Turns out, it is.

A police officer knocks on the door to request a private word with the detectives. They step out, closing the door.

Grateful for the break, Amelia rests her forehead on the table. She feels lousy—mouth dry, stomach queasy, head pounding. A hangover, Jessie had said earlier, when they were sitting on the hard bench. She has one, too.

She's in the next room, waiting for her turn with the detectives.

Lucky Jessie. If that woman had somehow turned out to be her birth mother . . .

Lucky Jessie. Her adoptive mother is on the way, rushing home through a storm to comfort her.

Amelia has never felt more alone in her life.

"You had a mother who raised you, too," Jessie had pointed out, right before they went to bed. The conversation is fuzzy now, but Amelia's been trying to replay it, because there was something else Jessie had said . . . something that troubled her, before she fell asleep.

The door opens again. Only one detective is back. He returns to the table, but he doesn't reclaim his seat. Instead, he takes the telephone from an adjacent desk, stretches it as far as the cord will reach, and plunks it down in front of her.

"Miss Crenshaw. When your name went through the system in association with this crime, it came back in association to a missing persons case in New York City."

"It . . . *What?*"

Her birth mother—birth parents?—have been looking for her all along? All these years, and she never knew . . .

"So I really was kidnapped?"

"Pardon?"

"They said I'd been abandoned, like I told you—that's why I'm here, so that Professor Moss can help me find my birth parents, remember?"

He stares at her like he has no idea what she's talking about.

"I thought . . . you said . . . if they filed a missing persons case on me, I must have been kidnapped, right? Or . . . lost, somehow?"

"I'm sorry. You misunderstood. Your father, Calvin Crenshaw, filed the report yesterday. He's been frantic."

"He . . . what . . ." She shoves words past crushing disappointment. "How do you know?"

He points to the phone. The hold light is red.

"He's on line two. I'll let you have some privacy." He leaves the room, closing the door behind him.

Amelia stares at the phone.

Calvin.

Not her birth mother.

Not kidnapped.

Not even put up for adoption. Just . . .

Abandoned.

Maybe her birth mother'd had a hard life, like Enid Skaggs. Maybe she's a despicable woman, too. Maybe not. But she chose to—

That's it! That's what Jessie had said last night, when they argued before bed.

"She didn't choose to leave you . . ."

She wasn't talking about Amelia's birth mother.

"She got sick."

Bettina.

Amelia's been so angry with her for months, dragging all that fury around, refusing to forgive her . . .

For the lie?

Or for leaving?

"You've suffered terrible losses," Silas had said yesterday, and the dam had fractured. She held back the tears then.

Now they stream down her cheeks.

She's lost two mothers. But only one took care of her. Only one tried to force-feed her homemade Southern food, and warned her about strangers, and sewed her that godawful pink dress with the uneven sleeves.

Her birth mother *might* have loved her, but . . .

Bettina *did* love her.

And now she's gone, and I'm angry, so angry . . .

But not alone.

Amelia reaches for the phone, lifts the receiver, presses the button for line two.

"Daddy?" she manages, before her voice is choked by sobs. But he's crying, too. Telling her he thought something terrible had happened to her. That he'd lost her.

She'd thought the same thing.

Something terrible had happened. And they'd lost each other. Now they'll have to find their way . . .

Not back. You can never go back.

We'll find our way forward.

She hangs up with a promise to call him again in the morning, opens the door, and sees that it's already here.

No, not morning.

Beyond a wall of glass, the world is bathed in soft gray light, shimmering in soft white snow.

Dayclean.

Sing Sing

SPONTANEOUS LIES TEND to spill from Oran Matthews's lips like well-rehearsed lines from a script, even when he's under pressure. Somehow, for him, the truth has always been much harder to come by. And sometimes when he tells it, he wonders why he bothers.

He glares at the two NYPD homicide detectives seated across from him. He isn't on the witness stand this time, testifying under oath, fighting for his life. He owes them nothing, yet he's giving them the truth—with a few omissions, yes.

Still, they don't seem to believe a word he's saying.

"No, I don't! How many times do I have to—"

"Sorry, Oran, but we want to be absolutely clear that you—"

"I don't! Don't know her. Don't know who she is. Never seen her before in my life. Never heard of her."

He maintains eye contact with the two men, keeping his voice steady and his cuffed hands firmly clasped on the table between them.

He doesn't know this Enid Skaggs woman they're asking about. He has no idea what might have motivated her bloody rampage. And he sure as hell won't allow them to see that he's shaken by the news that he's lost a child.

Emily. Such a beautiful name.

Such a terrible shame.

What about the others? He can only hope that Gypsy has found them by now, assembled them to wait, as he instructed.

"What about your daughter?" asks the younger of the two detectives, as if he's read Oran's mind. He tongs his double chins with a fat thumb and forefinger, waiting for the answer.

"Never met her, either."

A pause. "That's strange, because we're told she was here to visit you not long ago, and that she comes every Father's Day and every Christmas. So—"

"What? You mean Gypsy?"

"Gypsy Colt Matthews. She *is* your daughter, correct?"

"Yeah, she's my daughter. I thought you were talking about the dead kid up in Boston."

"Also your biological daughter."

"Guess so. How come you're asking me about Gypsy?" Saliva pools on his tongue. If he swallows, it will be a gulp.

"When was the last time you saw her?" the other detective asks. He, too, is jowly, his necktie too short above a fleshy gut, revealing the straining bottom button on his white shirt.

"And put a knife to thy throat, if thou be a man given to appetite . . ."

Proverbs, chapter 23, verse 2.

"Oran? When did you last see Gypsy?"

"Guess it was Father's Day. That's what you said, right? I don't keep track."

"Talked to her lately?"

"I don't *talk* to her. You think I have a damned phone I can pick up and call whenever I feel like it? I have to write to her. And no, I haven't. Not in a while."

"Do you know where she is?"

"How would I know? I'm in here." The words are slicked with defiance and spittle. He will not allow himself to falter.

The older detective leans forward. "Looks like Enid Skaggs and your daughter Gypsy spent some time in the same foster home, so we thought maybe—Hey, you okay, there?"

No, Oran isn't okay. And not just because the saliva has finally slid down his throat, making him choke.

Through the roar in his brain, he hears someone ask a guard to bring him water. By the time it arrives, he's retched the contents of his stomach, men recoiling all around him.

Body quaking, bile dripping down his chin, he closes his eyes. Ah, there she is—his fearless, clever little girl, with that striking violet gaze and raven mane.

"I like it just the two of us," she'd said, long after he'd removed her mother, before her sisters and brothers were born.

She's the only person in this world Oran has ever trusted.

Now she's betrayed him, just as Delilah betrayed the mighty Samson. Gypsy, too, is a beguiling beauty who conquered the seemingly invincible man of faith, robbing him of his strength, condemning him to imprisonment, blindness, and death.

He hears a spray bottle spritzing, smells disinfectant mingling in the air with his half-digested breakfast. Someone mops his face and holds a cup to his lips. He swallows tepid water, remembering Jesus and the sour wine.

It is finished.

He opens his eyes. A custodian wipes vomit from the table. The guards stand by. The detectives are still watching him intently.

"Need another minute?" the older one asks.

Oran shakes his head.

They resume their questioning about a connection between the dead murderess and his daughter. He assures them he knows nothing about it, nor Gypsy's whereabouts, and nothing about the murders.

The truth, all of it.

They thank him and leave, and he's led back to his cell, alone once more. He sits on his cot and stares at the pen and notebook he uses to write his sermons and letters to his daughter.

They'll look for her in northern Maine, he supposes, but he knows they won't find her there. They'll never find her. Nor will he see her again in this world, or the next.

Closing his eyes, he allows himself one last glimpse of her lovely face, searching for a hint of betrayal.

Seek, and ye shall find.

Her violet eyes have paled, glinting like the silver for which Delilah traded Samson's love; like a honed blade before it plunges into flesh and emerges wet with blood.

Oran opens his eyes and picks up the pen. It trembles in his hand.

He clenches his fist, steadies his grip, and thrusts upward, gouging first one eyeball, and then the other.

Continue reading for a sneak peek at

LITTLE BOY BLUE

On sale Summer 2019!

Chapter One

May 12, Present Day
New York City

Even before she opens her eyes, Amelia Crenshaw Haines knows she's alone in her bed, in the room, in the apartment. Sleep's mellow hush lifts, and she hears traffic honking on Amsterdam Avenue ten stories below, sirens in the distance, and the soft whir of the HEPA air purifier on Aaron's dresser.

It's beyond her, how he'd gone all his life without knowing he's allergic to cats. That became apparent only after she'd brought home, and fallen in love with, the first of many rescue kittens. She hadn't offered to return it to the shelter. Nor had he asked her to.

He hadn't offered to skip today's business trip. Nor had she asked him to.

But she'd thought maybe . . .

She opens her eyes.

A small gift box sits on the pillow beside hers. Telltale turquoise, tied with a white satin ribbon: Tiffany's. A year ago, her heart would have leapt. Today, it sinks.

She leaves the box where it is, gets up, and goes into the adjoining bathroom. Aaron's navy cotton pajamas with the white piping hang on a hook behind the door. Early in their relationship, she got a kick out of his real pajamas, the kind with matching top and bottoms.

"What else would I wear?"

"You know . . . boxers and a tee shirt, or something, or . . . nothing."

He laughed and pulled her into his arms.

She kicks the door shut and reaches for her toothbrush, alone in the white porcelain holder. His went with him to Chicago . . . or was it Denver today? Not LA. That trip is next week. She'd toyed with tagging along until he told her his schedule will be too jammed for time together.

Just as well. Sunday is Mother's Day. Business always picks up around then, for obvious reasons.

Amelia stares into the mirror above the sink. She'd read once that light-skinned black women don't age as well as their darker counterparts. Maybe it's true. Today, she notes the deepening lines around her eyes and mouth, the slight sag beneath her jaw. There are no longer any wiry gray strands in her sleek shoulder-length hair, but only because she had it straightened and colored last month as an early birthday gift to herself.

"Girl, you are getting old."

The woman in the mirror nods and turns away.

She takes her steamy old time in the new shower, with gleaming white marble and dual high-end rain heads. The contractor had slyly pointed out that there's plenty of room for two, but she and Aaron have yet to test that. He's taken to showering when he gets home at night, and she's tried not to wonder why. Nor has she asked him. She has never been, and refuses to become, a suspicious wife.

Wrapped in a fluffy new white towel, Amelia returns to the bedroom and lifts the shades. The two tall windows face east, and the first beams of sunlight have cleared the building next door, spilling over the unmade bed and the turquoise box on Aaron's pillow.

She leaves it, goes to her closet, and pulls out her most

boring—er, professional—outfit: a lightweight wool navy Brooks Brothers skirt suit and white silk blouse. She dresses quickly, adding panty hose, low-heeled pumps, a string of pearls, and matching earrings. Boring, boring. If she had her way, she'd be wearing jeans, boots, a splashy-hued spring sweater, and the chunky teal and purple beads she bought in Union Square last week.

But she has a new client coming in this morning, and she learned early in her career that when her wardrobe leans casual, people don't seem to take her seriously.

"So, an investigative genealogist? What is it that you do, exactly?"

"I try to find out who you are and where you came from."

That simple response doesn't satisfy most people, but in the end, that's the information they want her to provide. It's what she wants to know herself. Someday, she might uncover the truth about her own past. More likely, she never will. But it's been gratifying to help other abandoned children discover their own roots.

She makes the bed, though she's the only one who will be climbing back into it tonight. Second nature, when you grow up sleeping on a pullout couch in the center of a cramped Harlem apartment. There was a time, after her mother died and before Amelia went away to college, when she'd taken perverse pleasure in leaving a rumpled tangle of bedding in the living room every morning.

She'd been so angry back then—at her mother, for dying, at her father, for letting grief consume him, at both of them for not telling her she wasn't their biological child. She'd discovered that shocking truth by chance the day she lost her mother.

A scant few years later, she'd lost her father as well. She's been an orphan for most of her adult life—an orphan who might still have parents out there somewhere.

"But you have me," Aaron used to say, and he'd be wounded if she told him that a husband was not a parent.

"You have my parents, though, and my brothers and sisters, and all the nieces and nephews . . ."

No, Aaron has them. She's the in-law. Yes, they're her family, and she knows better than anyone that familial bonds don't depend on blood.

Maybe Aaron's large, loving family is part of the reason she was so drawn to him in the first place.

Maybe?

Part of?

She'd met him through his sister, Karyn, who had the home life Amelia had always longed for. Bettina and Calvin had been as happily married as her in-laws are, but they didn't get to live into their golden years surrounded by a large, close-knit clan, and they sure didn't have money.

Karyn invited Amelia to spend Thanksgiving in a leafy suburb, at the three-story brick colonial where her parents had raised her and her four siblings. Generations gathered around a long table, just like a Hallmark movie—an elderly great uncle, a pair of newlyweds, a firstborn grandchild, and handsome, brilliant Aaron, just graduated from law school. The weekend was magical, scented with wood smoke, pumpkin spice, and fallen leaves. Trivial Pursuit by the fireplace, touch football on the lawn, a moonlit walk with Aaron. He held the leash of his brother's frisky chocolate lab in one hand, and clasped Amelia's with the other. She returned to her lonely little urban apartment certain that he was The One. She wanted to be a part of his world. Part of his family.

And so she has been, for over two decades. She can't imagine life without her in-laws. But life without Aaron? Isn't that what she's been living?

They used to be so happy together. Life was full—of each other, work, family and friends. Too full to miss the children they'd decided not to have. They weren't parental types, they'd agreed early on. A dozen nieces and nephews more than filled any void, as did their careers.

Aaron made partner a few years ago. She rented office space downtown for her burgeoning business. They bought this dream apartment, a prewar two-bedroom on the Upper West Side and embarked on extensive, disruptive renovations: rubble, dust, noise, and an endless parade of workmen. They completed the bathroom last month and moved on to the kitchen. It's currently gutted and tarped off so that they can no longer even share a home-cooked meal. Aaron dines with colleagues most nights—or so he says—and Amelia gobbles takeout in front of some reality TV show he finds ridiculous.

"Haven't you ever heard of guilty pleasures, Aaron?" she'd asked, not long ago, when he walked in on her in sweatpants, clutching a white carton of greasy beef chow fun, riveted by a Real Housewives catfight.

"Sure I have, babe. But this would definitely not be mine."

What is yours, Aaron?

She was afraid to ask.

Now he's abandoned her on her birthday.

Abandoned?

No, your birth parents abandoned you. Your husband is away on business. There's a big difference. Remember that. And you might be wrong. He might not be having an affair. He might just be busy, distracted, stressed, same as you. Same as anyone . . .

Except, she's never wrong.

She picks up the shiny turquoise box. The white satin ribbon slips away with a slight tug. She lifts the lid, bracing herself for the sparkly diamond bracelet, sapphire earrings, some expensive bauble a philandering husband presents to his supposedly unsuspecting wife.

But inside, she finds a silver Tiffany horseshoe key ring.

It holds a set of keys.

What in the . . . ?

The heart-shaped charm is engraved with a Sutton Place address and 7:30 p.m.

You're never wrong, huh?

A slow smile spreads across her face.

SOME DAYS, AMELIA misses working from home. This isn't one of them, and not just because a plumber and several hammer-toting workmen arrived as she was leaving.

The city is glorious on this sunny spring morning. She bypasses the subway, treating herself to a birthday cab to her office on the Lower East Side. The driver cuts through Central Park, a sea of tulip blossoms, horse-drawn carriages, joggers and baby buggies. Beyond an awning of tender chartreuse foliage, the Manhattan skyline gleams a cloudless blue expanse.

Stuck in traffic on the southbound FDR, she snaps a photo of her new keychain and texts it to Aaron with a heart emoji.

Sometimes he responds instantaneously to her texts, but not today. He's probably on the plane. But he must be flying home tonight, to meet her . . . where? Googling the address on the charm, she finds that it belongs to a luxurious garden townhouse along the river. She has no idea why he wants her to meet him there, but one thing's for certain: he didn't buy the place as a birthday surprise. They're not hurting, but they can't afford eight-figure Sutton Place real estate.

She'd have reached downtown a half hour sooner had

she taken the subway, arriving just five minutes before her first appointment.

Her office consists of one third-floor room in a brick tenement on Allen Street just off Delancey. Hardwood floors, tin ceilings, and a fire escape window framed by swaying maple boughs rising from patchwork court-yards below. Every time she sees the brass door placard, she feels a prickle of satisfaction.

Amelia Crenshaw Haines, Investigative Genealogist.

Calvin and Bettina would have been proud; Silas Moss, her mentor, even prouder. She'd met the Cornell University professor at nineteen, having heard about his pioneering DNA research as it related to adoptees and so-called foundlings—abandoned children, like herself. Si's efforts to find her biological parents had never come to fruition, but she'd spent almost a decade in Ithaca, earning a college degree and then working as his assistant.

He's elderly now, but she visits him as often as she can—or so she tells herself. It's just hard to get away; harder still to see him as he is now, confined to a wheelchair, sharp eyes and brilliant mind extinguished.

Expecting her client any minute now, Amelia logs into her desktop computer to access the electronic paperwork the woman, Lily Tucker, filled out in advance of this appointment.

Lily had been found abandoned as a toddler at a suburban Connecticut shopping mall in 1990. She'd been well cared for, and didn't match the description of any known missing children.

She and Amelia have a lot in common. Lily is also African-American, and was raised by loving adoptive parents. But she was older when she was found, and might have some memory of—

Amelia's cell phone buzzes with an incoming call.

Aaron!

She snatches it up, but it isn't her husband. She grins, answering it.

"Happy maybe birthday to you . . . happy maybe birthday to you . . . happy maybe birthday, dear Mimi . . . happy maybe birthday to you."

Only one person in the world has ever called her by that nickname.

"Thanks, Jessie. You always remember."

"It's pretty much the only thing. I mean, don't ask me to stop at the store for milk, pay the electric bill, or remember where I parked my car in the downtown garage, because this middle-aged brain is more useless every day."

Jessie, middle-aged. It's hard to imagine, though they try to see each other at least once a year. At least two, maybe three, have flown by since they last met. Jessie, married with children, still lives up in Ithaca.

"So how are you celebrating, Mimi? Tell me you're off today."

"I'm off today," she obliges. "But actually, I'm not."

"Come on, nobody works on her birthday."

"I'm guessing most people do."

"Not when they're self-employed! Why didn't you give yourself the day off?"

"To do what?"

"Visit me. You haven't been to Ithaca in ages. Si's been asking for you."

"Really?" Last time they spoke, Jessie told her that Silas Moss hadn't strung together a coherent sentence in months.

"Well, not asking. But he misses you. And whenever I tell him about you, he smiles, like he knows. He's in there somewhere, Mimi. Come see him. Us. I have plenty of room."

"With four kids and a dog?"

"Okay, not *plenty*. But our door is always open. You and Aaron should plan a road trip."

"We don't have a car, remember?"

Plus, her husband isn't a fan of Ithaca. He finds it—and all of upstate New York—dreary and depressing. She told him that was because he'd never seen it in summer or fall, but when they remedied that with additional visits, it poured the duration of both.

"Why don't you come to New York instead?" she tells Jessie. "Girls' weekend at my place."

"What about Aaron?"

"He'll make himself scarce. He's good at that." Her laugh sounds brittle even to her own ears.

A pause. "Mimi, are you guys okay?"

"Sure, we are. We're actually celebrating my birthday tonight, and—" A knock sounds at the door. "Sorry, Jess, I have a client. I'll call you back later, okay?"

"Make sure you do. I miss you, Mimi."

"I miss you, too."

She hangs up and compartmentalizes a tide of wistfulness before opening the door to one of the most beautiful young women she's ever seen.

"Are you Lily?"

"Yes."

Even taller than Amelia, Lily Tucker must be close to six-foot. A model, maybe. She certainly has the willowy build and the looks. Her hair is cropped short, enhancing her delicate facial bone structure, glowing ebony complexion, and exotic wide-set eyes. She's effortlessly glamorous in a simple white tee shirt, black blazer, faded jeans, and flats, with sunglasses on her head and an oversized leather bag over her shoulder.

"I'm Amelia. Nice to meet you. Come on in and have a seat."

When Amelia first rented the space, she'd set up a pair of visitor chairs facing her desk. That arrangement had felt stilted, though, after years of meeting clients at her home. She's since replaced the chairs with a big, cushy leather couch and wooden coffee table.

"It doesn't seem very professional," Aaron said when he dropped by and saw the new setup.

"That's why I did it. People come in here and share their most private, emotional secrets. I want to put them at ease, not intimidate them."

She watches Lily set her bag on the floor and settle on the couch, lanky legs crossed. Leaving a full cushion between them, Amelia sits on the opposite end, her back propped against the arm of the sofa, like a friend settling in for a chat.

"First things first," she says.

"Oh, right. You take credit cards?"

"Not that." Amelia smiles. "You can pay at the end of the session. I just wanted to explain what I do, and why."

She tells Lily about her own past. How someone had left her, as a tiny baby, in a basket in Park Baptist Church up in Harlem.

She doesn't mention that it had happened forty-eight years to this very day.

This isn't her actual birthday. She might never know when, exactly, that is. But she's always celebrated it on May 12th. That had been Mother's Day, back in 1968— the day she'd been found by Calvin Crenshaw, the quiet, hard-working church janitor who'd gone on to become her father.

"He and my mother, Bettina, loved me with all their hearts, and I miss them both every day of my life," she tells Lily. "But I've also missed the strangers who brought me into this world. I've been trying to find them for almost thirty years now."

"Have you found any leads?"

She shrugs. "A few. And I won't give up. But we're not here to talk about my journey. I just wanted you to know that I get it. I know what it's like to be in your shoes."

"You know, it's funny. Until I found you online, I never knew there was a name for it—for what we are. Abandoned babies. *Foundling*—it's ironic, isn't it? Because most days, I don't feel found at all. I feel lost."

Amelia nods. "I understand. Tell me what you know about your past."

Lily recaps the information she'd shared in her pre-appointment forms, reiterating that she'd had a happy childhood in a wonderful adoptive home. She's staving off guilt, Amelia knows, over wanting—needing—to seek the parents who'd left her when she already has parents who love her.

"Do they know you're here today?" Amelia asks.

"Not specifically. But when I told them I wanted to look into my past, they gave me their blessing. They also gave me this." She reaches into the leather bag and pulls out a manila envelope, handing it over to Amelia. "It's full of articles about how I was found in the mall."

Amelia flashes back to Jessie, thirty years ago, showing her a scrapbook on the day they met. It, too, had been filled with clippings about an abandoned child. Her story, like Amelia's and Lily's, ended in a happy adoptive home. Unlike them, she's since discovered and met her birth mother. That's why, when Amelia embarked on this business venture, Jessie wasn't wholeheartedly supportive.

"You never know what you're going to dig up, Mimi. About your own past, or anyone else's. Just tread carefully. Sometimes, the truth is ugly. And dangerous."

Yes. But it's worth every moment of risk.

"Can I keep this envelope?" Amelia asks Lily.

"Yes. My mom made photocopies for me."

"She sounds pretty great."

"She is pretty great. Oh, I have one other thing to show you." She reaches into the bag again. "Only this, you can't keep."

She pulls out a small jewelry box. It's plain, white, not from Tiffany, not ribbon-wrapped. Passing it to Amelia, she says, "I was wearing this the day they found me. It's the only clue I have to who I might have been."

Amelia lifts the lid. A strangled little cry escapes her as she recognizes the object inside.

It's a little gold initial ring, with tiny sapphires set on either side of an engraved letter *C*, filled in blue enamel.